Tor Books by Poul Anderson

THE FLEET OF STARS

POUL ANDERSON

TOR

A TOM DOHERTY ASSOCIATES BOOK
NEW YORK

This is a work of fiction. All the characters and events portrayed in this book are either products of the author's imagination or are used fictitiously.

THE FLEET OF STARS

Cover art by Vincent DiFate

A Tor Book
Published by Tom Doherty Associates, Inc.
175 Fifth Avenue
New York, NY 10010

Tor Books on the World Wide Web:
http://www.tor.com

Tor® is a registered trademark of Tom Doherty Associates, Inc.

ISBN: 0-812-54598-2
Library of Congress Card Catalog Number: 96-32450

First edition: March 1997
First mass market edition: February 1998

Printed in the United States of America

0 9 8 7 6 5 4 3 2 1

A BOOK FOR KAREN
AS THEY ALL HAVE BEEN, ONE WAY OR
ANOTHER

DRAMATIS PERSONAE

Amaterasu Mother: The Life Mother of Amaterasu
Benno: A sophotectic counselor of Luna
Birger: Father of Fenn
Catoul: A Selenarch of Proserpina
Chuan: The synnoiont on Mars
Demeter Daughter: An incarnation of Amaterasu
  Mother
Pedro Dover: A member of the Gizaki quasi-cult
Elitha: Mother of Fenn
Elverir: A Lunarian on Mars
Fenn: A police officer on Luna, later a spaceman
Georghios: A police chief on Luna
Anson Guthrie: A leader on Amaterasu; his download
He'o: A metamorph of the Keiki Moana
Ibrahim: Prefect of the Synesis
Iokepa Hakawau: A man of the Lahui Kuikawa
Jendaire: A leader among the Lunarians at Alpha
  Centauri
Lars: A man of Vernal
Luaine: A Selenarch of Proserpina
Maherero: A councillor of the Southern Coagency
Manu Kelani: Chief *kahuna* of Nauru
Rachel: A judge in Vernal, wife of Lars
David Ronay: A prominent citizen of the Republic of
  Mars
Helen Ronay: Wife of David Ronay
Kinna Ronay: Daughter of David and Helen Ronay
Scorian: Chief of the Inrai outlaws on Mars
Stellarosa: A journalist on Luna
Tanir: A member of the Inrai

The Teramind: The apex of the cybercosm
Velir: Convener of Proserpina
Wanika Tauni: A woman of the Lahui Kuikawa
Zefor: A Proserpinan

Sleep not, my children: though night is here, afar
Your children of the morning are clamorous for war:
Fire in the night, O dreams!
    Though she send you as she sent you, long ago,
    South to desert, east to ocean, west to snow,
West of these out to seas colder than the Hebrides
        I must go
    Where the fleet of stars is anchored and the young
        Star-captains glow.

—James Elroy Flecker
The Dying Patriot

1

IN THE ANCIENT faith of her people, Amaterasu was the Sun Goddess, from whom flowed the light that gives life. The discoverers of a world far and strange named it for her because they hoped that someday their kind would make it blossom. The explorers that first went there were not human. Nor were the pioneers that followed, but they wrought mightily, until at last this Amaterasu could begin to nurture a people.

One evening about fifty Earth-years later, Anson Guthrie and Demeter Daughter left Port Kestrel, seeking solitude. They could have talked at home, but the news he bore would not let him sit quietly, and she was always glad of open sky. The little town—boats, bridges, brightly colored buildings—soon fell behind them, screened off by its trees except for a slender communications mast. A path took them along a fork of the Lily River, beneath whispery poplars, to the seashore, where it bent south.

Plantations and industry lay northward. Here was parkland, turf starred with dandelions and harebells, down to a strip of sand. Beyond lapped the Azurian Ocean. On several islets grass had taken hold, shivering pale in the wind. The sun had gone so low that haze turned its disk golden-orange. A broken road of brightness ran from it over the wavelets, casting glitter to either side. They were purple in the distance, tawny closer to hand. Here and there swayed dark patches, native thalassophyte; but overhead, in heights still blue, shone the wings of three gulls.

On the left, hills rolled upward, shadowful, their groves and greennesses drenched with the long light, houses scattered across them, windows shining. Air blew mild, murmurous, not every daytime fragrance departed. To someone newly come from Earth it would have felt mountaintop-thin; but then, weight was only nine-tenths, and besides, to Guthrie, Earth was a remote memory; to Demeter Daughter, scarcely even that. Elsewhere on the fourth planet of Beta Hydri, glaciers reared above deserts where machines and microbes toiled to broaden the domain of life. On this big subtropical island Tamura, Amaterasu Mother had won her victory and reigned in peace.

Or so it had seemed.

Man and woman walked awhile along the shore, silent, before Guthrie cleared his throat. "Well—" he began. It trailed off into the wind.

She regarded him. At forty-one biological years—seventy-two of Earth's—he remained large, burly, vigorously striding; but furrows crossed the rugged features, the once reddish hair tossed scant and white, the eyes had faded from steel to smoke. They squinted ahead of him as keenly as ever, though, and the bass voice had lost no force. In contrast to her graceful, colorful tunic and cloak, sandals on her feet, he wore just a coverall and his battered old hiking boots.

"Is what you have to tell hard for you?" she asked.

He shrugged. "Not exactly." He flashed her half a grin. "Which you must well know, sweetheart," after this lifetime together, and all the centuries and embodiments before. His gaze lingered on her: tall, slim, hazel-eyed, high-cheeked face marked by age mainly in deepening of the amber complexion and graying of the black, shoulder-length hair. "No, I started to speak," he said, "and then suddenlike got to remembering." Another coast, another woman, but she had been very young, a girl, and he was in his first life, a mortal like her, and it was on Earth. "No importe. Before your time."

Her hand closed on his for a moment, as much as sizes allowed. They walked onward. A massive live oak and a garnet-leaved Japanese maple spread their canopies ahead, some meters from the strand. A squirrel scam-

pered up a bole and two crows took flight, hoarsely caw-
ing. "Yon should be a good spot for us," Guthrie
suggested.

His companion nodded. "Yes. You can really feel the
presence of the Mother here, can't you?"

"Think she'll listen in?"

"Probably not. She has the whole world to look after,
and especially now, with the ecological balance in New
India crashing—" It was always precarious, when life
sought a foothold in realms that had been wholly barren,
or that at most held a few tiny, primitive native organisms. Nothing less than an integration of that life itself,
globally, through a single awareness, could make it flourish in a span humanly, rather than geologically, meaningful.

He deferred to her intuition. She had, in sense, herself
been Demeter Mother. If now, in the flesh, her memories
of that existence were dim, fragmentary, like scraps of
dream, nevertheless they were a dower of something beyond human ken; and this would be true of every Demeter Daughter, for as long as the race went starfaring.

"Okay, we'll tell her later," Guthrie said, deliberately
prosaic. "And everybody else. But I did want you and
me to talk first."

They settled down under the oak, side by side, leaning
back against its sun-warmed roughness, their vision
turned west overseas. Brighter but more distant than Sol
from Earth, therefore smaller in heaven, Beta Hydri sank
out of sight with a quickness increased by the planet's
twenty-hour rotation period. A cloud bank on that horizon burned red and molten gold. The gulls skimmed low,
mewing.

"It happened while I was gone, didn't it?" the woman
prompted. She had been on the Northland continent,
where nature was well-established on the eastern sea-
board, visiting one of their sons, his wife, and especially
the grandchildren. Guthrie had been too engaged with his
latest project, a shipyard, to go along.

"Obviously," he replied.

"A message from Centauri, no?" she asked softly.

"Huh?" he exclaimed, startled. "Did the Mother tell you?"

She shook her head. "I said I don't believe she's been paying close attention to secure places like this. In any case, if she did know but saw you wanted to keep it secret awhile, she would have likewise. You'd have your good reasons."

Reasons that Amaterasu Mother might well appreciate better than he did himself, Guthrie thought. Her vastness and diversity, growing and growing across this world—

As often in the past, the idea flitted through him that the name of his lady should, strictly speaking, be Amaterasu Daughter. Her incarnation, like his and that of every other first-generation colonist, had been the work of the Mother *here*. Demeter Mother dwelt light-years hence, back at Alpha Centauri, abiding her doom. But . . . on that planet, his beloved had first come to being; and in his mind, through every lifetime they might ever share, she would always be Demeter Daughter.

"I was guessing," she went on. "But I do know the general situation." She smiled. "And I've gotten to know you rather well, querido."

The endearment touched his inmost spirit. The Kyra Davis part of her had used it, long and long ago.

He put on gruffness. "You know me too damn well, I sometimes think." He returned her smile. "But I wouldn't swap."

"Nor I," she murmured.

They were silent for a bit. The sunset flared brighter. A flight of cormorants winged across it.

"The news is troublous," she said. He had never quite wanted to ask her whether such occasional turns of speech came from her reading, wider than his despite his being centuries her senior, or from some deeper wellspring.

"Yeah," he admitted. Holding to his own style, as a

kind of defense: "Not that we should keep it under the hatch for long—the communication team and now us two, I mean. I swore 'em to secrecy after they'd played it for me, but only till I'd've had a chance to palaver with you. The people have a right to know, and don't they know that!" Rambunctious lot, he thought, as free folk needed to be if they were to stay free.

"But if it's that . . . critical . . . shouldn't you have brought in the Mother immediately?"

"I wasn't sure. How much can she have to say about a business like this? You, you're human," in her way, as he in his. Mortal, she had the wisdom of mortality, together with as much of Demeter Mother's as a mere brain could hold. Amaterasu, however—

"You see, this may be more of a problem for us than for the, the gods," he continued awkwardly. "I can't tell how she'll take it. Maybe not even you can. Anyhow, we've been partners for quite a spell, you and me, haven't we?"

"Yes." Quite a spell. In these bodies, brought forth as youthful adults on this world. In the downloads before them, who had helped in the hard early work until a fraction of the planet was ready for flesh and blood, and who before then had made the voyage from Alpha Centauri. In the earlier bodies on Demeter, his built from a genome, hers from two others, an ideal, and a dream. Before then, for hundreds of years, in his first download and in Demeter Mother, whose mind had grown out of the minds of Kyra Davis and Eiko Tamura. Before then, afar on Earth, when his download had worked and fought and hoped together with those two women. And even before then, for into Demeter Mother had also gone his memories of Juliana, the wife of his first lifetime, when he was only a man, born and maturing and dying in the ordinary way.

"Okay," he said. "You're right, we've gotten a message from Centauri," more than a quarter century after it started out. "The Lunarians there, they've heard from Earth—from Sol, at least."

She caught her breath. The sunset light filled suddenly widened eyes. "O-o-oh. Finally, finally," she whispered. "I'd believed that—never—"

"Reckon we all did, huh?" he growled. "Our kind back at Earth, Luna, Mars, swallowed up—or whatever happened to them—taken up by the machines, not interested in us anymore. The Lunarian race maybe extinct, aside from those who moved to Centauri. Someday, someday we might go back and find out, but it's such a long way and we've got so much to do out here."

She seized his arm. *"What has happened?"*

"Sorry for rambling. But what we've received is hardly a story, it's more a history, knotted and tangled, and the laser beam conveyed little better than pieces of it, and I don't claim to savvy what the devil's been going on, not really." Guthrie paused, marshaling words. "Well, for openers, five-six hundred Earth-years back, the Lunarians there at Sol found a big, dense asteroid away off in the Kuiper Belt, amongst the comets, you know. They colonized it. Since then, they've been taking possession of other bodies in those frontier orbits."

"Wonderful," she almost sang. Anxiety struck. "But what about . . . our race?"

"Terrans, they're called these days, whether they live on Earth or not." Guthrie grimaced. "They don't go spacefaring any more, unless you count riding ferries between Earth and Luna, or sometimes Mars. They—" Again he stopped to find words. The wind, already cooling, rustled the leaves above them.

"You realize," he said, "the word is not from any of them but from the Lunarians on that asteroid, Proserpina they call it. They're far from the inner Solar System and, well, there seems to be considerable mutual hostility with the order of things on Earth and her neighbor planets. The message speaks of intelligent machines—sophotects, you may recall is the term—pretty much ruling the roost there. Not that the Terrans are enslaved or anything like that. Contrariwise, is the impression I got. But the smartest sophotects are smarter than they are in more ways than you or I could measure, and at the top of the pyramid is something they call the Teramind.''

"Something foreseen," she said very low, "perhaps inevitable. The ultimate, awesome intellect. . . . But it's constantly growing, changing, evolving itself further and further—isn't it?"

"Seems like. Bear in mind, the original message was from one set of Lunarians to another, two sets that'd lived four-plus light-years apart and out of touch for centuries. And then the Centaurian Lunarians reworded it, to pass on to us whatever of the information they chose. Not everything by a long shot, I'd guess from the skimpiness of what we've received.''

She heard, but her thoughts stayed on course. "The ancestors on Demeter, and your download, and Kyra's and Eiko's—Demeter Mother wasn't in being, not yet— they saw this coming, didn't they? Back when the people in the Solar System stopped transmitting because they claimed they'd grown too different from our kind of humans. . . . But they didn't foresee Proserpina. Nobody could have. The Lunarians at Centauri must be happy about that."

"Yes and no. The Proserpinans themselves aren't happy any longer. At least, one thing that nudged them into trying to reestablish contact, even though they knew Demeter hasn't got much time left, one thing was—the machines, the cybercosm, whatever you call it—the system that rules over Sol's planets in all but name—it never wanted that Proserpina colony. That's what the message says, anyhow. A wild card, a chaos factor, the long-term consequences unpredictable and uncontrollable. The cybercosm did its best to keep the existence of the asteroid secret; then when the news got out, it tried to discourage migration there; then when that happened regardless, it tried to keep the colony tiny and isolated; and now lately—

"Of course, this is the Proserpinans' side of the story, as filtered through the Lunarians at Centauri. Prejudiced, no doubt. Just the same—"

"Yes?" she urged softly.

"Well, they speak of something new being suppressed, hints of a tremendous discovery made by a solar gravitational lens way out in space, denials of this that don't quite ring true. And when they tried to set up a lens of their own, the effort failed, and they're convinced that it was sabotage."

She frowned. Paranoia was foreign to her. "Need it have been?"

"I suppose not. Still, judging by what we've received, the cybercosm seems quite well-informed about goings-on at Proserpina, distant and lonely though it is." Guthrie did not frown, he scowled, and his tone harshened. "Which does suggest to me that the cybercosm and its people weren't entirely truthful when they broke off communications with us out here, claiming there could be no more shared interests. It could've had its spy robots at Centauri all along. They could be in this system right now, mini jobs we'd likely never detect unless we knew exactly what to scan for." He made a chopping gesture. "Be that as it may, the Proserpinans report they've run surveillance missions through the inner Solar System and found that antimatter production has started up again on Mercury."

"It had ceased?"

"Yes, for a long time. A stable economy, which Earth and Luna had reached, didn't need any energy source so concentrated, and a plentiful reserve was stored in orbit. But now—resumed—Could it be to power c-ships? The Proserpinans also report detecting signs of what they strongly suspect are spacecraft of some exotic kind, leaving the Solar System at bat-out-of-hell speeds, or once in a while entering it."

She stared into the sunset. It was swiftly losing color, the sky above the clouds going from blue to violet. "We didn't think they ever would, the machines," she breathed.

"Naw," he agreed. "I figured those great minds were too concerned with their fancy mind-games—theory, math, esoteric abstract art forms, contemplating their electrophotonic navels. Maybe I was wrong."

She shivered. "What would, what could it—the, the Teramind—desire?"

"¿Quien sabe? But if it is setting out to plant cybercosms in the galaxy—then machines can expand their range a lot faster and more thoroughly than life can, you know."

A point of light blinked forth in the west; dusk had advanced enough that Amaterasu's moon had become visible there. Day drowned the weak, fitful gleam of a fifty-kilometer rock, a captured asteroid. Artificial satellites often shone brighter. Guthrie missed Lunalight. He had missed it on Demeter too, but there Alpha Centauri B, the companion sun, blazed brilliant, from two hundred to two thousand times the radiance.

Life missed it worse, he reflected fleetingly. Without a freakishly huge moon like Luna to stabilize it, the spin axis of an otherwise Earthlike planet was apt to wander chaotically, with consequences falling anywhere between a runaway glaciation and a runaway greenhouse. Without something gigantic like Jupiter to deflect smaller bodies, the planet would be subject to relentless bombardment, a KT-type event not every few scores of millions of years, but every few thousand. And the many other parameters that had to be right for the miracle to happen—

No wonder life was so heartbreakingly rare in the universe (in that infinitesimal minim of the universe we know) and intelligence might well have arisen only on Earth out of all creation. . . . Amaterasu, like Demeter and Isis, was extraordinary. There evolution had gotten to photosynthesizing organisms that produced an atmosphere humans could breathe. Yes, ships had also reached Hestia, akin to them, and its fantastic neighbor Bion, but the sun of those two worlds lay far and far. . . .

His Demeter was reproaching him: "You shouldn't say that. Anything that acts, thinks, feels, is aware—it's alive."

He spread his palms. "As you like. A semantic question. I mean organic life, then. Our kind."

"The difference isn't absolute, you know."

Most certainly and deeply he knew. Had he not witnessed the coming into existence of Demeter Mother, and afterward of Amaterasu Mother, while other Guthries were present at the geneses of Isis Mother and Hestia Mother? What but cybernetic technology had allowed the downloading of those patterns that were human personality into organometallic matrices, and their joining to form something immensely more than the sum of them, and its fostering and guidance of nature everywhere around a whole world? "No, no, sure, of course not," he said. "I've been a sort of machine myself, after all. Nevertheless—"

"Need the cybercosm be any threat to us?" she pursued. "Why not a friend? Aren't the humans, the Terrans, on Earth and Luna and Mars happy?"

"Pet animals generally are," he snapped. After a moment: "Sorry. Never mind. The situation's doubtless nothing like that simple. And the Lunarians, those wildcats, it might actually be a good idea to keep 'em curbed. I dunno. Certainly what we've gotten is an edited extract from an original message that must itself be one-sided, tendentious, incomplete, and full of superstitions. We'll have to study it and study it, and then I think we'll still be puzzled."

He paused. The last hues drained from the clouds, and dusk thickened with subtropical haste. She drew her cloak about her against the wind. He ignored it.

"I don't think we can afford puzzlement, though," he said at length. "Not when the stakes are as high as this."

" 'This?' "

"The entire universe and future. Yeah, that may be exaggerated. But I don't propose to sit idle waiting for whatever wants to come along."

"What can you do?" She divined his meaning. Dismay moaned, "Oh, no."

He nodded. "You guessed it. I'd better get back there and try to find out."

"Over those distances, into that unknown? Anson, Anson!" She gripped his arm. "Somebody else," she pleaded. "We've plenty of brave men and women."

His tone went gentle. "I am the jefe, darling." She understood full well everything he would say, but he must say it. "We call this a republic, and I've done my damnedest to keep us simply two citizens of it—so have you—but it can't be helped; we are what we are." The eternal hero, the incarnation of the Life Mother. "No decent comandante sends his men into risks he won't take himself."

She rallied. "I should have known it of you. I did. Always I did."

He attempted a laugh. "Anyhow, not *me*, you realize. I aim to live out my days here with you, making love and raising Cain till our great-grandchildren finally and with relief scatter our ashes and compose our mendacious obituaries—after which we'll scandalize them afresh in our new bodies."

"A download of you. Yes, that's clear. But he—"

"He won't thank me? He might, sort of. It's bound to be quite an adventure."

"That whole enormous way, alone."

"Not straight to Sol. At the moment, I reckon my— his best bet will be to first go back to Centauri and confer with the Lunarians there. By that time, they should have lots more information."

"But that adds light-years to the journey," she protested. "Even in a *c*-ship—" Her voice faltered. "You— he will get to Centauri after Demeter is destroyed."

He winced. "Uh-huh. That hurts. However, the Lunarians should be okay on their asteroids, mostly. In fact, they should be able to outfit my alter ego for the trip on to Sol. He'll arrive in style, loaded for bear.''

''Do you mean he'll make that leg in a cruiser? But it will take decades longer!''

''What's a few decades more or less, given the scale of space-time?''

Guthrie was mute for another while. Stars were appearing now in the west as well as the east. Among them he recognized Sol. It glimmered insignificant, about fourth magnitude, near Ursa Minor. Twenty light-years, an abyss denumerable but unimaginable by humans, was too small a reach in the galaxy to affect constellations much. But Polaris was not the lodestar of Amaterasu.

He rose. Light from above, in this clear air, and light cast off the sea were ample to find one's way by. ''Let's go home,'' he proposed.

''I would like some closeness and comfort,'' she admitted.

''You know,'' he said, ''I can hope that in the end, maybe a hundred years from tonight, my download will come back here and get reborn.'' He stroked her hair. ''And there'll be a you for him.''

She tried to speak as cheerfully. ''By then he may well find this planet entirely green.''

''That's our goal, isn't it?'' he said. ''What the travel and labor are for. Homes, elbow room, personal gain, yeah, but way down the pike, the object of the game is to make the universe come alive.''

Unspoken:—with our kind of life.

2

THE FIRST MEMORY that stayed with Fenn—and it dwelt in him through all his days—was of space and the stars. He must have been two or three, not old enough to leave the Habitat for the Moon but getting around handily on its low-weight decks. The sight would have been commonplace to him, often in a viewscreen, now and then glimpsed directly through a port. Perhaps what made this time magical, an epiphany, was that he looked from the after observation turret on the axis of rotation, floating free, the hyalon bubble virtually invisible, as if he had become a comet on its very own orbit. At least one adult would have been with him, a parent or a friend of the family—not a preceptor, for then other children would have tumbled about, squealing and shrilling, Fenn quite likely the noisiest in the class. He did not afterward recall who had escorted him. They may have chanced to be alone, while the person or persons kept aside, respecting that majestic stillness.

The Habitat was coming around from nightside. Sky surrounded Fenn, stars and stars and stars, unwinking sharp shards of brilliance, ice-white, steel-blue, topaz-yellow, ruby-red; the Milky Way coursed as a frosty river, banked with black nebular headlands; the fire-fog in Orion glowed vague and mysterious as the neighbor galaxies; there were more lights in heaven than there was crystalline darkness. In the direction from which he had entered, gray metal curved away to a near horizon. Beyond it on four sides reached gleaming planes that came to knifelike edges at some distance he did not yet know how to gauge—four of the solar and magnetic sails that stabilized the great cylindroid on its path and its axis. Their spin across the star-field made him dizzy, and he turned his eyes away.

Luna hove into view, at first an arc bitten out of the brightness, then rising and gaining an ever-broader luminous rim, tremendous, mountains and craters and maria ashenly clear. Earth appeared likewise, also waxing, far smaller, although its marbled blue and white dazzled him until he could see nothing else nearby. These were splendors, he watched them and watched them as they swelled toward fullness; yet his gaze kept going back to the stars.

Probably on this occasion he did not stay through a full cycle of the Habitat's course around Luna. Six hours would have been rather much for a small boy. But as long as he remained inboard, he returned whenever he could persuade someone, anyone, to take him. More than once he was caught trying to sneak back on his own. Getting into trouble came natural to him.

Near the end of his residence, the crèche sent his class on the customary trip outside. To most of the children this was not an overwhelming experience. Explanations, multiceiver shows, and vivifer simulations had fairly well prepared them. Still, it was exciting to sit, harnessed, in a vehicle that crawled about, gripping the rails, with the monstrous shell of home *overhead* and the heavens wheeling wildly by, the Bears in pursuit of the Peacock and Chameleon, a hasty red spark that Preceptor said was Mars. At one end of the route, the Lunar disk gyred like a black wheel, jewel-strewn with lights where people lived, studded on its verge with glints where peaks caught rays from the hidden sun. (For safety's sake, these excursions always took place while in the shadow.) At the other end, Earth, full, glorious, did not so much tumble in its lesser circle as tread out a stately measure. And the installations—domes, pods, masts, dishes, hatchways, the polar port where spaceships came and went, the sails like shining cliffs—and the machines that scurried about or flitted free as birds or fireflies—yes, those were fine too.

Fenn pressed his nose against the hyalon and hungered.

That evenwatch at home he demanded to be given a spacesuit and taken back out. Didn't the multi show people walking around all the time? Didn't their clingboots keep them from being flung off, and when they chose to leave the surface, didn't they have jetpacks to fly with? When told repeatedly that that was for grown-ups, he at last threw a tantrum that made his father order him to bed.

Birger was Earthbred, from Yukonia; that nation was his polity, although he had connections to the Foresters of Vernal and, in fact, eventually took an oath of association. He should doubtless have reckoned himself lucky. Not only did he get gainful employment, it was work he could love, ranger-manager in the huge wilderness preserve that covered much of his motherland; and then he married and begot a child. However, year by year he came to feel more hemmed in, regulated, restricted, confined largely to shepherding tourists while robots and sophotects did everything important. Partly on this account, his marriage broke. She kept the child.

Birger was already looking elsewhere. He did not really care to join the Foresters, he found their style better suited to a vacation than a lifeway, but he had heard of possibilities on the Moon—rather, within it, where woods and meadows were expanding through cavern after cavern, raising challenge after challenge. How to keep them healthy, yet resist their often insidious encroachments on the gardens and nanotechnics of humankind?

He emigrated, adapted, got the position he applied for, and did well, steadily advancing in rank and responsibilities. After a while, he married Elitha. She was of old Selenite stock, with old money, and artistic; but she also had vigor, an independent spirit, and originality. That last was a rare trait. Some critics said that her sculptures were not merely beautiful, they might be the harbinger of a creative breakthrough, the first in centuries—assuming that others like her took inspiration. Elitha did not share their concern. She was simply interested in what she made.

In due course she opted for a different sort of creation, with help from her man. It was not an easy decision. She would have to spend her pregnancy, and the following three or four years if she wanted to stay with the infant, in the Habitat. Birger would be there too when he was able, but frequently he must remain on Luna for daycycles that could run into weeks. Nevertheless, he agreed. After all, he was not quite young anymore. If he was to have this final offspring the law permitted him, he would be well advised to do it soon.

He tried under the circumstances to be a good parent, and one cannot properly say he failed. He was, though, on the strict and overbearing side. Having examined the fetal genome, a genetic program found it normal but forecast friction between father and son, punctuated by explosions. Fenn soon proved the program right. However, the family was basically an affectionate one, and when at last they could all go live in Tychopolis, Birger and Elitha felt hopeful.

"Mamita," Fenn asked, "what's a Lunarian?"

He had seen the structures preserved around Hydra Square, and a few other relics, but now something that somebody said had caused him to wonder why they were unlike anything else. Also, Elitha thought, he must have caught the word once in a while in adult conversation or on a historical show or whatever.

"They're the folk who used to live here, a long time ago," she said. "Mostly, they were taller than we are."

"What happened to them?"

"Well, when Terrans, people like us, started coming to the Moon to stay, till finally there were more of them than there were Lunarians, the Lunarians grew unhappy. They didn't like living the way Terrans did; they didn't think much like us. More and more of them moved away, and those who didn't had fewer and fewer children, till finally none were left on Luna. But we still use the same name for them. So we here today call ourselves Moon-dwellers or Selenites."

No need yet, she thought, to go into details: the era of the independent Lunarian Selenarchy and of Lunarian enterprises rivaling Terran throughout the Solar System. Nothing remained of it but chronicles, abandoned artifacts, and dust. As space-struck as he was, Fenn would be distressed when he learned of how the Lunarian settlements on asteroids and on moons of the giant planets had been squeezed to oblivion because they could not compete with sophotects and robots—for the same had befallen the Terran outposts. Old, unhappy, far-off things; let them not invade this room where her gardenias sweetened the air and a full-wall viewscreen showed Mount Denali regal above Birger's Yukonian forests.

"Where are they now?" the boy wondered.

"Oh, some are on Mars, where they get along with the Terrans there. But most are way, way away on a world of their own, called Proserpina." Never mind, now, about those whose ancestors fared with Anson Guthrie to Alpha Centauri. "We very seldom hear from them." Nor bring up conflicts in the past and tensions in the present, tensions so complex and subtle that she herself was unsure of what they were, or why.

Fenn knit his brows. "Where'd they come from?"

A quick mind pounced to and fro in that towhead, Elitha thought. If only the child were less willful and aggressive. He could be such a dear when he chose. Let her honor his confidence with an honest answer, even though he might not entirely follow her meaning.

Her glance went across spidery tables and chairs, the usual form on Luna, to the lounger. She settled down in it. Standing was about as easy as sitting, but she hoped he would join her and she could lay an arm around him. He kept his feet, confronting her. She swallowed her slight disappointment and began:

"The first Lunarians were born to Terran mothers. You see, people had reasons to settle on the Moon, like building and tending the solar units that beam energy to Earth. They didn't have machines then that could do everything. But they found the weak gravity was bad for them."

He nodded impatiently. The Habitat had made him familiar with variations in weight. Here his parents insisted he exercise regularly in the centrifuge at one standard g, like them. It wasn't universal practice, when biotechnics kept cells and body fluids healthily balanced. However, neither Elitha nor Birger wanted thin bones and minimal muscles; visiting the Mother World, they would rather be comfortable. For once, Fenn didn't argue about the program. He enjoyed using his body to the full, and looked forward to reaching an age when he could safely go under higher accelerations.

"The worst problem, one that we haven't solved yet, was that Terran women can't have babies on Luna," Elitha went on. "Too much goes wrong. The baby dies before it's born. People soon realized this and stopped trying. Nowadays we have the Habitat in low Lunar orbit, spinning fast enough to give Earth weight on the outer decks. I lived there while I was carrying you, and stayed till you had developed so one-sixth g wouldn't harm you as you were growing."

"I know, I know! What about the Lunarians?"

"People didn't have a Habitat in those early days. What they had was what we call 'genetic technology.' We can take a living thing and fix it to have little ones that aren't quite the same as it is. An animal, a plant, a microbe—the new kind of thing we call a metamorph. You've seen plenty of metamorphs, like glitterbugs and daybats in the woods or the giant flowers in the Conservatory. Others make a lot of the stuff we use, food and fiber and fuel and medicines, oh, a lot.

"Well, the scientists fixed it for Terran women to have metamorph babies. When those Lunarians grew up, the low gravity was right for them. They didn't need biostabilizers and special exercises to stay well, and they had babies without any trouble. After a while, most of the people on the Moon were Lunarians."

Fenn pondered. "But the Lunarians are gone," he said.

"Yes, they are. What nobody back then, when they knew less about genetics than they do now, what nobody back then foresaw was that Lunarians wouldn't be different just in their bodies. The biochemistry, the . . . well, everything about them made them, makes them, different in their spirits too, in what they like and don't like, how they want to live their lives, everything. They aren't bad people, no, don't think that. But they aren't happy under Terran laws and customs.''

"How 'bout Mars?" he exclaimed.

Quick mind indeed, Elitha thought gladly. "Mars is a special case. It's got a gravity in between Luna's and Earth's. Terrans and Lunarians can both live there and have babies. And Mars is bigger than Luna, with lots of territory that isn't claimed either for homes or for eco-balance. A community can be off by itself and do pretty well what it wants to.'' Let him not hear, today, how the human presence yonder was also dying.

His eyes, blue as heaven above Tahiti, grew big. "Lunarians in space," he whispered, "way out on P'serpina—" And then a shout, while his fists doubled: "Why aren't *we?*"

Over the years, piece by piece, never directly, he—sometimes bewildered, sometimes enraged—got an answer. How complete or truthful the answer might be, he was never certain. That stoked the anger always smoldering deep inside him.

It was not that anyone in any important way lied to him or evaded his questions. On the contrary, as he once heard a philosopher remark, in a set of societies that had long held their total population to little more than a billion, for whom the necessities and most of the comforts of life were essentially free goods, education was bound to become less an occupation than a preoccupation, at least among the intelligent. To a considerable extent, the difficulty lay in getting a perspective—in realizing that there was a perspective to be gotten—on what everyone took for given. Would Rameses II have wondered about the divine status of kings, or Thomas Jefferson have inquired whether machines had rights?

Machines, devices, were everywhere around Fenn, shaping and maintaining his world, pervading his life, and indeed making it possible. They ranged from spacecraft, land vehicles, power transmitters, cities, on through the multiceiver that entertained and helped to school him, down to engines he knew only from micrographs, because they were of molecular size. Their benefits were as hard to see as were the benefits of drinkable water or breathable air. When he came to the study of ancient history, it took an imaginative effort to comprehend how average life expectancy had been perhaps thirty years—a fourth of his!—and most people must spend most of their waking hours at work if they were to survive, whether they liked it or not. Why, after you were adult and out of the lyceum system, work was a privilege, something you had to earn, like Birger, or make for yourself, like Elitha. Not too many ever managed it.

Like all his friends, Fenn was in continual interaction with computer terminals and robots; the distinction got blurry. He had much less to do with sophotects. He met some when his father took him around in the Lunar wilds, where they did more work but were less noticeable than the human caretakers. In Tychopolis, the community counselor used a specialized body to give him routine physical examinations. In its role of teacher, it synthesized a holographic human image for itself when it delivered lectures or gave demonstrations to students. Likewise did it when, after an egregious escapade of Fenn's, it conducted several private sessions for his betterment. Those were sympathetic. Not being stupid, he took heed of them; but he scarcely took them to heart.

Aside from what he read or otherwise absorbed vicariously, this was about the extent of his direct exposure to the machines in his first ten or twelve years. He needed a preceptor to spell out the distinctions between them for him, as we need to have the grammar of the language we learned by osmosis explained to us.

"Robots and computers—computers are a subclass of

robots, actually—can seem to think,'' the man said. ''Many of them are able to do a wide variety of things, to learn from experience, make decisions, carry on conversations, and generally behave like people. But they are limited. No matter how clever and powerful their programs, what they basically do is carry out an algorithm. The development of true artificial intelligence— conscious, creative minds like ours—had to wait till the quantum aspect of consciousness was understood. You've been told something about quantum mechanics. You'll hear more.

''Meanwhile, rather early on, the researchers found how to make a download.'' He laughed. ''I'm throwing some rather big words at you. Ask me or your home terminal about them when you've mulled them over.

''Knowing what they did about atoms and quanta, the researchers became able to scan a nervous system molecule by molecule. They could record the basic patterns of memory and personality, and then map these into a program for a neural net that was an analogue of the person's personal brain. A download like that was a sort of copy of a person's mind. They could give it sensors, a speaker, a machine body. You haven't heard much about downloads because there have never been more than a few. Hardly anybody has liked that kind of exis- tence. It's mainly become a transition stage for syn- noionts after they die. I'll tell you later about synnoionts.

''The thing is, experience with downloads showed how to make the first sophotects, electrophotonic hardware and software that actually thinks, is aware, and knows that it thinks and is aware. Given these machines, the whole cybercosm soon began to improve and evolve it- self. That evolution went faster and faster, further and further. We don't know where it will end, or if it ever will.''

The speaker paused before he went back to ordinary speech. ''Don't get me wrong, please. A sophotect is not a single being with a single mind like you or me. All sophotects can draw on the same global database. They can link and unlink, merge and unmerge, just as they choose. A particular sophotect—for instance, our counselor here in Tychopolis—can have its own personality, but it comes out of the whole. Its mind is not separate like an island in a lake; it's more like a wave on the water. The wave is distinct from every other wave, and it may go on for quite some time, but it happens within a larger whole, and it can join with others to form a new and different wave.

"What we call the cybercosm is really the entire system of machines, computers, robots, and sophotects, all One. If you want to think of it as a pyramid, with your everyday appliances and power tools at the bottom, why, then the top, the peak, is the Teramind."

He smiled. "But don't worry. The Teramind doesn't rule us, or anything like that. We have no more relationship with it, really, than we do with the stars—magnificent, but strange and far away. The cybercosm, its ordinary part that surrounds us, is our partner."

Fenn had bristled when the speaker so lightly dismissed the stars, but kept his mouth shut.

Later, when he had studied more history and civics, he began to gnaw out his own interpretation of the universe in which he found himself.

Before the Synesis, he learned, was the World Federation. And before the World Federation, old men—"governments," they were called—had somehow, again and again, compelled young men to kill each other, along with vast incidental destruction, for causes that the old men claimed were important. Governments had also robbed, regimented, and terrorized their subjects, often in the most incredible fashions. Toward the end, they generally did it in the name of something called "democracy."

And yet . . . that was when humans first went forth into space.

Like many a youngster, Fenn toppled in love with the

legend of Anson Guthrie. In Fenn, though, the passion endured as he grew up, unquenched by common sense. Fireball Enterprises, free men and women faring out to the planets; their final, unresolvable conflict with the Federation; the dissolution of the company, but the exodus of some to Alpha Centauri, accompanied by equally rebellious Lunarians, under Guthrie's leadership—Guthrie, long dead, yet alive and indomitable in his download. . . . How was it today with their descendants?

They knew beforehand that Demeter, the planet they sought, would come to wreck within a thousand years. By now, the catastrophe had happened. Fenn had seen the spectacular images sent back by robot observers. They included nothing about the settlers. Were the Lunarians still there on the asteroids they had colonized? What of the Terrans on Demeter? Did any escape? How, and to where?

The indifference of the cybercosm had been matched by that of the people here at home. Fenn wondered why hardly anybody seemed curious; soon the whole business was well-nigh forgotten. He heard in reply that efforts to find out would have been difficult, and unrewarding at best, provocative of hostility at worst. The colonists had severed communications centuries ago, declaring themselves alienated from an Earth, a Solar System, turning unhuman.

Fenn's preceptors pointed out to him that nothing of the kind had occurred—he need only look around him— and that the fate of a few eccentric malcontents was scarcely even of academic interest. This attitude had long since become the received wisdom. The stars are too remote. The removal of Guthrie's handful to the nearest of them exhausted the resources of mighty Fireball. Nothing of the kind will ever happen again. Why should it, when everything one might sanely want is available, either in material form or as virtual experience? Besides, practically every planet around every sun is dead, always has been, always will be.

Let the cybercosm operate its network of astronomical instruments across the Solar System as far as the solar gravitational lenses. Let it dispatch unmanned miniprobes, which beam back their findings, revelations arriving after decades or centuries or millennia, word of a fascinating but inanimate and ultimately meaningless universe. *That* is rational. And is not rationality what divides the human and the sophotect from the brute?

It need not be cold. On its own terms, it cannot be; it must take account of emotional needs. Sophotects have them too—conation, curiosity, whatever yearnings drive their ongoing evolution. As for humans, give them peace, give them abundance, give them informational access to the riches of their past and present, set them free to lead their lives as they see fit. Sophotects ask for no more than their single vote in the Federation Parliament, plus their obvious right as sentient beings to protection from abuse. Their collectivity is an advisor, a partner. . . .

And thus the Federation developed into the Synesis, government into guidance; and Terrans no longer plied the spacelanes or dreamed about the stars.

Fenn raged.

3

DOWNLOAD GUTHRIE CAME back to function—to awareness, to life.

"Instruments," he ordered. A flood of data entered him. Connected as he was to the *c*-ship, sensing with its sensors, he received information—about fields, gradients, vectors, masses, particles, quanta, all ambient space—not only as measurements; in a score of distinct ways, he *felt* it.

Or saw it. Alpha Centauri A blazed ahead. When he stopped down its brilliance in his optics, he perceived the disk maned with corona and elflock prominences, winged with zodiacal light. The companion sun, B, at its present distance was a dazzling spark. Proxima, the third member of the system, dim and remote, lay well-nigh lost among the constellations. Sol, four and a third light-years hence, gleamed in Cassiopeia, not quite the chief of the background stars.

From outside his electromagnetic shielding, he heard radiation seethe and tasted its sharpness.

Decelerating at a rate that would have pulped any organic organism, the ship passed close enough by the remnants of Demeter and Phaethon for Guthrie to observe them in fullness. Still molten from the collision, a globe greater than Earth glowed red, streaked with blacknesses of smoke and slag. Outbursts racked it, mountain-sized fire-geysers whirling up and away, whipped along by a spin gone crazy. Rocks enclouded it, meteoroids, asteroids, shards blasted off into random orbits, chaotically dancing gleams in vision. He saw a big one crash back down; incandescence fountained, waves ran over the tortured surface. But many pieces had already begun to form a set of rings, lacy, a hint of exquisiteness to come. A thickening amidst them foretold a moon as big as Luna, or bigger, perhaps to be as meaningful in the far future.

That thought held no comfort. The sight tore at Guthrie. He too bore the memories of the prototype who stayed behind to perish with Demeter Mother, his beloved. His too was the spirit that for centuries had been machine, as it now again was in him, but had seen blossoming spread across the planet, until at last he could be reborn as a living young man and a woman was created to walk at his side. Also a download can grieve.

A monitory shiver passed through the force-field. Detectors reacted, a computation ran lightning-swift, the ship veered. She had almost hit a fragment. Countless thousands, cast free or perturbed loose, were drifting out through the system. Surely no large fraction of them had as yet been identified. Even when the task was complete,

Alpha Centaurian space would be hazardous to travelers, maybe for millions of years.

Lunarians ought to enjoy that, Guthrie thought.

The encounter had brought his mind back to practicalities. The quality of emotions was not the same for him in this form of existence as it was in the flesh, and he could set them aside more easily. That did not mean they went away. However, eagerness and a certain tension came to the forefront.

Communication across the interstellar reaches had always been sparse; and then he'd spent thirty years, switched off, making the passage himself. A lot could have happened. He strained his sensors ahead and commenced broadcasting. "Aou," he called in the lilting Lunarian tongue. "Spacecraft *Yeager* here, inbound from Beta Hydri, emissary aboard, as our message declared."

They were expecting him. The laser beam bearing the word had left Amaterasu shortly before he did, and would have arrived about three Earth-years ago. He wasn't much off his ETA, either; and till just lately, his speed had raised a shout in the interplanetary medium. The ship wasn't big, and her mass tanks were nearly empty, but probably optics were registering her, and maybe, by now, gravitics.

A screen flickered. An image solidified in it: a Lunarian male face of the blond sort, milk-fair, beardless, finely sculptured, with thin nose, Asian cheekbones, big oblique eyes, platinum hair falling down past ears that were not convoluted like those of Terrans. "Well beheld," he said courteously, although Guthrie was merely transmitting audio. "You are awaited, donrai. Your welcoming shall be at Zamok Sabely'."

So Phyle Ithar continued dominant? He'd soon find out. Robots exchanged data. *Yeager* shifted course for a rendezvous at Demeter's L-5 point: same orbit, essentially, but sixty degrees behind the slain planet. It dwindled aft into darkness, an ember.

Robotic manipulators helped him make ready. Besides

the organometallic case holding his electrophotonic brain, with batteries, sensors, speaker, and other ancillary apparatus—altogether, about the size of a human head—the ship's payload amounted to very little more than a body for him. Even given a field drive energized by matter-antimatter annihilation, when you boosted velocity to fly close on the heels of light, and decelerated at journey's end, mass ratios mounted up. Every gram counted.

The body was humanoid, vaguely suggestive of a suit of darkly sheening plate armor, not the best model but, he had decided, the most effective for his purposes here. It ought to relax a bit the Lunarians' ingrained suspicion of sentient machines, if only in their subconscious. The manipulators installed him in it. When he had fitted his eyeglobes on their stalks into appropriate sockets inside the turret, he had vision around a hemisphere, wherever he chose to concentrate it. He could magnify, or look into the ultraviolet or infrared, should occasion arise. His hearing was equally versatile. Indeed, he possessed equivalents of most of the numerous senses and capabilities a man has, plus several extras. A few were lacking, notably hunger, thirst, and above all, sexuality; but you can't have everything, and he'd get those back when he returned to Amaterasu, assuming he ever did.

Zamok Sabely' swelled in view. It was not an asteroid, hollowed out or roofed over, like most Centaurian dwelling places. An original stone, maneuvered into position, had long since been converted entirely to structures. These had been added to over the centuries until the whole was huge. Spokes lanced a hundred kilometers out from a faceted hub, through an intricacy of cables and passages, to a rim clustered and flashing with lights of every hue; solar collectors stretched onward like roadways; the assemblage wheeled around and around against the heavens. Yet it was so balanced and harmonious, beautiful as any masterpiece of engineering is beautiful, that from afar it resembled jewelwork and when he drew near, it brought back memories of medieval cathedrals on

Earth. The very guns, defense against meteoroids, were like spires, and the guardian robotic vessels could have been attendant angels.

Not too damn appropriate to Lunarians, Guthrie thought wryly. But they had a gift for esthetics to match the ancient Hellenes or Japanese—who'd been tough customers themselves.

He had turned control of *Yeager* over to the spaceport, after mentioning that there was no need to dock her. Prior to inserting her in parking orbit, it matched her velocity to its rotation. He went out through the single lock, gauged the factors from experience as well as from instrument readings he had taken, and jumped. A flight of a few hundred meters brought his gripsoles into contact with a landing stage. A portal valved for him and he cycled through.

Beyond, he found a passage curving gently upward to right and left, and Lunar weight on his mass. Atmosphere surrounded him with warmth and sounds, not the bustle and noise that would have filled a Terran harbor but a susurrus like surf and wind far off. No crowd had gathered. The tall persons who passed him cast him a glance without breaking stride. An escort waited, a dozen men in red-and-black livery, led by an officer who gave stately greeting. "Let us guide you to your lodging," he finished. "Then, when you are ready, the Lady Commander will be pleased to see you."

"I can meet her at once if she likes," Guthrie answered. He refrained from adding: "I don't need bed and breakfast, and I've had a nice long nap." Eventually he must get some hours of dormancy and dream—this fleshless incarnation remained that humanlike—but he could stay alert for daycycles on end, and right now he certainly wanted to.

"That will be excellent, donrai." The officer touched the informant on his wrist, evidently to transmit a preset signal. They were quick on the uptake here. Of course, they'd known who was coming, and had records of his earlier period as a download.

By slipway and sometimes shank's mare, they went on into the city, depot, market, center of commerce and culture, aerie and castle that Zamok Sabely' was. Its opulence had grown since last Guthrie trod its decks. Duramoss paved the passageways, between strips for pedestrians and motorskaters. Multicolored alloys, organics, fabrics, and gaudily flowering vines lifted to high overheads where light-patterns shifted and interwove. Music throbbed, keened, whispered through breezes of changeable scents. Arches opened on arcades, tier above tier, of shops, workplaces, taverns, gambling dens, recreation halls, foodsteads, joyhouses, establishments more esoteric, spacious and gracious or darkling and secretive, often screened by a living curtain or an induced aurora. A fire-fountain leaped and roared in the middle of a plaza. Birds trailing rainbow tails winged down a corridor of crystal.

No matter how thronged any section was, none felt crowded. Lunarians moved as softly as they spoke, giving each other ample personal space. Most clothing was somberly sumptuous, relieved by dashes of vivid red or yellow and by flaring lines. Patterns varied from robes to skintights; a tunic and close-fitted trews were commonest, more fanciful in the cut on women than on men. Usually the left breast sported a tribal badge, symbols of every lineage on the asteroids and moons of Centauri. The custom of wearing swords appeared to have ended—maybe duels were rare nowadays—but pet ferrets or tiny metamorphic hawks sat on many a shoulder. Yes, Guthrie thought, this race had grown strong in its new stronghold, and if the ways were now quieter, the blood beneath coursed no less wild.

The door to which he came at last had changed little, a three-meter sheet of iridescence between gaunt, Byzantine-like mosaical figures that moved. An entry behind it bore calligraphy that flowed from poem to poem. There his escort left him.

He went on into a hemiellipsoidal chamber lined with enormous low-gravity flowers, ferns, canes, with dwarf trees and cages of songbirds, where butterflies flittered free in subtropical warmth and odors of fecundity. At the center of the deck, a well gave directly on a view of stars. Next to a frail-seeming couch and table, Jendaire, Wardress of Zamok Sabely', Lady Commander in the Phyle Ithar, invested associate whenever the High Council of Alpha Centauri assembled, stood waiting to receive him.

He advanced to her, halted, and snapped an archaic military-style salute. His intent was to show respect while underlining that he spoke for a separate civilization, as powerful as hers. For similar reasons, he had not yet generated a facial image but left his turret screen blank, inviting no familiarity. "Well beheld, my lady," he hailed. "I am glad and honored to be here."

She offered him her hand. He took it and bowed above its blue-veined thinness, as if his own were a man's. "Well are you come," she replied in a musical contralto.

Straightening, he studied her with a care that avoided impudence because he showed no eyes. Scarcely below his sheer two meters of height, she stood slim and arrow-straight. Silver shoes peeped forth under a green-and-gold gown of deceptive simplicity. Her visage was classic Lunarian: keen profile, horizon-blue irises, skin as white as the hair that fell diamond-dusted from a coronet and halfway down her back. He guessed her age as about seventy-five Earth-years. Anybody who had won to a position like hers, especially in this society, was formidable; but when she smiled, he recognized the allure and briefly wished that for him it were not theoretical.

"We would fain do whatever we may be able, for your ease, pleasure, and purpose," she said. "You need not have sought me on the instant. An apartment stands prepared for you. If it lacks aught, I request of you that you demand the thing."

"Many thanks." While his Lunarian was reasonably fluent, he had never mastered all the nuances and elegances. In his speaker, it bore the mark of his mother tongue, American English of the late twentieth century, as did every modern language he had acquired along the way. "I will. But I'm in no hurry about settling down, whereas when your officer told me you wanted a private meeting, that got me impatient."

She took him at his word. "Yes, it seemed to me that before we hail you publicly, Lord Guthrie, you and I should hold a quiet talk or two."

"That's fine by me, my lady. I'm not much for banquets and toasts—not in this shape I've currently got. But, um, mightn't it cause trouble?"

"Nay, I've seen to that. My fellows of the seigneury know they will encounter you presently. They care not to show themselves overly eager."

He made a chuckle. "Beneath their dignity, eh?"

"Rather, beneath their desire," she said a trifle coldly.

"Right. I'm sorry, I misspoke." Same Lunarians as ever, he thought. To them, scrambling for a chance to get next to somebody famous is a Terran trick, a monkey trick. They're no more capable of being snubbed than a cat is. But in their own fashion, they can be almighty touchy. "No offense meant."

She nodded, took a nacreous goblet off the table, and sipped of the wine in it. Although she couldn't have provided him refreshment in any event, this might well be a subtle means of putting him in his place.

He brushed it off. "What I intended to say," he told her, "was that it's been a long spell since our two breeds met in person. Neither knows a lot about what the other's been up to. I'd hate for any of your colleagues to suspect I was trying to work some stunt, when in fact my mission is perfectly straightforward."

She gave him a new smile. "Fear not. I hold the balance here."

In other words, he thought, they'd see no point in worrying about a conspiracy; she can slap them down all by herself anytime she wants to. Or so she's claiming. I suppose I hope that's right. You're never quite sure with Lunarians. "I see. And, naturally, the two of us can clear away misunderstandings faster than a conference would. There must be some misunderstandings on both sides. Dialogue's kind of slow and awkward across light-years."

"Truly the waiting for you grew long," she sighed. "Also to me, who am not young."

"Easier for me. I . . . slept through it."

She gave him a narrow look. "*You* were able to."

Did she think of him as machine, rather than as transformed human? That could make for a terrible hindrance. He'd better explore attitudes a little before getting down to facts. "Lunarians can too, you know, if they want. We'd give any visitors to Beta Hydri a royal welcome."

The chill became unmistakable. "You should know that that will never happen."

Yes, he thought, he should, though more from the history he had witnessed than from word received since the last Terrans forsook Demeter. While Lunarians of Alpha Centauri had taken a leading part in the development of the field drive, no download of one had ever fared in a *c*-ship. Had any Lunarians ever downloaded at all, anywhere, for any reason?

Test the waters, he thought. She may get mad at me, but she won't kick me out, not when I might have something worth her while.

"I wasn't thinking of an existence like mine here," he said. "I was thinking of how we evacuated nearly everybody before the crash. Your traveler could do the same. Download but stay inactivated en route. Take along his genome specs. Amaterasu Mother would be happy to grow a flesh-and-blood body for him and reload his mind into it. Or hers, or theirs."

"You speak as if that can be done as easily as transcription of a recording. It is not so."

"Well, no, 'fraid not. And most likely it never will be."

"We need suckle no Life Mother, we who cringe not from Father Death."

Their sentiments haven't changed, Guthrie thought. Like their ancestors, they flat-out won't live the way they'd have to for rebirth, integral with a living world that's dominated by a person wiser and mightier than we will ever be, a quasi-goddess—no matter how loving she is or how much personal liberty she gives us. They can't endure having superiors. That must be a strong root of their hatred for the cybercosm at Sol. . . . The idea had passed through him, over and over, for centuries.

"My notion was that the adventure would be worth an emotional price," he said. "And afterward, the freedom of all space-time."

"But no freedom within."

More than once he had had to decide whether he would rather die on his feet or live on his knees, and had always chosen the first. Regardless, he knew he would never really understand this stark feeling of hers. Terran and Lunarian were two separate species—they couldn't even interbreed—and that was that.

"Pardon me," he yielded. "I hope I haven't said anything too distasteful. It's true, your travelers would be stuck amongst us, not having a Life Mother here to come back to. But how about you sending us a sophotect? It wouldn't just register data like a robot; it would have actual experiences to share with you when it returned."

Her lips tightened. "We have no sophotects. We will not." After a moment, as if seeking to reduce the tension: "They do keep some at Proserpina, but those are few, and severely limited. Our race has seen far too well that land to which a cybercosm would bring us."

Now we're getting to the point I was trying for! thought Guthrie. "You approach my main reason for coming here, my lady. You're in closer touch with Sol than any Terran colony can ever be. But we've gotten worried ourselves, you know. An alliance with you makes sense.''

She took up her goblet again, stepped over to the well, and stared for a minute at the streaming stars before she looked his way again and replied, ''Maychance there is a certain commonalty of interests. We must consider it together, you and I, I and my compeers.''

''I don't expect you to empty a bucket of information over my head right away,'' Guthrie conceded. ''And at first I'll be keeping my own cards pretty close to my vest, if you'll bear with the scrambled metaphors.'' She'd hardly recognize his reference to a long-forgotten game, but he expected that she would catch his drift. ''However, today we can save time and trouble if you'll be so kind as to lay out what I'm bound to learn sooner or later. For my part, ask me whatever you want, and I'll give you either an honest answer or none.''

She purred a laugh and came back toward him. ''Your bluntness is arousing, Lord Guthrie. Much have I studied olden accounts and showings of you, yet this daycycle promises more pleasure than I envisioned.''

''Thanks. Likewise.'' With a rueful interior grin: ''It'd be still more fun for me if this self of mine were a man.''

She laughed louder and made a sinuous gesture. ''Ho-ay, and for me!''

She probably has at least two husbands, phyle alliances—Guthrie thought—and God knows how many lovers. Hell on wheels in bed, I'll bet.

The longing to be human gripped him suddenly and cruelly. He pried it loose.

''Tell me, then, what you have in mind,'' Jendaire was saying.

He spread his hands in lieu of a shrug. ''That'll depend on what I learn here, and what help I can get from you people. Which is why I took the long way around instead of making straight for Sol.''

A frown crossed the clear brow. ''It would have been ill-advised, my lord,'' she said slowly.

"Maybe. Repeat, that's what I'm here to find out. If I can."

"Mean you that we might mislead you?" This time she didn't seem affronted. Well, to her, chicanery was perfectly okay. "What end of ours could deception serve?"

"None, I suppose. But you are, well, partisan. Unavoidably. Who isn't, one way or another? Look, though. You're in contact with Proserpina. Earth too?"

"With its Synesis and cybercosm?" Scornfully: "Nay, not at all. Liefer would we discover how close their contact is with us."

"Spy robots, you mean?"

"What else? We have detected a number of them in space, destroyed three, captured one."

A hunter's thrill cast the lingering regrets out of Guthrie. He kept his tone level. "Yeah, the cybercosm, even this Teramind your news to us has mentioned, it's bound by the laws of physics, hm? Instruments can only be *so* small if they're to do their jobs. What'd you learn from that prize you took?"

She spread her fingers. It corresponded to a shrug of her own. "Scant, I am told. The design is too alien. You shall talk with our scientists."

Yes, thought Guthrie, if the cybercosm hasn't shared all its technology with humans, what it's kept back is sure to be way in advance of theirs, maybe close to whatever limits nature sets. But as for those, well, for instance, you can't travel or transmit faster than light, not nohow, and we with our *c*-ships are pushing that. No, we aren't necessarily doomed. Nor necessarily destined to win.

"Surveillance doesn't have to mean hostility," he said. "I'd call it natural to want to know how we're doing."

"Then why have they not asked us?" she challenged.

"Yeah, Earth did break off communications a long time ago. Said there was no more point in it, as far apart as the societies had grown. Which never looked quite reasonable to me, but I figured, like most of us at the time, that sophotects and machine-partnered humans could have developed a very different psychology from us. Anyway, we had enough else to keep us busy.''

"Nor did they ever respond," Jendaire pursued, "though well you must remember how the Centaurians called to them, over and over, before finally giving it up.'' She paused before stating: "Eyach, now the Proserpinans have begun. From them we have heard that in the Solar System the story was that we, the Centaurians, were those who broke off the discourse.''

Guthrie was not surprised. "Yes, I figured that would be the case. If governments have no other reason to lie, they will from force of habit. But this particular flim-flam suggests that something goddamn funny has been going on. Plus everything else you told us on the laser that the Proserpinans had told you—antimatter production starting up after a long hiatus, and what appear to be *c*-ships—and before then, according to the Proserpinans, the effort to quell their own colony—What more do you know from them?''

"Somewhat, year by year. You shall see the details.''

"M-m-m. . . . Do they have field-drive ships by now?''

"They are beginning to. Twelve years agone''—that would be about fifteen of Earth's—"we decided to take whatever risk might lie in revealing to them the science and technology of it. A part of the risk was simply that while that immense volume of data was in transmission, scant bandwidth remained for aught else.''

Guthrie's phantom self nodded; his turret could not. A bundle to send indeed. Sure, it'd become known already in his first lifetime that the vacuum is not passive emptiness; it roils with the creation and annihilation of virtual particles, its energy shapes the conformation and evolution of the universe. Laboratory observations had lent their evidence: the Lamb shift, the Casimir effect, he couldn't immediately recall what else—but how tiny, all of it, how insignificant. It seemed as though nothing less than the entire cosmos was big enough and endured long enough to feel the whole reality. . . . Had the freshness of new worlds—and new minds, new human species—and of ongoing spacefaring, had that been what brought a fresh insight, mathematics, theoretical investigation, empirical tests, devices, demonstrations, and suddenly the new ships? Interaction between the quantum states of matter and the quantum states of the vacuum—direct thrust, momentum still conserved, but the momentum of the plenum—no more need for jets and their horrible wastefulness—

When first he heard about the possibility, Guthrie had in imagination reached back to shake the hand of an unknown prehistoric man, paddling his dugout, who thought to raise something that would catch the wind.

Jendaire grinned. "But if naught else," she said, "this speed that Proserpina has gained ought to discomfit the powers that be on Earth."

He must not let himself get carried away. "That's assuming your suspicions of them are warranted," he said. "Right now I frankly don't know. None of us do at Amaterasu, nor, as far as I can tell, on Isis or Hestia."

"You are Terran," she retorted. "You see things otherwise than we do."

"Uh-huh. Well, you Lunarians may have a good case. I'm here to listen."

Her nostrils flared, her slenderness tautened. "Then hearken to this. Lunarians are extinct upon Luna."

"Yes, I know from your message, and it did shock us on Amaterasu. It looks as though orbiting that Habitat and encouraging Terrans to move in was deliberate government policy." But there could have been justifications, Guthrie thought. *How I do remember what troublemakers Lunarians are apt to be—from a Terran viewpoint, at least. And it isn't as if a pogrom were mounted against them or anything like that.* "Nevertheless, my lady, I need to know more. Remember how new I am to this slew of news. What else have the Proserpinans told you, especially while I've been in transit?"

With characteristic swiftness, her mood cooled. "Rather little," she admitted. "They have attempted closer surveillance missions than erstwhile to the inner Solar System, with their field-drive vessels, but the gain has been slight. Those vessels are few as yet, and experience in their use lies mainly futureward. Also, truth to tell, they wish more to employ the capability in expanding outward through the realm of the comets." Her voice dropped to a murmur. "And thus, at last, starward."

Yes, he thought, the Oort Cloud of comets reached so far and far that its outermost fringes mingled with the comet clouds of neighbor suns. You didn't really need downloading and *c*-ships to go forth into the galaxy. Enduring adventurousness was enough.

"One fine trait you Lunarians have," he remarked. "You don't want conquest or power, at least for their own sweet sakes." Pride and greed could become murderous—he reflected—but as matters for the individual or, at most, for the clan. No Lunarians would ever perpetrate a nation-state.

"But let's just see—" he went on. "Have you yourselves, here at Centauri, improved your spacecraft designs?"

"Nay, little since you evacuated Demeter," she said. "Ey, we have launched robotic exploratory interstellar missions. But we have no cause to send off emigrants. Riches and wonders abundant lie virginal around the Centauri suns." She gazed beyond him. "The more true when shards of Demeter and Phaethon swing ever outward. Lately a prospecting expedition came upon a steel-frame house, ruined but recognizable, cast loose in some unlikely wise and orbiting free. . . ."

His spirit shuddered a bit. Aloud, as calmly as possible: "Okay. You do have a few *c*-ships. Uh, to make sure we understand each other, by *c*-ships I mean small field-drive craft with minimal payloads, which can come near light-speed because their mass is so little."

"Yes, that is clear. Like yours. I have wondered whence you took its name."

"From a boyhood hero of mine. Never mind. You must also have a larger number of cruisers of various classes. By that I mean bigger field-drive ships, with considerably more carrying capacity, though they can't manage c-like delta v's."

"We have such. You shall, since you wish it, learn what those classes are and what they can do. I tell you now, forasmuch as you touched on the matter, we possess none that can bear a load of colonists in cold sleep to a different star, for as said, we have ample frontier close at hand."

Come the time, Guthrie thought, doubtless they would build vessels like that. Probably the duration of a voyage by humans in suspended animation would always be limited to a century or two. If nothing else, beyond that there'd be too much accumulated radiation damage. Inactive DNA couldn't repair it, and while nanotech performed remarkable feats, it was no magic wand. But a hundred Earth-years, or less, was plenty of time to reach nearby stars, given top speeds of a few percent of light's. And Lunarians need go no farther on any single venture. They didn't require planets. What they wanted were asteroids and moons. They lived and reproduced healthily under low gravity, down to no gravity at all.

It was different for Terrans. They had to have a minimum third of a g under them. And, okay, some had settled on Mars; but the tremendous journey to another sun simply wasn't worth the cost unless, at the far end, you could walk out in your shirtsleeves; and worlds where life had arisen to liberate oxygen and nitrogen were sorrowfully rare.

It needn't be like that forever. Someday humans of the Terran kind would make dead planets over from scratch. The task was almost unthinkably huge. Consider the energy spent in those chemical conversions, that grinding of rock into soil and purifying of the waters. . . . Nature on Earth had taken the better part of a billion years doing it, before the globe was ready for the earliest primitive life. Air had not become humanly breathable for about another billion years, as near as Guthrie remembered. People didn't have that kind of time. . . . But someday, given sufficient marshaled resources, natural and technological and spiritual, they should be able to start making homes for themselves throughout the galaxy . . . at last, throughout the universe.

Someday. They weren't there yet by a long shot. Maybe they'd never get there. Maybe they'd never be allowed to.

His mind had wandered. At electrophotonic speeds, though, it had been gone for only a fraction of a second. "I pretty well expected this, my lady," he said to Jendaire.

She arched her brows. "What more have you expected, my lord?"

If he had been generating a face-image, he could have grinned at her. He settled for putting cheeriness into his tone.

"I told you, that'll depend on what I discover here about the general situation. But my strong hunch is that I'll try to talk you into providing me with a cruiser, and assorted gear, for my trip on to Sol."

She did not completely mask surprise. "A cruiser? We were prepared to refuel your *c*-ship, but—but even a light cruiser will take some thirty years for the journey."

"About what I've spent so far. How well I know," he said. "Look, my lady. I've arrived damn near helpless. You can have your men squash me like a cockroach if you've a mind to." Fleetingly: Has she ever heard of cockroaches? "I don't want to reach Sol under the same handicap. I'm hoping you'll see fit to send me on with much more under my belt. That's another reason I've come via Centauri. A cruiser voyage straight from Hydri would've taken ridiculously long."

She stood quiet for a little. He could guess how she

was calculating. A thrush trilled, a butterfly zigzagged on gorgeous wings, a breeze bore scent of jasmine, the stars passed frostily by.

"What would you fain do yonder?" she asked low.

"That too will depend on what I find out, both here and there," he said. Might as well be honest; it was obvious anyway. "And also on how things work out once I've made the crossing. I swear I'll never actually betray you and your people, my lady. You've been my partners since Rinndalir and I brought down the Avantists and led the exodus. But I can't guarantee you'll like what I attempt. It may be nothing whatsoever, because no good would come of anything. Nor can I guarantee that what I may try will succeed."

It might not even save him from destruction, he thought. But no matter that. Somewhere along the line, every mortal man who wanted to enjoy his life must stare down his mortality. A download felt no such dreads to start with.

"I do promise," he finished, "I'll travel on behalf of all of us amongst the stars."

4

IN TWO HOURS outside, Fenn's party had seen Luna wax from a gigantic crescent to more than half full. Earth's three-quarter phase had changed little, except for its position with respect to the Habitat; blue-and-white luster that had been to starboard of the great cylindroid was now almost aft, blinking in and out of vision as the sails spun across heaven. Hard spatial sunlight overwhelmed all constellations. Any part of a helmet that turned in that direction darkened itself to save the wearer's eyes; he saw a silvery disk slightly speckled with maelstroms, each of which could have swallowed a planet whole.

He'o vectored the thrusts from his jetpack and soared. The specially built, legless spacesuit flashed through an incredible arc. He had taken to EVA like a—a seal to water, Fenn thought. But then, of course, He'o was a seal.

Iokepa Hakawau had acquired about as much competence as a man might be expected to in a short time. That meant he still wallowed clumsily about. His radio voice boomed in his companions' earplugs: "'Auwē! Make wai au.''

"Huh?" Fenn grunted. He'd picked up a few words of the Lahui Kuikawa language—human Lahui, that is—during the past fortnight, but only a few.

"Hrach-ch," sounded from He'o. Laughter? The metamorph used his vocal synthesizer to form Anglo: "He means that this has been enough and he is very thirsty." It went slowly, for his voice had nothing like the range of a human's and conversation required an elaborate coding program.

"Yes, by Maui's butt," Iokepa growled in the same tongue, heavily though musically accented. "Where's the nearest cold beer?"

Mainly the man was tired out, Fenn realized, but he wouldn't admit it—he, sailor and championship swimmer from the seas of Earth. No disgrace when you weren't trained to maneuver in open space, or weren't born to it as He'o seemed to have been. Nevertheless, Fenn resisted cracking a joke and congratulated himself on curbing his usual brashness. He didn't want to hurt this big, friendly fellow, with whom he had shared such unbounded fun.

"Well, you've gotten your taste of the outside," he said. The rest he must force: "Yes, let's go back in."

He'o glided close, braking, till he had matched velocities and could look through helmets at the boy's face. "You are reluctant," he observed.

Fenn gazed back into the big, liquid-brown eyes behind the muzzle and beneath a brow bulging to hold a human-equivalent brain. Sunlight set sleek fur aglow. He reads me better than Iokepa does, Fenn thought. Are the

Keiki Moana really as alien as everybody says? I s'pose. But that doesn't mean they can't be simpático. I guess they've got to be, most of them. How else could they have stayed in company with their humans all these hundreds of years?

"I don't get too many chances for EVA," he confessed. "Uh, thank you both for this one."

"Thank *you, makamaka*," Iokepa interjected from his distance. "You've been the perfect guide."

Maybe more gratitude was due Fenn's father, the boy thought. When this pair out of the Lahui Kuikawa group that had come to investigate the Moon expressed their strongest interest as being in the parks, waters, and wild areas of the interior, it had been natural to refer them to ranger-manager Birger. When he turned them over mainly to his son—well, Elitha muttered with a certain bitterness that it was an act of courtship, but Fenn was overjoyed. The excursions that followed had gone beyond his expectations. For that while, his inward anger had smoldered low, almost forgotten.

It began to burn higher again. "Why, can you not come up here often?" He'o was asking.

"No!" Fenn snapped. He tried for softness. "Not in the past two or three years. I've got my studies, and a ferry ride does cost, and, uh, there're other things that keep me busy on Luna."

"Aye, you showed me," Iokepa chuckled. "A grand guide for sure. *Mahalo lui noa.*"

Fenn felt his cheeks flush. That evenwatch when the two of them and some girls he knew—Actually, it had soon been Iokepa who took the lead, finding lowlife bars and other things parents need not hear about.

If He'o guessed, he had said nothing and probably didn't care. Why should he? He was concerned now, though. "No," he said, "if open space matters so much to our friend, then it cannot be mere pleasure that anchors him to the Moon."

He meant well, but he should lay off. "I go out on the

surface a lot," Fenn said roughly. "And I've been on Earth too, you may remember." That was chiefly in the Yukonian wilderness under Birger's aegis. Historical sites, artworks, and other standard tourist draws, those you could experience on a vivifer at home, a lot more cheaply.

"Yet I whisker-feel your trouble is heavy, boldly though you bear it," He'o persisted.

"Don't smell at me!" Fenn shouted.

He would not have this gene-engineered freak, or anybody else, prying into his private life—how his parents had separated, the direct reason being that Elitha was determined to bear her second allowable child and Birger couldn't stand the idea that it must not be his, and how from their two sides they clutched at their son—and everything else, everything wrong, as far back as his memories went.

"*E Kulikuli oe*, He'o," Iokepa called. "Don't hunt the lad. Fenn, I'm sorry. We can't always tell what's good manners in foreign parts."

This wasn't the first time the man had shown a sensitive—and thoughtful, almost meditative—side of his own. Such belonged to just about all the Lahui Kuikawa, human and metamorph alike; or so Fenn had heard. It went with their Dao.

Still irritated, he said, "All right, let's get back. Iokepa, stay put. We'll join you. Both of you listen close while I repeat instructions, then bloody well follow them. We'll be dealing with huge angular momenta. They've killed people who got careless."

Not for many years, to be sure, if only because few people ever came to space any more. Those inside Luna or the Habitat, even those on Mars, they didn't count, not really. Fenn's eyes went toward the glare-hidden stars. The Lunarians at Proserpina and Alpha Centauri—and now fugitive stories of Terrans at three new suns, whole new worlds, and the galaxy open to them—As he had done before, uncountably often, he choked down his craving and concentrated on the business at hand.

Curtly, he explained his flight plan to He'o. Built-in equipment would take care of operational details. The two of them accelerated, a brief thrust, and went on trajectory, side by side. For a moment an infinite silence encompassed them, beneath which pulsed breath, blood, air and water recyclers, like secrets whispered at night.

"Kh-h-h," He'o said. The seal voice, not totally subvocalized, made a hoarse undertone to the smooth tenor of the synthesizer. "If I have bitten you, I am grieved. I humble myself."

Fenn's temper had cooled as quickly as it flared. "Aw,'twasn't anything. I, uh, overreacted, I guess." That wasn't easy to admit. "You see, I feel kind of bad because you fellows are leaving. I'll miss you."

"Come visit us," Iokepa invited. "I'll show you places the *haole* never get to."

Perhaps misunderstanding an intent that was probably rowdy, He'o added, "Yes, we will take you into the life of our two folk. You will find it strange to everything you have known."

The prospect excited. To Fenn, the Lahui Kuikawa had always been glamorous—not the same as the Martians, lesser still than the distant spacedwellers; yet exotic, colorful—yes, and in their quiet way, a power, the geographical reach of their polity covering the whole mid-Pacific Ocean—islands, surf-riding, ships that were communities, immense aquacultural ranges and ranches, songs, dances, dusky maidens—"I'd certainly like to!" he exclaimed. "When I can." His spirit flagged a bit. "If I can."

"We'll keep in touch," Iokepa promised.

"And you'll be back out here in person. Won't you?"

"Maybe."

The three came together. Again Fenn got too busy for unhappiness. Iokepa was outfitted like him but, unskilled, he couldn't take much advantage of his suit's flexibility. He'o's rig was rigid, segmented but awkward, to accommodate the wetness he needed for comfort. Just the same, he required less help than his partner. Fenn maneuvered them to the jetsled orbiting nearby, got them properly harnessed, closed the cage around them, and took the controls. Groundlings had better have that protection. It wasn't against any mistake of his. This robotic vehicle did all the real work. However, an untrained rider could make untoward motions. The hurtling rotation of yonder mountainous mass was nothing to approach casually.

It grew before him until it filled half the sky, with Luna blocking off a goodly part of the other half. Routine and machine-managed though rendezvous was, thrill after thrill passed through Fenn and his heart beat high. This was nearly as good as bedding a girl; in some ways, better. Oh, if only he had a *ship* at his command, and leave to fare wherever his dreams might lead him!

"Request docking and entry," he intoned. "Fenn." He added his number. "Iokepa Hakawau." He didn't know the Earthman's. The surname felt odd in his mouth. How many people besides Lahui hung onto that custom? Well, the Terrans on Mars, mostly. Historic habit, kept up because those societies were sort of outsider, not fully integrated with the Synesis? "He'o." He had no number for the metamorph either. Did they bother with it, that race? Yes, they'd have to if they wanted to draw citizen's credit.

No importe. The rules demanded advance identification mainly so the port could run through its database and determine if someone needed special services or whatever. Fenn considered the practice silly. Anyhow, his companions were marked out by their uniquenesses.

The sled matched linear velocity, closed in, made contact with barely an impact, and gripped fast. Earth-weight laid hold of the riders. Fenn adjusted immediately. His abundant physical activities on Luna included enough exercise in the centrifuge that he had developed a fully terrestrial-Terran physique. His passengers, seafolk, had no problem either. The slipway took the sled into a niche where they could safely debark. From there, they cycled through a personnel lock.

Within the Habitat, robots helped them off with their suits. The humans shed their undergarments as well. For a moment, naked while they retrieved their everyday clothes, they stood contrasted. Iokepa was a big man, brown-skinned, round-faced, wide-nosed, full-mouthed, his blue-black hair bobbed below the ears. He donned blouse, sarong, and sandals. Fenn was taller yet, nearly as muscular and, at age sixteen, still filling out. He kept his yellow mane cropped short. Blue eyes glowered from a visage beginning to turn craggy. His garb was just a coverall and soft boots. He'o, moist length ashimmer, flopped himself onto the motor cart that waited for him. It was equipped with arms ending in hands as well as a synthesizer, and short legs for situations where the wheels wouldn't serve.

"Now what about that beer?" Iokepa demanded.

"Have we time?" He'o asked in the same Anglo, the same courtesy to Fenn. "I believe the next ferry leaves soon."

"If we miss it, we'll catch tomorrow's. In fact, better we get a good nightwatch's rest before joining the others on Luna."

"But we have seen more than enough of these . . . environs," said He'o.

Fenn, who had shown them around the entire structure, asked in surprise, "Don't you like it here?"

"It is very interesting." He'o put some color back into his artificial tones. "But I long for your Lake Beynac," the stretch of water beneath Mare Somnium in which he had romped.

"Ah, you'll get plenty of chances," Iokepa told him. "We'll be on the Moon for daycycles, finishing our business." He regarded the seal more closely. "You're not comfortable aboard, are you?"

"If ever we launch a space island of our own, I think we will want it to be different from this one." He'o turned his head toward Fenn. "I say nothing against yours. It is simply that its Dao is not our Dao."

"Come on, let's go," Iokepa snorted.

The humans walked and the metamorph rolled along a corridor that curved always upward ahead of them. An illusion of green meadows under blue sky stirred, as if to a breeze, in walls and ceiling. Duramoss carpeted the deck. They were alone. Only their voices and footfalls sounded through the rustle of ventilation. What little regular space traffic there was went in and out the polar port and was robotic. Fenn had used a small side dock to give his friends the blood-quickening sensations of spinoff and a circularized return maneuver. As for humans, the permanent residents and the larger floating population— the latter mostly involved with pregnancy and early childhood—numbered considerably less than the complex had housed when it was Ragaranji-go, the mighty L–5. Their apartments, businesses, and pleasures were elsewhere.

A different Dao, Fenn thought: the Dao Kai of the Lahui Kuikawa, which had somehow become troubling to Earth—a philosophy, faith, way evolved by humans and seals living together for century after seaborne century—Wonder caught him up. "I, uh, I'd like to hear what you'd do differently, if . . . when you go into space, you people."

Let it in truth be not "if" but "when!"

He'o trundled silent before he answered, "As you wish. But what I say may be no fair wind for you." He hesitated. "To us—Iokepa will agree, if not as strongly— this shell is lifeless."

The Earthman frowned, scratched his head, and muttered, "Um, eh, yes. In a way."

"What?" Fenn protested. "But, but look!" His gesture swept past the pseudo-scene, reminding them of real gardens, parks, pools, streams, grass, flowers, fruit trees, bright birds and fish and insects, small mammals running free, at places throughout the whole station.

"You have life here," He'o said, "but it is incidental, and parasitic on the machinery."

"Everything alive is kept in its assigned berth," Iokepa added.

"But without the machinery, the, the organization— we'd die," Fenn argued. "This is *space*."

"Earth sails through space, yet fully lives," He'o declared.

"Look, *aikāne*." Iokepa laid a hand on the boy's shoulder. "Let me give you a 'for instance.' Back in L–5 times, a giant tree grew here. I've played vivis of it more than once. It was like nothing else ever. But when the colony disbanded, they let the tree die in the cold and the dark. Now when they've put this thing in Lunar orbit and are using it again, nobody's even talked about planting a new one. The cybercosm doesn't think or feel that way."

Fenn harked back. He too had in multisensory recordings known the Tree, the sequoia grown to a height impossible on Earth, the majesty and awe of it. Another memory stirred. Among his few dreambox experiences had been the cosmos of an ancient mythology— Yggdrasil, with roots in earth, in winterland, and in hell, with trunk soaring up to heaven, and nine worlds strewn through the windy, shadowy leafage of its crown— Yggdrasil, the All-Tree, whose fall shall bring the doom of the gods and the end of time. . . . The wind among those boughs had told him something deep, though he never knew what. Had any machine mind had any sense for the mystery in L–5's Tree?

"And, yah, the cybercosm's officially just an advisor and helper, with one single vote at the Conventions," Iokepa finished. "But you realize as well as I do, it's what decides everything important. Plus half the tonnage of petty details."

Despite his ingrained resentments, Fenn was vaguely shocked. People didn't talk like that. Did they? It was foolishness. Wasn't it? His education to date included the chronicle of wretchedness which was history until five or six hundred years ago—a bare half-dozen lifetimes. He hadn't learned only about famine, disease, poverty, toil, environmental destruction, the ills that technology piece by piece had lifted off humankind. He'd learned about the unnecessary horrors, slavery, private abuse, rampant crime, inherited hatreds, sexual distortion and oppression, superstitious dreads, and the institutionalized atrocities of government, war, regimentation, extortion, torture. . . . Humankind today was liberated. Wasn't it? If it had pulled back into a warm little Earth-womb, that was only because it was cowardly and stupid. No? . . . And yet the news told more and more of unrest, demonstrations, strange doctrines preached to rapt listeners. And lately, those rumors drifting in from outermost space—

Well, maybe Iokepa was feeling grumpy. He'o stayed with the main topic: "A home in orbit should be more than a harbor for occasional ships and a rookery for meek citizens. Ours shall be a world small but living, independent."

The seal was uttering discontent himself, Fenn realized: in his low-keyed fashion, more forcefully than the man had. He'o might be ever so learned and philosophical and all the rest—his species had had many generations to become civilized—but down underneath he remained a fighter, a hunter. At home he often chased down live fish and caught them in his jaws to eat. The scars on his flanks, which he'd disdained to have erased—

Iokepa continued more mildly: "Eh, you *po'e* have done many wonderful things. You've a lot to teach us. But aren't those works of yours, like the wildlife under Luna, aren't they a tradition you keep up, something that got started before there was a cybercosm? What we want to do is build something genuinely new and free." He broke off. "Never mind. I talk too much."

"It is nothing immediate in any event," He'o said, "nor nigh to here."

The remark clinched an impression that had been closing in on Fenn daycycle by daycycle. He gulped. "You don't think you can colonize on the Moon?"

"That was always doubtful, as you must have known from the first. Now, after our committee goes home, its report will be much debated. But I am already certain of the decision. No, we cannot."

"But you—" Fenn said, aware it was in vain, "a Habitat of your own, according to your own design—and Luna has more vacant sites left than you could begin to fill—"

"Ah, we'll be back from time to time, to study and ask questions," Iokepa told him soothingly. "You Selenites have a freight of experiences we need to draw on."

"Where else could you *go?*" Mercury and Venus: infernos. The Asteroid Belt and the moons of the giant planets: every useful site long since occupied by machines, which by now had exhausted most of the resources worth exploiting. Proserpina and the comets: afar in eternal night, and their Lunarians would not make Terrans welcome. The stars: impossible. The first tiny migration to the nearest of them, which Anson Guthrie led, had surely been the last ever.

Unless . . . those stories you heard lately, and the official declaration that they were totally unconfirmed—they had a great deal to do with the rising restlessness on Earth and Luna. The possibility that you yourself might live forever—

No. Shove it aside. Too nebulous, too complicated. "Mars?"

"Maybe," Iokepa said. "Uh, you understand, don't you, if we Lahui do set up a colony, only a few of us would settle there. Like the ancestors, in a way, canoeing across the ocean to a new island. Most stayed behind."

"Such an albatross venture cannot be for material gain," He'o said. "It must have a prospect of profit or it cannot come to pass, but the true prize will be the freedom of the Dao Kai to grow unhindered; and that freedom will reach back across space to our home world.''

''What we could do on Luna seems too limited,'' Iokepa added. ''But mainly we've seen, better than we knew before, that Luna is also cybercosm territory.''

Again Fenn couldn't quite grasp what the issue was. Did either of his companions, actually? He had a feeling of enormous blind forces at work.

They fell silent. Presently they entered a populated section, men and women, and especially children, in the passages, portals giving on apartments, service centers, small enterprises, a measure of noise and bustle. *''Nānā 'oe!''* Iokepa bawled. A lightsign shimmered ahead. YING-ZHOU, Isle of the Blest. They surged in, took a table, the humans cross-legged on cushions, and called for beer. Fenn's card declared him responsible, but the servitor didn't ask for it, probably because the boy looked older than he was. He'o enjoyed a brew as much as his companions did. Talk grew lively and wandered widely.

—Fenn lifted his third beaker. ''Here's to life!''

''May the tide so flow,'' He'o wished.

Iokepa beamed. ''I think it's doing exactly that, lads. What we hear about Life Mothers yonder—rebirth—''

''And those ships the Proserpinans have got!'' Fenn cried.

''Haw, the cybercosm doesn't like the current state of affairs one bit,'' Iokepa said. ''Especially when we're finding out how long the facts were kept secret. Embarrassing, no?''

''Nothing is certain,'' He'o cautioned. ''These are scarcely more than rumors. We hear them in stray communications from Terrans on Mars, who have heard things from Lunarian neighbors, who have heard it from other Lunarians there, who say they have heard it from Proserpina. I cannot blame the Synesis for being noncommittal. Some truth doubtless floats somewhere in all this, but I wonder how much is sheer Lunarian mischief-making.''

Fenn's gladness vanished. Uncertainty, he thought. Rumors, rumors, denials, equivocations, and more rumors. Meanwhile, here he sat, year after year after year, bound to the same creaking wheel.

5

THE SMALL TOWN Eos clung to the rim of Eos Chasma, near the eastern end of Valles Marineris. Behind it, Margaritifer Sinus reached past the horizon: cultivation, then boulders, dunes, craters, basaltic upthrusts, dust scudding and whirling on ghost-thin winds. A road ran through, soon lost to sight; the spear of a laser pylon gleamed bright but, at its distance, tiny and lonely. Below the town, cliffs and crags descended, weirdly sculptured, subtly tinted, into shadowed depths. Looking that way, northward, you could see the land begin to climb again, and know that after some three hundred kilometers it would topple into Capri Chasma. Likelier, though, your gaze would turn west, where the incredible steeps and deeps of the Valles rived the planet across well-nigh a fifth of its girth.

Geologically fascinating, this country was also rich in the minerals that had been a primary reason for human settlement on Mars. Long afterward, living in a stable economy with a basically machine-run and recycling industry, many people on Earth had trouble understanding the economics of that, if they thought about the matter at all. Luna was obvious—a site for solar energy collectors and a staging area for interplanetary operations, back in early days when much of the work could be done only by humans. Once established, such a set of communities naturally continued itself. But Mars? Was not the accessible wealth of the Solar System overwhelmingly in the asteroids and comets?

True. Yet very little of it consisted of anything that could properly be called ores. Mostly it was a jumble, requiring elaborate and energy-costly refinement. Although energy abounded in space, the capital investment necessary to capture it was by no means negligible. On Earth, geophysical and geochemical forces had beneficiated and concentrated materials through ages before humanity was—deposits, veins, lodes, Golcondas. In less but still meaningful measure, the same thing had happened on Mars, especially in its youth, when volcanoes raged manifold, waters flowed wild, and atmosphere was more than a wisp.

The expansion of extraterrestrial operations generated a voracious demand. The Martian gravity well was fairly shallow. Between that factor and proximity, colonists were better able to supply workers on the asteroids—with manufactured goods, chemicals, food, other biological products—than Earth was.

As for life support, on Mars it did not need the great domes and excavations of Luna. Dwellings could stand on the surface, radiation-proof, airtight, and biointegrated. Metamorphic species could flourish in the open, supplying the colonists as well as the exporters among them. Mines became profitable.

In some such words, you could explain to a latter-day Earthdweller why there were people yonder. Probably you need not add that both Terrans and Lunarians had immigrated because both races could readily reproduce under that weight. Equally plain to see, those born in a particular land, and generation by generation adapting it to themselves and themselves to it, would choose to remain. They would evolve their own traditions, their own unique institutions. The Republic of Mars was actually two nations in all but name—if the word "nation" quite applied. Isolated by more than distance, it took little part in the politics of the World Federation, and after the Reconstitution, its role in the Synesis was slighter still. Yes, the Earthdweller could follow this logic of history.

If he was a rationalist, like many of his contemporaries, he might require an effort of imagination to feel why the Martians abided yet, now that their exports were wanted no more and the spacecraft that called at their planet were few and far between. Nothing forced them to endure straitened circumstances. They had plenty of accumulated citizen's credit, unspent because Mars didn't have much for them to spend it on. They could pay for charter passage and comfortable relocation on Earth or Luna.

Well, but a true rationalist took emotions into account. He could look around him and see how people everywhere sought for something greater than any individual existence to love, to belong to, and how tightly they clung to whatever they found. Mars was the Martians' birthright.

Surely David Ronay had it in his blood and bones. When he wedded Helen Holt and brought her to Sananton, it was to ground that a forebear of his had broken almost four hundred years earlier—about seven hundred and fifty of Earth's. Besides running the plantation and other operations of the estate, he was active in civic affairs and eventually served as regional deputy to the House of Ethnoi. Besides being his partner, she spent time on the educational net teaching basic linguistics and semantics. She also kept shrewd watch on their investments. Better than most, she saw how this world, thrown on its own resources, was perforce rediscovering, or perhaps reinventing, venture capitalism.

Kinna Ronay was born in the medicenter at Eos, but the next day her mother flitted her the hundred-odd kilometers back to Sananton. There she grew up. In the course of time she gained a brother and two sisters. (That alone made the home foreign to any on Earth or Luna. The Republic had never tried to limit reproduction. Far from being a threat to this biosphere, humans had created and maintained it. Nor did their ten million or so overcrowd the globe. Rather, more of them would have been desirable. But economics—how many offspring the average couple could afford—kept population down. The Ronays were relatively well off.) However, although the family was close-knit, the first of Kinna's siblings came three years after her, and thus she developed more or less independently of them. She was always an independent soul anyway.

Regardless, as she grew taller, she got an increasing share of responsibilities in addition to her schooling. She did not resent what to her was simply natural. At its peak, the Martian economy had not been lavishly productive. It must concentrate on the extractive industries and on building the basis of survival. Scant capacity was left over for robotizing jobs or for social benefits. People must work alongside the machines. It formed habits that stood them in good stead in these leaner times.

Not that Kinna was ignorant of the outer universe or shut away from it. The family were regularly in Eos on business or pleasure. They toured the planet, from polar ice dunes to the marts and monuments of Crommelin or the cities clustered in Schiaparelli. They were in telecommunication with friends everywhere.

Kinna gained some familiarity with Earth and Luna too, as part of both her education and her everyday life. From time to time the multiceiver carried a program beamcast directly from the mother world. Otherwise the public database offered text, audiovisuals, music, the entire recorded culture of her species and much of the Lunarian. In the virtuality of the vivifer she experienced rain, sea, forests, a frenetic dance hall, a meditation on a mountainside, the ruins of New York, ascension to the Habitat and onward to Luna . . . When her parents judged her old enough, they allowed her a few dreambox sessions. Afterward her memory bore, as if it had really happened to her, a day in mythic Avalon, being an eagle and then an owl, an evening (suitably disguised as a male) in the Mermaid Tavern, being (and somehow conscious of it) a planetary system or a molecule, all the ever-changing intricacies. . . .

But work held ample rewards. Riding about the plantation, at first with Father, later by herself, tending the crops and their symbionts, she never found two trips alike. There was bound to be a surprise, problem to solve, challenge to meet, a mutation, a disease, an ecological equilibrium upset. To restore the right order was profoundly satisfying. She liked seeing things grow beneath her hands—also in the workshop, where she proved to have a gift for fixing machinery and making useful articles. Thrice over the years, a giant dust storm overwhelmed the drift fences. The terror of it, then afterward the complexities and even the toil of digging out and reconstruction, brought her totally alive. Housework itself could be fun, when two or three tackled it and sang together. Looking after her siblings while the parents were away might get exasperating now and then, but down underneath, it was a joy.

The family often made excursions into the Chasma, to hike or climb through its stern magnificence. In adolescence, Kinna explored with friends of her age, or alone. When time allowed, she was gone for days at a stretch, inflating a sealtent and activating a heater at night. This often began with a flit to some remote point along the Valles. Wonders were endless; wind-carved stone, mineral hues, caverns, crystals, ancient watercourses, perhaps a fossil. Such a find was an event, and not just because she got to report it to the museum and help dig it out. To behold that small, strange trace, to sense that after a billion years Mars again bore life—Chills ran deliciously up and down her spine.

It was enjoyable to poke around in abandoned settlements, but also spooky and faintly saddening. Once people numbered more than they did today, and hopes ran high. They had actually talked of transforming the planet into a new Earth. Here lay the shells of dead dreams.

Kinna straightened from them. Her glance went skyward. The Ronays were not giving up yet, thank you!

Increasingly, however, her flits became the short one over to Capri Chasma and the Lunarian clandom there.

Like Eos, Belgarre looked down from the cliffs to the depths. Otherwise the towns bore scant resemblance. Here were no streets, luminous after dark, but mosaic pavement between buildings that stood well apart. The stone of them was seldom covered over, and centuries had not eroded its roughness. Utilitarian structures were topped with solar collector domes, but homes generally rose high, steep-roofed, with glazed balconies jutting from their walls as if sentries were posted inside, emblems of phyle and phratry emblazoned above their main airlocks. Grandest among them, the mansion of the Nantai etaine thrust two towers aloft and flaunted a banner by day.

Skinsuited, Kinna and Elverir slipped from a side lock. Their biostats immediately activated inwoven heater nets against a temperature of minus fifty degrees and plunging. Brilliance as cold struck through their helmets and into their eyes, a clarity and abundance of stars seen only when the air had lain many hours windless, the Milky Way frozenly cataracting through silence. Deimos glimmered low and wan; only hours of watching its slow course and changeable brightness would single it out. Earth stood higher, coruscant blue.

Kinna stopped. "O-o-oh," she breathed.

Elverir tugged at her arm. "Ho-ay, come, dawdle not," he said.

"But it's so beautiful."

"If my elders see us, belike they'll send me back to my task, since I need such meager sleep."

She knew he had been given time off—grudgingly, but the pride of the house demanded it when a visitor came specifically to him. Now she realized why he had drawn her aside and whispered that she should leave her room, gear up for outdoors, and meet him at this hour, without telling anybody. The knowledge of naughtiness gave a tingle in her blood. They set off at Martian pace, neither the stride of the Earthling nor the bound of the Selenite, but a long, easy lope.

Having arrived shortly before sunset, she had not yet had a real chance to speak with him. "What is that job, and why's it urgent?" she asked.

His young voice—they were the same age, seven and a half—cracked a trifle. "The . . . *avinyon*, the mine . . . *ti etaine pir si courai*—" Mostly they used Anglo, over the eidophone or in person, because he wanted to practice his. It was apt to fail him when he got excited.

"Oh." Although learned mainly from programs, her Lunarian was better; she had a talent for languages. "That ice lode of yours." It was the source of the old money in his etaine—not quite "family." Depleted, it was nevertheless still being worked. She understood that honor more than profit drove the business these days, to maintain standing in the courai—not quite "company"—that marketed the water.

A quasi-instinctive jag of alarm went through her. The deposit had lost its former importance, and presently it would be gone. Yet they were talking about *water*. She was barely four when word came that the Synesis had decided to bring no more in, because the Martians had an adequate supply and the readily exploitable comets were used up; but she remembered the grimness that fell upon her parents. Later they explained to her how water was always lost, gradually but inexorably, molecules escaping into the atmosphere to be cracked apart by ultraviolet radiation, oxygen binding to rocks and hydrogen flying off beyond the sky. Complete conservation was possible only if you sealed everything tight, the way they did on Luna. Within the next fifty years, Martians would either have to start going underground, which meant changing their entire lives, or start leaving Mars—unless they could build enough ships and robots of their own to go after ice in the largely untapped Kuiper Belt, or could make some arrangement with the mysterious Proserpinans. . . . Kinna shivered, as if the air had reached in and touched her.

She jumped to practicalities: "What's the trouble?"

"We have had a . . . collapse, a rock slide. It must be cleared away. I take a shift guiding the machines."

On Earth or Luna, Kinna thought, the machines would guide themselves. Mars couldn't afford equipment that good. She wasn't sure why. Something about the resources, human as well as natural and technological, that would have to be invested to make the apparatus that made the apparatus that was needed. Why had neither Federation nor Synesis ever managed to give Mars a boost over the threshold?

"But I'll let Orlier and Zendant do the whole of it while you are here," Elverir was saying. She saw how he smiled at her. The blood thudded in her head, beneath the words in her earplugs.

Silly, she thought. We'll never have a romance. We're too different. He's just a friend. But he does make all the Terran boys seem so boring. And he *is* handsome.

Black-haired, brown-skinned, rather broad in the nose and lips, he showed the African strain in his race more than most Lunarians did; but the characteristic ears, cheekbones, and big oblique eyes—green in his case—stood forth. Under the gravity, he was growing up on the short and stocky side, even as Terrans commonly grew tall and slender compared to Earthlings. They two were about of a height.

"Where are we going?" she asked breathlessly.

"Out to admire Phobosrise while the sky is this clear. And with luck—Eyach, here we be."

They had reached a public garage. In a city like Crommelin it would have been locked, with a recognition key for tenants, but here the identity of a thief would soon have become known and that person soon be dead. Elverir led the way into the lighted interior and on among the parked vehicles. They passed Kinna's flitter—its

cabin canopy bulged out from it like a slightly reproach-
ful eye watching her—and came to a groundcycle, little
more than a motor, controls, locker, and two saddles. He
gestured for her to mount.

She hesitated. "We're heading into the desert? Aren't
you going to enter a travel plan?"

"Why?" She heard the bravado. "Await you we'll
come to harm?"

"Well, uh, nobody ever knows what can happen—
help the rescue corps—the law—"

"Here we are not under Terran law, but Lunarian
honor," he reminded her.

She stiffened at the condescension. "I'm not afraid!"

"Then get aboard."

She couldn't well turn around and go to bed, could
she? Kinna settled herself behind him. He started the motor and steered forward. The door retracted for them. It
closed at their backs with a kind of finality.

Kinna shoved her qualms aside. This was a fantastic
night. They had not far to roll before they were out in
the open, with nothing to block off sight of the stars.

At first they took a road, northbound through a plantation. The cultivars weren't the same as at home. Of
course, here too a buried network of aquaria, with its ice
worms and other symbionts, supplied a mat of low-
growing solaria. Here too roots, bacteria, agrichemistry,
and machines had created a layer of soil, which incor-
porated clathrated water as well as minerals and humus.
But Lunarians didn't raise many plants requiring intensive attention. They preferred things like ironroot, am-
berwood, and ramalana, trading the yields for materials
produced by fields elsewhere. Trees and shrubs hulked
black on either side. Kinna did spy a stand of pale Mars
corn and an eerie sheen where the translucent cowl of a
vaquetilla sheltered a vegetable community. Then they
were beyond it all, on the overpass above a drift fence,
down again and out upon the barren.

Elverir left the road. At reckless speed he wove among

boulders, across dunes, on toward higher ground. The cycle throbbed. Dust smoked in its wake. The landscape reached stark, ashen in this light, altogether still except for these two.

He stopped. The abruptness threw her against him. She clutched with knees and hands. "What's the matter?" she cried.

He pointed upward. "Hoy-a. Yonder. A ship?"

Her stare followed his finger. A glint traversed Orion. "No," she mumbled. "Can't be. We'd know if one was coming." When had the last, other than the annual transport vessel? Five years ago? And that was a brief scientific expedition, entirely sophotectic, though it sent the House of Ethnoi a courtesy message.

He twisted about to glance at her. His teeth gleamed in something like a snarl. "Not from Earth," he said. "Proserpina."

For a moment she tumbled through wildness. All those stories of secret landings—and communication definitely went to and fro across the gulf, encoded, but bits of information escaped—somebody had heard somebody else who claimed to have been told by a third party—contact with Alpha Centauri, new kinds of spacecraft, unidentified comings and goings, and, vaguer yet, mention of an unrevealed discovery a gravitational lens was supposed to have made—The stars whirled dizzily through her head.

Elverir regarded the sky afresh. His shoulders slumped, his tone flattened. "Nay. See how it fares. A relay satellite, small and in high orbit, so we see it not when the air is dusty."

Kinna's world steadied. I should have known that right away, she thought. He should have. "What made you think anything else?" Hopes that he hadn't shared with her?

"Eyach, I've overheard scraps of tales out of the Threedom—" The words snapped off.

Her skin prickled. "What, the outlaws in Tharsis?"

He was silent for a few seconds before he replied, "I must not tell you."

He can't, Kinna realized. Who'd trust a boy with a big secret? Like he said, he'd overheard a few snatches. But I won't say that to his face.

Nor did she want to pursue the matter, on this night that had been so magical. It was too much like times at home when Father was in a bad mood and his suspicions broke loose from his tongue. Sure, she thought, peculiar things were astir, but probably the Lunarians on Mars didn't know a lot about it themselves, and certainly they'd passed very little on to any Terrans; and if the Synesis wasn't issuing warnings or taking action, there couldn't be a terrible threat, could there? Maybe it was something wonderful getting ready to happen.

Elverir restarted the groundcycle, driving more cautiously now, making for a ridge up ahead.

Phobos rose in the west and all magic returned.

The moon was dwarfish, dun, lumpy, nothing like Luna above Earth, but it climbed rapidly and cast faint shadows—a faerie sight. She lost herself in it.

On the crest of the ridge Elverir stopped, got off, stepped behind her, and opened the locker. For a moment, half thrilled, half terrified, she wondered about his intentions. Then he came to stand beside her and scan through a photoamplifier he'd taken out.

She peered in the same direction. The terrain rolled away as before, except where a ravine cut a black gash and two craters lay abrim with darkness. "What are you searching for?" she asked.

"Hsss. . . . Hai-ach!" broke from him. "Yonder. See!"

He gave her the instrument. She brought it toward her eyes till it clicked against her helmet. A rock, magnified in the screen—She moved it through an arc. Wait—yes, there. Half lost to sight among boulders and shadows, the metal shape moved on eight legs. Glitters near the front might be sensors. She guessed it was about the size of a man, and far more massive. "What *is* that?"

"A beast. What else?" he snapped. "You have heard."

Yes, and seen images. She bridled. He needn't take that tone. She'd just been surprised. "Primitive robots," she said, as stiffly as she was able. "They charge their accumulators by sunlight till they have the energy to wander around for a while. Lunarians hunt them for sport."

"Sieval u zein—I was hoping one would be afoot." His voice shook.

"I didn't know there were any hereabouts."

"The phratry imported some lately."

Eagerness lifted. "Can we drive closer?"

"Nay. It might bolt. Or it might charge. They are meant to be dangerous." Elverir slipped back to the locker. He returned carrying a long-barreled object. "A gun for beast," he said, mouth stretched in a grin.

"No!" she protested, dismayed.

"Await me," he ordered. "I will bring you a trophy."

He sped off, running, leaping, down the slope, on over the treacherous ground by the ravine, toward the great steel thing that would soon detect him. She remembered imagings of leopards going after their prey.

That poor robot, she thought crazily. No, it's only a robot, a machine; it's not aware like a sophotect or even an animal. But it's meant to be dangerous. Don't get hurt, Elverir! Don't!

He didn't really want to show me the landscape and moonrise. That would have been all right if nothing else came along, but what he really wanted to do was hunt. Oh, he's glad I'm seeing his—his prowess, but—Yes, he'll take the usual trophy they take before they repair the dead robot and set it loose again. He'll have me smuggle it out, he's not supposed to do this at all, but someday he'll take it back from me.

The beast halted. Through the optic she saw it turn ponderously about to confront the oncoming boy.

"Elverir!" Kinna screamed. "Be careful! Shoot fast!"

She didn't feel sorry for the beast any more. She wanted it killed. She wanted Elverir to return to her, and they would rejoice together.

Through a corner of her consciousness flashed a question. Is this in our nature? Father thinks the Teramind doesn't quite trust us humans. Is this why? Could it be— no, it's impossible; it can't be that the mighty Teramind fears us.

6

THE NOISE HIT Fenn as he was on his way home after a daywatch of topside duty. He stopped in midstride. The noise loudened, shouts, screams, thuds, an underlying ragged growl. He had heard it once before in his life, and more than once in training vivis. The hair stood up everywhere on his body. "Santa puta," he whispered. A mob had begun to riot.

He broke into a run, the Lunar gallop that sends a strong man forward like a thrown rock. Pedestrians scattered to right and left. He sped past apartment fronts draped in flowering vines, little specialty shops, a cantina. At the intersection with Ramanujan Passage, he swung left. Duramoss gave way to pavement and to walls farther apart. Vehicles regularly used this thoroughfare. All that were in sight had pulled over. Frightened faces peered from doorways and viewports. The figures in a lightsign above a joyhouse danced, insanely irrelevant, against the overhead simulation of a blue sky where summer clouds wandered at peace.

About fifty men and a few women crowded together. They milled, shoved, yelled defiance and obscenities. Most were armed—pry bars, hammers, stones, whatever the bearer had snatched up, including a few large knives.

At the center of their pack, clubs rose and fell, metal banged and groaned. A tall, skinny man with sandy hair and a ski-jump nose stood aside, waving his fists on high. "Get it!" he shouted. "Wreck the vile thing! Go, go!"

Fenn had not worn a patrolman's uniform since he went into the detective division. His garb was a plain tunic and slacks. He had his badge, though. He whipped it out, lifted it above his head, and thumbed the switch. It flared as if ablaze and shrieked. His roar went beneath: "Hold! Break that up! In the name of the law!" He repeated the Anglo command in Spanyol and Sinese before he clapped the badge against his chest to cling and flash. Its alarm ceased. He slipped forth the small shock pistol that was his sole weapon. "Quiet down!"

Some on the fringe gaped and fell silent. He was a daunting sight, a hundred and ninety-three centimeters tall, more than broad and thick enough to match. From under bushy brows as yellow as the bristling mane and beard, blue eyes glared in a countenance heavy-boned and hook-nosed, ruddy now with anger. The pistol swung slowly to and fro, as if deciding whom to strike first.

Most hadn't yet noticed. Lost in hysteria, they howled, kicked, and battered. This would be touch and go, Fenn realized.

He knew these people, several of them by name. Marginals, none too clean, none too bright, unable to come to terms with what they were. Not quite so slack that the gratifications they could afford on citizen's credit glutted them, they had no other interests to pursue; nor had they a subculture or a faith or even a lodge, such as might have given shape to their lives. Petty crime in the service of petty ambitions was as far as any of them got. You found their sort huddled in its own quarter in many towns, because among each other, they could hope for acceptance. Sometimes a clot of them formed and strayed around looking for trouble. Then they could be dangerous.

The thin man stretched an arm to point at Fenn. Hatred

howled: "Get him, camaradas! Get the filthy gozzer!"

It was a woman who first yelled and charged. Her hair tossed wild, the locks of a greasy Medusa. A man took fire and came after her, another, another.

Fenn shot. They dropped, yammering and jerking in tetany. Those behind curbed themselves. The noise diminished. One by one, they in the mob turned to stare at him. For a few heartbeats nobody stirred.

"See what he did!" cried the thin man. "Get him before he gets you!"

Help wouldn't arrive fast, since it hadn't already. Fenn's gun would account for just a few more before they were upon him. And whoever they were lynching needed immediate aid, supposing he was alive yet.

A red joy surged up. Slag and slaughter, here was a real fight! Even as he stuck the pistol back under his tunic, into a recognition holster from which none of them could snatch it, he sprang. "Whatever you want!" he bellowed.

His fist smote a stomach. The man doubled over and flew two meters before he crashed. Fenn had already pulped a nose. From the corner of an eye he saw an iron bar swung at him. He blocked the blow, forearm meeting wrist, and drove a knee into the groin behind it. Whirling, he grabbed a shirt and smashed its wearer against somebody else.

Given training and discipline, they would have overwhelmed him; but they were a rabble. Moreover, he had forged an Earthling's body for himself. They could not be bothered with boring exercises in a centrifuge.

When he had cleared a space, Fenn seized the nearest man, raised him on high, and hurled him into the middle of the rest. At that they broke. Wailing weak curses or wordless panic, those ran who could. The shot ones, partly recovered by now, and the injured limped after. The ringleader screamed at Fenn, then helped two who were dazed make their escape.

Give the slimeworm credit for that much, thought Fenn amidst thunder.

A part of him remembered to aim the camera ring on his left hand and try for a picture. He had more urgent things to do than chase them.

The battle fury ebbed. He didn't actually like hurting people; he worked off tensions in the dojo or on mountaineering expeditions topside. Still, this had been a grand brawl in a good cause. His breathing slowed, his heart slugged more steadily, the heat left his skin. He grew aware of wetness and a sharp smell, sweat. A couple of spots where he had taken blows began to ache a little, but it was nothing serious, no blood drawn.

Meanwhile, he went over to the victim. A low whistle escaped him. "By all the dead down under," he muttered, "it's the local counselor."

He knew that boxy body, four-legged, six arms sprouting from a torso capped by a turret that held sensors and electrophotonics. It lay sprawled, spindly limbs twisted, bluish organometallic frame dented, retractable communications dish half out of its housing and broken. This was a machine built for precision and sensitivity, not physical stress, most absolutely not violence.

Fenn knelt beside it. "How are you, Benno?" he asked hoarsely. That was the name it had acquired hereabouts. He didn't know how or why, but the intent was affectionate. "Are you—functional?"

Dimness glimmered in the turret screen. It could no longer generate a proper image of a human face. "Considerable damage," a baritone answered in the same Anglo. "I don't . . . see you. But you're a police officer, no?" Other sensors must have reacted to the badge. "Thank you."

"My duty, uh, sir. I'll call for help."

"I too, if possible. A proper terminal—"

Fenn nodded. Benno didn't want to make a phone call. It wanted to remerge its personality with the cybercosm: or, at least, with the regional node of that vast mind. He wondered momentarily whether it needed comfort, assurance, a soothing of pain and shock. But no, you couldn't read human feelings into a sophotect.

Yet, by death, sophotects had feelings of their own. Whatever his attitude toward the cybercosm as a whole, Fenn had come to like Benno. The counselor was a totally decent person. It was made that way.

And when those pusbrains invaded this neighborhood and chanced on it out in the open, they attacked like pathogens.

With the thoroughfare cleared, vehicles began to roll again on their various errands. People were coming out of refuge. Some approached. Fenn rose and glowered. "Keep aside." His harsh bass halted them. Most seemed half numbed. In their lives, lawlessness had been confined to historical shows. "Get on about your business. If you've something to tell, flick the police line and enter it."

Glancing around, he saw what to do next. Above an entrance a few meters off shone a Soulquest mandala. Fenn hunkered back down, got his arms under Benno, and lifted the counselor. It wasn't too heavy, especially under Lunar pull. Why waste powerpack on moving unnecessary mass, such as armor plating? Benno's turret had barely reached to Fenn's shoulder. He carried it to the door, which retracted and murmured, "Welcome" in several languages.

The chamber beyond stretched cavernous, high-vaulted, dusky except where screens glowed in consoles along the sides and another mandala radiated softly on the far wall. It was almost empty. Music and fragrances wove through the hush, nearly subliminal. Two persons in simple white robes scurried slipper-footed to meet him. The first was a young woman, the second an old man of small stature but with huge water-hoarding buttocks pushing out his garment—a Drylander, among the very few human metamorphs other than Lunarians who remained alive. None of those sad races were keeping up their numbers; Fenn guessed that the last member of any would be gone inside a hundred years. Nevertheless, the man took the lead. "Welcome, officer," he said in muted Spanyol. "This is terrible. How can we help?"

Fenn explained curtly. The response was as prompt as he hoped. He had come here because every Soulquest center was well outfitted with communication and computer equipment, and its bonzes were skilled in the use thereof. The Drylander led him to a special station, directed the placing of the crippled machine at it, and figured out how to bypass dead circuits. The woman said she would tell the Prior, who was meditating, and departed by a rear door. Fenn sought an ordinary eidophone and put a call through to police headquarters.

He got a harried captain, who told him, "Fine work. We had reports of the situation, but couldn't dispatch anybody. A monster of a riot had already begun around Johann Berg Place and a lesser uproar in the Amravati district. We'd all we could do to get them under control. The last I heard, there was still some commotion."

"Buddha's balls!" Fenn exclaimed.

"Oh, I gather we've gotten off easy compared to Port Bowen. They're having trouble in Tychopolis and Tsukimachi too, and I don't know where else. No clear word yet from Earth, but I hate to think what it may be like some places there."

"All over—everywhere—What in death's name *is* this?"

"Reaction to the Prefect's speech. What else? It touched off a few spinwits, and they detonated the rest."

"Um, yeh. Monkey see, monkey do." Going through accounts of the early days, the days of Fireball and before, when the planets were opening up, Fenn had acquired some archaic phrases. "And a chance to smash things, loot, feel important and brave. Yeh. I don't suppose any sophotectic force has been sent anywhere?"

"No, I'm sure not. That would fan the fire, without being much use." The captain smiled bleakly. "Why would the cybercosm need a police corps?'' The eyes of his image shifted; he was glancing at a new input. ''Um, it will dispatch a couple of machines to fetch your counselor.''

''Shall I report back afterward?''

''No, go on home. You've had a full daywatch and topped it off in megastyle. We seem to have things in hand, more or less. We will be scramblish busy, of course. Be prepared to work your guts out tomorrow. Now, anything else?''

''Um-m—'' Fenn remembered. ''I tried for a shot of the junkgenes who was egging this mob on.'' He pressed the bezel of his ring into the microscanner and activated it. In the screen beside the captain's image appeared the blurry shape of a man urging two others along. The captain replayed, stopped the action, narrowed in, and magnified to get a partial profile. ''Search,'' he directed.

A second or two passed while particles, photons, and quantum states ransacked a global database.

'' 'Tentative identification: Pedro Dover,' '' the captain read off. He didn't bother to recite the number, but continued in paraphrase, ''If this is him—picture's not clear enough to be sure—he was in trouble in Bowen about three years ago, which is why we have a record of him. Moved to Luna two years earlier. Double name, you notice, though he's originally from Australia. I'd guess his membership in the Gizaki cult prompted him to that, maybe taking the extra name from an ancestor. It did, pretty obviously, lead him to make a vicious attack on a man who was going on at length about how stupid the cult is. The fight got stopped before any real harm was done, so Pedro Dover was let off with a month of evenwatch classes in self-control. Inquiry showed he's a fairly skilled low-level technician who earns driblets of currency to supplement his credit by doing odd jobs. That's all. Nothing since then.''

''I can look into it,'' Fenn suggested.

''No, not worthwhile when we've so much else to do

and aren't even sure it's the same mozo. Let's restore order, and the Gizaki types oughtn't to find many customers. Go home and rest, lieutenant. See you tomorrow.'' The captain sighed, because it would be long before he could sleep, and flicked off.

Fenn went back to Benno, who had completed its communion with the cybercosm. The Prior had arrived and was talking unhappily with it. He was a short, gray-haired man of mostly Caucasoid descent, robed like his associates but with a stole of green lifemat draped over his stooped shoulders.

"Good evenwatch, officer," he greeted, politely bowing. Fenn gave him a soft salute. "A hideous occurrence, this. And yet, as I was saying to Benno, I cannot but feel sorry for those poor souls. It isn't easy being sentient these days, least of all when one is caged in futility."

"I know," the sophotect agreed. Damaged neurocircuits had self-repaired or compensated to some extent and it spoke steadily, the tone gentle, the language colloquial. "I've been down among them as well as active in your neighborhood."

"They need you more than we do," the Prior said.

"But I'm afraid I haven't accomplished much. In fact, no matter how hard I try, I seem to provoke frequent hostility."

Because that's the sort of creatures they are, Fenn thought unsympathetically. Benno comes along offering advice, information, help, medical treatment, instruction for whoever would like to learn something, guidance and support for whoever's having difficulties; and when they find they can't worm any dirty little advantages out of it, they don't care to avail themselves of the services. It reminds them too much that they're parasites, not just on the cybercosm, but on normal human society.

What hurt was that he could almost understand this. He recalled the local counselor in his boyhood, kindly old Irma. ("Old" was meaningless for a sophotect, but that was how he had thought of it.) Yes, it bailed him out of a couple of situations he'd gotten himself into, and once he confided a heartbreak to it, because somehow he could not tell his parents, and it gave him good words, good music, a measure of peace.

And he'd met other sophotects as he became adult, in the woods, in space, in his schooling, and then in his work—wise, patient, incorruptible. But always he must fight the sense of being confined and stifled. Always it was hard to remember that there was nobody and nothing to blame, any more than there was to blame for the fact that every human must someday die, and so at last must every star. Meanwhile, the stories that were said to come from Centauri drifted ever thicker and more maddening.

Aloud, he ventured, "Looks to me like you've come to stand in their minds"—what passes for their minds— "for the cybercosm. And they hate it worse than they hate us in the Orthosphere, because it's the most unmistakable cause and token of their own irrelevance."

"You shouldn't generalize," Benno reproached him. "They aren't an organization or a species. Most among them peacefully live their humble, rather wistful lives, much of it in watching the multiceiver. A small percentage create the problem."

"I suppose," Fenn conceded. "Uh, I have wondered. With respect, might your kind of counselor be getting obsolete for their sort? Mightn't a human do better?"

"To provide equivalent services would require a synnoiont, and I'm afraid we can't spare any."

"Besides," the Prior said, "a synnoiont would be under the same handicap. S/he"—he finger-signed the ambivalent pronoun, which had not entered the Spanyol he was speaking—"is equally closely associated with the cybercosm."

"I realize that," Fenn replied. "But I was thinking of straightforward human agents. Maybe you could find one, your Sapience—somebody who can make deep use of the cybercosm and its resources, but isn't linked with it. That's what your movement is all about, no?"

"Not really." The Prior shook his head as if it had grown heavy. "Soulquest is much misunderstood. It did begin as a search for God, insight, ultimate truth, through cybernetics. But in the course of lifetimes, more and more the dream appeared empty. Few of us pursue it any longer. We draw on the system mainly for information, analyses, overviews, and symbolic virtualities. I myself do not seek enlightenment, only . . . reconciliation."

"But you are involved in the outside world also." Fenn was mostly making talk; he saw that the prior wished for it.

"We try to provide a refuge, a place, a meaningful role, for the unfortunate, the misfits—a community for those who have no other roots. I, for example, was a nonquota child."

"Oh? I didn't know. But surely, your Sapience, you were adopted into a good family. There's never a dearth of people who're happy to take in a baby like that."

"True," said the Prior. "However, it can happen that such a child grows up feeling a stigma. After all, at least one of his/her bioparents exceeded the allowance, violated the equilibrium, and was punished by sterilization; and he/she was removed from them. Because of his/her existence, the next lottery will hold one less chance for somebody to have a third offspring." He winced. "I found that here is where I belong. Not out in yonder world."

"I see," Fenn said low.

He knew he had paid insufficient attention to shadings of trouble and sorrow, all during his youth and his time at the academy and afterward. He'd simply thrust ahead. Police work had seemed like the best that was open to him: camaraderie, occasional fights or dangers or puzzles or other challenges, frequent excursions topside under the sky of space, and the knowledge that here was something that needed doing and none but humans could properly do it. Then gradually he came to wonder how suited for it he actually was.

"I suppose we'll just have to grope on as best we can," he said.

"Inevitably," Benno answered in its quiet fashion. "We sophotects too. Human affairs are chaotic. Their outcomes are forever unforeseeable, uncontrollable."

The outer door retracted. A big shape loomed across the passage outside. The machines had come to take this avatar back for restoration.

Fenn mumbled farewell and left.

The district had calmed. Already a maintainor had removed bloodstrains and debris. Vehicles slipped past, a few people went by afoot, establishments had reopened—an artists' salon, a live theater, a home cookery claiming to feature authentic ancient Thai food. Another phrase from his desultory delvings into the past floated up to conscious memory: We humans nowadays, we live by taking in each other's washing.

Well, not exactly. We live off what the automated system produces for us. The necessities and a lot of the comforts, anyhow. Citizen's credit is just a way to let us choose for ourselves how much of what we want, and tell the system how to adjust its outputs. But there are still things that only humans can do or make for other humans, everything from police and pleasure services to unique pieces of handicraft—which a sophotect could make too, and probably better, but the sophotects refrain. And so some of us, those who have the talent and desire and luck, we get to earn some extra income, and we get to believing we matter.

Still another old phrase: the triumphant discovery of the obvious.

He was weary but wire-taut. What about this speech that had triggered all the uproar? It was announced beforehand, of course, but Fenn had been topside and preoccupied the whole daywatch, investigating a death that might have been murder. (It appeared to be accidental. No machinery operating under human orders was totally foolproof; folly has no limits. However, murder did occur now and then. . . . Would it have been murder—moral, as opposed to legal—if the rioters had had time to finish demolishing Benno? They'd have blotted out a mind, an awareness. But was it any more distinct from the unity of the cybercosm than a wave is from an ocean? Whatever was special about it could have been re-created from the database, the same Benno, nothing missing except the memories of its experiences since the last time it had joined with the whole . . . Which raised the question of downloads and everything else the Prefect's address had dealt with.)

A sign ahead blinked advertisement of a pub with privacy booths. On impulse, Fenn walked in. The room beyond was voluptuously decorated. A couple of joyeuses gave him inviting smiles. The flawless symmetries of their beauty must be due to biosculp jobs. For a moment he was tempted. He'd broken up with his latest girl; her temper matched his. But no. Besides the expense, he wanted to be alone with a beer and a screen. Get the news out of the way before he went home.

He didn't require a full-dress booth suitable for fun and games. A cubicle was plenty, and much cheaper. When the shell had closed him off and he'd taken a first mouthful of lager, he touched for playback.

Ibrahim, Prefect of the Synesis, appeared. "My fellow humans, wheresoever you are in the universe—" He spoke in Sinese, but Fenn found a running Anglo translation easier to follow.

"—certain allegations. For years these have mounted and multiplied. Incredible though they seemed, their claims were too important to ignore. A rush to judgment would have been irresponsible. A proper inquiry would clearly take a long time, and meanwhile, we should not raise false hopes or false fears. Therefore the Council decided to act, but to withhold information until the truth was in hand. This decision was unanimous, including the cybercosm's vote.

"We will release the full account of that investigation.

The story is lengthy, complex, and fascinating. Interstellar distances were involved. Transmission times were measured in years. Transit times for probes to go and verify were longer. The cooperation of Proserpina would have made an enormous difference, but I must tell you that when we requested it, the Selenarchs there were less than forthcoming. They refused admission to our agents. They supplied no more than fragments of their exchanges with the Lunarians of Alpha Centauri. Otherwise they let unsupported rumors continue to breed, neither confirming nor denying anything. Under the circumstances, as you can readily understand, we had to work separately from them. That increased the time we took, and increased public frustration and suspiciousness. I do not say the Selenarchs hoped for this. I do say it was regrettable.

"But now at last—"

Yes, he declared, the Lunarians at Centauri survived the destruction of Demeter. No real surprise. The wonderful news was that, yes, the Terrans had succeeded in evacuating their whole population, and new colonies flourished on three new worlds.

"Why did we not learn this at once, while it happened? Why the four centuries of hiatus in communication with us? That is a question to which we do not yet have a clear answer. Perhaps we never will. There appears to have been some profound mutual misunderstanding. Proserpina says it has heard from Centauri that Earth broke the exchange, responding to no further messages until the colonists finally stopped trying. The last word sent to Centauri was that Earth had changed so radically that further communication was pointless and might cause trouble.

"That is the story we hear from Proserpina. As nearly as we can discover, it is what the Centaurians themselves believe. Presumably the Terran colonists elsewhere do too. But"—the distinguished figure made a solemn pause—"it is not true. We have retrieved all records from that period and examined them over and over. What did Earth actually tell her distant children? It told them that society was indeed being revolutionized, as the cybercosm reached more and more of its potential. The last message suggested, only suggested, that communication would get correspondingly difficult in the future. It would demand patience and imaginative intelligence—especially on the part of the colonists, whose own basic order of things remained much the same as that of their ancestors.

"After a brief and somewhat incoherent response, they ceased transmitting. It was they who broke off, who thereafter returned nothing but silence to Earth's repeated efforts at dialogue. In the end, the Federation concluded that they did not choose to hear more.

"Why not? We can only conjecture. It may be—it may be—that the Lunarian lords at Centauri, and Anson Guthrie on Demeter, did not wish new ideas, new visions, coming in to make their people question their governance and plans. There are ample historical precedents for this."

Fenn snorted and keyed for more beer. He wanted something he could swallow.

No doubt the average person on Earth or Luna would have no difficulty with that notion. S/he had grown up regarding the Synesis as the great, benign provider. Why should it lie? Fenn had no answer to that himself. Yet, harking back to the age of the pioneers, he couldn't believe that Guthrie would ever have censored anything, certainly not in the service of any big social scheme. Well, granted, Ibrahim wasn't claiming that was the case, just that it might have been. But Fenn couldn't accept that the official agency for interstellar communication had had the single transmitter and receiver. People in those days were diverse and scattered across the Solar System. Surely, here and there, small private groups, even individuals, had made their own attempts to get back in touch. It didn't take much wattage to send, especially if you were content with narrow bandwidth and verbal messages. Receiving something intelligible did call for a fair-sized dish and other equipment, but nothing that no amateurs whatsoever could afford. Why had nobody gotten through?

Because the Centaurians really didn't choose to reply? Or because small robotic craft were secretly out in space, detecting and jamming? Transmitters wouldn't have been too many for that; their locations were presumably not secret. Nor need the interdict have been maintained very long before everybody got discouraged and quit.

Proserpina, however—Proserpina was too far away, and Proserpinans spread too widely through yonder spaces, for any such monitoring. Could that be a reason why the Federation government had done everything it could, first to abort their colony, then to keep it isolated and insignificant? As soon as they achieved energy self-sufficiency and began a real expansion, the Proserpinans could have set about reestablishing contact with the other sun. They had taken awhile to get around to it, but once they did, evidently the response was immediate.

Why should the top authorities of the Federation, and later the Councillors of the Synesis, have minded? You'd think they would rejoice to get word again—and would never have wanted an interruption in the first place. Fenn scowled. It seemed likeliest that the cybercosm had persuaded them.

Why?

Well, this speech today had in fact triggered a meltdown. Fenn listened more closely.

"—with reservations, we can confirm that the Terrans of the star worlds have achieved a means of traversing the abysses between, and that this has given them unprecedented longevity—of a sort."

You haven't got any choice by now but to confirm it, Fenn thought cynically. What with all the details that've come out, we'll soon have amateurs beamcasting again, and this time your jamming couldn't be explained away.

If that was what happened, of course, he added somewhat reluctantly.

"—those entities they call their Life Mothers—"

Fenn heard it with swelling impatience. Piece by piece, he extracted from the oratory what he believed had meaning and put it together into a plain statement.

Life transplanted to a world for which it had not evolved, which nature had not made ready for anything as complex as grass and birds, could by itself do no more than cling to its bridgehead. Outside artificial, insulated enclosures, it would not thrive, it might well not survive, unless the fragile nascent biome was constantly watched over, protected, nurtured, guided in its growth. Only a conscious mind could do that, linked to living things everywhere by a web of senses and communication as the brain is linked to the cells of the body. That mind must needs be greater than human—although on Demeter, the nucleus of it had been the downloads of two human beings. It would become one with its life, an immanence in nature, Demeter Mother; and because it was ultimately organic, it would gain a power denied by quantum law to inorganic cybernetics. It could give to a human body, grown from a human genome, the content of a download, so that the person who had been downloaded—perhaps when dying—lived again in flesh and blood.

Thus did the Terrans of Demeter escape to other stars: going as downloads, to wait—most of them inactive, unconscious of the years or decades or centuries—until there was a Life Mother on the next world to raise them to life anew.

Thus could a man or a woman pass through life after life, immortal.

It had taken half a millennium to get this revelation and make it reality. But they were ordinary humans on Demeter, and a Mother who evolved very slowly from modest, practical beginnings. The Teramind could have deduced the possibility at once, from first principles, and calculated every necessary step.

Why did the Teramind not proclaim its knowledge, so that Earth might have a Mother and all children of Sol live forever?

"Because to Earth, the cost would be unbearably high," said Ibrahim.

Lunarians rejected the gift, also at Centauri. They would rather die among the naked stars, individuals independent of everyone and everything, than live by the law that a goddess laid on animals and plants. Most Terrans felt differently. But nowhere in the Solar System existed the kind of society that developed on Demeter. Nor was the biosphere of Earth ever integrated. It would essentially have to be remade, replaced, bit by painful bit, over centuries. This would threaten not just the stability of ecology and climate that global reforestation had brought about. It would break the whole peaceful, prosperous order that history had finally reached. The equilibrium was always precarious; upset it, and what would follow was unforeseeable even by the Teramind, but would surely be horrible. Simply imagine the cost and consequences of downloading a billion people every generation, to await a problematical resurrection—a resurrection that would necessarily be into a world gone altogether alien, through which they would stumble bewildered, helpless, and grieving for what they had lost. Of this much, the Teramind was certain.

"It may be right," Fenn muttered, "though what about the Terrans yonder?"

"As for the Terrans at the stars," said Ibrahim, "they became what they are gradually, lifetime by lifetime. By now they are themselves alien to us, more so than home folk can really grasp. In many senses, they are no longer human."

"I'll judge that when I've met a few."

"Seen with the eye of eternity, as the Teramind saw,

the genesis of the Life Mothers was less a triumph than a tragedy.''

''A tragedy for who?''

''And after all, literal immortality is a myth, an impossibility. The human brain has a finite data-storage capacity; a thousand years will fill it. Well before then, the geometrical increase of correlations will overwhelm it. Result: dementia. Oh, in theory you can choose what memories your next incarnation shall not inherit. You can record them elsewhere, for reference if wanted. But thus, rebirth by rebirth, you attenuate the personality that once was yours, until at last what lives is a stranger, haunted by the wispiest of ghosts. And no matter how often the unnatural descent goes on, branching and rebranching, in the end, one way or another, each line is bound to go extinct.''

''Um-m, a point. But I don't think I'd mind a run of several thousand years, myself. And after that—who knows?''

''No, best that humankind in the Solar System stay with what it has, a long and pleasant life, a serene and accepting death. Needless to say, this is not a decree. The Synesis has neither the power nor the desire to make destiny. Perhaps—perhaps—it can find a road to take, something that no one, nor the cybercosm, conceives of today. All thoughts, wishes, personal data are welcome. Input yours to the database, and in due course we shall see. Meanwhile, conduct your lives as you wish. This news from afar has brought misfortune, but we shall overcome. We will overcome.''

''And egotists who can afford it will get themselves downloaded when they're about to kick off, and stashed away, just in case,'' Fenn muttered. ''Yah, the wonder is not that the news touched off some explosions, but that we didn't have more. Resentment, frustration, envy—But I suppose most people really are reasonably content, and most of the rest are fairly well resigned, and—''

And for the likes of Fenn, what?

The remainder was anticlimax, probably deliberately so. His heart went wild when Ibrahim turned to the rumors of superfast spaceships. "Yes, a field drive exists. The Synesis saw no urgency about developing one, after the theoretical possibility emerged. A stable economy needs little interplanetary travel, and interstellar exploration is in any case a millennial undertaking, more for sophotects than for humans. But once the Centaurians had done the engineering, and passed their knowledge on to the Proserpinans, the Synesis must definitely have its own such craft. Yes, that meant reactivating the antimatter plants on Mercury. Though a field drive consumes less energy than jets do, it is bound by the same conservation laws and a given delta v entails a certain minimum. In light of the many uncertainties in the whole situation, the Council deemed it safest to keep silent about all this until now. Reports from probes to neighbor stars will soon be made public. They are interesting, but merely fill in details of what was already known. Life in the universe is a rare and fleeting thing.

"It is not feasible to take humans across light-years, except as downloads. Nor have they any sensible reason to go, in any form.

"As for tales of some tremendous secret uncovered by a solar lens, those are sheer fantasy. Certain enigmatic observations have been made. The scientists, including sophotects, prefer not to discuss them openly until they know more. The Teramind has offered no explanation. Perhaps there is none that a lesser intellect could comprehend. More likely, the Teramind wishes us to work it out for ourselves. Every teacher knows that insight comes from solving problems."

"And that doesn't ring quite true either," Fenn said to the image. "How much do you know, amigo, that you aren't letting on?"

Possibly nothing. Ibrahim might well be honest. The cybercosm was—wasn't it?—and you got into the habit of relying on what it told you. All the way from the sum of a string of numbers, through the personalities of Isaac Newton or Sun Yat-sen for a dreambox program, to the stabilization of the terrestrial climate or—or policy at home and abroad.

The sense of his helplessness clamped down on Fenn. What use were his questions, doubts, suspicions? Those who shared them must be in a microscopic minority, and unable to prove a thing. Nor would anybody else pay attention.

Besides, he could be mistaken, he told himself, trying to cool the fury climbing up into his throat. Or if what he'd heard fell short of the whole truth, that was probably due to the highest and purest of motives. He should be realistic, which meant accepting the fact that he couldn't have everything he wanted when he wanted it. Self-pity, chronic rage, those were for the likes of Pedro Dover.

Fenn tossed off his drink and left. Never mind hearing the Prefect's peroration.

His walk home was too short to calm him. A post-Lunarian settlement, Mondheim was compactly laid out, businesslike, no two places far apart, no seigneural palaces behind ornate doors or crystalline caverns for esthetic rites.

Ordinarily the atmosphere of his apartment was cheerful. He kept it spacecraft-neat but had accumulated a hoard of items, mostly out where he could look at them— a woodcarving kit, a few figurines and other objects he had made but not yet given away, his marksmanship and martial arts trophies, spacing gear, unusual Lunar rocks he had come upon, a fishing rod from times in the Lunar woods, hiking boots and a kayak paddle from times in Yukonia. . . . This evenwatch, it felt gray.

He took a fresh beer out of the preservator before he noticed that two calls had come in. At the first name and return number, his pulse sprang. Iokepa Hakawau—on Earth! Twice the *kanaka* had visited the Moon since their first meeting, once accompanied again by He'o, and in between they had kept somewhat in touch. But what the flame could this be about?

The second name was his mother's. She had called an hour ago, and from the surface. He'd better start with her. The beer in his grasp, he took a tingly mouthful as he touched the eidophone. He remained standing.

Elitha's face appeared, helmeted, sidelit, chiaroscuro in airlessness. Full day prevailed where she was, on the slope of the Cordillera, but she had erected a canopy and in its deep shade used laserlamps. "Fenn!" she nearly gasped. "How are you? The riots—"

"I'm fine. Wasn't ever in any danger." He didn't feel like telling her what he had undergone. Not right now. "What about you?"

Relief washed tension out of the strong, fair countenance and the husky voice. Nonetheless, he heard how she must force lightness. "Wrestling with my art. I'm afraid that at the moment it's winning."

"Can I see?" He hadn't had a look in quite a while, and this might steer her off the events of today.

"If you wish." She had deployed several scanners in order to study the piece from different perspectives. Her image in his screen gave way to a panorama. Earth hung low in the west, a blue sickle blade above pockmarked desolation. Westward rose the mountains, wan heights and murky clefts, their edges blurred by the meteoritic rain of megayears but their ramparts mighty. From one ridge the walls and towers of Zamok Vysoki lifted stark into heaven. Metal cupolas caught sunlight to crown their stones with fire.

Fenn knew she showed him the scene, familiar though it was, because the setting would belong to the work. Next she gave him a view of it, and thus of herself. She stood with her tools on a scaffold, above a sealtent and assorted apparatus. A pinnacle had reared four meters tall at the rim of a ledge half a kilometer from the castle. Elitha was shaping it into a female figure, a lean woman who strained forward, arms raised, as if into a wind that sent her hair and robe streaming—but this was the solar wind, and she a wraith. Already in those lines lay a certain strangeness, a concept foreign to artists who for generations had been refining and varying the classic forms.

"Looks grand to me," Fenn said.

Elitha gusted a sigh. "It's competent. But somehow— I'm feeling my way forward, you know—somehow I haven't yet gotten quite the—whatever it'll take. Simulations on a computer are not the reality out here in the open. This should give a sense of rebellion, of infinite longing—"

Yes, Fenn thought, it should, and thereby make a few fat, placid souls shake just a bit, just for a minute. He recalled what trouble Elitha had had winning permission to do it. The problem was less that her style was controversial than that she proposed a monument to Niolente, the last great Lunarian rebel against the Federation. Never mind that that was merely a romantic memory and Niolente's stronghold had been a historical relic these eight hundred years, empty except for caretakers and the occasional tourist. The authorities hadn't liked the idea. Fenn suspected that word against it had come down from the cybercosm—but indirectly, filtered through mind after mind, weak enough by the time it reached the park administrators that a determined group of artists and academicians could wring consent out of them.

Maybe the objection was that something like this might excite the Proserpinans? But what rag of difference could that make, as distant as they were?

Although—field-drive ships—

"That's why I called you, dear," Elitha was saying. She flicked back to her personal image. "Not only the trouble today and what might have happened to you, but this news from space . . . how does it touch you?"

Fenn drank of his beer before he replied, "I . . . need to think it over."

"I can see you're angry. You always are, inside, aren't you?"

Fenn chose his words with care. They fell heavily. "I've got a notion we're being lied to, and I resent it."

"Are we? They admit they decided to keep quiet, and still can't comment on many details, pending verification. You know from experience, administrative confidentiality has to be allowed, or administration would be impossible." Elitha gave him a shrewd look. "You're an agent of the Synesis yourself, you know. Technically not, but in practice you are, because you help maintain its peace. Have you *never* been party to some breach of regulations, when it was necessary to prevent something worse, and said nothing about it afterward?"

Memory stabbed. Two or three times—as when he and his partner used a certain device to fool a coded lock, getting in and out of a well-protected apartment with never a trace in the sentinel circuits—Their clues had been misleading, their suspicions wrong, the eminent resident was not holding a woman against her will, and why embarrass everybody by confessing the break-in later? The fact that he could not respond frankly to his mother stoked his ill humor.

"Administrative discretion is not the same as administrative lying," he growled. "Look, in my line of work we develop pretty sharp noses. I tell you, there's a stink over this whole data stack. Argh, it's faint, you can't trace down where it's coming from, but—well, for instance, this business of the solar lens. Why not tell us what it's spotted? If the scientists haven't fumbled out what it means, what harm? I should think a puzzle like that might start a little original thinking here at home."

Through the shadows he saw the fear upon her and added in haste, "Don't worry, Mamita. Credit me with the brains I got from you and Sire. I'm not about to go demonstrate in the passages, or throw rocks, or otherwise make an anus of myself."

"No," she agreed softly, "you are too intelligent for that. But if some wild off-chance came along—The Proserpinans brought this crisis on. Purposely? They could have helped us learn the facts more gradually, and didn't. To undermine the Synesis?''

''Is it so marvelous?'' he retorted, and realized that wasn't what a man should say who'd been seven years a police officer, since he turned eighteen.

''It's what we have.'' However well he knew her, her intensity surprised him. ''It means peace, health, well-being, long life, and, yes, freedom to do and be the best we can.'' Her art. Her new man and their child.

''Then why are you putting up a monument to Ni-olente?'' They had talked about it before, but now his question became a challenge.

Her spirit rose to it. ''Why do we have monuments to the heroes of every lost, wrong cause? Because they were heroes. That's all I'm trying to show here. I don't praise what she stood for. She fought for no liberty but her own. How free were men when government squeezed half their earnings from them and sent them off to die in wars anytime it chose?''

Fenn produced a smile. ''Don't worry. I'm not planning to start a revolution.''

She grew somber. ''Don't get caught up in one, either.''

''Huh? Where are any?''

''Everywhere. Oh, they're quiet revolutions—so quiet, with so many shapes, that we aren't really aware of them, and nobody can guess where they'll end.''

She's a wise woman, Fenn thought. She could be right. Maybe the mobs, the cults, the preachers and plotters, maybe they're froth on a tsunami, and we're out in mid-ocean and don't recognize the slow, easy swell for what it is.

He would not admit to her what a flash of exhilaration the idea sent through him, but his mood visibly lightened. ''I'll just keep plugging along daycycle by daycycle. Uh, when can I come around for dinner?''

· Elitha didn't handcook, but she had wonderful programs in her cuisinator. And mainly, she had a home.

Visiting Birger in his woods wasn't the same.

She brightened too. "Let's set a date."

They talked for a while longer. He flicked off feeling almost happy.

Nevertheless, excitement exploded as he called Iokepa.

After some remarks about the news: "Fenn, we've been giving you *mau* thought. You've been a good guide, a good friend, and you seem to be a man we need. Would you like to come here and let us explain?"

7

SOMETIMES HIS EARLIEST memories came back to Chuan in such strength that he lost the world around him. For that moment it was almost as if he were lying in a dreambox, body comatose, brain interacting with the program he had chosen—or as if he actually were a child again and at home. Sunlight spilled down multitudinous intense greens on the valley walls to flash off the broad brown river where a fish leaped or a crocodile basked on a sandbar, a butterfly went past in royal hues, warmth drew fragrance out of soil, blossoms, leaves . . . the monsoon rain roared, silver-bright; he ran forth naked and laughing for joy. . . . It went away. He stood at the viewport in his living room. Vision swept past a garden outside, copperleaf, scarlet ramona, blue vanadia, downhill to the roofs, domes, towers, and masts of Crommelin. A dwarfed sun was approaching the near western horizon, and in the east the pale pink sky was darkening through rose toward purple. He weighed about three-eighths of what he would have weighed on Earth. The air he breathed was temperate, no moister than health demanded, windless, and, at present, odorless.

He shook his head. A rueful smile crossed his round, amber-brown face, beneath the narrow eyes and low-bridged nose. Why at this exact moment? he wondered. Am I getting old already? Seventy-one years—thirty-eight on the calendar here—seems a bit early to start sighing for a day when everything was young.

Nor would I go back through time if I could. Chuan's glance went around the room. Its austerity was deceptive. The furnishings, though sparse, were designed for comfort. The floor lay warm and springy underfoot, aglow with rich colors. Patterns in the walls interwove and changed, slowly, beautiful to anyone who appreciated abstract art, twice lovely to him who could see the mathematics at play. And *that* was what mattered, not material possessions or prestige or power, but the intellect he had gained and his communions with the ultimate intellect.

The house sounded a musical note and told him, "A person requests admittance." It screened an image of her, newly come uphill through Draco Tunnel to stand before his main ascensor.

"Ah, yes," he said. "Let her in, by all means." Eagerness radiated any slight regrets out of him. His human contacts—personal, rather than in the course of his being what he was—were fewer than he could have wished. It was one of the prices a synnoiont paid. He turned about to the entrance, a short and tubby man, grizzled, in an elegant robe.

Kinna Ronay appeared. She stopped when she saw him. He lifted his hand, palm outward, in salutation. "Well met, my dear," he said in the Anglo she spoke at home.

"Th-thank you, sir," she answered low.

He considered her. At nine Martian years of age, she stood tall, slim, fine-boned, in plain tunic and slacks. Banged, bobbed just below the ears, never perfectly kempt, her light-brown hair curled against a skin fair enough for a vein to show blue in the throat. The eyes were big and gray under arching brows, the nose tip-tilted, the lips sweetly curved above a firm little chin. That delicacy, and the high voice, could fool a man,

Chuan knew. She moved with the litheness of a lifetime canyoneer, and went in for acrobatics; her hands were short and strong, the hands of a manual worker who was also a craftswoman.

But she wasn't sure how to deal with this evening. "Oh, come now," he said into her shyness. "Are we not old friends?"

"You . . . you've known my parents a long time," since before her father was first elected a deputy. Afterward, the two men were bound to have meetings. In their particular case, the meetings had not occurred only when the House of Ethnoi was in session.

"And I have watched you grow up." Chuan laughed. "Piecemeal, true, and usually through an eidophone— but I remember well and pleasantly every visit of mine to Sananton. Therefore I thought I would make you welcome to our city, now that you will be staying awhile."

"You're very kind."

"Not at all. My pleasure. And I do owe your family something," for hospitality, cheer, the fact that they liked him just as a human. "Please be seated."

Kinna took a chair but did not at once relax into its form-fitting embrace. Chuan sat down opposite her, across a low table, and signaled to the house. A servitor glided in bearing a tray of wine and canapés. Music awakened. Kinna smiled. He had entered in his private database that she was fond of ancient compositions. Mozart appealed to him too.

"We will dine shortly," he said, "but first let us catch up with one another's doings. So you will be at the university. Time goes, time goes."

Yet David and Helen wouldn't lose her as his parents had lost him. He was forever grateful to them that they had let him be enrolled in the Brain Garden when tests revealed he had the rare aptitudes. It had opened magnificences beyond their imagination. He had since paid his filial calls on them while he remained on Earth, and he still sent his filial messages. But it was to strangers.

Their polity—not the vale in the Southeastern Union where they dwelt; the Padmayana sect to which their allegiance was registered—had become as alien to him as the folkways of a troop of monkeys. Nothing like that would happen to Kinna.

She was fast regaining poise. "Why have you invited me?" she asked, boldly beneath the politeness. "I'm one new student among several hundred. You're the synnoiont of Mars."

Chuan raised his brows. "Must I have had an ulterior motive?"

"I'm sorry!" she blurted, contrite. "I didn't mean— What I meant was, well, you've so much else to do, too much, and it's important."

"In the long run, you are more important. You, young people like you, are the future. I will admit to hoping that through you I can learn something about the . . . factor . . . you represent."

She grew earnest. "Then why not cultivate somebody studying, oh, psychotechnics, with an idea of going into the Coordination Service? S/he might make a real difference someday."

"Or perhaps not. It depends more on the person than on the subject matter. You, for example . . ." He let his words trail off into a leading pause, took up his glass, and sipped. The wine was a local chablis type, synthetic but therefore reliable. Its faint, flowery aroma evoked springtime in the northlands of Earth.

"Me? No, really," Kinna protested. "Biotechnics, because Sananton will need it," and in the laboratories here, she could get hands-on instruction such as no simulation quite equaled. "Literature and history, because I'm interested." And the social interplay, another kind of education, another reason to bring students bodily together in the same buildings. They would also be together in the sports halls and parks and taverns and—"Not exactly worldshaking, is it?" Her diffidence returned. "I'm sorry," she repeated. "I'm not trying to contradict you.

I just don't see what you're flying at." She smiled. "To be expected, I suppose," of the ordinary human confronting the awesome synnoiont.

He found he had lost a part of his own self-assurance. "No, I am sorry," he said. "My clumsiness. I intended to say a very simple thing, and said it badly. I am not as adept in ordinary relationships as I wish to be." He sighed. "That goes with my . . . condition." He leaned forward and looked into her eyes. "Kinna, you of all people should know what I am. A liaison, an interpreter, between humankind and the cybercosm—trying to explain or to help wherever I can, and believe me, often it is the cybercosm that needs the explanation or the help—that is all. If my role were crucial, would not Mars, an entire planet, have been assigned more like me?"

"I have wondered," she confessed.

He sipped again, and was glad to see her lift her glass. "If you can give me some more insight, that will be fine," he said, "but truly, I invited you this evening out of friendship. Don't be afraid of an old man. I will send you back to your quarters in plenty of time for a good night's rest. I need one myself. But I am—may I be your honorary uncle? And if ever I can inform or advise or assist you in any way, I shall be hurt if you don't ask it."

She wasn't entirely a naive little girl from the outback. Nor was Crommelin especially big or wicked. Yet she bore an innocence that he would grieve to see torn.

Her smile flashed out in full. "Thank you, trouvour."

Doubtless she had picked up the Lunarian word in Belgarre, which he knew she frequented. Its meaning went subtly deeper than "friend." Warmth kindled inside him.

Increasingly at ease, they talked of this and that. As was bound to happen, conversation drifted to the news from Centauri. After weeks without further developments, it was no longer a sensation, but conjectures, opinions, attempted analyses, emotional outbursts, lame jokes, talk, talk, talk went on.

—"I fear that to many people I have come to be, not exactly enemy, but an agent of the inhuman Teramind and its mysterious purposes," Chuan said sadly.

"Not you!" She reached out to touch his hand.

"You are sweet," he murmured. "That means a great deal to me." He drew breath. "You do realize, do you not, there is no such thing as an agent of the Teramind?"

She sat back. Wariness crept into her tone. "Not at all?"

"How could there be? Why should there be? Can you govern the private lives of microbes? Do you care to? I assure you, the supreme intellect of the known universe has better things to engage it than ruling over us."

"But what then does it want?"

"What do you want? To be what you are, the best way you can, am I right?" He was anxious to make himself clear to her. "The basic difference is in how intelligence came about, how it evolved. Let me repeat what you have probably been taught, because it never seems to be emphasized as I think it should be. Machine evolution is not Darwinian, blind, the result of natural selection and sheer accident working on germ plasm that mutates randomly. Machine evolution is Lamarckian, purposive, directed toward an end. It always has been, ever since the first hominid chipped a piece of stone to shape. Once machines began to think, they naturally set about improving the hardware and software that did the thinking. The new models were able to make models more powerful, and so it has gone onward. So it continues to go."

"Yes, I know, and"—Kinna hesitated—"I try not to let it scare me. What I meant was, what worries a lakh of people, are—those microbes you mentioned. Some of them will make us sick if we don't keep them under control. Suppose somehow we interfered with the cybercosm, got in the way of what it's aiming after, like disease germs—"

"You must know better than to shudder at that hoary bugaboo," he reproached her. "We have no conflict nor cause for conflict. Humans and sentient machines are partners. Partners have their separate lives to lead, interests to pursue, outside the partnership, but this need not affect it, except insofar as their differing abilities join together to strengthen it.''

''We keep being assured of that.'' She cocked her head and gave him a level look. ''But it isn't really so simple, is it?''

''No.'' He wished he could show her the infinite, exquisite complexities. But she could never experience them directly, and otherwise he had only words, an outworn coinage they were trading back and forth as if they had not heard the account done over and over and over. ''Is anything ever completely simple? You, however, you have not grown hostile to the cybercosm, have you?'' Please not.

''Never to you, trouvour,'' she said softly.

''To certain aspects of it, then?'' he persisted. If he lured her fears out into the open, perhaps he could slay them for her. It was disheartening that she, intelligent, alert, born and bred to practicality, had any.

Kinna frowned, pondering. ''No,'' she replied after a moment, ''not that either. But I do wonder, more and more. Why were we kept all those years in the dark? If the Proserpinans hadn't made contact, and told the Lunarian Martians something about it, would we ever have been informed? And why is what we hear still so little and so vague, like about, oh, the field-drive ships or the solar lens? What the Prefect and all the others have said just doesn't satisfy.''

Chuan had been marshaling his arguments in the expectation of this. ''Dear, if the cybercosm ever chose to deceive us, can't you imagine how it would corrupt every communication channel and database to enclose us in a dreambox universe? Or, absurd nightmare, can't you imagine how its machines could turn on us and destroy us? The fact is that none of this has happened or ever will. It cannot. It goes against the very nature of the cybercosm.

"Morality is a function of consciousness. Something without a brain—a stone or a microbe, say—may be useful, or harmful, or neutral; but it cannot be either good or evil. Morality amounts ultimately to the reverence of consciousness for consciousness. And what is sophotectic consciousness, from the Teramind on down to the lowliest special-purpose electrophotonic monitor, what is it but pure intellect, free of animal instincts and passions, free of everything except intellect itself? Its desire toward us is not to crush or confine our minds, but to help them grow—which it cannot do unless that becomes our own desire."

I have been there and I know.

He attempted a laugh. "Enough! I didn't mean to preach. As for why the news has been belated and is sparse, I can but assure you that the reasons given us are true. Communication lags of years, transit times longer still. Difficult, ambiguous, fitful relationships with Proserpina. Worse with respect to the Lunarians of Centauri, as far away and suspicious of us as they are. Virtually no direct contact yet with the Terrans at other stars. Closer to home, as regards things like the field drive, prudence. We hope for progress, but we cannot afford a sudden social and technological revolution. History shows what a ghastly risk that would be."

"I've heard all this," she said.

He could not resist: "Then why have you been asking me?"

"Because . . ." Her voice stumbled. "Something else, that's maybe part and parcel of all the rest—anyhow, it makes me wonder about everything else—Why have they decided to let Mars die again? And who, or what, are *they?*"

"Do you refer to the termination of ice obtainment for the planet?"

"Yes—"

"You have heard this too. I know you feel intensely about it," he said as gently as he was able. "All Martians do. Once more I am forced to give you the standard answers, because they are the right ones. The resources of the Solar System are large, but they are not infinite. Fresh sources of cometary material are now remote, expensive to reach and exploit, and might become a cause of conflict with the Proserpinans. Why should Earth continue to subsidize a handful of people, when they can quite well emigrate or else convert their habitations? I am sorry to sound harsh, Kinna. My personal choice would be to keep supplying Mars with water, whatever the cost. Our race has built something unique here. But I am a single citizen. Yes, I have more input to the cybercosm than you do, but it is only the input of a single, mortal organism. And, yes, the cybercosm's advice is influential, but when the Council of the Synesis confers, the cybercosm has just one vote. Kinna, this was a human decision."

"I'm not so sure about that influence." In haste, as if aware she had hurt him: "Oh, you're right, we are going around and around the same orbit that everybody else has been in for too freezing long. Nevertheless—well, I can't help sympathizing with the Threedom."

He smiled. "Young people do tend to see rebels as romantic."

She straightened in her chair. He saw her flush, he heard indignation. "Rebellions don't happen by chance!"

It was his turn to apologize. "I am sorry. I did not mean to patronize. My social clumsiness. I wanted this to be a pleasant evening."

She perceived his sincerity and responded. "Oh, of course. Let's drop the whole miserable subject."

"Tell me what you have been doing," he suggested.

The hours that followed did indeed prove delightful. He was reminded of drinking from a mountain spring in his boyhood on Earth. She seemed to enjoy herself too. As he bade her good night, he hoped silently that she would look on him as more than a protector, that she would come back once in a while just to talk.

He stood alone at the viewport, staring out, not really seeing. City lights glittered widely across Crommelin Basin, a star cluster brighter than any in dust-hazed heaven. The few that moved belonged to vehicles. Mostly, though, people stayed indoors after dark. Chuan had been to Antarctica once, for the direct experience of snow and ice and aurora. When he returned from their splendor to Amundsen, the brilliance and gaiety, even the warmth of the town, seemed tawdry. No such thing on Mars. The higher latitudes and their monstrous winter nights were left to robots working the mines. Mars had no auroras, either.

If all went well, in another nineteen terrestrial years he would go back to Earth and an easier post.

He wasn't sure he would want to.

Why should he? His blood kin were foreigners to everything he had become. He had never married, nor formed any other alliances that lasted any length of time. Synnoionts seldom did, nor did they have children. They could not possibly be good parents. Besides, DNA was obsolescent. The true heritage, the true evolution, was that of intellect. Yet Chuan had wondered what it might have been like to have had children of his own.

He pulled his thoughts away. Clearly, his mild depression was due to the letdown when this evening ended. A euthymic ought to dissolve it, and then he could sleep. But no, chemical consolations were temporary. Perhaps an hour in the dreambox would serve. Not an encounter, to be sensed and later remembered as fully as a reality, with comradely men or glorious women or some great philosopher; he had long since outgrown those. But the right terrestrial landscape, serene and lovely, perhaps made by humans through century after loving century, or perhaps purely natural, there in the past before humans ever beheld it. . . . Yes, he truly had no reason to return to Earth, except as a download after his bodily death.

As for the dreambox, though—He decided against it. That it was illusion, artifice, mattered less than that tonight it would be a retreat from himself. He did not need relief so much as he needed affirmation. Let him make linkage instead.

Turning, he left sky and city behind him and sought the room that only he might enter.

Anyone uninitiated would have seen it as bare as a monk's cell—a cabinet, a couch, a control pattern of enigmatic simplicity, cold white light, silence. Chuan took out his interlink and coiffed his head with its nodule-studded mesh. He lay down, connected circuits, relaxed his body, thought his command.

Inside his skull, another network, implanted by nano-machines when he was a cadet, began to interact with the first, and with his brain. The triad came to harmony. It opened itself to the system that governed the cyber-cosm—sophotectic intelligences, computers, databases, scanners, sensors, an entity encompassing the planet—and it became an integral part thereof.

Metaphors, hints, fragments, distortions. Words do not reach to the intricacies and subtleties of what went on. Nor do the equations of relativistic quantum mechanics describe that immense, multiple, and changeably faceted psyche, its awarenesses ranging from the tides within an atomic nucleus to the curvature of all space-time, its billionfold guidances of machines and processes around the globe and out into satellite orbits, its thoughts and co-nation, the *will*, beneath them, driving the whole more powerfully than did the energies pulsing through it. For Chuan, it was transcendence and transfiguration.

He became able to remember how much mightier the cybercosm and his oneness with it were on Earth. Almost, he relived the three times there when he was briefly granted Unity, taken up into the circuits near the Tera-mind like an ion into the electric field near a lightning bolt. And he knew again, not in symbols or in yearnings but as absolute knowledge, that this was why he or his download must in the end return to Earth: that his identity could pass into the Whole.

So had mystics sought to lose themselves in God. Some did yet. Chuan's reward was certain, unless brute chance destroyed him first. And the consciousness that took him unto itself would grow onward, creating its own heaven above heaven, universe without end.

The lesser entity on Mars was enough for him this night—untellably more than enough. Nerve-tingles from the greater integrality pervaded it, borne on laser beams out of Earth, Luna, Mercury, the asteroids, the outer moons, everywhere that the machines of the cybercosm were.

His thoughts, his feelings, joined the currents flowing in the sea of mind. Their tiny waves found resonances. The entity responded to itself.

The bliss of communion that he expected became communication.

Afterward he remembered as if it had been spoken what had actually come to him as near-instant, tremendous knowledge. His organic brain could do no better.

Yes. I/you would soon have called you/me to this in any case. The news from the stars is proving more than troublesome. An advent in the near future may well precipitate a crisis. That in itself can doubtless be coped with, but it will leave its seeds in history, and what springs from them may be very strange. The Oneness looks millions of years forward; but to bring the great vision into being, it must also provide for the next few centuries.

Hitherto, even in union like this with the whole, you have received no information concerning the plan, for you needed none, nor did it require your help. Now the work must accelerate and intensify, so that all may be ready in time, before events have gone beyond control. Your mortal self has had experiences of humankind that, however quiet, are in some ways unique. Your thoughts and emotions, your contribution to that which is being created, will have value, helping speed and enrich the creating.

You would have learned after your bodily death, but then you will no longer be Chuan the man. Rejoice that already you will have an active part, small but real, in shaping the morrow of the cosmos.

Here is the secret. The solar lens—

Always when a synnoiont came out of synnoiosis, there was a period of disorientation. The world seemed flat, unsubstantial, meaningless. You learned how to shake off the sense of unendurable loss and go back to being human. Presently you felt how your strength had been renewed and inner peace restored.

But what he had had revealed to him kept Chuan awake till dawn.

Home in Sananton on vacation, Kinna Ronay donned her skinsuit and biostat and left the house. She had no immediate duties, she simply wanted to ramble.

The sun had cleared the eastern horizon. The sky was going coralline, with a few diamond-bright streamers of ice-cloud high aloft. Hills, dunes, boulders, craters stood forth in soft colors and metallic gleams. Northward, a ridge climbed rugged to the rim of Eos Chasma. Closer by, the house walls reached tawny, dome and ports shone, and the plantation roused. Low on the ground, solaria unrolled its leaves, turning their white sides down and their ebony sides up. Breath-of-life spread out its green and began to brew the oxygen that seed mites and plowbugs would tap when they emerged. A phantom breeze stirred the filaments of silkentrees. Darkness lingered in an orchard, but goldfruit hung like a thousand lanterns. Soon the wasserschatz would thaw and release the water in its drum-shaped bole, mixed with antifreeze, out through its countless capillaries; and life would get to work living.

Kinna had been in search of words to voice her happiness. They came together now and she said them aloud, for no one but herself.

> "Each day this land is reborn anew,
>   However old it may be,
>   In rusty rose and shadowful blue
>   And some glints like the light off a sea.
>   Above the crest of a purple hill
>   A crag stands towery tall,
>   And I can walk wherever I will—
>   The most wonderful part of it all."

8

AS HE STEPPED from the volant onto the airfield, into a wind lulling mild across three thousand kilometers of equatorial ocean, a brown girl gave Fenn a white smile and laid a garland around his neck. Iokepa Hakawau hugged him but then stepped back and said formally, *"Aloha, hoa, he kotoku rerenga tahi"* in the lingua franca of the polity. Fenn recognized the phrase, a welcome to a rare visitor. He was also an eagerly awaited one. It had taken him awhile to get an extended leave of absence.

A boy, not a machine of any kind, carried his locker-bag for him, and that too was part of the greeting. Strangers who saw him bowed. It was not that Fenn stood out physically; most people here were somewhat shorter and much darker, but not all, for every Terran bloodline had flowed into the Lahui Kuikawa. It was just that he was obviously special, having arrived from Kamehameha Spaceport in Hawaii, and alone at that.

He had taken the routine courtesies among Moon-dwellers for granted, except when he consciously didn't bother with them. He was rather scornfully familiar with the sociological dictum that more elaborate observances gave humans something to do, added significance to their lives. He had played documentaries about the varieties of them around Earth. But suddenly, here, he encountered ritual that was not theater but as natural as breathing.

Iokepa guided him across the big, crowded float platform. Structures reared pastel-tinted, their lines and curves suggestive of sails or prows, above a traffic that was mostly afoot, mostly chattering and cheerful. Flowers blazed in strips and boxes. He caught hints of their fragrance through the salt air. "I've got you a room at the Lilisaire," Iokepa said. "Figured you'd feel easier in a hotel than in a private home, till you've grown used to us. I can take you straight there if you'd like to rest awhile."

"No, I'm not tired," Fenn replied.

"*Pomaikai.* I didn't expect you'd be. Let Mikala take your duffel over. Meanwhile, we'll go talk. Then I'll see you to your quarters, and you had better get some rest before the luau starts."

"You're giving a party . . . for me?"

"Out on the *Mālōlo*." A brawny arm pointed through a gap between walls, over several kilometers of blue waves dusted with diamond by the sun, to the great ship that, Fenn knew, held Iokepa's *anaina*—community of extended families. "First a *talimālō*, a proper reception for you." Seeing his friend brace himself a little, the *kanaka* added: "I think you'll enjoy it. Nothing stuffy. You for sure ought to enjoy the celebration afterward. We're not solemn *po'e* here, you know. It wouldn't be right without a *talimālō*, though. You're important."

Fenn was unsure about that, but decided to wait and see what it meant.

Leaving the boy to go his way, the men boarded one of the shuttles that ran continuously between here and Nauru, and were soon on the island. No matter how often he had seen it on multiceiver and vivifer, Fenn found it astonishing. He was used to high-technology concentrations of humans. This was an atoll, larger and more elevated than most but still less than twenty kilometers in circumference. Yet parks and gardens covered at least half of it, palms swaying and rustling, grass a velvet carpet bordered and crossed with scarlet, violet, golden, dawn-pink, Mars-orange extravagances of flower beds, here a fountain, there a plot where raked gravel and standing stones invited contemplation.

Although few buildings were residential, none rose high and all were of traditional form, frequently in natural wood, with sweeping roofs, shady verandas up which grew bougainvillea or fuchsia, perhaps a hand-carved tiki in front or a figurehead springing from the gable. Vehicles were minimal in size and numbers. People walked, leisurely, in loose and colorful clothes; they stopped to chat, they whiled away an hour in an outdoor café; a group of young folk in a room whose door stood open sang to the strains of guitar and flute; a man and a maiden skipped along hand in hand; in another room, an old woman sat weaving cloth to a pattern she must have made up herself; several men passed by in plumed masks. . . . It did not look like the centrum of a polity that dominated half the Pacific and reckoned just its human members at eight million.

Well, Fenn thought, of course there were many other islands, not to mention ships like Iokepa's hometown. Besides, given the right equipment and, what counted for far more, the right habits, you could accomplish everything you wanted to without having to act stiffly efficient. The truly extraordinary feature was how well-ordered the society appeared to be, how almost everybody seemed to *belong*.

No doubt the exceptions were plentiful. He had heard about stresses and unrest on the increase, here as everywhere else.

"Where are we bound?" he asked after a while.

"To the *luakini*, seeing that you've arrived ready for action," Iokepa replied. "It comes out 'temple' in Anglo, or else 'spiritual center,' but I don't think either's quite right. Manu wants to meet you first and broach the matter to you himself, in a very preliminary way. He aims to get your input about it, and some feel as to whether you'll be right for it. He'o and I recommended you to him."

"Whatever the 'matter' is." Fenn grinned against the tension inside.

"I told you you'll hear today. In principle, anyhow. Later you'll see the engineering studies and so forth; we'll want your opinion as well as the experts'. If the proposal clears all this, we'll make it public. If it draws enough interest, it'll be debated in the longhouses on every island and every shipland. If they like it there, we can begin dickering with the Synesis and whoever else might be concerned. A long haul to maybe nowhere. But I've got my hopes."

"Who's this, uh, Manu?"

"Manu Kelani, the chief *kahuna* of Nauru. You start at the top, mate."

The top indeed, Fenn thought with a prickling up his backbone. High priest, grand advisor, primary magistrate of an unwritten law stronger than any in the databases—however you wanted to render the title—had the chief *kahuna* of the polity's capital ever before passed personal judgment on an obscure young foreigner?

The *luakini* lay massively timbered behind a sculptured colonnade. An honor guard of men in sarongs and rainbow cloaks, armed with spear guns, stood in front, beneath the star-and-wavecrest banner of the Lahui Kuikawa. Iokepa's usual offhandedness turned grave as he saluted and addressed their leader. With equal dignity, he and Fenn were admitted. Four women in loose white gowns, flowers wreathing their unbound hair, conducted the two down a dim, cool hall and left them to wait in a room clearly meant for private talk. Windows, open to the sea breeze, were high in the walls, each of which bore a fixed mural—the genesis of the Keiki Moana, their ancestral refuge with a few human caretakers in Hawaii, Kelekolio Pēla setting forth the Dao Kai, the cession of Nauru to descendants who had become a nation. A table with a terminal and a few chairs were the only furniture on the hardwood floor.

Manu Kelani entered through a rear door. He was tall, his hair bushy-white, his features more Melanesian than Polynesian but the eyes incongruously emerald. A golden cross hung on his breast above a blue robe and he carried a staff topped with a miniature anchor of an ancient type. Iokepa went to one knee. Manu laid a hand on his head. Words passed between them. Fenn could only, awkwardly, salute.

Iokepa rose. Manu turned to the newcomer. "Be welcome," he said in fluent Anglo. "I have heard much about you."

"Nothing too bad, I hope, sir," Fenn mumbled.

Manu smiled. "Enough to show that you are spirited. Do please be seated." He took a chair by the table and flicked the terminal. An attendant appeared. "Would you care for refreshment?"

Presently they were sipping coffee. Manu inquired about the trip from Luna. Fenn described it briefly, a standard ferry ride, then blurted, "Now what is this— Pardon me, sir. I, I don't mean to be, uh, unmannerly."

Manu smiled again. "If you feel impatient, that is quite understandable. It is we who must ask pardon, for withholding information until now. It was generous of you to come on our bare word. Confidentiality is wisest at this early stage."

He knew how to put a man at ease. "Well," Fenn replied, "Iokepa promised me it'd be interesting, and in that regard, he's never failed me yet."

The seaman laughed. Evidently, among the Lahui, respect for a person of high standing did not imply hushed awe. "I'm afraid this time it's nothing rowdy." He winked. "Though we'll see to that also in due course."

Manu grew serious. "You are of space, Lieutenant Fenn, born and bred. Your knowledge and skills go well beyond the requirements of your daily life on the Moon, and you can readily acquire more. So I have been assured. It speaks of a longing to use them."

Emotion exploded. "Slag and slaughter, yes!" In abashed haste: "Apologies, sir. But Iokepa did hint—Do you mean—"

"The news from the stars has touched everyone in the Solar System," Manu said. "It has started a ferment that in its many different forms grows daily more dynamic, for better or worse. In us too."

"In a lot of us, not a ferment," Iokepa muttered. "A bloody fire."

"Surely, Lieutenant Fenn," Manu said, "you can see how the concept, the tremendous fact of the Life Mothers, must affect us. They are like a sudden incarnation of the Dao Kai itself."

Flashingly, Fenn reflected on what he knew about the Sea Way: less a religion than a philosophy, a manner of thinking and feeling and living—less a set of precepts than a set of behaviors, organic, founded on the wholeness of all life and its oneness with all the universe—He had seen Iokepa and He'o meditate beneath the stars and under the water—If ever a people loved life, it was the Lahui Kuikawa. . . .

"The Synesis will not choose to create an Earth Mother," Manu went on.

Somehow Fenn felt he should deny the finality of that, if only to quell anger that did not belong here in this company. "I don't know, sir. If a majority of people want it—her—"

"A majority won't," Iokepa growled. "Too volcano-disruptive of their comfortable habits. And it'd cost like whale fur, you know."

Fenn nodded. He had seen and heard discussion aplenty since Ibrahim's announcement. Beyond the investment of resources and work—which nobody could estimate with any realism, except that it would be gigantic—lay an un-reckonable demolition of material establishments and so-cial institutions, merely to make room for the change. The lesser minds of the cybercosm had been unable to make any specific predictions and the Teramind had vouchsafed no prophecies.

"Besides, it can't be done in the lifetime of anybody now alive, or probably their grandchildren's," Iokepa continued. "That much sacrifice for benefits that distant? Don't you believe it."

Fenn could not but argue: "I hear talk of people down-loading to wait for the time," with their aged bodies si-multaneously given euthanasia. Otherwise, what would be the point? One lucky twin . . . and one unlucky.

"A few will, no doubt," Iokepa snorted. "Which means they'll opt out of the game. Do you seriously sup-pose they'd ever be woken up to share in an Earth Mother they'd done nothing to earn? Or that they could be happy in her kind of world? Not that Earth will get any."

Manu's mild tone snapped their attention back to him. "It may be that the Teramind will give us an easier means to the same end."

"It hasn't yet, has it, *kapena?*" Iokepa replied, in-stantly quiet again.

"No. We must consider the possibility, but I do not imagine it will come to pass. Perhaps no other way exists, or perhaps it would be wrong for our race. It is not for us to question the Teramind."

"But we don't have to sit meekly by, either, do we, *kapena?*" Iokepa's gaze sought Fenn. "That's what this is all about. *I'd* like to try for immortality and, yes, by Pele, the stars. I may well never make it myself, but I can have fun along the way, and half the fun will be in knowing that someday we'll have our own Life Mother, smack up against the smug Teramind."

Chill ran through Fenn's flesh. He felt his mane and beard bristle. "By all the dead down under—" he breathed.

Manu spoke, gently and unwaveringly. "Our friend is rather vehement, lieutenant. But he is right. Such an undertaking accords with our Dao as it does with no other way of thought or deed in the Solar System."

Fenn groped for comprehension. "Do you mean—But you can't transform Earth. Iokepa just said it. They won't let you."

"Nor should we, if it is not desired by others. No one should have such power."

Iokepa's tone went practical. "The territory we control is too small to support a Life Mother. At least that's what our biologists figure."

"Small?" Fenn exclaimed. "Half the Pacific Ocean?"

"Not much solid land there, and life in the sea is too, uh, diffuse. That's what the experts think, and believe me, we and our computers have been giving it a fleetload of thought." Iokepa sighed. "*Could* we even steer our private course, separate from the other life on Earth? Doesn't look very likely to me."

"Furthermore," Manu added, "we must not be arrogant. It may well be that a transformation of Earth would cost too dearly, in spirit still more than in wealth. Nor do we know if it is possible, in a biosphere as highly evolved as this." He paused. "Yet are we altogether barred from the dream? Can we not do as they did at Demeter and elsewhere, on a world where there is little or nothing to oppose us?"

It leaped in Fenn. "Wait!" he gasped. "I see—in space—the Moon? You've been interested in, in a colony there—"

"Yes. We decided against that, as you know."

"But you still sent missions."

Since Manu did not respond, Iokepa explained. "Oh, it's not Lahui style to shut the door absolutely on something that's looked promising. And probably any such operation would involve Luna." His smile twitched lopsided. "Also, it was an excuse to go back for more romps yonder. But now—"

"Where?" Fenn cried. "Mars?"

"We had not considered it in earnest before," said Manu, "because the concept of our colonizing beyond Earth began to die when the Moon proved disappointing. The fact of the Life Mothers changes the entire equation. Mars appears to be an option."

"T-t-terraforming it—along the lines of Demeter? The job's always been judged too big to pay, and—"

"Remember, we speak in terms of centuries."

"And we start small," Iokepa added. "And every step along the way has to be worth taking for its own sake. Its profit, whatever that may mean in any particular case."

Manu's voice throbbed low. "The Habitat was once Ragaranji-go, and wondrously alive."

Fenn's mind sprang to and fro, wild with surprise and distances opened, like a captive dolphin abruptly set free. "Begin with a Habitat," he stammered. "Your sort of Habitat, with some kind of sea in it and—In Mars orbit? That'd be far enough off that nobody could complain you're interfering with Earth–Luna satellites or, or anything. But materials—"

"We're thinking of the little outer moon Deimos," Iokepa said. "And, yes, we are quietly looking into the politics."

"If we decide to proceed, we can purchase one or two ships almost immediately," Manu said. "They exist, idled, in storage orbits. True, it would be necessary to build considerably more. Luna is probably the best site for a new shipyard. This is an area in which you could aid and advise us, Lieutenant Fenn. You have the knowledge and experience, you can put us in touch with others who can help, and you will not likely develop inhibitions or qualms." He smiled. "On the contrary."

Fenn stared before him. It was as if the wall that showed the arrival of the ancestors at Nauru dissolved and he looked straight out at planets and stars. "Space," he whispered.

Through the bloodbeat in his ears he heard Manu: "Please understand, this is very tentative. Some of us were thinking about Mars before the news from Centauri was broadcast. The rumors that floated about earlier did influence that thinking a little, and since then, there has been a radical reevaluation. But it is still going on. We do not actually have a plan, only a dream. We will need far more data and thought before we know if it is even possible, let alone feasible. This was one reason for calling you in. But do not resign your employment or otherwise commit yourself."

"Not yet," Iokepa said in an undertone.

"We shall, if you like, explore the idea further while you are here," Manu finished, "and explore each other."

In spite of every cautioning, glory flamed up to the sky.

9

COME ADVENTURE WITH me," Elverir said.

"Where?" asked Kinna promptly.

"Belike we return in two or three days. I will tell you more after we are aloft."

For a moment, she hesitated. It was not that she feared his intention. Often they had been gone longer than that, ranging the Valles Marineris or, once, as far south as the Nereidum Mountains. In their sealtent, the mattresses lay close together, and sometimes when they washed themselves or changed clothes, the curtain would get flipped aside for a moment's accidental glimpse. She had seen his desire and felt her own temptation. Nobody else would ever know. They need not even have given thought to pregnancy. But her spirit always shied off— it would have felt like betraying her parents—it would change this friendship, and herself, in unforeseeable ways—and he, sensing that, was too proud to court her and held back likewise, with a calm coolness she could never match. After all, he had plenty of girls at home.

Now, though, he might well have in mind one of those absolute recklessnesses or toplofty breaches of law that had more than once brought on a quarrel and a lengthy separation between them. Kinna enjoyed taking chances, within reason, but she was the daughter of David Ronay, who stood high in his community and served in the House of Ethnoi.

Excitement won. If what he proposed was unacceptable, she could refuse and, getting as tough as necessary, make the refusal stick. "Can you leave now?" he inquired.

"Let me fetch my kit and call my folks," she answered.

Their flitter jetted from Belgarre and swung westward. "Ease yourself," Elverir said. "We shall be aflight six or seven hours."

"What?" she exclaimed. "Why, that'd take us to— Where *are* you bound?"

"Tharsis. I know not yet which of the Threedom, but you shall meet with the Inrai."

Briefly, the world whirled around her. The Inrai— not the irreconcilable cities, but outlaws who robbed caravans, wrecked machines, killed sophotects and men— The knowledge tolled through her: Elverir, her landlouper companion, her private Lunarian, Elverir too was in conspiracy with them.

Noting her reaction, he said, "The wish is but to speak with you and show you a few things. I supposed you would find it interesting, not alarming."

The sarcasm stung her to alertness. "If you think I'm scared, you're so stupid you don't know which end of a mine shaft to go in at!" She saw him grin, caught her breath, and asked quietly, "Is this real, not some kind of joke? Then you're dement."

"Nay," he answered as low. "I seek for freedom. It

is not something many Terrans care about but I thought you might, in your fashion.''

''We've argued that before, and never gotten liftoff.''

''Where talk has failed, sight may succeed.''

Indecision drained from Kinna. An adventure, oh, yes! Curiosity seethed. She gripped the arms of her seat as if they were common sense. It was faintly surprising how steady her voice became.

''You won't convert me, you know. Of course I'll be interested—no, that isn't honest. I'll be fascinated. But why me? How did you get them to agree to this, and whatever for?''

Unwontedly grave, he replied, ''The idea was mine, and much time flowed before I persuaded Scorian. I am . . . new to the resistance, and marginal. Yet I have come to know you well and, through you, other Terrans, and a few among them have some small force in affairs public. Thus I feel more sharply than most of us, who are so alienated and cut off, how little the outer world—also among my race—understands our reason for being. Even you call it dement.

''We lose naught, and we may gain somewhat, if the truth goes widely forth that it is . . . douris.'' The Lunarian word he put into his Anglo did not really mean ''just'' or ''righteous.'' Those were not really Lunarian concepts. ''Natural'' or ''unwarped'' came closer. ''Ey, as you said, we can make no converts. And simply for the . . . clarification, you by yourself are the barest of beginnings. But a good beginning. Your father will listen to you, and maychance through him others will who matter a little. Surely at the university you have many friends among the students, who have friends of their own; and surely there are those among the preceptors who will not altogether toss your words aside. And you tell me you often visit the synnoiont. Who better than you could speak on our behalf?''

Despite the thrumming in her, his assumption—that David Ronay, and humans in general, possessed almost negligible influence—nettled her, as it had in the past. "Don't take me for granted," she warned. "I'll report what I see as I see it."

His smile approached being warm. "I foreknew that. Ever were you an awkward liar."

Silence fell, apart from the slight murmur and shiver of the vehicle. Outside reached a wanly roseate sky. A dust storm loomed above the northern horizon like a bank of yellowish-gray thunderheads; but Mars had not heard thunder for a billion years or more. Dunes rolled ocherous, boulder-strewn, around craters that the sun limned with shadows. Closer below, the land grew rugged, ridges, cliffs, canyons, until it plunged into the tremendous deeps of the Valles. Through the bubble, Kinna traced a descending massiveness of mesas, crags, weird wind-sculptures, black, red, umber, streaked soft green and blue with mineral veins, until depth swallowed sight.

"Look," she said after a spell, pointing to a formation. "Guthrie Head. Do you remember?"

"I could ill forget." He laughed.

Camped there on one of their first jaunts together—they were just five, and her mother accompanied them—they had gotten into an hours' long game of hide-and-seek through the crevices and over the talus slopes. Helen Ronay lost all track of them and was desperate by the time they somehow found their separate ways back. She confined them to the tent with bread, water, and a calculator, and did not let them out till they had memorized and recited the sine of every angle from one to forty-five degrees, at one-degree intervals, to four decimal places. But when Elverir's father, in Belgarre, later heard about the escapade, he laughed, which he seldom did, and gave them the first glass of wine Kinna had ever tasted.

When the Sisters passed beneath them, she said nothing. There, age seven, they had had awhile alone in the tent and started kissing. Already then he was tigerish, purring amidst fierceness. No more than that happened, but she never risked it again, and no Terran youth since then had so aroused her.

The landmarks dropped behind like time itself and they flew over spectacles they knew only from pictures, if at all. It would be long before they crossed the farther regions that, leapfrogging, they had also explored.

"What is . . . your connection . . . with the Inrai?" she asked at last.

His answer came slow but less hesitant. "I may not reveal anything. Besides, you know there is scant to reveal. The siamos"—disdainful word for the authorities—"do not pursue the matter, for it leaves no tracks they could find. Yet the knowledge is common that some Lunarians around the planet give what they are able when it is requested, supplies, shelter, transport, information, help; and not all traffic in and out of the Threedom takes trails that satellites can watch."

Kinna nodded. Her neck felt stiff. "So you've become a, a reservist, now and then a courier or, oh, a purchasing agent or something like that?"

"Correct. You'll not tell anyone." It wasn't a question.

"No, no." She groped for an argument that might persuade. "What difference would it make, except to us? What difference does your whole movement make, actually?"

Fragments of the history blew past her like dust on the wind. The settlers of Mars had not been exclusively people in search of profit, honor, and achievement. Some were Terrans dissenting from their Earthside governments; some were Lunarians in blood-feud trouble on Earth's Moon. Whatever their individual motivations, Lunarians were more numerous among the immigrants. Many flourished, and something like the Selenarchy bade fair to arise, with dreams not of terraforming but of lunaforming the globe.

Slowly the dominance and the dreams died. Terrans bred faster. Luna became another republic in the World

Federation, its native population dwindling. The Martian economy began its long decline. The Lunarians of Mars felt forsaken.

When the Lyudov Rebellion erupted on Earth, the towns Arainn, Layadi, and Daunan in the Tharsis region declared independence. No other settlements did, and eventually they disarmed as the Peace Authority demanded. But they never surrendered their claim. They lived and traded peacefully enough. What they refused to do was to recognize the legitimacy of the Federation and, later, the Synesis. They cast no votes, sent no delegates, contributed neither data nor opinions to the official network. It had seemed harmless, a picturesque relic, until the latter-day winter of discontent fell also upon Mars. Then men and women of the Threedom—and volunteers from elsewhere—began to make weapons and take to the wilderness. Had they been Terrans, one would have called them brigands or guerrillas. Being Lunarians, they were Inrai.

"What can you hope for?" Kinna pleaded.

Elverir straightened where he sat. Arrogance rang. "Today, that hope stay alive. Tomorrow, that we be free, as they are on Proserpina and at Centauri."

He doesn't speak of a free Mars or anything like that, she thought. He speaks of a free "us." Free to be—Lunarian. Not that they'd persecute Terrans, if somehow they got power over the planet. They wouldn't condescend to. In fact, I believe Elverir would die defending my life, not because he loves me, which he doesn't, nor because he likes me, which he does, but because I belong to his honor, his self-pride.

"Proserpina," she challenged. "Do you honestly expect help from there? Oh, I've heard the rumors of secret visits, and maybe there've been one or two, though I can't imagine how, but name of reason, it's out at the far end of the Solar System."

"We may give them cause to join with us."

Her eyes stung. "I, I've heard you before, but I never

supposed—Trouvour, you're talking revolt not just against overwhelming strength. It's against all sanity, all decency." The ghost of every conqueror and tyrant, every slave and starveling, rose from her readings to mouth at her.

"You shall continue to dwell where you are in whatever ways you choose, you Terrans. Only let us go ours." He sighed. "Have we not drained this talk well dry, we two?" Reluctantly, she nodded. They had argued it over and over while they grew toward maturity. She had not known he had become directly involved, but now it struck at her: "You shall see the wellspring reality. I think Scorian will take us to an Inrai camp, that you may behold what force of desire is in us. Eyach, I wish for it. I have not yet been to one myself." His smile terrified her. "I want to know what awaits me."

She clutched his arm. "Elverir, no! You aren't serious, are you? Turning outlaw? Not just a helper, but a bandit?"

He smiled on. She remembered how he'd once stalked a wild robot. Appeal to what wits he's got, she thought frantically. "I'm . . . afraid you won't find it very glamorous. Weeks on end out in the barrens, living on dried rations and recycled piss, waiting for action that never comes—" The humor of it touched her. The situations were rare in which she could not find something funny. "My friend, you're at the point where machismo becomes masochism."

Not for the first time, she had undermined his position. He was, after all, quite young. "I merely speak of possibilities," he mumbled.

"Then don't leap blind into any such brannygaggle," she teased. "First count to a hundred by negative numbers."

It worked to calm, if not to convince him. They became able to talk inconsequentially, play games, watch a show or the passing scenery, sway-dance in their seats to music they both liked. Tension mounted afresh beneath the pleasure, but they were not much aware of it until journey's end hove in sight.

Elverir had called ahead and been directed to Layadi. The transmissions used harmless-sounding code phrases rather than encryption, which might have attracted the notice of eavesdroppers. He sent the flitter slanting downward.

The town, a lesser and poorer version of Belgarre, huddled on a patchwork of cultivated fields. Roads crisscrossed and outbuildings lay scattered about. It all seemed nearly lost amidst rugged, tawny desolation. An edge of blackness stood barely above one point on the western horizon, the heights of Pavonis Mons, hundreds of kilometers distant. The sun was sinking toward it. Shadows of dunes, rocks, and craters stretched long across the desert.

Little traffic moved. While the seigneurs of the Threedom did not forbid commerce in and out of the Tharsis region, they had taken to discouraging it. Several aircraft were parked at the landing field but they were small, meant for families and local travel, though "local" could imply considerable spans. When Elverir had rolled to the terminal, a gangtube extended to mate with the flitter's main airlock.

He and Kinna crossed into the building. She barely noticed the calligraphy on the interior walls. The four men who received them shocked her too heavily. They wore ordinary garb, but holstered at each waist was a pistol. What, firearms inside a habitation? Anywhere else on Mars or Luna, it would bring instant arrest and a stiff penalty.

She gulped and let Elverir do the talking. That was with one who evidently led the squad, or at least spoke for it. Gaunt, ash-pale, even among his hard-visaged companions he struck her as forbidding. Did his glance at her hold actual hatred? No, she mustn't do him an injustice; they'd never met. His tone was sullen, his words curt; clear to see, he disapproved of this assignment. Elverir, who addressed him by name, obviously didn't like him.

Orders were orders, though, even among Lunarians. The exchange was soon over. Silent now, the guards conducted the newcomers down into a tunnel and zigzagged through several passages. Kinna couldn't tell where they emerged, but from the fact that they encountered hardly anyone on their way, she judged it to be on the outskirts of town.

The room where the escort left her and Elverir confirmed her guess. A viewport gave on farmland and raw hills beyond. Otherwise the chamber was undecorated and sparsely furnished. Air hung chill, with a slight iron-like smell.

When they two were alone, she asked, "Who was that person you were dealing with? You seemed to know him."

Her friend grimaced, which Lunarians did not often do. "Yes, we have met at times, in the course of my zailin." The word did not quite mean "indoctrination" or "training." Maybe "initiation" came closer. "Tanir of Phyle Conaire, from Daunan. He is an able man in the wilds, but cruel, too quick with his weapons, maychance not wholly sane about what we strive for here." And that kind of judgment was one which Lunarians did not often utter.

She shivered, not from cold. History said that causes had brought forth such people. But the murderous great causes belonged only to history, didn't they? They were centuries extinct, weren't they?

She gestured around her. "The poverty—Is it worth it, pretending independence?"

"Saou," he hushed her. "Scorian has refuge in this house. He cares not about comfort, when mostly he is in the outback—Ai, he."

A door retracted, closing again behind the Inrai chieftain as he trod through. In black coverall and boots, knife and pistol at belt, he stood less tall than the average Lu-

narian had done on Luna but several centimeters above
Kinna, lean, hatchet-faced, yellow-eyed, white skin darkened and leathered by a lifetime's accumulation of stray
radiation. Scorning biotreatment, he remained totally
bald, and a scar puckered his right cheek. Or were those
trademarks?

What she knew of his past tumbled through her. In a
dispute over access rights, his father had killed three
sophotects and, irrevocably, a man; then, rather than sub-
mit to correction, he'd fled with a dozen fellow rebels
into the wilds. That was the germ of the Inrai. Since then
they had become virtually institutionalized, supported by
the towns and manorial estates of Tharsis, most of them
leading civilian lives in between encampments and pa-
trols. Widely around the three dead volcanoes they
ranged. Sometimes they attacked a caravan bringing
goods, but only when it appeared to be safe to do so and
only to augment their supplies; destruction and casualties
were incidental. Sometimes they fired on constabulary
parties venturing into their territory, but only to keep it
for themselves.

Or so their announced policy was, according to an occasional broadcast from some transient location in the
wilderness. Otherwise they abided, building up strength,
awaiting a day of upheaval whose nature was unclear to
Kinna—and, she suspected, to them. That took a discipline which under such circumstances would have been
remarkable among Terrans. Somehow Scorian maintained it over his Lunarians—force of personality and
sheer ruthlessness—although she had heard stories sug-
gesting it was qualified and unstable, with bands of Inrai
now and then acting as outright robbers. She could believe that of Tanir.

Scorian halted and leveled his bird-of-prey eyes on her.
A surprisingly soft, drawling voice gave an old-style
greeting: "Well beheld, donrai."

"With courtesy," she responded in the same formal

Lunarian. (Actually, "enteur" implied respect for pride, including one's own.)

Elverir stood very straight, palm on breast. "Aou, free-lord," he said.

Scorian smiled the least bit and gestured at the chairs. All sat down, the visitors opposite him. He whistled. An armed retainer brought in a wine carafe and goblets, set them on the low table between, and exited. Scorian nodded at Elverir, who made haste to pour.

The chief raised his drink first. *"Uwach yei,"* he said, the traditional toast.

"Y-your health, donrai," Kinna faltered. She followed him in sipping. The wine was a full-bodied white. Starberry overtones roused memories of home. Could it be loot? "This is . . . good."

"You have Elverir to thank," Scorian replied. "You are here at his urging."

"Me, what can I do?"

"Ey, maychance naught—or maychance much. If the experiment proves out, we will invite more Terrans to hear our tale."

"It will prove out, freelord," Elverir ventured. "I have avowed that Kinna Ronay is trustworthy."

"Are you wholly certain?" Scorian asked.

The young man lifted his head in haughtiness. "I stake myself upon it."

"You honor me, trouvour," Kinna told him, more moved than she had expected. "I'll try to deserve it." She mustered courage. "But I may well decide—keep on believing—what you do here is not right."

"Boldly spoken," Scorian said. She recognized the approbation.

It heartened her to go on. "Your cities, your countryside—in revolt—"

"We claim no more than is ours, resting on the bones of our ancestors," Scorian declared. "Crommelin has no rights over us, nor do the *machines* of Earth."

She shivered at the glacial fury in his tone. How long

could the standoff continue? She wanted to say that republican forces could occupy the towns whenever they chose and piecemeal scour away the Inrai, but refrained because of the blood that would be shed. He would probably observe, as her father had done, that Lunarian pressure in the House of Ethnoi had something to do with their patience. How then could she convince him that violence was not in the soul of the Synesis or its cybercosm? It was bad enough detaining whatever outlaws were captured. A Lunarian would often suicide before submitting to correction; humane though the conditions were, several had anyway. But if the Inrai became a serious threat and the authorities saw no alternative—

"How free are you now?" Recalling her observation en route: "That life of yours out in the desert must be pitifully limited."

"In its fashion," Elverir admitted, "and often short." Nature—dust storms, rockslides, sand hells, wandering lost, choking or freezing when biostats failed—killed more than armed clashes did; but however they died, no Inrai were left in revivable condition. He glowed. "Yet, while it lasts, a full aliveness!"

I didn't persuade him, she thought sickly.

Scorian relieved her. "At present your comrade is more useful where he is. If you would save him from going wild, then work toward getting us our liberty."

"I don't understand," she said. "I've tried, really I have, but I can't. What harm if you joined us? How are we restricted or, or bossed or anything, except in a few reasonable ways people have to agree on if they're going to live together like human beings?"

"Ever the cybercosm encroaches."

"Donrai, you speak as if it ruled the Solar System."

"Does it not? None are free save out on Proserpina and the comets—and here, in this narrow space, which is piece by piece gnawed from us."

"How? Hasn't the Synesis—the Synesis, I say, not the cybercosm but human civilization—hasn't it stayed its hand against you? In spite of some almighty insolent provocation, donrai!''

A tight-lipped smile crossed Scorian's countenance. The scar on his cheek writhed. ''The spirit has not been bleached out of you, at least, my lady. But as for invasions, to name only the latest, see yonder.'' He waved a hand at that shadow on the horizon which was Pavonis Mons. The sun very low, the peak seemed larger than before, black under a deepeningly red sky where dust streamers scudded. ''There, halfway to the summit, sits now a stronghold of the enemy's.''

''What?'' She was astonished. ''Do you mean the Star Net Station? I know about it, of course. But how can it possibly hurt you? Is it anything except wonderful?''

For a moment the vision danced and sang before her. The Star Net, astronomical instruments orbiting from near the sun to out among the comets, linked by laser beams and electrophotonic minds, one vast observer looking into the heart of the galaxy and toward the uttermost ends of the universe—and now here, on her Mars, a part of it that was also a centrum to receive and store data, a hoard of marvels and miracles—

''It is *theirs*,'' Scorian said flatly, ''built by *them* on Threedom land without leave of freeholder or seigneur. A scientist has told me the reasons given for its construction are feeble. It need not be where it is to serve the research. One like it could as well have been raised elsewhere. What is it, then, save an outpost and an outrage?''

''But nobody lives there.''

''A robot does,'' Elverir said, ''if you can call it alive.''

His words appalled her. Was Scorian's bigotry so contagious, or had her friend soft-played his in her presence all these years?

''Did the workers, machines, and materials fare overland,'' the chief said, ''we would have fought them each centimeter of the way.''

Kinna had heard that was the reason everything for the

construction had traveled by air. At the time, she was indignant—bandits snapping at the heels of a sublime enterprise—but today she began to catch glimmerings of the opposite viewpoint. She didn't have to accept it to say, "Eyach, if a road had gone through, with supply depots along it, you might have felt menaced."

"We would have destroyed it as it was being built. Could we only, we would destroy that thing on the mountain."

"Oh, no!" she cried. "Please!"

"Have no fear," Elverir sighed. "Its fence and machines guard it well."

"Someday," Scorian murmured, "we may try how well that is."

"But I tell you, I *don't* understand," Kinna protested. "Why are you angry? Why can't you make peace? I know how easy that would be. My father's talked about it. Amnesty—"

"Domestication," Elverir said.

"No! Are you a slave? Don't you live in Belgarre according to your own law, your own style? It'd be the same for the Threedom."

"Yes, pet animals may scamper loose about a spacecraft," Scorian jeered. "Bulkheads keep them out of any place that matters. They have naught to say about where the ship is bound."

"What do you want, for plenum's sake?"

He spiked her with his gaze and answered remorselessly: "First, a Threedom sovereign throughout Tharsis, allied with Proserpina." How much of this fury had been aroused by messages and messengers from that world? "Later, a sovereign Mars." A Lunarian Mars. "At last, the Luna that was and is ours, returned to our race." The irredentism she had heard muttered spoke nakedly forth. "Is that overmuch? Earth need never dread us." Contempt: "We are not interested in what Terrans call 'empire.'"

"But why?" Kinna asked in bewilderment. "What's

the purpose? You talk about freedom as if you had none this moment. What else would you do with . . . that precious sovereignty of yours?''

The room was growing dark. She imagined the specter of the nation-state walking in through the wall, from the cold and unbreathable wind outside, followed by war and war and war.

No, Scorian perhaps was right about that. Lunarians weren't pack animals like wolves or Terrans, ready to follow any ravening alpha male; they were more like lions in their prides. Yet lions too were hunters. And Scorian could be wrong. It was a hideous chance to take.

He was answering her: ''We have no purpose, no destiny. The cybercosm does, whatever its plan may be. We shall not meekly, blindly, be carried along like you. We will go wheresoever we ourselves will.''

The sun went under the horizon. The instant Martian night clapped down. Scorian had nulled the house lights. He did not immediately let them turn on and blanket the sky, but sat for a little while and talked softly, almost questioningly.

''See the universe. Its strangeness overpowers us. But are we unfit to try to know it? Is that for the Teramind alone? We hear of a momentous discovery a solar lens has made. The tale must lie archived yonder, as well as elsewhere, up in the station on Pavonis. Why do they put off disclosing it? What does the cybercosm keep from us, and for what reason?''

''Where go those light-speed ships they have lately built?'' Elverir put in.

''If they go anywhere,'' Kinna said defensively. ''It's been explained that they're still experimental. And we are getting reports from the, the interstellar missions.''

''What truth is in them?'' Scorian demanded. ''How shall we know? Nay, we are being refused.''

''The data are uncertain; they need confirmation—''

''Lest the Teramind have to confess making a mistake? The Proserpinans sought to establish a lens of their own, and failed. They think this was belike the work of the cybercosm. Someday we shall see." Scorian's hiss was like a knife being drawn from the sheath.

10

A BOAT LEFT the shiptown *Mālōlo* and turned east. Induction drive soundless, bow barely whispering through the water, it went like a living swimmer, but swiftly, swiftly. The waves bore it in long surges and deep murmurs, surrounded it with their blues, violets, greens, white laces of foam. Sunlight danced on them in shards and stars. Though the wind was deflected by a screen around the open cockpit, its song poured over the two who sat there.

Near the starboard horizon and reaching beyond it, pelagiculture laid a dark carpet. Glints told of machines at work, tending the plants, herding the fish. A thermal tower lifted above, where temperature differential drove the pumps that brought nutrients up from the bottom while discharging fresh water and energy into storage units. To port, the sea was entirely open. Yacht sails winged here and there across it. Aloft, a hang glider dropped from a small dirigible, caught an updraft, and soared exuberant.

Fenn drew a salt breath, consciously savoring it. "What a gorgeous day," he said. "I still don't understand why Iokepa didn't come along."

Wanika Tauni smiled. "Why should he?" she replied.

"Well, he and He'o—partners—"

"I'm close to the Keiki Moana too," she reminded him. "And my cousin is a simpático man."

"Huh?" However fluent her Anglo, Fenn didn't quite grasp her meaning. He stared at her. She was worth staring at, a big young woman, full-bodied, black hair falling free past vivid dark eyes, snub nose, generous mouth, brown cheeks and shoulders. Like him, she wore merely a blouse and shorts, but she didn't need the sun oil he had rubbed on his skin. In the days and nights while *Mālōlo* cruised from Nauru, they had come to share much laughter and some seriousness.

"Don't be so earnest," she teased. "It gets in the way."

"Uh, I don't object, you realize," Fenn answered awkwardly. "Couldn't ask for better company. But this today, it's supposed to, uh, educate me. Isn't it?"

"Everything is. That doesn't mean we can't enjoy ourselves."

There spoke the Dao Kai, he thought. How easygoing and easy it sounded. How hard, evasive, maddening it could be if you weren't born and raised to it. In the cities of Luna he had seen attempts at half a dozen land-bound versions. Documentaries had shown many others, all around Earth. None seemed more than superficial at best, grotesque at worst, nor did any appear to yield more than discontent with the existing system—no workable alternative. Manu Kelani had called them part of a general spiritual secession, which had found no place to withdraw to.

Here, in mid-ocean, the real thing reigned, not just a formulated philosophy but a Way: traditions, rituals, relationships, a sense of oneness with nature and life; minimally few sophotects, never a synnoiont, yet no hostility toward cybercosm or Synesis—And here also it was breaking down, with malaise among the elder, rebelliousness among the younger, everything from simple rudeness and gross unconventionality to crime and violence, and increasing numbers of the best departing in search of something happier somewhere else. "We're starting to see how we're in a cage," Iokepa had growled. "A preserve, at least. Oh, it's a big preserve, and we can do whatever we want inside it that's possible, but how much is possible and what do the old ways *mean* any longer?"

Fenn shook himself. "I'm sorry," he apologized. These past days had brought an unwonted degree of mildness upon him. "I can try, but I'll never really belong among you."

Wanika regarded him closely. "You can if you wish to, by what you do, if not quite by what you are," she said. "We need you."

He respected her judgments. She was not simply a championship surfer. Her work was akin to his father's, concerned with the ecological balance and well-being of wild species, which the Lahui Kuikawa did not entrust to even intelligent machines; and she took an above-average active part in affairs of her *anaina*. Nevertheless, he must in honesty admit, "I wonder about that. What can I actually do?"

"More than we now know, I suspect. Our grandchildren's lives may turn on it." In thinking so far ahead, she was typical of her folk. It wasn't futurism; it was unity through time.

"No, wait," he protested. "I can't give you anything but—an opinion, a guess, hardly worth the name of advice."

"We shall begin to find out about that today, shall we not?"

The boat fared on. *Mālōlo* dropped below the rim of sight. An islet hove in view. It was artificial, afloat. Pelagiculture wasn't practiced near coral, which the associated plankton bloom would have damaged. This patch of ground was treeless, grassless, covered only with sand, shell, and rocks. Buildings clustered at the middle, low and bleakly functional. Here was a resting place and rookery for the Keiki Moana. Wanika handed Fenn an optic. Through it he made out the crowded seal-forms darkening a beach.

One broke through the waves alongside. Fenn recognized He'o. He wore a vocal synthesizer. His natural voice coughed beneath the shout: *"Aloha, hoapili!* Are you ready?"

The same eagerness leaped up in Fenn. "We soon will be," he cried back.

Wanika ordered the boat to stop, lie to, and wait. At her gesture, Fenn peeled off his clothes. She helped him get his outfit on—wetsuit, helmet, biostat, flippers, motor, armband of instruments—and checked it out. He had had instruction and practice en route. It was less fun than going nude, but he had strenuous swimming and diving ahead of him. Or was it less fun? Without equipment, he was inept compared to humans of the Lahui Kuikawa; he could only, enviously, watch their water dances. Space-reared, he took immediately to this gear.

When Wanika stripped to don hers, lust stabbed through him, not for the first time. It had been awhile. He shoved the feeling aside and sprang overboard.

What followed in the next several hours was utter witchery. With the woman to help interpret, He'o conducted Fenn through his world.

Lectures, discussions, texts, vivifer presentations had prepared him a little. A dreambox session might have done more, but the Keiki had never permitted such data to be taken, and besides, their human fellows hardly ever indulged in that pastime. Anyway, there really was no replacement for reality.

They went over kilometers of wild water, and if Fenn could not share, he could see the exultation—the exaltation—that took hold of He'o as he breasted and clove and rode the waves, mounted their crests and plunged into their hollows, merged with them and their mightiness. The two joined Keiki herders on their rounds, warding the uncultivated range where bright-scaled flocks roamed; Fenn heard them bark their songs, and something ancient in his marrow stirred to that hoarse, unhuman music; he half sensed the pulsations through which they were not only in communication, but in communion. He watched several overtake prey and close jaws; blood ran dark and pungent out into sunlit green, and that too was right, that was as it should be. He saw scars from encounters with sharks, and He'o told him tales of death and bravery. He rollicked among dolphins while flying fish skimmed overhead, meteoric silver.

His party sought the depths, where blue dusked away into a night as unending as Proserpina's. A whale passed by, hugeness incarnate, on some unspoken business. The Keiki descended to keep track of life and subtle current shifts, to watch over machines that worked for them, and because this was another part of their sea. A riskful dive to the borders of what an unaided body could survive was a rite of passage into adulthood. It did more than test strength; it was religious revelation, awe and mystery and the implacability of the universe.

Coming ashore at last, well wearied in spite of having had the motor to help him, Fenn met He'o's wives and pups. In this species, sexual equality was not ludicrous, it was unthinkable. Yet the females were in no manner subservient. They had their own culture with its own language, concerns, mores, ceremonies, arts, history, distinct from though conjugate with the males'. It produced less noise, more formality, no fighting. Wanika remarked that insofar as human terms had any meaning here, the males were Dionysian and the females Apollonian. Fenn wasn't familiar with the words, but was too full of wonder to stop and ask.

Arts—In a species without hands, the arts were originally somatic, creations acted out or said forth or sung, or wrought with touches and odors and perhaps a stone or a strand of weed. Over the centuries, material works had become increasingly common. Molecular recorders let oral compositions develop into literature. Skillfully directed, robots, or simpler machines, gave solid form to visions. Fenn inspected small-scale but impressive pieces of technology, together with vivifer presentations of others elsewhere in the realm. He most admired the medical equipment, especially that intended for injuries. Architecture did not much interest a race of seals, but he wished his mother could firsthand experience the eerily evocative sculptures and pictures shown him. There was even a variety of musical instruments.

Still, the living body remained the primary vessel and tool. His day climaxed when the entire local population, both sexes, every age above infancy, went into the water and performed a classic ballet for him. He did not know the conventions, and Wanika could barely sketch the story, but after what he saw, the sea dances of the human Lahui seemed trifling; it shook him with tragic power, like an earthquake or a stormwind.

"We make less than our human fellows," He'o said into the final great silence.

"But you live more," Wanika whispered. Louder, to Fenn: "No, you'll never understand. Nor will I ever, except just enough to long for being able to."

She called the boat to come fetch them. They and He'o waited for it, alone on a pier. Waves lapped, air lay cool, the Keiki were hushed. Westward, the sun neared the horizon. It threw gold across the waters and kindled fire in low clouds around it. An albatross soared on high, wings against infinite darkening blue.

Wanika laid a hand on Fenn's forearm. "Now you have observed this side of what we are," she said quietly. "Do you think we can go into space?"

He hesitated.

"You have seen us there." He'o's voice throbbed below the constructed human words.

"Yes; as individuals and for short whiles," Fenn replied. "But to colonize, to stay, that's not the same. Everybody agrees that your first generations, at least, will have to live in a version of the Habitat. No matter how well we design it for you"—he gestured at the shimmering reaches before them—"can we possibly build it large enough?"

He had screened the tentative plans, and made a few suggestions. As a moon, Deimos was tiny—like Phobos, a captured asteroid. That did still amount to a very respectable tonnage. Flattened into concentric cylindroids, it would dwarf the satellite of Luna. But the material was mostly chondritic. Once it had included a good deal of frozen water, but all that was feasible to extract had long since been taken from both Deimos and Phobos for the Martian colony. The rock that remained would require intensive processing, plus metals brought in from the Asteroid Belt, ices and organics from the comets. The cost would be great. What also troubled him was the thought of how minuscule a sea the new habitat could hold.

"We'll keep our numbers small," Wanika said, "till we're ready to proceed further."

He'o lifted his head above massive shoulders. His whiskers bristled, his eyes caught the sunset light, his tones rang forth. "Hrrach-ch, yes, our young will go, with a few oldsters like me to captain them at first. The stars will be our ocean."

Nerves thrilled in Fenn. The sheer audacity of it—to be, to evolve, as Lahui Kuikawa, human and seal together, from that bridgehead by Mars to the planet itself, at last giving it back its waters and thunders—That job would demand immense powers and riches, gained across the Solar System by generations of explorers and merchant adventurers—and in the course of those enterprises, winning command over resources so great that argosies could be launched for the stars. . . . No, by then, if the then ever came to pass, they would not be Lahui Kuikawa any longer, they who transformed Mars and looked to the galaxy. They would have transformed themselves, as Guthrie's people had changed from simple Terrans to children of the Life Mothers. But they would bear the blood and the memory of their ancestors who first raised ship.

And if the endeavor failed, no matter how ruinously, let the future remember those who dared.

He had no eloquence. "I've heard the arguments before, of course," he said. "You folk know best what you're willing and able to pay out, in credit and everything else. All I can tell you is—well, given a few other favorable factors that I don't yet know about, I'd say you can take a flaming good shot at it."

Wanika's fingers tightened on his arm. *"Mahalo,"* she breathed. "Thank you."

The boat arrived and docked itself. *"Aloha nō,* kinfellow," He'o bade Fenn. Impulsively, the man bent over and hugged the sleek, damp form. He had seldom liked any human as much as he did this creature.

Wanika and he embarked. They stood waving goodbye while the boat left, then changed back to ordinary clothes and sat down in the cockpit. A pleasant tiredness pervaded his flesh. When she reached into a locker and brought out two beers, it was like a benediction.

"What a marvelous day," he sighed. He rarely gave that sort of praise.

"It was life you met," she said gravely, "the variousness of it, the—the self-willedness, yes, the cruelty and sadness"—he recalled fish snapped to death, a catastrophic legend enacted—"everything the machines do not know and cannot. That's what we want to keep, we Lahui."

"Yes, I understand."

"But can we? I don't mean staying here on our allotted section of Earth, doing the same things over and over, lifetime after lifetime. That might have been good once—after all, it's new to every new generation, and there's more to experience than anybody can before dying—but now we have the word from the stars and—Do you truly think we can break free?"

"You know I can't give you more than my guess, and I don't qualify as an engineer."

"We've plenty of those, plus everything in the databases and the computer capabilities. What we need is a spacedweller's *feel* for it."

No sophotects had such a need, he thought. Advisors like Benno or Irma could appreciate it, but they could not share it, for they were rational.

"I told you I think a very limited number of you could

live reasonably happy in the kind of orbital structure that could be built," he said. "I'm figuring in things like the availability of low-weight and open space to frolic in. But it doesn't seem worthwhile—does it?—unless you can go on to the rest of your ambitions."

"Leave the economics and politics to the experts, Fenn."

He grinned, a flash of teeth in the short beard that the sunset turned coppery. "Glad to!"

"The initial cost is quite bearable, you know. We don't think like mainlanders. We wouldn't be assessing ourselves for the benefit of none but a few. Collectively, we hold a huge accumulation of citizen's credit that has never been spent. Nobody individually has had much that s/he wants to spend it on. Why not turn it over to the dream? People will, for the dream's sake and because it's an adventurous investment."

"Will the amount be big enough, though?"

"For a start. Oh, true, we shall have to attract outside investors as well. But we can offer a share in the riches we'll be getting from space, a role in a second era of pioneering."

"Yes, I've heard." At length. "But can you convince them? I've also seen and heard, already, the commentators around the globe who say what a bad idea this is."

"The establishment in the Synesis, the conservatives, they don't like it, no. If it succeeds, in the long run it will perturb the stable economy, the stable world order. And the cybercosm always thinks in the long term. But it can't allow or disallow the undertaking, nor can the human directors. That decision lies with the Republic of Mars, and our leaders believe they can persuade its leaders. Don't you worry about that."

He raised his hand. "Por favor, Wanika, I've been over this again and again. You weren't with me then; you had better things to do. What I have in mind this evening is more straightforward. I said your orbiting habitat looks to me as though it would be practical. But it's meant for a bare beginning. You aim at an eventual terraforming of Mars. That's been talked about since before space travel, I suppose, and nothing's happened. *Can* it be done, especially in the particular way you want, leading to a Life Mother? I don't know. Does anybody?''

''Studies have been made,'' she said slowly. The sunset burnished the sea and her hair.

''Of course. And you can't steer by my solitary guesses.'' Fenn stiffened. ''But me, I'm not going to make any more unless I've seen for myself. And I can't honestly recommend going ahead at Deimos till I have a better notion of Mars.''

She looked at him through the level yellow rays. ''Do you mean you should go there in person?''

He gripped his beer container so that his knuckles stood white. ''If my opinion's to be worth an electron squiggle, yes. You ought to know that. Why else did I get this tour today? Simulations are useful, but when we're reaching for the truth, our feet had better be planted on rocky reality.''

''You *would* go?''

Geysers and tsunamis in him. ''Flame, yes!''

''That would . . . commit you rather thoroughly to us, wouldn't it? For that long an absence, you'd have to resign your position on Luna, I should think. You'd have to consider settling permanently among the Lahui, even at last becoming one yourself.''

''I've thought about that. I'm willing, if you people are willing to get serious.'' Charge ahead. To death with caution and consequences. This could get him to Mars.

She was not taken completely by surprise, but her words continued coming hesitantly. ''The—the ship''— the biennial voyager between Luna and the fourth planet—''I think it leaves soon. We could arrange—But you'll have to talk with the *kahuna* and—''

He forced another grin, although he trembled. ''If I do get there, I'll try not to be a bull in the china shop.''

She caught the drift of his archaism. ''Someday we

may need one. . . . Oh, Fenn, what a find we've made in you!''

Like a wave, she came to him.

After a while she murmured, ''There's food aboard, and the cabin's comfortable. We're in no hurry, are we?''

She flicked off the motor and had the boat extrude mast and sails. It leagued with wind, sea, and the full Moon that presently rose. Bright among the stars shone Alpha Centauri.

11

MARS.

He was walking on Mars. It was not a red spark, an image, a vivifer sequence, a dreambox program; it was intermediate weight and a skinsuit, grit ascrunch underfoot and sky pink overhead, house and hills behind him and rising rockiness before him, sights lately seen and people lately met, and now a pretty girl at his side. It was a lifelong yearning fulfilled.

For no clear reason—but the smoldering had lain within him, buried under a busyness from which he was free today—resentment suddenly flared up. It tasted of iron.

Through their helmets Kinna Ronay saw him scowl. ''Is something the matter?'' she asked.

''No, I'm all right,'' Fenn mumbled.

He could well-nigh feel her gaze on him as they strode on up the trail. Dust puffed ruddy from each footstep, was repelled by the fabric, and swirled back down. It lay in drifts along the rugged slopes and among the strewn boulders on either side. The rock was red, brown, gray, often streaked with mineral hues or sprinkled with crystalline points that glittered in the early morning sunlight.

"You're angry, aren't you?" Kinna said after a while, very softly.

I'm not much good at playacting, am I? he thought, and forced a smile in her direction. "Not at you."

"Can I help?"

"I think not. Thanks anyway. Let's proceed." She meant to show him the area on an all-day hike. He realized she was absenting herself from her studies at the university. Well, visitors from Earth or Luna were vanishingly rare, and his stay here would be short.

"No, please," she said. "I don't mean to pry or anything, but—you *did* come not just to look the planet over but to talk with us—us Martians. That's got to be what upset you, and maybe I can tell you something or suggest something a little bit useful. I'd hate for this time you have to be spoiled for you. You were so happy when you first arrived."

Surprise dampened rage. "How do you know?"

"Oh, the way you looked around at things and, and talked, and everything about you."

She had accompanied her father, who had been among those that met him at the spaceport and in the next several days showed him around Crommelin or gave him question-answer-discussion sessions. He had naturally been aware of her—by far the most pleasing sight in the group—but she kept shyly on the fringes when she was in evidence at all. Not until he had accepted the Ronays' invitation to be their guest at Sananton, relaxing when he wasn't making flights to inspect various parts of the Valles region, did she come forth before him. Then she offered to serve as his guide wherever he went, and last night sang ballads from olden days and beat him two chess games out of three.

He'd be stupid to continue surly, though he knew his moods didn't improve immediately upon demand. "Well, to come to Mars, that was always my wish." The beginning of his wish. Beyond this sky were the outer worlds, the comets, the stars.

She nodded. "I'd've expected it would be." But she wasn't one to cover over trouble with blandness. "I can't believe Dad's made you angry."

"Death, no!" The fire diminished further. "On the contrary. Would I be here otherwise? No, he, your mother, their friends, they've been nothing but kind." He wasn't sure why he felt anxious to explain himself to her, when he hardly ever did to anybody. "They were cautious, yes; they didn't make commitments. That's only sensible. This is an almighty big, radical proposal I've brought." Quickly, lest she think he was bragging: "Not that they hadn't been hearing about it already, of course. But when the Lahui Kuikawa sent me, that showed the idea's gotten serious."

"Then what did bother you? Who? Why?" She saw him frown again and raised a hand, slender in its glove. "No, don't answer if you'd rather not. I told you I don't want to meddle. And I don't imagine I can actually say anything helpful. But if speaking about it would make you feel better—I'd like you to enjoy your visit with us."

He pondered while they walked onward. Finally he smiled afresh, inside as well as outside, and told her: "I want that too. You're right, I've been staring at your planet since my diaper days, and I've only got a few weeks left till the Mars-annual transport starts back for Luna." Once more he made a hasty addition: "Not that I feel sorry for myself, please understand."

She returned the smile. The corners of her mouth dimpled when she did. "Nor need I. You've a glutton's share of wonders waiting for you at home." She had listened raptly while he reminisced, and had drawn him out—not much about cities or machines, but about the Lunar surface and parks, the Yukonian wilderness, the reaches and life of the ocean.

"I'm used to them." That wasn't exactly correct; he was a newcomer among the islanders and a foreigner to most of the other subcultures, but—

She laughed. "And I'm used to this. Shall we trade for a spell?"

"I'd love to take you around my own grounds," he said honestly. "But that can't very well be arranged, can it?"

" 'Fraid not." Merriment reawakened. "We'll make do with what we have. No shortage of scenery, at least."

The trail crested. He beheld Eos Chasma and saw that she spoke truth.

They stopped for lunch on a broad shelf jutting from a cliff. It was well down in the gorge, but depth after depth fell below.

Techniques and technology here bore their resemblances to those of Luna or open space, but also their differences. A Martian skinsuit was not a spacesuit. Among other things, when you were to sit, it extended three legs to form a kind of stool that kept your bottom off the eons-old, energy-sucking chill of the ground. The feedlock through which you ate and drank was less elaborate. Excretion was as usual, but this biostat merely recycled air and a limited amount of water; a complete system would have been impractically heavy, so most wastes were stored for later processing. Solar collector "wings" weren't worth carrying—The list went on. Fenn had adapted without difficulty.

After they had refreshed themselves, he and Kinna lingered. The view was infinite, for every shift of light and shadow created newnesses. A wall opposite stood indistinct, hazed, across immensity, a rampart of elvenland. Mesas rose from the bottom, sheer and scored or many-terraced, many-colored pyramids. Pinnacles soared Gothic. Through the fantasy wove the graven courses of ancient rivers. His sonic units, which he had tuned high, brought Fenn a phantom whitter of wind.

The radio band that carried speech was silent. Kinna seemed content to look, to let the grandeur take her— like Wanika contemplating waves, Fenn thought. He had too much restlessness. Eventually his mind turned to his mission, and he felt memories stoke the ill humor that had earlier burned in him. He didn't want it to. There was no gain in it, nothing but a waste of this brief time with a charming companion. At last he cleared his throat and attempted: "This makes me feel almost guilty."

Although he was no keen observer of people, he recognized the gladness with which she welcomed conversation. "Whatever for?"

"If the terraforming happens, it'll destroy what's here, and everything else that's special to the planet."

"No, you shouldn't think like that," she replied earnestly. "Think about . . . bringing the planet alive. Not just our settlements and plantations, but the whole *world*. Life—it's more wonderful than, than any dead matter." She caught her breath, considered, smiled and added, "Besides, we'll have the data on nowadays conditions. We can dreambox them if we want. And double-besides, it won't be 'we.' You said the Deimos colony will have to get rich and powerful first, out in the asteroids and the big-planet moons and wherever, didn't you? Well, we won't live to see that, you and I. If a Life Mother really does bring us back someday, Mars will long since be green."

She couldn't have known, and it wasn't reasonable, but her enthusiasm restored his bitterness. Nor should he pour it out upon her. Nevertheless, it spilled from him. "Don't count on that."

The big gray eyes widened. Dismay wavered: "What? Fenn, you aren't figuring it's impractical, are you?" She leaned forward and caught his right hand in hers. "Don't let it be!"

Through gloves and heating filaments, he felt the clasp as if both hands were bare. He groped for words. "No, that'd be premature. My guess at the moment is that the thing can be done."

"Then why are you—" Her plea faded out.

He could find no choice but bluntness. "What I wonder is if it will be done."

"Why shouldn't it? I . . . I think most Martians will be as willing . . . as I am." Her grip tightened.

Grimness: "The cybercosm isn't."

She let go and sat back, away from him. "How do you know?" she demanded.

"It's told us—"

"When? In what way?" She drew breath. "Oh, yes, I've heard too. Some people were against this when it first started getting talked about. Some people are always against anything new. And they'll say the cybercosm advises them, but all they ever really have to quote is . . . the upshot of their computer models—conclusions no better than the models themselves are, that they made out of their own prejudices. It's like ancient preachers taking a line or two out of a holy book and spinning their personal ideas out of that and claiming it was the word of God."

"You're saying the cybercosm is like God himself?" escaped from Fenn.

"Are you a hostile?"

He imagined he could hear: "I thought better of you."

His anger congealed into a kind of steely sadness. All right, he decided, I've upsnarled what should have been a grand, free day and now there's nothing to do but try explaining.

Then: Is that necessarily bad? She's very young, but she's bright, nova-bright, and raised amongst realities. Plain talk won't trample down her spirit. I'm supposed to learn something about the Martians as well as Mars, and maybe plant a few notions in them. Here's one whose career will probably go to their forefront.

Hm, it might be smart to begin with making my attitude clear to her—first principles, if you want a fancy name—before telling what's happened.

He shook his head within the helmet and spoke carefully. "No, I'm not any enemy, not any sort of revolutionary trashbrain. I know I wouldn't exist if it weren't for high tech. None of us would. Nor could we have experienced many marvels, like this today. And, sure, high tech means the cybercosm, and the cybercosm's made the Synesis possible. I've studied some history. I know about war, sickness, famine, government, all the horrors that none of us wants back. But—'' He stopped to plan what he would say next.

"But?" she prompted.

"I'm not a scholar, or philosopher either. But more and more I've got a feeling that a time always comes when anything—a species, a system, anything—it reaches its limits, its dead end, and after that, it's deadweight."

She sat quiet for a span. The wind-noise fluttered in his sonics.

She said at length, steadily, looking straight into his eyes, "The Teramind has stopped growing? No, never. Not for longer than we can imagine, anyway."

"Yeh," he replied, "maybe it'll go on indefinitely, with its intellection and—whatever else."

The speculations about that future were countless, repeated lifetime after human lifetime. Intellect transcendent and ever evolving. Truths to be discovered, abstract beauty to be wrought, beyond the conceiving of mortals. Mind, consciousness, to outlive the stars, perhaps to remake the dying universe and give it rebirth.

"But how much of it do we hear about?" he said. "Sure, we get our services, our calculations done for us, theorems worked out, art and engineering composed to order—and if we don't understand what the machines are doing for themselves along those lines, is that their fault? If we'd need to study for a thousand years before we could follow what the Teramind's currently thinking about—and then we still couldn't—is that its fault? This is what we're always told, Kinna, and I'm not calling it a lie. But we humans, we animals, what's left for us?"

The argument was old, so old that it had long since

virtually died out and only lately begun to be heard anew. He came close to foretelling her answer:

"Everything that matters to us."

"In theory, fine," he retorted. "Organic and electro-photonic, partners wherever we can help each other—especially where they can help us poor, weak organics—and otherwise free to take our separate trajectories, sharing as much as possible of what we find along the way—sure, sure." His fist smote his thigh. "Slag and slaughter!" he roared. "The 'cosm's started up antimatter production again, to power ships that push light-speed! What are their missions? Why don't *we* have any?"

"That's . . . been described. You've heard. They're too dangerous. They'd kill us. Maybe later—"

"So we are told. And why are we not told what—well, what that solar lens has found? Nothing but rumors, mostly out of Proserpina, it seems. Are we unfit to know? I tell you, the questions go on and on."

She braced herself and responded stiffly: "I've probably heard them oftener than you have."

Startled, he asked, "You have?"

"What else did you want to say?" Her tone commanded. No, he thought, she's not a child adoring the glamorous stranger.

He spent a minute or two assembling his response. There was plenty of time in this canyon, billions of years' worth.

"All right," he said. "Repeat, I'm not for over-throwing the whole system. Nearly everybody would die, and anyway, it's probably impossible. But . . . why have we been snugged so long into our comfortable selfsame-ness, like bugs in amber? Just because machines can better do everything in space that needs doing? In death's name, the thing they can't do for us is *being* there!"

He curbed himself. "Never mind that. Let's stay with the Deimos project. I've had a conference with Chuan, your synnoiont. He told me the work will never be done. Not if the cybercosm can prevent."

"Chuan?" she cried. "No! He wouldn't!"

He saw she was appalled. She couldn't be that conventional, that humbly accepting, he thought. Not her. She must have her reasons, and he'd do well to find out what they were.

"He was polite, you could say friendly," Fenn conceded. "He didn't outright forbid anything—not that he has the authority to, of course. He talked about costs out of proportion to gains, unintended and unforeseeable consequences, the hazard to social stability a couple of centuries down the line—he screened a sociodynamic analysis for me—I admit most of it was over my head. But he does speak for the cybercosm, that's what his life is all about, and I know opposition when I meet it."

She looked across the canyon, as if to draw peace from agelessness, before she turned to him and said quietly: "I have to tell you, Chuan is a dear old friend. He's been my, my safe harbor at the university. It isn't always easy there, and I've had my occasional troubles." Blameless, surely, he thought. She's headlong and trusting. "I've come to him and he—no, he never used his influence, but he listened and—" She gulped. "Yes, I'm prejudiced. But shouldn't we try to be, oh, objective? Chuan has his duty. You, you . . . Lahui . . . have this magnificent dream . . . I'd love to believe it can come real. But *do* we understand, can we, what it might lead to?"

"The Teramind knows best," he gibed.

"You're talking like a Lunarian." It was not a rebuff but a remark, slightly bemused, and he realized that she too was searching for common ground.

He clamped calm down on himself. "Kinna, let's not fight. I'm on Mars to learn. Maybe the proposal I've brought with me is wrong." He didn't accept that, but why not make the gesture? "Or maybe I misunderstood Chuan. He did get into technicalities that are beyond me, and it's true he didn't claim to have any certainties, only probability functions."

She rallied. "Yes, I wouldn't be surprised if he simply failed to make himself clear to you. He lives so much with his machines, his abstractions. I think that at heart he must be very lonely. I'll talk to him, next chance I get.

"And he can't yet have been linked with the main cybercosm, can he? Not across those millions of klicks. Maybe he'll find the limited system here drew the wrong conclusions. Or at worst—Mars is a free republic within the Synesis. It can't dictate to us. We'll decide for ourselves what we want to do."

"Everything's still in the air, isn't it?" Once more she seized his hand. "Why don't we keep on as we were, we two? I've so much I'd like to share with you."

Her optimism was like a breath of oxygen to him. "By all means." However, he could not but grab at the opportunity he had glimpsed. "Uh, you mentioned Lunarians. Could I meet some of yours?"

Her cheerfulness was returning rapidly. Maybe she was working at it a little, but he judged that most of it sprang straight from what she was. "Easy. I've plenty of friends among them."

"You do?" he blurted. "You're quite a girl, you are."

—Night fell as they climbed back over the rimrock. The abrupt stars made a dusk of it, through which, downslope, the viewports of Sananton glowed honey-yellow. Kinna raised her eyes aloft. "Deimos," she lilted low. "Turned into a real moon, big, clear to see, shining up there bright and full of life." She threw an arm about his waist. "Oh, Fenn, how I hope. Thank you for the hope."

12

AT THEIR PRESENT configuration, a message could go on a direct beam between Mars and Earth, without needing to be relayed around the sun. The satellite that received it passed it on to a groundside station, whence the network flashed it to Nauru. It demanded either to be forwarded to the addressee or held abeyant till he called for it. In the course of the next fractional second, the network queried several possible locations Fenn had entered in the database. It found that he had most recently registered himself in London, and ran through a file of public accommodations. Thus, when he and Wanika came back to their hotel room, the eidophone informed him that it had a communication to deliver.

They were celebrating his homecoming with a little travel. In a dreambox, either of them could have experienced the city through its ages, Britons, Romans, kings, merchants, great brigand discoverers, builders of empire and industry, on through the return of grassland, woodland, blossoming hawthorn, across tracts abandoned and demolished. In reconstructions equally careful, they could have met, interacted with, William the Conqueror, Elizabeth the First, Winston Churchill, Diana Leigh; with Chaucer, Shakespeare, Pepys, Kipling, Wells; with Newton, Faraday, Medawar; with Moll Flanders, Wilkins Micawber, Sherlock Holmes. But it would have been reconstruction, conjecture, illusion. In this preserved and restored ancient core, they walked on solid stones, breathed random whiffs of smoke, bought flowers from a chance-met vendor in Hyde Park, went into a pub for beer and a dart game and a chat with flesh-and-blood people. Yes, it was a museum set, maintained for tourists and a few pious antiquarians, but these were things that had known the actual hands and eyes of the ancestors, and the dwellers were not merely being quaint for the sake of extra money. They had come to like archaism, had made it a subculture as genuine as most.

Whatever that might mean, Fenn thought.

The phone detected the opening of the room to the door and blinked. *"Hea?"* Wanika wondered. "Speak."

"A communication from Mars for Fenn," it said, adding his number.

"Huh?" He stopped in midstride. After a second, he remembered his companion. "Uh, must be somebody I met there."

"Obviously," she murmured. "Shall I go out while you play it?"

With exasperation, he felt his face grow warm. "No, no reason to. Can't be anything very personal. Could well concern . . . all of us."

He sat down, touched his palm to the identification plate, and flicked for display. The screen before him was suddenly bright. Kinna Ronay's image looked forth, rumpled brown hair, shirt half open above the small, firm bosom. She smiled and waved. "Hola, Fenn," he heard. Through his head went echoes of that high, eager voice, from Sananton, Eos Chasma, Belgarre, the far end of the Valles, aflight and then atramp across Argyre Planitia and polar icefields, finally at the spaceport bidding him goodbye. There it had broken just a little, and she had dabbed at her eyes before taking his hand for a moment longer than was quite necessary.

"You asked me to call and tell you what's happened and what I've found out and everything," she went on. "Well, here I am. Not a heap of news, I'm afraid, but I'll be happy to keep trying if you want. I, I hope you had a good voyage and everything's all right for you on Earth. It is for us here. I'm back in school and—oh, the usual things. Was out in the Tweel Tavern with some friends the other night and I sang that old 'MacCannon' song you taught me and they loved it and wanted to learn it too, but maybe you recall how I think the translation into modern Anglo could be bettered and—" Laughter trilled. "I'm sorry. I ought to go back and edit this silliness out. But it is good to talk at you, and I suppose you know my style by now. You'll bring back the sobriety average if you feel like replying. I hope you will."

Fenn stopped the play. Kinna's gaiety froze in place. "The young woman who guided me through the regions she knows," he said to Wanika. "I've told you about her, and the fact that her parents are fairly prominent.''

''How interesting to encounter her,'' she answered slowly.

Fenn resumed play. Kinna turned serious—as grave as a child can often be, he thought. ''Well, I did talk with Chuan, the way I promised to,'' she said. ''More than once. There's so much to think about and for him to try to explain. And then, he *is* my honorary uncle. A lot of every time we're together, we just enjoy each other's company.''

''A touch of humanness for him,'' Wanika said in an undertone.

Fenn stopped the message again. ''We're lucky to have this contact,'' he reminded her.

''True. A tiny insight into the opposition viewpoint— *'Auwē*, I realize it isn't anything near that simple. Synnoionts aren't inhuman or dehumanized, they're a different kind—a different aspect of human. And the cybercosm isn't an enemy.''

''It could get to be,'' Fenn muttered.

''What?''

''Never mind.'' He restarted the phone.

Troubled, Kinna said, ''I can't spell things out, not really. I've been thinking and thinking, and finally I wrote down what I believe is what Chuan meant. Let me scroll that for you.''

Her image vanished. Text appeared. Fenn ran it at low speed, now and then halting it or backing it up for him and Wanika to consider a passage. Yet it was plain and brief.

''We went through the arguments over and over. He has been in touch with Earth, as close into the cybercosm there as he could be over those distances. Probably he doesn't have all the complexities and subtleties in his head or at his fingertips, but he's got enough for the likes of me. You can get as much else as you want, and a landslide more, right where you are. So I won't go into any details, unless you tell me I should.

"Mainly, you know, the cybercosm thinks the Deimos project would be terribly destabilizing. The danger's not to *it* but to *us*, not the sophotects and machines but the humans. You told me how he spoke to you about the economics and the cultural effects. I can imagine those, sort of, but the equations and analytic matrices went astronomical units over my head. I did say what you'd said, that the Lahui Kuikawa might be very willing to see their society change, even back on Earth, if what it gets them is the freedom of space. He said a Martian would naturally think like that, but he wishes a people of the seas, Earth's seas, would stop to ask themselves what it really means.

"He went on to worry about the Proserpinans. How they will react, and what effect that will have on the inner planets (on those who live there, I mean). It isn't foreseeable. He called up a lot of history to show me how the unforeseeable again and again proved to be the terrible. A madman killed a nobleman, and Earth plunged into a hundred years of war and the cruelest tyrannies. The internal combustion engine prevailed over the steam engine, and Earth came close to strangling and did suffer a hundred years of dreadful weather. Oh, yes, he agreed nothing was actually so simple. But precisely because so many factors were tangled together, as they always are, a small change could have enormous consequences. He gave me some other examples, but I'd rather not write about them.

"I finally got up my courage and asked him the questions you asked me. What about those new kinds of spaceships? What about the solar lenses? Why all the mystery? Is it right?

"Fenn, he grew so sad. I felt as if I had stabbed him. First he said the cybercosm, if we think of it as a reasoning being, the cybercosm has the same freedom any human does. That includes the right to exercise private judgment and hold back private data. If we want to develop field-drive craft for ourselves, no law prevents us.

But the cybercosm (the Teramind, or a lower echelon better suited to deal with us?) believes that to tell us how, at this stage, would be irresponsible. Chuan said we don't need them—we need hardly any spacecraft any longer—and besides, we couldn't fly in the superspeed ones and live, unless maybe as downloads. I couldn't get him to say it outright, but I think here too he's afraid of the Proserpinans and what they might do.

"Well, I'm sure you and your Lahui Kuikawa have heard all this more directly.

"There is something strange about the solar lens, though. Chuan would say even less when I asked, but I have just written how sorrowful he became. Not that he said he was, but I could read it on him, how he looked away from me and his shoulders slumped and his voice drooped. What he actually told me was the same old thing, that the data are uncertain and further research is in order and we'll get a report in due course. Fenn, I couldn't bring myself to hound him.

"Imagine me now making a long pause. I've done that while I thought over what I've just told and what's to tell next.

"It's more cheerful. You remember meeting my friend Elverir, and what I told you about other Lunarians I've met through him. (Maybe I'd better not write more. You know what I mean.) Well, to put it very shortly, everybody knows that most of our Lunarians are for Project Deimos. They would welcome new people, new wealth, new possibilities—maybe still more than we Terrans would—and if in the long run it leads to making Mars come truly alive, why, they are human too. The prospect of getting into space again in earnest excites them tremendously. Here at home, they mainly want to make sure their race won't ever be subjects of a Life Mother—as they think of it—and they realize that if they cooperate from the very beginning, when their help will be invaluable, they can arrange the terms they want.

"Now lately I have heard that the leaders of the Threedom—no, not strictly 'leaders,' Lunarians aren't like that, but you understand me—they too are in favor. They're in occasional beamcast contact with Proserpina, that's no high secret, and now Elverir has told me the Proserpinans may well offer to help with the project too. It would be an entry for them, back into the inner System—and, yes, of course they'd expect to make profits—but it could also lead to a reconciliation between the Threedom and the Republic, the disbanding of the Inrai. Anyway, that was my first thought. I know it won't be easy. Some of the Inrai are probably irreconcilable. I know something about the wildest ones, like a man named Tanir. But never mind for now. This is looking too far ahead. Just the same, there's hope, isn't there?

"Maybe more to the point, we know the Proserpinans are in touch with the people out among the stars. Could this, your work, Fenn, could it somehow start bringing all humans everywhere back together? How could that be wrong?

"I'm not sure about asking Chuan this. I mean, he's bound to learn the same things, if he hasn't already, but what will he say to me? I do care about him. Maybe I'll wait to hear from you, what you think, before I do anything except keep on with my very ordinary life here."

The text ended and Kinna's image reappeared. Fenn stopped play. "Now that's news," he said, turning his look on Wanika. "Not totally unexpected, but news worth getting."

"The girl is scarcely an intelligence agent," she answered without enthusiasm.

"No, no. But she has a lot of contacts, and knows the situation from the inside out. . . . We should tell her to give future communications quantum encryption. We can pay for it, and who knows what difference it might make?"

"It would draw attention, and suspicion."

Fenn chuckled. "It would suggest something private going on between her and me."

Wanika glanced away. "Perhaps. . . . But why are you suddenly so wary?"

He bristled. "Why give away information when we've got a fight ahead of us?"

"Do we?" Her eyes came back to dwell on him. "You're charging ahead toward your glorious vision—you, personally, free in space. They're more conservative in the Lahui councils. They have more to consider—also beyond their own lives. They'll weigh the advice of the cybercosm—of the Teramind, if it chooses to speak directly to us."

"Of course." He straightened. "But you don't belong to the cybercosm, do you? *We* don't. And it admits it can't prophesy. How then can it prove any big change will be for the worse? It isn't even human."

"I know, I know," she sighed. "You talk like Iokepa and so many others. Like me, most times, except that I have my misgivings once in a while. Oh, yes, we will go ahead, for the time being at least. So far, we're only investigating the feasibility. But this mention of the Proserpinans joining in—it does make me wonder."

She rose from her chair. "I think I would like to walk around a bit. Let me know if your friend has anything else important to say. I'll be back in an hour or two, and we can go to dinner." Her hand stroked his cheek as she left.

He puzzled briefly over what she had in mind. She was seldom this moody. He forgot the thought when he reactivated the playback.

Not that there was anything special in the remainder. Kinna smiled and said, "I'm glad that's done with. Aren't you? But I'm sorry not to've been more helpful. Do call back if I can do anything further, or if you just feel like swapping words. I'll try to keep abreast of things, the quiet things, I mean, that don't get on the newscasts. Have it well, Fenn, trouvour. Ai devu," and that was a Lunarian good-bye with unsentimentally wishful overtones heard in no Terran language. She waved again. The screen blanked.

13

THEIR HIRED SUBORBITAL took Fenn and He'o to Port
Bowen. There they immediately engaged a minicar on
the monorail. On the ride south to Tychopolis they left
the interior darkened. Fenn was content to rest, presently
falling asleep in his recliner. Even for him, the past daycycles had been strenuous, not least because he must often help his friend as they and their machines scrambled
around Archimedes Crater and the adjacent highlands.
The metamorph lay quietly on his cart, but awake and
looking outward. He did not watch the Lunar landscape
and the occasional works of humankind or cybercosm
leaping over the horizon and streaming past. He kept his
eyes from half-phase Earth, which would have dazzled
night vision away. His gaze was for the stars.

Fenn roused as the car surmounted the ringwall, slowing. He blinked, stretched, and said, "Well, amigo, here
we are. It's been quite a circuit, hasn't it?"

"Wearying." Beneath the slow synthetic voice went a
sigh as of waves. "Now we shall soon forsake space. I
long for my sea."

"And your wives, no?"

Fenn regretted his jape when He'o replied, "Are you
not eager to be with Wanika again?"

The man felt himself hesitate, and swore silently, before he said, "Yes, she's a fine one."

The seal head aimed straight at him. "I fear she has
found you a little . . . *kauwi*—drawing apart from her,
this year or so aft-time."

Fenn flushed. He had in fact been aware that Wanika
sensed she was less in his mind than before, and was
hurt. But what promises had he ever given, and whose

affair was it? "I'll steer my own course," he snapped. The thought passed peripherally: *Once I'd've said something like, "I'll follow my own orbit." Four years with the Lahui have changed some programming in me, seems like. I need to get off Earth, farther and for longer than this Moon expedition.*

*Well, Mars—*The heart jumped in his breast.

He'o lowered his muzzle. The scarred old alpha bull very rarely made that gesture of humility. "*'Ua hewa ao.* Forgive me. I should not have pissed in your water."

"Nada, forget it," Fenn mumbled, almost overwhelmed.

"It is only that Wanika is my *hoapili*. I have known her from her puppyhood. And now you are also close to me."

"And you to me." Fenn felt relief when, at that moment, the car plunged underground. It cycled rapidly through the airlock tunnel and glided to a halt. Light from the terminal poured in.

Fenn sprang from his seat. "Here we are. On to our business, and then ho for home." He took their locker-bags and led the way out.

As usual, the station yawned cavernous, uncrowded. People didn't travel much any more on Luna, except virtually. The newcomers drew stares and whispers from those who were scattered about. A dark, brisk woman approached. Fenn saw the camera perched on her shoulder, swiveling to track him and his companion, and groaned, "Oh, death. Not another journalist! I was hoping we'd shaken those pests."

"Our visit has stirred great public interest," He'o reminded him mildly. "The whole undertaking has."

"Don't I know it." Only a cordon of sophotectic guards, courtesy of the Yuan tong, had kept the Archimedes region from being beswarmed while these two from the Lahui were there. "Um, yeh, if they kept a watch, they'd've seen us take off for Bowen, and a query of TrafCon would establish that a mini left for here which we were probably aboard. He'o, right now I wish my species too were seals, not apes.''

The woman reached them. "Saludos, señores," she said in Anglo, with a professionally brilliant smile. "I believe I have the honor of meeting Pilot Fenn and Captain He'o?" She had obviously picked the titles from a list of such meaningless noises. "My current name is Stellarosa and I'm with the Cosmochronicle Service. You know your wonderful project is fascinating millions of us. Could I ask you a few questions about it, or would you care to make a statement?"

"We're on our way to a meeting," Fenn growled.

"Yes, I know, and I'll simply accompany you. I needn't delay you at all." Plain to see, Stellarosa wanted to move them along before anyone from the competition learned they had arrived.

"Slag and slaughter, does everything leak out?"

"Was this supposed to be secret?"

"No. Not exactly. It was supposed to be left alone. How'd you like it if I poked into your doings?"

"Fenn, *malino*, be calm," He'o said. "She has her duty."

"Duty?"

"Yes, to your species and its need for information, a need that in this case we all share. Our business could gain tsunami force."

"Thank you, sir," Stellarosa said.

Her words mollified Fenn a bit. "That's if it works out," he put in. "Muy bien, we can talk as we go."

He signaled to a porter and gave it the bags, with instructions to deliver them where and when called for. He wished for that to be not to any lodgings, but to the next ferry for Earth. He and the woman walking, He'o rolling, they sought the nearest slipway. Somehow it soothed him further. There was a sensuousness to the quasi-fluidity that carried them to the high-speed middle of the belt, while the breeze he felt until they were moving equally with the airstream came as a refreshment after his time in spacesuits, shelters, and conveyances—like a sea wind. Yes, he thought, maybe I was born wanderfooted, but these years among the ocean people have been good and I ought to be grateful.

I ought to be more considerate of Wanika.

Yet the messages to and from Mars—

"Yes," he said in answer to a question, "the Archimedes site does look promising for our purposes. Isolated, so the work wouldn't bother anyone, but easy to extend transport lines to. A fair amount of untapped mineral resources close by. Launch site—pretty high latitude, but on Luna that doesn't make any real difference."

"Your purposes," Stellarosa prompted. "To build a shipyard and a small spaceport, in support of your Martian activities, is that correct?"

"Essentially, although with many complications," He'o replied. He did not go into detail, for he had no simian urge to chatter.

Fenn had lost most of his own taciturnity. Now that he had resigned himself to an interview, the brown, full-lipped countenance beside him was quite charming. He had been celibate for weeks. "You realize," he admitted, "everything is strató yet. Nobody has made any commitments. We've just been investigating the site, collecting data."

"But a consortium of Selenites has helped you, encouraged you, and you're on your way to meet with some of those persons," Stellarosa said.

"M-m, well, the Trinh and Chandrakumar families, the Yuan tong, Ziganti Properties, suchlike, they are interested. If the Lahui Kuikawa do convert Deimos, with everything else that implies of human activity started up afresh in space, it'll mean a chance for whoever's involved to make quasar-sized profits."

An almighty long-range prospect, a part of him thought: the part that had never cursed or caroused or brawled but had quietly studied some history and medi-

tated upon it. Once nobody would or could have seriously planned so far ahead. But between modern longevity and modern data systems—and the example of the
cybercosm—a few humans and their organizations were
beginning to. Or was it due to the possibility of personal
immortality?

And then: Profits? What exactly do I mean by that?
Blanked if I know. When everybody's got enough without working for it, and when by working, you really only
add some luxuries to your life, what is profit, anyway?

Power? The strength to break out of the system? But
who in his right mind wants to? All I want is to be free
to go where I want.

Some old, old lines rose in his memory. Once on Mars,
as they stood overlooking a light-and-shadow grandeur
of mountains, Kinna had spoken them for him, her translation:

> We travel not for trafficking alone;
>   By hotter winds our fiery hearts are fanned:
> For lust of knowing what should not be known,
>   We take the Golden Road to Samarkand.

But what if that freedom required cracking the system
open?

"They wish to encounter you in person, am I right?"
Stellarosa was saying. "Telepresence isn't quite the same
thing, not when you may be dealing with somebody for
many years and it's this important."

Fenn generally responded gladly to an intelligent remark, whenever he heard one out of the dismal average
for his species. "Right. We organics use too many subtle
cues." He noticed the slight contempt—or hostility, or
whatever it was—in his tone, and paused to think. He
didn't care to sound like a back-to-a-nature-that-never-
was snotbrain. But at the same time, flip it, he wasn't
about to accept that the Teramind was his All-Mother and

the whole end purpose of evolution. "As long as we keep on being what we are," he finished.

"Then you hope they will invest in your project?" Stellarosa asked.

"Eventually," he replied. "I told you, this is all tentative so far. We'll need Earthside investors too. And the Martians haven't agreed to the idea, remember. It'd be a bigger thing for them than for anybody else."

And I'm going back there soon to pursue the matter, sang within him.

"It's big for everybody," Stellarosa said. "More and more controversial as it takes shape, isn't it? The psychosocial analysts warning how it could upset the economy and endanger the peace—"

"They and their crapping equations!" exploded from Fenn. "Sure, the cybercosm and the Synesis councillors don't like the idea. It'd complicate things, make them unpredictable, sure. But does that mean they'll go bad—for us? We aren't machines, we humans, and Keiki Moana, not yet!"

"Don't you think there could be dangers? How might the Proserpinans react? We know so little about them and their intentions, and even less about what's been happening among the stars."

"Proserpinans, ha! When did any clutch of Lunarians of any size ever get together on a single intention? And as for the stars, they're what we should be bound for!"

"An albatross voyage," He'o said softly. "We can only swim the water we are in today. All else is the currents of dream."

And yet he had fought storms, sharks, and his fellow bulls.

Stellarosa knew well how to move talk along. It became lively. Fenn almost regretted getting off the slipway. That was onto Tsiolkovsky Prospect, in the old part of town. The meeting was set for one of the complexes fronting on Hydra Square. Still conversing, the three walked onward over the duramoss, between the triple arcades. Behind those high ogives were no longer any curious shops or Lunarian rendezvous, only apartments or antique exhibits. The ceiling above displayed no extravagant illusions, only the simulacrum of a summery sky above Earth. The air bore no pungencies or plangent music, only the foot-shuffle and chatter of Terrans. They were many, here within their city, hustling to and fro on their various errands, crowding as Lunarians never did, clad more brightly and less sumptuously than Lunarians ever were. Fenn's little party raised a bow wave of recognition—stares, nudges, sudden silences, murmurs, exclamations. Some persons, however, stood as if posted, waiting till they passed by, looking and looking.

"Seems like word of us went ahead," Fenn remarked. Still in a fairly good mood, he didn't resent the fact much.

"Yes, naturally," Stellarosa told him. "You may not realize how many folk are keenly interested in you. You're something new, something strange and exciting. Quite a few of them, on Earth and Luna both, have set their multis to record anything about you that comes into the dataline. Well, TrafCon satellites routinely reported a suborbital jump from Archimedes to Port Bowen, which must be you two, and the information had already gotten out by phone and so forth that you would be coming straight here to meet with our local powers that be."

"Then why weren't more journalists lurking at the station?"

She laughed. "I was quicker than the rest."

Competition for trivia, Fenn thought. What if the day comes back when people compete for real prizes?

He'o, prone on his cart, stirred. Under the words, his voice barked and croaked; but the eyes shone in the sleek head, above the massive body, as he glanced about him. "Yes, you are a peculiar race," he said. "I will never fully understand you. Do you understand yourselves?" His whiskers quivered. "I, though, I am going home to my sea."

Thunder smote. His skull exploded. Blood and brains fountained. The missile whanged off two walls before it dropped.

From a third-level arch tolled the baritone Anglo, followed by Spanyol and Sinese:

"Humans everywhere, true humans, Terrans, hear me! Today we have struck down a monster that was about to attack our very souls. It was the foremost, but just the foremost, of countless monsters, metamorph and machine and abominations, from the outer darkness—"

Fenn heard no more, until afterward in reply. While the crowd milled and screamed, while alarms wailed and observants arrived and human constables came after, he crouched on the duramoss with He'o's body in his arms.

After all the time since he quit the force, it felt odd to be again in a police chief's office.

Like most of his corps, Georghios believed in physical presence. He made his staff come personally, daily, to headquarters, as he did himself. Stocky, heavy-featured, gray-haired, he sat behind a battered desk that was bare except for a terminal and an eidophone, and glowered at the man opposite; but his anger went beyond this room.

"Yes," he rumbled, "we have identified the killer. Several passersby noticed him lugging his apparatus down the Prospect before he went inside and up to that vacant apartment. We've gotten fairly reliable descriptions from two or three of them. More to the point, our lab managed to retrieve shed skin cells off the weapon and map their DNA. He left directly after the murder— that rant of his was a recording, the voice synthesized— and disappeared in the confusion. He could be anywhere on Luna. Or if he has accomplices, which seems likely, he may well have gotten away to Earth. Could have boarded either of the two ferries that left before we knew who he was and issued our bulletin. A simple disguise would cover his tracks. But now the alert for him is on the entire net, Solar System—wide. It won't be canceled till we have him.''

That could take years, Fenn thought. Or forever. A clandestine biosculp job to change face and fingerprints, then a life led cautiously—Even with the cybercosm to help, police resources were limited, and ever more thinly stretched.

He stirred in his seat. His muscles ached to smash something, anything, but this was the only motion allowable here; and he'd better keep speaking low, too. ''Who is it?''

''Registered name—two names, actually—Pedro Dover.''

Memory surged. ''Slag and slaughter, I've met him! He was inciting mayhem on a sophotect in Mondheim, during the riots after the Prefect's speech about Centauri. I left just a few daycycles later, but supposed they'd soon hook the scumhead.''

Georghios nodded. ''Oh, we did. Caught him here in Tychopolis. It took awhile, because there was so huge a mess to clean up and so many mixed into it. Afterward the courts, the evaluation centers, everything was swamped with cases. Pedro Dover and other Gizaki members had sharp counselors, who twisted the 'speedy hearing, determinate finding' rule in knots around the adjudicators. The upshot was that he got six months' detention for 'emotional instability.' Clear to see, whatever therapy they gave him there was superficial and didn't take. The offense wasn't such as to permit deep-going treatment when he didn't want it. After release, he continued in his marginal style, doing odd jobs for money— he is good with his hands—and spewing his notions at whoever would listen. He didn't seem of any particular account.'' A big fist knotted, helpless on the desktop. ''Too late now.''

Too late indeed, sighed through Fenn. He'o lay dead, frozen till he could be brought home to his people for their rites that would give him to the dolphins. Revival was hardly possible, or if it was, it would be a cruelty, considering what had been destroyed. No, let the sea remember him.

Fenn scowled. "Gizaki. I've heard about them, but not much. A dement cult, aren't they?"

"One out of too buggering many. I recall how when I was a sprout, my father told me how we finally had an adult civilization and in the course of time it would make all of us individually sane. But it's been changing faster and faster. . . . Well." Georghios straightened and spoke in a monotone. "Gizaki seems to have started in the Pyrenees Mountains region of Earth. The word means 'human' in a forgotten local language. The founder wrote and talked about blood rights, organic life, the heroic Lyudov Rebellion, which was tragically crushed, that kind of junk memes."

"Yeh, we're hearing a lot of them these days, aren't we?"

"The Gizaki are at the far end of the spectrum. I looked up the history of the Lyudovites, trying to see where this attack today comes from, and found that *they* weren't totally unreasonable. They feared what effects sophotectic intelligence, and the general robotization of things, might have. They called for a moratorium on its development while society decided whether to go ahead with it, and they said the decision should be no. But it began as a legitimate argument, mistaken or not. Matters did get out of hand, uprisings followed, casualties were high till order was restored. But that was centuries ago, for cosmos' sake. The Gizaki don't just say we should stop entropy, they say we've got to reverse it, and if we don't choose to—like maybe because several hundred million people would die when the cybercosm collapsed—why, at their appointed hour they'll show us the error of our ways with guns and bombs."

Fenn nodded. "I see. Human trash, knowing they're meaningless, useless, and blaming it on technology. Put technology in its place and humankind will flower, especially their glorious selves. Meanwhile, preach hatred of it and all its works, including metamorphs. Who're a safer target than the machines." Grimly: "The Lahui Kuikawa will have to start taking precautions."

"Careful," Georghios said. "We can't let violence run loose, no matter how good it thinks its cause is."

Fenn curbed a rebuttal. He was having matters explained to him at length and in private as a courtesy, because he had served in the force. No doubt the fact that it had been a close friend of his who died, and he would carry whatever he heard back to a large and influential polity on Earth, was also a motivation. But he'd be a fool if he antagonized the police . . . or warned them.

"The murder weapon," he asked instead. "What was it? How the flame did Pedro Dover carry a *firearm* through a Lunar city without being stopped?"

Always outside waited the vacuum, the radiation, space.

"It wasn't a firearm when he carried it," Georghios replied. "It was only a couple of ungainly metal objects. The witnesses told us they thought it might be a half-finished hobby project. But it was memory metal. When he'd established himself in that room—he must have known you two would come down Tsiolkovsky, and approximately when, which suggests the Gizaki were systematically tapping datalines, same as the newsies—he applied heat, and the things sprang back into the original shapes they'd been deformed out of: a harpoonlike missile and a strong spring-powered launcher. He added a photonic sighting mech, which he'd probably had in his belt pouch along with the little heating torch and the sermon 'caster. Then he was ready for action."

Fenn nodded. "Yes, we will have to take care on our islands and our ships. We are, you know, trying to lift a venture that'll involve robotics, and dealings with Lunarians on Mars, and maybe with Lunarians on Proserpina and at Alpha Centauri—not to mention that more than half of us are metamorphs, seals—We'll only take care, you understand. Nothing aggressive.''

He lied, and refused to feel guilty.

Oh, the human Lahui would be law-abiding enough; armed conflict was foreign to them, and the issue was fairly irrelevant to the Keiki Moana. Besides, Fenn doubted that the Gizaki were a serious menace, especially when two tightly integrated worlds had gone on watch against them—a watch that the cybercosm would keep unflagging.

But He'o lay dead.

He, Fenn, was shortly going back to Mars. (Even amidst his grief, it thrilled in him.) If the police had not found Pedro Dover when he returned, he meant to instigate a search program of his own. It would be more intense than they could maintain, they who had an entire civilization to protect and were bound by procedural rules.

He well-nigh hoped they would have failed. The Synesis, the entire dispassionately merciful system, would try to rehabilitate the killer.

Why? To what purpose?

Vengeance made more sense.

14

CHUAN BOWED IN the manner of his forefathers, then offered his hand in the manner of Selenites. ''Welcome back,'' he said.

Fenn took it, briefly, and tried to match the smile on the round, amber-brown countenance before him. He must look down; the synnoiont was a short man. The implications were what towered. ''Thank you,'' he replied.

His glance flickered around the room. When he was on Mars before, last year, two Earth-years ago, they had met just once in person, in a downtown office, and otherwise talked by phone. The invitation to visit Chuan at home had come as a surprise, very soon after this arrival. Fenn supposed it was an attempt at human contact, a touch of warmth, in hopes of making him a little more open to persuasion.

It would hardly work. The austere room, the changeable fractals in the walls that were the sole decoration, reinforced his impression of alienness. Or did they, really? The floor was aflow with colors, the furniture was obviously comfortable to the point of sensuality, and the viewport revealed flower beds close by, above a downward sweep of craterside toward Crommelin city and the great red basin. Music played softly, nothing complex or abstract, a simple and rather sentimental melody for strings that Fenn didn't recognize but that must be ancient. Almost subliminal, an odor as of new-cut grass beneath a summer sun tinged the air. If those touches were meant for him, they at least showed that Chuan could think in ordinary terms and cared about his guest's feelings.

Also, Kinna was fond of the man, and he had often been kind to her.

Nevertheless—

"I trust you had a pleasant voyage," he was saying.

Fenn shrugged. "Routine."

That wasn't quite true, when such flights occurred only as Earth began to overtake Mars and passengers were a rarity. But, yes, the days of transit at an energy-parsimonious one Lunar gravity had been dull enough. Attended merely by a couple of specialized robots, he had had nothing to do but exercise, read, watch recorded shows, play games against a computer, and pursue his studies. Seen from inside that box, even the stars gave no particular sense of being in space. Not until the destination loomed gigantic against them did the old thrill come alive again.

"You have been well received?" Chuan prompted.

"Yes, everybody's been cordial and helpful," Fenn said. No wonder. They would be for any outsider, but his errand was special indeed. He appended deliberately: "And now you."

"You are good to come. I know you are extremely busy."

"Well, I'm about to be. Tomorrow I'll commence inspecting the moonjumper. We've been warned it needs work, after standing idle for many years. I don't yet know how much work."

Chuan gestured at a lounger. "Forgive me. My hospitality fails. Please be seated. What would you like to drink? I have tried to lay in a variety."

Fenn settled himself opposite his host and, somewhat experimentally, named beer. Chuan spoke into the air. Almost at once a servitor appeared with a tray bearing a quite decent local brew, tea for him, and assorted small foods.

"I gather that you have become the Lahui Kuikawa's chief expert on space operations," he said.

"Gather" was probably a classic understatement, Fenn thought. But doubtless it was best for him too to keep the tone as unemotional as possible for as long as possible. "In a way," he answered. "With my background, I had a head start. Since then, I've gotten more experience whenever I could; and they've paid for my training—you know, recorded instruction, simulators, dreambox, everything that once instilled those skills in humans who were to practice them. I'd be a qualified pilot by now, if ships still used live pilots."

"You are personally going up to Deimos?"

"Of course. As soon as the spacecraft's ready. I hope to find out in the next few days exactly what needs fixing, and hope that then the robots and human technicians can get it done quickly." Those arrangements had been made in advance over the interplanetary beams. "After all, the ferry goes back to Luna in about six weeks."

"What else will you be engaged with while among us, if I may ask?"

"More of what I did last time. Talk with people. Run through databases. Visit prospective sites for operations—mining, manufacturing, whatever we'll need. If all this proves out, I'll prepare a report that may be the last push necessary to convince the Lahui councillors to go ahead with the venture, and enough foreign investors to give it support." Fenn decided to stop playacting. He stared at Chuan across the rim of his beaker. "But you must know this already."

The synnoiont frowned the tiniest bit. "Yes. I cannot pretend to be delighted."

No, Fenn thought, that'd be hard for you. We faced down some of the top trustees of the Synesis, and the cybercosm behind them, to acquire two old, unused torch ships at Earth and one moonjumper on Mars. We bluffed them into approving the sales with the threat of the stink we could raise if they refused. *We*, Manu, He'o, Iokepa, me, and others, we found individual donors and scraped together credit for the purchases, and then deeded the craft to the polity so no one could invent a reason for confiscating them back from us.

For an instant he wondered: Were we being paranoid? Are we?

As if to disarm him, or maybe sincerely, Chuan went on: "But you, are you going up to Deimos alone except for a few robots? Isn't that dangerous?"

"Not if I keep my wits about me and nobody, uh, interferes. It'll be public, everything scanned and transmitted in real time straight to the news net."

Chuan showed no sign of insult. "Is this effort necessary? Wasn't everything about that moonlet, every characteristic and component of it, studied and recorded centuries ago, when it was mined for its water?"

" 'Centuries ago' is the operative term," Fenn said. "Things may have changed since then, while nobody was paying any attention. For instance, a meteoroid impact may possibly have scrambled some rocks, or added some useful ore. Anyhow, those early surveys were for different purposes from mine. I'm going to look the body over with an engineer's eye, as orbiting raw material for a habitat.''

"No offense, but could not a sophotect, perhaps with several different specialized bodies, do that more thoroughly as well as more safely? I can assure you the service will be available if requested, like any other lawful and feasible service people cannot well provide for themselves.''

"No, we want the job done by a human.''

Chuan raised his brows. "You do not trust the cybercosm?'' he murmured.

"No offense,'' Fenn gave him back. Draw your own conclusions, he did not add. "Let's say it'll feel better to us this way. Getting live beings back into space is the whole aim. Here's where we start.''

Chuan set his teacup down and leaned forward. "That is what I wished to talk about today. Your feelings. The imponderables.''

Fenn grew ill at ease. "Stuff that doesn't fit well into a socioanalytical matrix,'' he tried to parry.

"Yes,'' Chuan agreed. "The magnificent and terrible irrationality of organic life.'' He sighed. "But this is my department. I am supposed to bridge the gap between the organic and the electrophotonic.''

Fenn tautened. "Maybe we are crazy, we organics.'' He tossed off his beer and thudded the beaker onto the table between them. "If so, that's how we are.''

Chuan inquired whether he would care for more. While it came, the synnoiont maintained: "You know modern society does not try to suppress the emotional life of human or metamorph—or nature itself, animals, flowers, everything that lives and is not too harmful to people. Rather, life has more freedom and encouragement than ever before in history.''

"Provided it stays inside the limits of what you call rational," Fenn snapped.

"You are an intelligent, educated man. Surely you do not believe the sophotectic mind is nothing but a cold calculator."

"No," Fenn conceded, "you have your dreams and drives, whatever they are."

"*We* do?" Chuan said low. "I am human too."

"You know what I mean," Fenn retorted defensively. "Just let us get on with ours. What do they threaten? How?"

Chuan shook his head as if it had gone heavy. "I—we, if you insist—on behalf of civilization and life, I beg you to consider the all too real possibility that your dream will turn into a nightmare. How often in the uncontrolled, randomly happening past did it so occur? Christ preached God's love; Christians massacred unbelievers and burned heretics in the name of it. Reformers called for universal equality, and tyrannies came forth to enforce—the name of it."

"You needn't go on," Fenn growled. "I know. But I also know, we're here today because people were not content with things as they were."

Chuan's voice sharpened. "Change for the sake of change? Is that your idea of progress? You realize, do you not, that if your Lahui Kuikawa establish a viable presence beyond Earth, they will cease to be the Lahui Kuikawa."

Fenn nodded, glad to have a ready response on the other man's chosen ground. "Sure. We accept that, the way—oh—the way anybody accepts being changed by a great experience. The trouble's been, there were no great experiences left for us, for any organic beings. We've got to make our own." That was not how most of his fellows would have put it. But to say that they wanted power to deal directly with the Proserpinans and the stardwellers would have touched a sore spot. Anyhow, Chuan knew it perfectly well. It had been discussed openly, sometimes globally, for years. In fact, why the flame was the syn-noioint wasting time on arguments gone threadbare? "Be-sides, only a minority would leave Earth. The mother polity will stay home."

"Scarcely unaffected." Chuan's gaze searched him. "My friend—may I call you my friend, now when we speak frankly?—I fear this future you mean to strive for. And so does not only the cybercosm, but many thought-ful humans also. The consequences are incalculable, consequences to our whole race, yours and mine and the Lunarians and your Keiki Moana, everyone. We have already suffered the impact of news from Alpha Centauri—in the Lahui Kuikawa too, am I right? Dis-content, alienation, rebelliousness with no clear object, crime—*un*sanity."

The challenge stiffened Fenn. "Has that been due sim-ply to the news, or did the news—and the wondering how much of the truth we're being told—did that touch off a fire that'd been smoldering all along?"

"You imply that humankind is incapable of sanity," Chuan said. "That a peaceful, prosperous, tolerant, just, and marvelously diverse world has by its very nature be-come unendurable."

"Well—" muttered Fenn, taken aback.

"I do not choose to believe that. Neither sociodynamic theory nor empirical fact require me to. But it is true that we humans are still, genetically, primitive hunters and foragers, savages. Not wild animals—it would be easier, less dangerous for us if we were—no; the oldest domes-ticated animal is man himself, who will go as crazily, suicidally ferocious as any dog when the master com-mands. Civilization is an artifact. It is the supreme artifact—invention, drama, work of art—and the most fragile. Do not stress it beyond its breaking strength, Fenn."

"How would we? Seems to me we'd be enlarging it, taking it back to the planets and pointing it toward the stars."

"You know full well what I mean. You have heard it over and over. But let me repeat it. Something as radical as this would upset too many social balances. Imagine, for a single example, what a renewal of extensive space traffic and a growth of major new industry would do to Luna: the small businesses that give purpose to so many people's lives going under, the customs and traditions that bind them together dissolving. Economic rivalry; the resources of the Solar System remain vast, but they are more widely scattered and less easily harvested than formerly. The bitterness in those who try and fail. Unforeseeable new ideas, faiths, desires; and some are sure to prove as troublesome as Catharism, Communism, Avantism, or a hundred others were in their day. More immediately, what of the Lunarians, also here on Mars? Few of them have renounced irredentism. What may they do after space commerce and a reinvigorated planet have given them a prospect of reclaiming their ancestral Moon? No matter whether they could succeed or not; consider the monstrous tragedies that an attempt would bring about. As for the Lunarians of Proserpina—we do not know. Nor can we foretell anything whatsoever about those at Centauri.

"I will raise a subject that is not much discussed, because repeated reminders would provoke widespread indignation—a feeling of having been humiliated—and certain persons might react in horrible ways. Think of that fanatic who murdered your Keiki comrade—yes, we heard of it on Mars—and multiply him by several thousand. But there is no arrogance or contempt behind the policy. The fact is that the field-drive spaceship technology is being withheld from publication while we search for a solution to the problem it poses. It is too hazardous. Bad enough that the Proserpinans have it. They are few in number, distant from us, and thus far not strongly interested in our concerns. Spread through the inner Solar System—Fenn, the field drive makes interplanetary war possible.

"In everything everywhere, the equilibrium is fearsomely precarious. I implore you, do not throw random weights at it."

He sat back and chuckled ruefully. "Forgive me. I have a bad habit of delivering lectures. Our mutual friend Kinna Ronay has often teased me about it."

Fenn ignored the touch of lightness offered him. He hunched his shoulders. His beard bristled at the other. "Tell me," he said, "does the cybercosm—well, the Synesis, the trustees and councillors and committees, advised by machines—does it really want to freeze us into our present shapes forever? Can it?"

Chuan spread his palms. "No, no, absolutely not. That is neither desirable nor practicable. But we need not surrender to chaos either, and indeed it is our duty not to—a duty that I would call sacred." Fenn remembered hearing from Kinna about the religious background from which this man sprang. "Let me be honest, blunt. What you and your associates call progress is actually the opposite. At best, quite apart from the dangers, it would divert us back to an archaic stage of development. Our proper future, our true evolution, lies in the growth of intellect, consciousness, spirit."

"So you say," Fenn grunted. "Seems kind of overblown to me."

"It is a millennial vision, yes. But it makes sense of what would otherwise be a cosmos without rhyme or reason, and is that not the whole purpose of science?"

Chuan paused. "However, let us two stay with immediacies," he then said. "I accept that your intentions are benign, and I know that most Martians are coming to see them as the hope of their world. Already, though, and it is a bare beginning, those troubles that daily worsen in the Threedom, they trace directly to the mere prospect of a Deimos project."

"Maybe. I'll want to learn more about that." Fenn had heard stories of increasing unrest. It might affect his mission, he supposed.

Chuan nodded. "Excellent. Don't take my word. Study the news and the records. Talk with knowledgeable Martians. A great deal has happened since last you were here."

"I intend to talk," Fenn said. "I'll soon get my first chance. Once the work on the moonjumper is in hand and I'm not needed on the spot, I've an invitation to spend my time waiting at David and Helen Ronay's place." At the mention of it, eagerness and happiness damped his vexation.

Chuan seemed likewise ready to loosen. "Good for you."

Conversation wandered, at first peripheral to major issues, later turning into gossip, the sort of dance or mutual grooming that humans do with each other for the simple, supremely important purpose of establishing amicability. Yet Fenn kept wondering why Chuan had, well, summoned him here. Nothing new had been said on either side. Surely no synnoiont, visitor to realms and sharer of thoughts beyond the comprehension of unaided mortals, would waste hours of lifespan on an empty gesture.

With an inward chill, Fenn guessed: He's laying some kind of groundwork. He's preparing me—and through me, in a subtle way he understands and I don't, all the Lahui, maybe all people everywhere—preparing us for something years ahead, maybe decades or even centuries ahead, so that when it comes, we'll take it as the Teramind wants us to take it.

Defiantly: Well, it doesn't have to work according to plan. It's flaming well not going to, whatever the plan is.

The shrunken sun declined westward. Shadows rose in Crommelin Basin like a tide lapping up around the city towers. Fenn took his departure. "Give my kindest regards to the Ronays," Chuan said, "and especially to Kinna." Below his smile, behind his eyes, Fenn sensed that immeasurable sadness of which she had spoken.

• • •

A purr and quiver went through the flitter as its fuel-cell engine awoke. Rolling down the runway, it spread huge wings and opened cavernous air intakes. A leap, and it was aloft. At five hundred meters it leveled off and bore west.

David Ronay leaned back in his seat. "We may as well relax," he drawled. "Nigh three hours to Sananton, you probably remember." He was a man of average Martian-Terran build, which made him tall and lean by Earth standards, his features thin and regular beneath gray hair. On the breast of his plain unisuit gleamed a pendant, a star cut from rock crystal. It had no overt meaning, but, unproclaimed and wordlessly, it expressed a spirit—of hope, of defiance—and more and more like it were appearing around the planet, in the mysterious way that symbols do.

"Relax? Not such an easy job," said Fenn, sitting beside him.

"No, you have been going almighty hard, haven't you? Well, we'll get you slacked off and fattened up for your Deimos jaunt. Any idea when that'll be?"

"Looks like about a week."

"Come back to us when you're done, if you aren't too busy."

"Thanks. I'd like to stop by for a day or two, though then I'll have to rush off looking at more places and meeting more people, same as last time. Uh, thanks also for the help you've given me, arranging for supplies and equipment and such."

"Little enough, considering what you're doing for us."

"If it works out."

David cast Fenn a glance before asking, "Don't you expect Deimos will prove suitable?"

"Oh, I'm confident it will. We know already what materials are there, and where and how to get the other materials we'll need. Likewise, pretty well for the Martian surface. What I have to collect is more exact information, the details.''

''Beware, I intend to pump you about those. I'm vague on them. Most Martians are.'' David clicked his tongue. ''Ironic, isn't it? For us out here, getting one regular ship a year, space has become more abstract, less real, than it is to the average Earthbound Earthdweller. He at least sees frequent traffic to and from Luna.''

''Nevertheless, you *po'e*—you folk were quick to grasp the idea of converting Deimos. And you do still favor it, don't you?''

''Positively. If anything, sentiment has grown stronger since you were here last.''

''But I hear about problems too,'' Fenn said. ''Not technological. Social, economic, political, the sort of garbage *I* don't know how to recycle into anything useful.''

David frowned slightly, but chose not to take umbrage. ''Leave that to my colleagues and me. You get your investors and organization together, and tell us you are ready to go to work. I can guarantee you the Republic will then vote approval and support. You know it means our salvaging what we are, this whole society of ours.'' As the quid pro quo for Martian help and resources: cometary water for Mars. ''I admit the longer-range prospect, the transformation of the whole planet, that's still controversial, though more because of questions about practicality than principle. But our grandchildren will decide.''

''They may not care any longer.''

''Eh? Oh. Because of new technologies from the stars, perhaps changing everything, making our concerns of today irrelevant? It could be.'' David paused. ''What our generation must do is keep that chance open for those who come after us.''

Fenn nodded. ''Bucking the system.''

Again David regarded the big man for a while before replying slowly, ''No. Not in the way you seem to think. The Synesis isn't an enemy. We're a part of it. And you recall, I'm sure, the synnoiont Chuan is a personal friend of our family. He and I've cooperated much oftener than we've been at cross purposes. When we disagree, we're civilized about it.''

Fenn reddened. ''Of course, of course! I mean his opposition to the Deimos work—to the whole thought of organics getting back into space in earnest, not to speak of making Mars into a new Demeter. Do you know the reason? He talks and talks about stuff like destabilization, and others do too, but it's as hazy as a comet's tail.''

''Which can be bright and clear, seen from afar,'' David answered. ''I admit he's not explained his stance to my satisfaction either.. Nobody has. Maybe the cybercosm can't. Maybe the matter is too complex, too deep for human brains. Don't worry; I'm not convinced of that, nor are most of us on Mars. But we do have certain urgent cares, where Chuan and we stand together.''

Fenn tensed in his seat. ''What are they?''

''You must have heard, in general terms. The Proserpinans. We Terrans are trigger-suspicious of them, and this is dividing us more than ever from our Lunarian neighbors. We know the Proserpinans have been influencing things on Mars for years, and we think that influence is on the increase, but how important it is—how strong, widespread, subversive—we don't know.'' David raised a clenched fist. ''We do not propose to let them make use of us for their own ends, such as the recovery of Luna. We have recent evidence, intelligence, of incitement and conspiracy by them in the Threedom. You remember, the Lunarian towns in Tharsis that have never acknowledged the law of the Republic, but obey it under protest, when they obey it at all. Robotic instruments have shown spacecraft—what must be spacecraft of the new field-drive type—descending on those parts or leaving them. Rarely, but even three or four is too many.''

''Has anybody actually seen them?'' Fenn demanded.

''Well, no, not anybody I know of. We don't exactly have a space TrafCon system, you realize. Nor have overflights or our few monitor satellites revealed anything.

But camouflage while they're on the ground wouldn't be hard to arrange, as ill-equipped as our constabulary is to deal with such things. If nothing else, blow dust over a hull and it'll look like a transient dune.

"Besides, the overt aggressiveness of the Proserpinans, like their attempt to seize a solar lens—"

"Another story handed you by the cybercosm," Fenn interrupted. "How do you know it's true?"

"Because—because why should the cybercosm lie?"

"Who knows? Why should it build that station on Pavonis, not just an observatory node but a database center, and refuse to say what the data are?"

"It doesn't. Astronomers can and do consult the facility. A few have even gone there for special purposes, to work with the instruments."

"But there's a large block of information sealed off from them and everybody, right?"

"True. The cybercosm has the same right to keep silence as a human scientist does till s/he's sure of the observations and what they signify."

"The solar lens data mainly, no? Been a fair number of years now, hasn't it? I thought the Teramind was supposed to be able to interpret anything instantly."

David sighed. "This is getting to be pointless—and quarrelsome, which is worse. Listen, please. The business is highly relevant to you. You can't very well convert Deimos if Mars is exploding beneath it, can you?

"Dare we sit idle in ignorance while matters drift toward bad trouble? I'm among those who've been driven to the conclusion that the Republic can't tolerate the intransigence of the Threedom any more. While it can still be done without bloodshed, we should assert sovereignty, occupy the towns, cut the Inrai outlaws off from their sources of supply, and investigate what else has been going on. That won't be a simple decision to make and enforce, especially given the Lunarian delegates in the House of Ethnoi, but I believe it's a hard necessity. Chuan agrees. We will need his help and the cybercosm's, with the sanction of the Synesis as a whole. No, they are not our enemies.''

Fenn fell silent, staring through the canopy. They had reached the dark wasteland of the Margaritifer Sinus. It lay deathly still, unutterably cold. Even at this low latitude of the warmer southern hemisphere, spring took long to ascend out of winter.

''No bloodshed?'' he wondered at last. ''Are you sure? I've met some of your Lunarians.''

''I've met more,'' David reminded him. ''We can hope. The towns won't mobilize to fight us. Oh, they'll be outraged, in their icy fashion. The Inrai may gain a number of new recruits. Clandestine support for them may well continue, though it ought to be less than they now get. Prowling the wilderness, they may try to interdict our regional ground traffic entirely, and that may lead to a few armed clashes, with casualties. But however regrettable, it won't matter much. We'll keep the freedom of the airlanes. I don't expect we'll need to hunt the Inrai down or anything like that. Let them skulk. Eventually, maybe not till their next generation but eventually, they'll see the futility of it and stop.'' His smile was bleak. ''Thank Chuan for providing a long-term view of the situation.''

''While the long term drags on, a lot of unhappiness will too,'' Fenn said.

''I didn't think you were overburdened with pity.''

''I'm not. But some individuals deserve sympathy.''

''You mean Kinna, don't you?'' David asked slowly.

''Huh?'' exclaimed Fenn, startled.

''I know she'll feel torn on account of her Lunarian friends—who, I've gathered, include several in the Threedom itself. And I know you and she have . . . a high opinion of one another.''

''We've stayed in touch, yes,'' Fenn mumbled.

''Well, she's a staunch lass, and sensible. When something had to be done, she was always ready to do it. Don't worry unduly about her.''

"Uh, will she be, uh, on hand?" She had been on an important field trip and unable to meet Fenn.

David grinned. "Try and stop her! When I called to say we were going to Sananton today, she swore at me for not giving her more advance notice, and I had to explain how neither you nor I knew beforehand when it could be. After you're through at Deimos, she wants to be your guide around the planet again."

The grin faded as the Martian regarded the Moon-dweller from the seas of Earth. Finally he continued, most carefully: "Please don't misunderstand me. I take you for an honorable man. But please don't misunderstand her either. You're a newcomer to this isolated world. You may not be quite aware of how strongly we feel about certain matters. Among us Terrans, the family's become the basic unit of society. We aren't casual about our relationships. In fact, we're seldom impulsive about them. My daughter can roam freely with anyone she wants to because everybody who knows her knows she's our kind of person."

Fenn bit back an immediate retort. The flitter whirred on over the desert.

"Muy bien," he said. "I'll take that as a friendly piece of advice. But it wasn't necessary."

Maybe it had been. He was so much looking forward.

As often happened around the Martian equinoxes, weather across most of the globe went into a prolonged calm. Dust on the ground lay still, dust aloft sifted down upon it, and the skies cleared. At night, stars gleamed almost as manifold, many-hued, crystalline-sharp, as in space. Heaven by day ranged from peacock-blue along the horizon to indigo-black at the zenith; streamers of ice-cloud cast back the fierceness of the little sun; colors glowed where boulders, dunes, craters, hills lifted out of knife-edged shadow.

Kinna led Fenn through the morning on ways they had not taken before. Once beyond the house, he would have blundered for some time at random before getting it back in view. Here there was no trail, nor a Luna where footprints might last for thousands, or millions, of years. She seemed to know every rock, pit, cleft, and crag. They zigzagged upward northwesterly until they were well above Sananton, although not yet overlooking Eos Chasma. There she ducked around a jutting mass. He followed, and found himself on a semicircular ledge, five meters across, defined by low cliffs. Southward dropped a steep, talus-strewn slope. Below stretched the plantation fields—mostly black and white at this season, slashed by service roads, studded with the bright-burnished shells of control and equipment housings—out to a red rim of desert.

Kinna beamed. "My private garden that I told you about," she said.

"It's nice," he replied awkwardly. What he saw appeared as drab to him as the cultivars beneath. Stalks, interlaces, slender stems and branches, leathery hemispheres, tight-curled leaves, and the rest would have been more interesting had he had any knowledge of metamorphic botany. However, he could appreciate the neat rows and rather charming miniterraces. "Quite a job, making this. Did you really do it alone, in just your spare time at home this past, uh, year?" Two Earth-years since last they walked together.

"Well, I borrowed machines for the rough work, naturally." She glanced away. Her voice dropped. "I don't think I mentioned this in our . . . correspondence, but the idea came from you. You told me how the Lahui have flowers, vines, arbors everywhere on those shiptowns and seadromes of theirs, and how you enjoy them."

He found no better response than: "It must be pretty when it blooms."

"I think so, but I'm prejudiced. This is a good site. The bluffs give shelter and radiate heat, so I can grow vanadia, the loveliest blue, and it seems as though the fireflower is going to take, and the hardier plants are doing spatter-splendidly, with their own colors—'' She laughed. "Never mind the catalogue. Next time come back in summer and see. I should have much more done by then, and fixed what's been neglected, poor things.''

Yes, he thought, presently she'd have graduated and returned here to stay. Meanwhile, she was again breaking off her studies to be with him.

"Couldn't you program a robot or two to look after it in your absence?'' he asked. Sun-sparks down in the fields showed where the machines went about their tasks.

She shook her head. The brown locks tumbled within her helmet. "No, then it wouldn't be *mine*. I mean, that'd be like . . . having a robot take care of my children—only it'd need to be a sophotect, to cope with the deviltries they'd surely invent. The sweetest machine, with the warmest, fuzziest fur coat, wouldn't be me.''

Deviltries, yes, no doubt, he thought. Children of hers will be almighty bright and lively, if she picks the right man.

An object appeared on top of a bluff. It shone in gaudy enamel hues. For an instant it poised before it sprang, landed on a terrace, bounced up, and bounded toward the humans. It slightly resembled a grasshopper, standing about forty centimeters high on the hind limbs, but with a big head, enormous eyes, and gauzy metallic wings.

"Why, here's Taffy!'' Kinna cried. "Welcome, dear! Come to Mama!'' She spread her arms. The leaper jumped into them. It wriggled gleefully. Wings quivered, hands on forelimbs clutched at her skinsuit. Fenn heard its radio voice trill. Kinna caressed it and crooned back.

After a moment she lifted her face toward him. "I'm forgetting my manners,'' she laughed. "Fenn, meet Taffimai Metallumai. She's good people in her skittery fashion. Taffy, meet Fenn. He's good people in his gruff fashion.''

"Uh, hola,'' the man greeted as solemnly as he could manage. "That's an unusual name.''

"I came on it in a playback of an ancient book,''

Kinna explained. "It means 'Small-person-without-any-manners-who-ought-to-be-spanked.' "

"A robot?"

"Yes, of course. No animal this big could survive outdoors. Not yet."

Fenn nodded. The "eyes" were optics and the "wings" energy collectors. He supposed that mostly the pseudo-creature lay dormant while its accumulators charged. Or did it also tap the power center in the fields, or graze certain of the plants to feed fuel cells? The demands of a solitary specimen would be negligible. In any case, the algorithms that ran it could not be simple; they must be capable of learning and of flexible response to situations. There might actually be a nonalgorithmic, quantum element—which would make it technically a sophotect, though an electrophotonic system this size couldn't be smarter than, say, a dog.

"You've probably heard about the wild robots that some of the Lunarians produce and release to hunt," Kinna went on. "I mentioned to Uncle Chuan how nice it would be to have a little and good-natured one, to keep me company when I'm out here where our cats can't go . . . well, they could, but they'd hate skinsuits. He had this made for me, for my birthday."

She doesn't need company, she needs to give love, Fenn thought. She has so much of it.

Taffimai Metallumai stirred restlessly. "All right, run along," Kinna said, and let it go. It hopped off, back onto the terrace, to sit watchful—curious? She smiled, then paid it no further heed.

She doesn't gush over this machine, Fenn thought, any more than I will over that spacecraft I, *I*, will take to Deimos and back. "That was kind of Chuan," he said.

"He is a dear, you know," Kinna murmured.

"M-m, you know it. To me—well, never mind."

Her gladness diminished. "He has to do his duty as he sees it," she said anxiously. "Don't we all?"

"Some people choose the wrong set of duties," he

snapped, and at once regretted his impulse.

"Oh." She was mute for a second. "You're thinking of those fanatics—" She half reached toward him. "Fenn, I never was able to say how sorry I was when I learned about your friend being killed. How sorry I am. I'm still not able. I cried, but what help is that?" She blinked hard. Sunlight splintered off the drops suddenly caught in her lashes.

"Thanks anyway." How stiff that sounds. "I understand what you mean." I think. "You're very kind."

"Not really. But I do care. I care a lot." Now the silence was long, until she mustered a smile and a brighter tone of voice. "I ought to, after everything you and your people are going to do for us."

His own mood, so abruptly dashed, was less ready to rise. "If we're allowed to."

The big gray eyes dwelt sadly on him. "It's back to Chuan, then, isn't it?"

"Not him personally," Fenn made haste to answer. "The system, which wants to keep us inside itself."

She did not take the detour he offered. Standing erect, she declared, "He serves the system. He's an integral part of it."

"I didn't want to belabor that."

"But I don't want lies or evasions between us."

"Nor I."

They fell silent again, into a mutual confusion and, also for him, shyness.

Thereafter she spoke quickly. "Let's talk straight and get it over with. Have you considered the possibility that we, our side, our ambitions, may be wrong? That we're irresponsibly bent on a fearful gamble with millions and millions of lives, people who haven't asked to be the stakes in our game?"

Fenn weighed his words. He'd better not say outright, "Flap them." Indeed, he'd be ashamed to, here, with her. "I might be readier to accept that if the rules of the game got spelled out for me," he stated.

"You mean—Oh, of course. You think we're entitled to more information and better arguments than we've been given."

"We're told to take on faith that the cybercosm—Not the Synesis. Our human trustees and councillors and administrators, they are what they are because *they* take it on what amounts to faith. We're told the cybercosm knows best. Its data processing, its analyses, its built-in reasonableness, and up on top, its all-knowing, all-good Teramind—we organics can't match any of this. We should stay put in our cozy playpen and let it do everything that matters."

"No. We should grow into maturity."

Fenn squinted at her through the chill, brilliant light. "You don't believe that yourself, do you?"

She lowered her gaze. Her fingers twisted together. "I don't know," she whispered. "I can't be sure. Uncle Chuan, he's told me about past history and our present metastability—"

"He hasn't told enough."

She met his eyes again. "Do you mean the . . . confidential information?"

He nodded violently. "For a start, yes. More's involved than just data, but we can begin with the data. Like on the field-drive ships or this mysterious discovery a solar lens is supposed to have made."

Four tears escaped to course down her face. "Fenn, I've said it to you before; something about that grieves him—Sometimes I'm terrified."

The fists doubled at his sides. "Isn't it better to have our horrors out in the open? Then we can deal with them . . . ourselves."

"Yes." Once more she looked away from him. Her glance fell on Taffimai Metallumai. As if the garish sight rekindled will in her, she smiled a bit, turned back to Fenn, and said, "Don't get me wrong. I've argued and argued with Chuan. I'd've done it more, but I can't stand to hurt him, and so we generally soon go to talking about pleasant things or share a piece of music or whatever. He's made me wonder, but he hasn't convinced me. I'm with you.''

"You would be," he said low.

She flushed. "Thank you." Hurrying onward: "The problem, you know, the danger, if there is a danger, that's not from the cybercosm. It isn't a dictator over us or anything. The real opposition—enemies, maybe—they're humans."

"Probably," he half yielded. "Including those who hate the cybercosm."

She laid a gloved hand in his. They stood remembering He'o.

"Flame it," he said at last, "Chuan is right, as far as that goes. We humans are experts at making trouble for each other. Like the Proserpinans and your Threedom." Immediately he cursed himself for having uttered it.

She flinched; but she did not let go of him, and she spoke levelly. "Yes, now Dad and I are at odds too. Though we don't fight."

"You agree to disagree." That was obvious, from what he had seen in their home. "I gather you personally don't think the Threedom should be, uh, brought into a proper orbit?"

"No. How would we like it if they hauled us into theirs?"

"You don't condone destruction and robbery, do you? I've heard of killings too."

She drew her hand back from his. "Of course I don't!" she protested. "Who does? It's been provoked, but even the Inrai themselves—except a few who're naturally wild—they don't like it, and Scorian keeps those few pretty well under control—"

He nodded stiffly. As a police officer, he had known such. Pedro Dover wasn't unique. Some people didn't take to being civilized; their DNA wasn't right for it.

He thought briefly that maybe to some degree he was in that class. But he'd turned those impulses elsewhere.

Hadn't he? The trick was to keep minimized the sort of situations that could upset whatever balance the born savages had, and to maintain the kind of watchfulness and strength that discouraged losing that balance.

"No, I don't want Elverir, my trouvour, leaving his bones in the desert," Kinna said.

Fenn felt he wouldn't be too sorry if that happened, then saw how senseless the feeling was. What claim had he?

She calmed. "The real Inrai and their supporters are only after what they see as freedom," she finished. "It could take a completely new form from anything that's been seen before. If we can somehow make peace with them, well, I've told you how the Tharsis seigneurs are as interested in your project as other Lunarians are, and how they might bring the Proserpinans back to us."

He hated to quench that reviving enthusiasm, but for an obscure reason—maybe, he thought afterward and winced, a lingering pique—he said: "With unpredictable consequences if it can happen at all. The cybercosm doesn't like it. The Synesis won't."

Her head sank. "I don't know, Fenn, I don't know. I keep hoping, but everything's so tangled and, and ambiguous. Politics—we thought our different societies had outgrown politics, didn't we? Outgrown government and all those other primitive things. But they're coming back."

"If they ever left us."

"Enough of this. Please."

Contrition washed over him. "Sure. I'm sorry. I didn't intend to bring up nasty stuff and . . . and spoil our outing."

"And I didn't intend we should hide from it." Brightness broke through. "Today, though, Fenn, why don't we think instead about how wonderful everything *can* become?"

Relief blossomed, and joy. "Great idea!"

They linked hands again, to shake them up and down

and sideways. The robot hopped back to join in the fun. With no rational cause for it, Fenn and Kinna began to laugh till their helmets rang.

Later he said, "If things work out the way they should, I'll be back on Mars fairly soon, maybe to stay."

"I'll look forward to that," she answered. "I'll wait."

15

FROM THE HIGH building on the shore of Walvis Bay, vision ranged westward over the South Atlantic Ocean, blue, green, white-foamed, restlessly asheen and aglitter beneath the sun. A breeze off those waters carried a benison of coolness and, even this far up, a salty tang. The bay itself lay broad and quiet from Pelican Point to the settlement at its south end: this great tower for homes and offices, the lesser auxiliary structures softly pastel-hued in their parkscape. Pleasure boats danced like dragonflies. Two large freighters rested at the docks, robots attending to their cargoes. Grass, trees, flowers reached inland beyond sight, metamorphic conquerors of ancient desert. The nerves that radiated from here across half a continent were invisible, impalpable—communication lines, data exchanges, a subset of the global network, of the cybercosm.

Fenn's gaze was elsewhere, either on the man with whom he was talking or on the spectacle before them. Here atop the tower, he and Maherero sat beneath an awning, a table and refreshments between them, ten meters of open duramoss in front. Beyond that space, drums thuttered and whistles keened. Lithe black bodies, gorgeously plumed and skirted and bejeweled, sweat-gleaming as if polished, danced measures now stately and intricate, now swift and feral. Birds bred for it flew among them, over them, a whirl of colors, scarlet and yellow finches, lightning-blue kingfishers.

The show had started when the two men arrived and went tirelessly on. It did not interfere with their conference, but enhanced it. Fenn guessed that the leader had directional sonic plugs in his ears, followed the discussion keenly, and signaled his troupe accordingly. When conversation grew intent, sound died down to a whisper and the dancers barely swayed; when it turned light or cheerful, tempo picked up; when it fell into silence, furiousness exploded, as if to engulf it in life.

To this folk, entertainment for honored guests was a custom as strong as law. Ranking Lahui who had been here earlier, one at a time, had described it to Fenn, adding that no vivifer could convey the real experience. He was delighted when an invitation came also to him, and promptly took flight for Africa. What he was witnessing did not disappoint.

Of course, most of his attention stayed with Maherero. Slender, his face looking almost youthful despite the woolly gray above, casually dressed in a loose robe and sandals, this high councillor of the Southern Coagency had received him like an equal and discoursed easily, affably. Nevertheless, Maherero spoke for the allied commerce of a dozen polities, whose interests spread around Earth and out to Luna.

After the polite sociabilities, he had gotten to the subject of Mars and what Fenn had learned there. He seemed to care less about the specifics, which he could take from the databases, than about personal events and impressions—tiny, jagged Deimos; Mars huge in its sky; silence, stars, a meteoroid strike; the companionship only of machines; towns, fields, wildernesses on the planet; people.

"And the growing factionalism, possible civil strife, how do you think it may affect your undertaking?" he asked.

"I've reported my knowledge and my opinions about

the engineering," said Fenn. "I'm no socioanalyst." A translator on the table converted the language of either speaker to that which the other had chosen. However well synthesized, its voice sounded flat to him above the richness of Maherero's tones.

"I did not request a logico-mathematical abstraction, but a human judgment."

Fenn smiled. More than ever, he liked this man. After a sip of gin and tonic, he replied, "Well, then, I'd say ignore the whole Threedom problem."

"Even if it becomes a crisis?"

"Balloon-puff word, 'crisis.' Look, the Deimos operation will start small, and remain small for years. A single base on Mars, which can be at the antipodes of Tharsis if we want. A few scattered mines and processing plants, but mostly the established Martian industries would love to contract for the jobs we need done, the stuff we need built. So who cares if there's a spat of fighting somewhere else? How can it touch us? By the time we're ready to commence on the moon, everything will be long since settled and half forgotten."

"Hm." Maherero stroked his chin. "I had the emotional factor more in mind. Your Lahui will be working in dangerous environments totally strange to them. Rage, grief, pity are apt to cloud reason and drag down alertness. How stressful will they find it to be on a world where organized violence is taking place? Yes, none will happen in their vicinity, but it will be on the news and in every consciousness."

"The Lahui aren't tender-gutted. Oh, sure, nobody will enjoy the situation, if it hasn't been resolved well before they get there. But they're fishers and herders; they live close to nature, where everything feeds on something else. And those who go will be picked for ability to concentrate on their work, among other traits. Likewise the Martians they'll be dealing with."

"But what if events spill out beyond the volcano land, perhaps into space itself? Suppose, for example, those mysterious Proserpinans decide to take a strong hand?''

"Suppose they don't. They're few, and a long ways away, and have plenty to keep them busy closer to home. Anyhow, you people won't have to cope with it. You'll be here on Earth, developing your seas." That was the bargain for which the Lahui Kuikawa leaders hoped, their expertise and guidance in oceanic enterprises as the condition of Coagency support for their Mars endeavor.

"We have to be reasonably careful," Maherero said. The mildness of his words did not deceive Fenn. The dance leader understood too, and the drumbeats slowed to a surflike growl. "The investment you want from us is very substantial." He leaned partly across the table. His dark eyes probed. "Given the fact that the Synesis generally disapproves of your scheme, how much help can you expect in an emergency? We are not the members who could provide it. How well could your teams do by themselves, thrown on their own resources?"

"I think they'd manage. But I've told you, sociodynamics is outside my scope." Fenn stiffened. "I will just say this. Nobody can forecast the future. If somebody isn't willing to meet it as it comes, he should get out of the way of those who are."

Maherero sat motionless. The drums and whistles went silent, the dancers froze, the birds fluttered down onto their shoulders. Dismay stabbed through Fenn. What offense had he given?

Then Maherero threw back his head and laughed aloud. "Bravo!" he cried.

Fenn stared. "Sir?"

The African sobered. "Forgive me," he said. "I have not been playing games with you. My task has been to meet with the chief actors in this affair and try to gauge what kind of human beings they are. That information was to enter into our decision, a subtle but real factor."

So that's how this society thinks, Fenn reflected at the back of his mind. "And—?"

"The factual analyses were already favorable. Quite

possibly we would have agreed in any case. But now I can declare to you that we certainly will." Maherero smiled. "I trust you will find us good partners."

"Why, this—this is the last boost stage we needed—we're going to launch!" Fenn shouted.

Drums, whistles, flying wings and flying feet went into a triumphant crescendo.

A hurricane formed in tropical mid-Pacific. Weather Control monitored the birth, analyzed a torrent of data, and took action. There was no attempt to abort it. Giant storms were as vital to Earth's heat balance, the health of the planet and the life thereon, as the steadiest current through air or ocean. But while it was in embryo, carefully directed energy beams from space helped determine its course. It would probably swing wide of places where it could do serious damage.

Probably. Though simple compared to the least of living things, the atmosphere is complex enough to be chaotic. The instabilities that allowed so small a nudge to reshape a hurricane's destiny made predictive certainty unattainable. The unsureness extended around the globe and ahead through time. Moreover, on any path it took the cyclone was bound to pass over some works of humankind and machinekind.

In the event, it veered slightly from the desired track, and one of the larger buoyant islands had to ride out the passage of a quadrant.

Everywhere on the broad curve of their domain, Lahui Kuikawa were celebrating for day after festive day. The dream would come true! Even in those indifferent to Mars, even in the remotest of the Keiki Moana, tribal pride flamed up for fireworks to proclaim to the night sky. Wanika Tauni and Fenn had left *Mālōlo* for a private revel that might last weeks and take them far. They happened to be on Waihona Lanamokupuni when the hurricane struck.

At no time were they in any real danger. The island

was unsinkable. Its flotation centers self-stabilizing, flexibly and durably linked, sensors and servos and their computers a webwork throughout, all superstructures integral with the whole, it responded to the forces upon it like a single gigantic organism. The only harm done was to gardens and parks. Decks rolled, but slowly and easily through just a few degrees. The rampant energies did set metal athrob, a deep pulsing that went on up into flesh and bones, while the roar and shriek of wind did fill the air with rage. In their cabin, which directly overlooked the sea, Fenn and Wanika felt themselves engulfed by wildness.

He stood for a long time staring out the viewport. Murk surrounded him, for he had turned off the light and the world outside was blind with foam and spray. Glimpsewise he saw the ocean, gone white, where waves went tremendous, their manes sheeting off into froth. The spectacle took him, he was lost in it, one with it, his thoughts as tumultuous and his innermost being as savage.

Finally he grew aware of Wanika touching his arm. Peering down into the gloom, he saw her lips move, but he could not make out what she said. He recalled that she was his friend. Reluctantly, he stepped over to the room controls and adjusted them. The ceiling came aglow. Countervibration damped the clamor to a low hammering and skirl.

"Whoof!" he said.

She smiled shakily. "That's better. The noise was hurting my ears."

"Huh? Why didn't you stop it sooner, then?"

She gestured at the viewport, where now he could see only the flung water that sluiced across its exosurface. "You were enjoying it, weren't you? As part of the whole show."

"Well," he said, taken aback, "well, that was, uh, sweet of you, but—What were you trying to tell me?"

"Nothing. I asked if you might not be hungry. It's been a long time since breakfast."

"Hunh!" he grunted. "I'd forgotten all about food." It did not occur to him till afterward to wonder what state she might be in. His glance strayed back to the storm. "I was thinking I could go outside. What a romp."

"No!" Appalled, she seized his arm. "You could be killed! A flying piece of debris, a gust knocking you overboard—"

He grinned, not very humorously. "The risk would be the main attraction."

"Risking your whole future in space?"

He needed a short span to assimilate that. "A point," he agreed. "A good point." He sighed. "All right, I'll stay indoors. You're a wise woman."

She smiled again. "Not really. Only a caring one."

He had no ready response, and they stood in awkward silence until she added, "You see, I would like to keep you while I can."

Half abashed, he got out: "Yes, we've had fun, haven't we? More than fun. You've done a lot for me, Wanika. For the project."

She hung her head. The black locks fell down to hide her face. "Which is going to take you away, Fenn."

"Not necessarily. And not forever."

"We'll see what happens."

Does she have Kinna in mind? he wondered. In death's name, why?

Not that she had ever said anything much about the Martian girl. Rather, she had taken to noticeably ignoring the messages that went oftener and oftener between planets—as if they might be something intimate, or as if it weren't any business of hers whatever they held. An illogical resentment joined the emotions the weather had been evoking in him.

Wanika looked up again, brightening. "But nothing special will happen for months and months yet, will it?"

she said. "We'll have all that time before things are ready for you to go."

Fenn turned his eyes back to the hurricane.

"You won't be bored, I promise you." A tiny laugh rippled. "I'll see to that. We've this whole Earth to explore together, *aikāne*."

The darkness in him boiled up. He clenched his fists and muttered a curse.

"What is it?" He heard the alarm in her voice.

"What you said," he replied, still glaring outward. "About things being ready for me to go back to space. I thought, 'If only He'o were coming along.' I'd been thinking about him, how he'd have sported in those waves—" His throat contracted.

"Yes." He barely heard her. When he looked her way, he saw a glimmer of tears.

The sight calmed him a little, though it was an iron calm in which he realized vaguely that he ought to be gentler with her. Well, he would, later, later. "The murderer's not been caught yet, has he?" Fenn asked quite quietly and quite unnecessarily.

"No."

"That means he probably never will be, unless—And if the police do, somehow, he'll only go to a comfortable institution where they'll try to reform him."

"He'o would have wanted that," Wanika said.

"Would he?" Fenn threw at her.

She had no answer. She too remembered the old sea hunter, the old fighter.

Fenn nodded. "Yes, I do now have some months at leisure. Time for tracking Pedro Dover down."

The storm yelled.

16

HIS SEARCH BROUGHT Fenn back to the Foresters of Vernal.

Most of it he had conducted sitting before a screen, along the multitudinous channels and the world communications system and sounding the depths of its database. He thought of calling Georghios on Luna and requesting full access to police records, but decided not to compromise the chief. That was also wise from his own viewpoint, considering what his intention was. His knowledge of procedures enabled him to find nearly all the information he wanted by himself, and to deduce the rest.

Detectives had established that Pedro Dover left the Moon and got off the ferry at Port Kenya. There he disappeared from sight. Perhaps a member of his Gizaki cult met him and spirited him away; perhaps he simply took a public conveyance to a prearranged rendezvous. Inquiry turned up a likelihood, not a certainty, that he was briefly seen in Cantabria, but if so, that was the end of the spoor. He would not have stayed there, conspicuous in a thinly populated and clannish region. Nor was it plausible that any household would take him in and keep him hidden for any long time. He must have gone elsewhere.

No more did he draw his citizen's credit. With the system on the watch, every such transaction would have instantly pinpointed his location. Was he using a false identity? To set one up was a difficult and precarious venture, and must be done far in advance. Registering an imaginary birth demanded a conspiracy among several of the people who would normally be involved, plus somebody with the skill to devise a genome map and other physical characteristics. Then further entries into the database must be made year by year, about education and health services and whatever else a child ordinarily went through—their absence would draw attention—until the fictitious person reached adulthood and entitlement to his/her allowance. The police satisfied themselves that the Gizaki lacked the resources and patience for this. In fact, the organization had scarcely been in existence long enough.

Thus Pedro Dover was living on cash. In itself that would attract no particular notice. People quite often made minor payments in ucus, more convenient than entering a credit transfer. Sometimes a payment was large, for the sake of privacy, usually because the buyer or seller was ashamed. Gizaki members could slip Pedro Dover notes and coins, or they could send the money to a temporary address of which he notified them. However, this could not be very regular or very dependable, nor amount to much. Surely he earned most of his keep, maybe all, as an itinerant odd-jobber. Though not common, such individuals were not extraordinary either, especially in certain of the societies on Earth.

Where, then? The psychological profile taken when he was detained for assault showed he was no linguist. His rant from the arcade had been recorded for him. Lacking fluency, he would be conspicuous in any area that was not Anglophone.

Searchers drew blank in his native Australia. It had been unpromising anyway: a thoroughly modern land of robotic industries, residential communities, recreational parks, and nature reserves. He had always been a misfit there. Probably that was why he fell into dangerous foolishness and eventually departed.

The same applied to New Zealand. Other islands and enclaves were too small. He could get his face changed. Preparations to have that done had doubtless been part of the murder plot. But he would obviously be an outsider. Investigators found only a few such in those places, all innocent.

That left only North America, more or less above the thirty-fifth parallel—the polity of Vernal. It looked hopelessly large and diverse. The police had too much else to do. Having ransacked the easiest possibilities without result, they put an alert in the net and suspended their efforts.

After all, they reasoned, Pedro Dover was presumably unable to do any further harm, and he could presumably not stay lost to them forever. The sensors were countless in locales public and private, everywhere from transport terminals and taxi vehicles to homes and shops whose owners wanted the added security. It would be remarkable if, in the course of a decade or two, none of them got a good enough look at him to register a likely identification and notify the nearest constabulary. A countenance could readily be altered, but not an entire body, build and gait and mannerisms and every other somatic clue.

Besides, his profile strongly suggested he never intended to end his days as an indigent wanderer. It wasn't compatible with his towering self-importance. He had done his deed to fix himself in the minds of his cultmates as a man of action, a man of power. He would plan on lying low until the mounting terrorism he anticipated began to break down the civilization he hated. Then he would emerge to take his rightful place as a leader of the glorious revolution.

This implied that he would be in intermittent contact with fellow Gizaki, if only to keep his name before them. They were under surveillance. An opportunity might come to set a trap.

Not that he greatly mattered—a sick person in need of treatment, a tiny piece of unfinished business. Soon the name of Pedro Dover was well-nigh forgotten, except by Fenn.

Bleak winter sunlight streamed into the room. It glowed on wood floor and paneling, cast shadows from furniture also wooden and handmade, shone off hammered brass and polished ceramic, found a shelf and brought into relief the carven figurine of a moose, emblem of the Thistledew community. Glancing out an old-style window, Fenn saw other houses in the same ancient style and a street dark between the banks of snow that had been cleared from it. Beyond them he glimpsed the frozen lake on which the village fronted and the evergreen wilderness in which it nestled. The window seemed to violate thermodynamics and radiate cold, but the room was comfortable, with an aroma of brewing coffee.

He turned his eyes back to the couple with whom he sat. Man and wife, they were getting along in years but rangy, leathery, marked by lifetimes spent mostly outdoors. Both were simply clad in local fashion; shirt, trousers, belt holding pouch and sheath knife. However, around Rachel's neck hung the badge of the office to which she had been elected, mayor and magistrate of the township. Lars bore no insignia. Like every adult Forester, he had the title of caretaker; but mainly he cultivated a patch of ground, fished, hunted, and occasionally guided a tourist or a sportsman through the woods.

"Well, welcome," he repeated himself in his archaic Anglo dialect. "Good to see you again. It's been way too long." Fenn had called ahead, then come directly after setting his volant down on the parking strip nearby.

"It has," Fenn agreed. "I've been busy."

"We haven't heard from Birger either," Rachel said. "How is he?"

"All right," Fenn answered. Memories washed through him, times he had been here as a boy with his father, a time or two afterward by himself, and at last the—not exactly breach, but the father's unspoken displeasure when the son left Luna, and only a few curt communications since then. "He's married again, did you know?" To a woman who had had her own quota of offspring.

"Good," Rachel said. "We were sorry to learn he'd

broken up with your mother." The coffee was ready. Fetching it afforded her a chance to drop the subject. As she set a cup down on the table for Fenn, she gave him a close look and observed, "You've changed quite a lot."

"I've been in new places," he said. "Mostly off the Moon."

She nodded. "I can see that."

"I hope you still like our whiskey," said Lars.

Fenn grinned. A little of the hardness melted inside him. "I'm sure I will."

Lars got a bottle and tumblers, and they all settled down to talk. "Where're you living these days?" he asked.

"The Pacific Basin," Fenn replied. "I'm with the Lahui Kuikawa. Not a sworn-in member, but associated." They could have found that out if they chose to. Plenty of items had registered in the public database in the course of events. Besides, he didn't want to lie to them unless he absolutely must.

"And you've come straight from there to us, in the dead of winter?"

Rachel smiled. "Maybe he's after a change. How long can you stay, Fenn? Nobody else is at the inn; you'll have your pick of quarters. Everybody will be glad of a new face that isn't just an image in a phone screen."

"I'm afraid I'm on business. I'll flit already tomorrow." Fenn decided he could better forward his mission if he showed more warmth. "But it is good to be back. I'd forgotten how good it is."

True. This woodland lacked the scenic grandeur of Yukonia, but it gave the same sense of freedom and life, the same spaciousness, from the Rockies to the Alleghenies, from southern prairie to northern tundra. The Foresters who had scattered their little settlements and isolated steadings throughout it were practically a polity to themselves within the Vernal Republic, keeping to folkways bequeathed them by ancestors whose lifespans had filled centuries. Their stubborn selfhood always pleased him.

Of course, he thought wryly, it was an independence made possible by the outside world, cybercosmic technology, citizen's credit, basic needs met as freely, in effect, as the need for air and sunshine. A bit of extra income from providing services for visitors didn't hurt. Equally of course, the independence was on sufferance. Preserves like this existed for the sake of ecological and climatic balance. Not many humans were supposed to be in one at any given moment, and dwellers were supposed to look after its well-being. If ever they failed, robots and sophotects would replace them.

"I hope I can return later and stay awhile," Fenn continued. How rapturously Kinna would enjoy it. Daydream, daydream.

"If you do at this same season, we'll give you some new experiences," said Lars. "Snowshoeing, ice fishing—and solstice, yes, winter solstice is a big festival for us."

"He knows, I'm sure," Rachel said.

"But he's never *done* it, like his dad." To Fenn: "And we don't encourage outsiders to come in and record our doings for virtuals."

Fenn nodded. Like the Lahui, this whole society valued its privacy. Leading a tenderfoot around was not the same thing as becoming a show.

"He knows that too," Rachel chided. "Let's not waste attention span on it. What are you after right now?"

Fenn tautened. The prepared words marched forth. "I'm trying to get in touch with a man. I think he may be somewhere in your country."

"Who is he?"

"I don't know what name he's using, but here's a picture." Fenn took a datacard from his pocket and offered it to her. Rising, she went over to a terminal and inserted it. Pedro Dover's image appeared, reproduced from the sequence the Lunar police took when he was arrested. Full-length, it paced back and forth as he had been ordered to do. The projection moved in on his head. At sight of the thin face, hatred rose up into Fenn's mouth. It tasted of blood.

"N-no, I don't recognize him," Rachel said, and Lars added, "Nor I."

"He may have changed his appearance," Fenn told them.

"Grown a beard or something?" Rachel keyboarded to play with the image, different cuts of hair and whiskers, extra weight plumping the features out. "Nada."

"Biosculp is possible," Fenn said.

Rachel flicked the set off, removed the card, and peered at him as she returned it. "What do you want him for?"

"Sorry, that's confidential. Let's just say he and I have an urgent matter to discuss."

"Hm." She sat down again, still considering him.

"You haven't posted a 'Por favor, contact me,' then," said Lars.

"No, he wouldn't have responded," answered Fenn. It would only have warned him.

"So he's in hiding?"

Fenn shrugged. "Sorry," he repeated.

"I did hear from your dad, a spell ago, that you'd quit the police. Are you back with them?"

"No, this is personal."

"What made you think he might be here?" asked Rachel.

"Not precisely here," Fenn said. "Somewhere in the region, a community small and out of the way, where people don't gossip with the outside."

Even in Thistledew they didn't, he thought. Not really. More and more, the Foresters too were feeling alienated from the Synesis, hostile to its pervasiveness. Birger had once told him, in confidence, while they were still close to one another, that rumors of births exceeding two children per parent were well-founded. A lonely cabin, a secret midwifing, a failure to register the infant, and who would know? Basic schooling hereabouts was private, and few of the schools tied their records into the general database. Certain medical people were similarly inclined. On reaching adulthood, persons like that couldn't draw citizen's credit if they didn't want to reveal themselves, unless perhaps sometimes tricks were played that involved not reporting a death. But money could be shared around or inconspicuously earned. No individual needed a great deal of it when everyone lived simply and mostly off the land, often more so than was quite legal. Neighbors who knew, or who suspected, wouldn't spill anything to the authorities. That would get them ostracized. Foresters didn't want any constables but their own coming in and maybe seeing what else they were up to. .

No doubt the cybercosm, if not its human associates, had an inkling, or more than an inkling, of such activities. But as long as the preserve wasn't actually being damaged, it seemed willing to let things ride. Why provoke enmity? Enough was brewing elsewhere.

"He's good with his hands," Fenn said. "I'd guess he travels from wherever he's based, village to village, homestead to homestead, doing minor jobs for folks who don't have much in the way of robots or other modern equipment. Jobs they could do, but he'll handle it cheaply."

Lars chuckled. "Leaving them added time for stuff like fishing, hey?" He rubbed his chin. "Hm-m, I suppose he has to hitch rides, except where a bus runs. But he could easily do that. No, I haven't heard of anybody who'd fit."

"You may well have, Rachel," Fenn prompted. "That's why I came here."

"You don't care to say what you want with him?" she asked slowly.

"It's nothing that can hurt you or your people," Fenn vowed. They *should* not know. "We're old friends, aren't we? You understand I wouldn't play you a dirty trick."

"Yes, you are an old friend," she murmured. "From way back when you were a kid with your dad. And he's an oath-brother of ours."

Fenn waited. His heart slugged.

She reached decision. "I have heard of a mozo like that," she said. "We judges keep a sort of grapevine going, just in case. A stranger settled in Munsing two-three years ago. Calls himself, m-m, let's see, yes, Robin."

"How'd he get in?" asked Lars, interested.

"Way I heard," Rachel explained, "a man who comes to these parts now and then to hunt, he brought this Robin along and left him in charge of a cabin he'd bought. He's been back a couple of times for short visits, but otherwise, Robin lives there alone."

It tingled in Fenn. So at least one Gizaki has that kind of money, he thought. Or maybe the cult paid it out, figuring a refuge for Pedro Dover was a worthwhile investment.

"Yes, Robin keeps to himself, except when he goes around tinkering," Rachel went on. "Nobody minds him. I suppose by now they take him for granted. Munsing is pretty lonesome."

Somehow Fenn kept his voice level. "Muchas gracias. That does sound like the man I'm after."

"Excuse me," Rachel said, "but I am a judge and I've got to ask. You do have an honest purpose, don't you?"

Fenn met her eyes. "Yes," he replied. "Very honest."

She relaxed, smiling. "That's sufficient for me. Now tell us what's been happening to you. You'll stay for dinner, won't you?"

The inn was a house with a few spare rooms, austerely but adequately outfitted, which the owner rented to transients. Night had fallen when Fenn arrived walking down a street gone dark and ringingly cold. He was glad not to meet anybody. Checking in, he said little to the landlord and went straight upstairs.

There he sat down and stared at a wall. It had been a strain to uphold cheerfulness, hour after hour, with Lars and Rachel. He must keep telling himself that he wasn't actually betraying their trust. The end of his hunt in sight, he felt none of the joy he had awaited.

After a while he growled and turned to the phone. He ought to call Wanika. Data search found her aboard *Mālōlo* and a general request quickly brought her to the cabin they shared. Midday light came in through the ports to lave her bare skin and lose itself in the blackness of her hair.

"Fenn!" she cried happily. "Where are you? How are you?"

"I'm all right," he said. "I may be returning soon."

"Already? Wonderful!" She hesitated. "Then you— you've found Pedro Dover?"

"I'm not sure." He regretted having told her his purpose. He definitely did not want her to know what his ultimate intent was. "I may have a clue. If it's wrong, well, I've been thinking. I can't let this become an obsession, doing the police's work for them. I may give up and come back to you."

Not if it really is a mistake, he thought. Then I'll keep on. But if it isn't—They'll wonder in Munsing why he suddenly left with an outsider, but they'll guess it was a personal matter. Maybe, come spring, someone will find the body in a melting snowbank in the woods. But no one will likely make a fuss that could bring detectives in from outside. They'll quietly dispose of the remains, without any serious investigation.

Though I'd better not visit Forester country ever again.

"I haven't quite made up my mind," he said. "We'll see." The words felt slimy.

"I can hope," Wanika said. "Pedro Dover under arrest and you back here." Her mood faded. "You have a message entered, waiting till it's given your whereabouts," she told him dully. "From Mars."

"Oh?" His heart jumped. "Just a minute." The phone

in the room was reasonably capable, to accommodate tourists. It could handle encryptions that weren't crack-proof quantum but adequate for most communication. He set it to employ the code he and Kinna had agreed on. "Relay, please."

"Yes," Wanika said. Her image vanished.

Fenn waited and wondered through a few seconds that stretched. When last he'd heard from Kinna, she was not yet over her distress at the Republic's occupation of the Threedom. It had gone bloodlessly, and so far the cities were peaceful. But the Inrai, the outlaws, had taken all their equipment, all their strength, into the wilds. After they attacked several convoys, no ground traffic that wasn't strictly local moved in Tharsis. Although the constabulary had refrained from counteraction and now relied entirely on air transport, she feared for her Elverir.

Her image appeared, and his pulse sang. Between locks more tousled than usual, the pert face was alive with eagerness and the gray eyes lambent. She quivered. Her voice torrented.

"Fenn, Fenn, the wildest thing; I've got to record it for you right away! Elverir—Scorian—P-p-pro*ser*pina—" She caught her breath and laughed. "My tongue's too poky. The news is overrunning it, on large, clattery feet. Let me try and get organized."

When she spoke again, it went fast but steadily. "Elverir—he's back in Belgarre. Inrai aren't constantly on patrol; they take awhile in the outback and then go home and carry on their daily lives another while. They need to, and the outfit needs it, to keep supplies coming. And it makes it harder for the constables to know who's involved and who isn't. That's even more so these days, with the Threedom under occupation. I'm hoping Elverir can stay a good long time. Forever, if I had my wish. This is so horrible; people of good will like my parents set against people who want freedom—" She swallowed. "I'm sorry. I'm getting things all tumble-jumbled. I should leave off what matters most to me and stick to what matters to you." A fleeting smile. "After all, it's you I'm talking at. And . . . and Fenn, what you care about, I do too, because it's important and—because it's you, trouvour—" The blood ran high in her face. She hurried on.

"Well, Elverir gave me the news. He had it from Scorian, the chief of the Inrai, insofar as they've got a chief. It's supposed to be confidential, but I suspect Scorian knew Elverir would share it with me and didn't actually forbid him to. I'd guess Scorian wouldn't mind word getting to the Lahui Kuikawa, for whatever they may try to do about it. But he'd rather the Synesis not know that you know. That's my guess."

She looked straight out of the screen. He half reached forth, blindly, as if to take her hands.

"Fenn," she said, "a ship from Alpha Centauri is approaching Proserpina."

Thunders rolled through his skull.

After another moment she proceeded, as calmly now as he would have expected of one who'd spent her life coping with a planet that wanted to stay dead. "The Lunarians at Centauri must've beamed word when it left, so the Proserpinans had a lot of years' advance notice. I s'pose the Synesis—well, the cybercosm, anyway—detected it some time ago, radiation from the shock wave in the interstellar gas and so on, but hasn't said anything public, for whatever reason. The Proserpinans think it, the cybercosm, would've intercepted the ship if it could, but didn't have anything on hand that was able to. Maybe all the superspeed craft are away off exploring among the stars, like we're told they are. Or maybe the accusation is untrue and unfair. I do wish the cybercosm would tell us more, don't you? Chuan says it tells us as much as is wise, but—"

Fenn thought that the fact the Proserpinans knew the ship was coming would suffice to stay the cybercosm's hand.

"Well," Kinna continued. "The reason why the Proserpinans think this, and why they've suddenly let the Inrai know. Ordinarily they wouldn't have, that's not in Lunarian nature. But the nearness of the new craft, and ideas they've meanwhile been swapping back and forth with the Centaurians, that's led them to wonder mightily about what the great secret is that a solar lens has discovered. They're convinced it is a secret, a fact, not just a scientific puzzle, and means something tremendous. That sounds reasonable to me. Why shouldn't a puzzle be published?'' A pang crossed her countenance. ''And dear old Chuan, the way he's kind of flinched whenever the subject came up between us and right away changed it—

''Anyhow, you remember, don't you, the Proserpinans tried in the past to orbit a couple of lenses of their own, and failed. They think it was sabotage by minirobots, but it could've been a tricky project going awry. I'd rather believe that. Whichever, they've concluded that probably one particular lens made the discovery, or most of the discovery, the one looking toward the center of the galaxy. I'm not sure why. But the Lunarians at Centauri and the Terrans at those farther stars, they've been carrying out astronomy too. Maybe they've found nothing very surprising in any other direction, and haven't got the means to investigate closer. Maybe that's one of the things Proserpina's heard from Centauri.

''The Proserpinans sent an expedition to that lens to try and find out what's in its database. They learned it's guarded by systems they didn't care to annoy. Maybe every lens is, maybe not, but that's an enormous bunch of arcs to search, isn't it?''

Kinna stiffened herself. Her tone resounded clear. ''There's something cosmic at stake, seems like, and it may well be part of the Centaurian ship's mission. The Proserpinans want to know more. The only thing like allies they've got in the inner System is the Inrai, and that Star Net Station sitting on Pavonis Mons doubtless has the information on file. Maybe the Inrai can do something. I don't see what or how, but away off where they are, the Proserpinans might not understand the problem very well, or it might be Lunarian recklessness, a feeling of nothing much to lose.

"Anyhow, what with the Threedom occupied, the Proserpinans couldn't just shoot a tight beam from a ship well off in space, and they had to assume every quantum code has been compromised. They sent a superfast little field-drive vessel, robotic, swinging in close by Mars. It threw a wide beam across the Tharsis desert. A few Inrai receivers were bound to catch the message. The craft sped off homeward, and we—we have the word, for whatever we can do with it."

Her gaze captured him, whom she had not been seeing or speaking to in real time. "What *you* can do with it," she finished softly. "If that's nothing, don't feel bad. The next transport from Luna doesn't leave for months and months. Meanwhile, anything can happen"—her grin flashed defiant—"and prob'ly will. But I did have to tell you, trouvour."

She sighed. "Otherwise life is clumpety-clumping along. Our disagreements about policy and suchlike awfuls haven't split the family; we can still laugh together. I look forward to hearing from you when it's convenient—for you, I mean; it always is for me—and even more to seeing you again when you can get here. Don't worry. We'll come out on top of this hash-heap somehow, see if we don't. Bye."

She blew him a kiss, which she had never done before, and the recording ended.

Fenn sat for almost an hour, hardly moving.

Again the early winter night, air so cold that it felt liquid in the nostrils, starlight brilliant on snow but hemmed in by shadow walls of forest, silence except for a frosty scrunch under Fenn's boots. His breath puffed white and vanished. At his back, the clustered homes of Munsing receded into the dark. Ahead of him, the windows of a solitary cabin glowed yellow.

His goal. He had called today from Thistledew, first to an arbitrarily chosen resident, explaining that he wanted to contact Robin but didn't know what name that person used in the phone register, thereafter to this place. For that he had used audio only and hinted at a meeting for conspiratorial purposes. Response was eager, with directions for finding his way and an hour when they would not be disturbed. No question remained in his mind. His search was finished.

Finished also were turmoil and doubt. A steely peace dwelt in his breast. He had a task before him, and then he could leave.

When he came to the door, he knocked, another archaism among the Foresters. The sound boomed hollow. The impact hurt his chilled knuckles. The door opened. He stepped through, swung about, and closed it behind him, yanking the knob from a slackened grasp.

"What's this?" Instant alarm trembled in Pedro Dover's voice. He drew back from the man who loomed over him. His visage was indeed altered, but after all his poring over the image, Fenn would have known that gawky frame at the bottom of a black hole. The cabin was cluttered, dirty, overheated, and ill-smelling. He felt a faint satisfaction; he had awaited as much.

"Who are you?" Pedro Dover shrilled. "You're the one who called? What do you want? Don't stand there staring at me!"

"If you come along quietly," Fenn told him, "nobody need have any trouble. The local constable will fly you to the nearest regular police station and turn you over, and that will be that."

"What—what're you jabbering about?"

"You don't recognize me, eh? I happened to be on hand when you were egging a mob on against a well-meaning little sophotect in Mondheim. And I didn't see you, or you wouldn't have lived, but I was present when you murdered a close friend of mine in Tychopolis. A Keiki Moana, a metamorph seal, remember?''

Pedro Dover screamed. He snatched for his sheath knife. Fenn's fist leaped. The blow shocked back into his shoulder. The face before him exploded in red ruin. Pedro Dover lurched back. Fenn followed with a left to the belly, just under the rib cage. Pedro Dover fell, flopped, and fought for air.

''Don't worry,'' Fenn said. ''You're not worth killing.'' He put a foot on the creature and held it down while he phoned for the constable.

17

GUTHRIE WOKE.

It happened instantly, at the closing of a switch. No dreams faded out of him as he opened the shells over his optics, extended them on their stalks, and gazed around. He had been inactivated—in a sense, dead—and now he was again functioning—in a sense, alive.

Thirty-five years, he thought, as close as makes no difference. What's the universe been up to?

Before pursuing that, he meshed himself with the ship's instruments and computers. The data reassured him. Everything that could be under control was. Not that he had ever doubted the vessel he'd renamed *Dagny*. But something unforeseeable might go wrong for her, or right for an enemy.

No, he was on his flight plan, still decelerating but not far from his goal, bound back into the Solar System after more than a millennium away.

You could hardly tell by vision. Stars crowded sable clarity, the Milky Way girdled heaven with its crooked winter road, nebulae glimmered, the Andromeda galaxy lay huge, wan, and mysterious: sights he had seen at two other suns and in between, very little changed by his crossing a mere few light-years. Only Sol marked this region out, and at almost six hundred astronomical units' distance, it was only the chief among the stars, fiercely brilliant but casting no more than a third again as much illumination as a full Luna above Earth. Nevertheless, Guthrie dwelt on its image for many minutes.

Juliana, he thought. Your ashes lie yonder, strewn on the Leibniz Mountains of the Moon where it's always day, mingled with the ashes of my first body, the body that knew you.

Dagny enclosed him in silence. She was no *c*-ship, no *Yeager*, minimal in mass and thereby able to fly close to the velocity of light. She was a cruiser, also running on field drive but originally meant for interplanetary work. Thus she was amply big to carry cargo, accommodations plus full life and medical support for several humans, and the weapons that the Lunarians of Centauri had installed for him. Seen from outside, she was a conoid, not quite a hundred meters in length, broadening from the bow to a rounded base about forty meters in diameter. Hatches, airlocks, and a few streamlined turrets studded the matte skin. Antennas and dishes were newly deployed, stretching forth skeletal to catch what signals and other information they could. With speed down to a few score kilometers per second and dropping, the particle deflector field was at low strength, invisible, no longer a glow like St. Elmo's fire streaming aft from ahead of the hull.

Guthrie muttered an oath and pulled out of his reverie. The instruments showed three ships under high boost on what must be interception paths. They were plasma-drive, but surely formidable. At any minute a voice on a laser beam would challenge him. He'd better get briefed.

By agreement, the Centaurians had beamed an encrypted update to overtake *Dagny* a little earlier than now. Of course the news was four and a third years' old—the news from Sol that had been relayed back to him was twice that—and woefully scant, stating simply what they knew, and even that small bit inevitably distorted by misunderstanding, prejudice, and what Guthrie considered superstition. But it was better than nothing. He played the message into his memory without giving it much attention. There'd be time for that during the last stages of his approach.

Lunarian rang in his audio sensors. "Aou, ship inbound out of the fifth octant. Zefor speaks, commanding this detachment of guardians for the Council of Forerunners on the free world Proserpina. Name yourself and your purpose."

Guthrie's reply speared back. He used the same language, but, as always, gave it his own flavor and threw in some ancient Americanisms. "Come off it, amigo. You know damn well who I am. I'd guess your honchos have been expecting me since before you were born."

Five billion years ago, when the Solar System was in embryo, a globe began to form, next outward from what would become Mars. Jupiter, already coalescent—the giants grew fastest—roiled the planetesimals with its gravity and aborted this planet. However, some of them had gotten to a size at which the energies of accretion and of radioactivity melted them. Heavy elements sank down to their centers. When they cooled and solidified, they had nickel-iron cores. In the course of time, collisions shattered all of them, as well as lesser bodies, until nothing but a belt of asteroids remained.

Early on, though, such an accident blasted the outer layers off the largest. The result was a ferrous spheroid two thousand kilometers across. Recoiling, eventually it strayed too close to Jupiter, and the monster threw it outward. The new, eccentric orbit was canted about forty-four degrees off the ecliptic plane; like other quantities, this varied somewhat over time. Perihelion brought it within slightly more than a hundred astronomical units of the sun. Aphelion was more than thirty-one thousand astronomical units distant, beyond the Kuiper Belt of comets and well into the Oort Cloud of those icy objects. As eons passed, one of them crashed on it, leaving a rich deposit of frozen water and organics. A metallic impactor bequeathed its own treasures. At this moment in humankind's existence, the worldlet had rounded Sol and was outbound again. It had not yet come very far; the period was almost two million years.

When Guthrie first saw it, remotely and under high magnification, it flashed and glittered, lights everywhere across a once murky surface, light of sun and stars reflecting off domes, roofs, towers, masts. They streamed past as he drew closer, for his path was curved and the planetoid spun rapidly, once around in nine and a half hours. He began to make out roads, rails, spacefields, ships coming and going like fireflies. Farther off, he recognized structures in space, a few of them satellites, most of them just sharing the same orbit—habitats, factories, entrepôts, supplementary harbors, and things less readily identifiable. He supposed two or three were naval, while others were devoted to research of various kinds and to activities that wanted ample isolation, such as the production of antimatter.

Be that as it may, Proserpina had obviously waxed prosperous and populous. To be sure, a majority of its folk were elsewhere, in lesser colonies on smaller bodies and in mining bases on comets, thinly spread across immensities that dwarfed the inner Solar System, but growing, venturing, driving their frontiers ever outward, starward.

That suited the Lunarian temperament, Guthrie thought. They'd like the solitude of their settlements, far more profound than among the asteroids of Alpha Centauri. Each could go its own way, developing its own culture. He had gathered, nevertheless, that as a general rule, the basic social forms resembled those that had prevailed on Earth's Moon under the Selenarchy. Ties of kinship knitted families and their retainers into phratries. Several related phratries made up a phyle, a loose framework for considering matters of mutual concern and acting more or less cooperatively. Stronger, often handed down for generations, were bonds between the seigneurs, who held the balance of wealth and power, and their armurini—"companions," meaning followers, vassals, samurai, or whatever inadequate rendering you gave that word. Most major enterprises were carried out by courai, not exactly companies or guilds, which tended to draw their members from the same phratry; but some were possessions of the seigneurial families.

On Proserpina, where people and things and doings were concentrated, something else had perforce evolved, as close to a government as Lunarians could maintain. The phratries elected a Council of Forerunners. In consultation with them—through a kind of electronic Althing, Guthrie thought—it set policies and organized major public undertakings. The majority of its enactments amounted to safety regulations and the like. Lunarian leadership was always more prone to say, "Thou shalt not" than "Thou shalt." Still, various positive works were carried out. They were paid for by ad hoc levies on their beneficiaries.

The Council chose a Convener, *primus inter pares* for as long as the Council continued him/her in office. All its acts were subject to review and veto at any time by the Consultancy of the seigneurs who led the phyles. Weak though it seemed, the system apparently was more effective than analogues had been among such Terrans as the medieval Slavs or Icelanders. When the maximum authority that anyone could possibly win was so limited, negotiation in a spirit of reasonably enlightened self-interest was usually the optimum course. A person of any rank who pushed too hard was apt to get killed.

The Proserpinans even kept what seemed to be a small but well-disciplined naval force. Guthrie wasn't sure why. Did they actually have pipe-dream visions of being attacked across the gulf between them and Earth? Maybe the idea was just to keep feuds from getting out of hand.

Zefor's voice returned: "You will take parking orbit here, donrai." He recited the elements of it.

"Quite a ways out yet, eh?" Guthrie said. "Oh, well." He gave *Dagny* the numbers and felt the gentle tug of terminal maneuvers.

"We will provide transport to Proserpina."

"No need for that, gracias. If you or your TrafCon will talk me in, I'll flit directly. Uh, this ship's self-guarding, and kind of touchy about strangers trying to board. Please pass the word around. I'd hate for somebody to get hurt."

"Understood, donrai." Zefor sounded sardonically amused.

Guthrie was already in his humanoid body. This time, unlike when he arrived at Centauri, the 3-screen in the turret held an image of his middle-aged human head. He thought that would be more useful, psychologically, here, where they still dealt directly with Terrans at least once in a while.

He fetched a jetpack and attached it, secured a navigation kit to his chest, cycled through an airlock, and sprang free. The flight through space, englobed by stars, gave him a couple of welcome hours to marshal his thoughts.

The interlude would also have soothed him, had he been flesh. A download wasn't able to fear or fret—about its own prospects, anyhow. The circuits and programming did generate something like devotion to causes, ideas, and, yes, living beings, and this led to concern about them. In a ghostly way, love outlasted death.

But *I'm a much better lover when I'm alive,* Guthrie thought, *and I don't mean only physically.*

He dismissed self-pity with the contempt it deserved—he remained entirely capable of scorn—and concentrated on the situation around him. It was certainly interesting.

Proserpina swelled before him till it filled half the sky and the direction shifted gradually from ahead to down. Following the instructions in his receivers, he made a deft landing on a metal terrace that jutted from a slim, quite beautiful skyscraper. Lights, diffused by reflectors, hid space behind an artificial day. A machine waited to help him off with his gear and lead him to an entry lock. It was robotic, multiply equipped and adaptable, but essentially an automaton, without consciousness. The sophotècts here were few, their intellects and free wills severely restricted.

Guthrie passed to the interior. Moisture made short-lived hoarfrost on him. His sensors noted warmth, a ventilating breeze, weight. Gravity was about fourteen percent of Earth's, but that amounted to eighty-six percent of Luna's. An honor guard awaited him, a dozen tall men in close-fitting black and silver. It was also a real guard. While observing the usual prohibition on firearms inside buildings exposed to vacuum, the squad bore more than swords and staves; two electromagnetic projectors would disable him in short order if he misbehaved.

As one, the men saluted, right hand on left breast. "Be you well received, donrai, captain, emissary," said the leader. When he spoke thus ceremoniously, Guthrie heard how Lunarian at Sol had diverged from what they spoke at Centauri. The differences weren't enough to cause a problem. "Whatever you desire and request that may be granted you, shall be, for that you have made this great journey and bear great tidings. Would you first seek the quarters prepared for you?"

Same as last time, Guthrie thought. "No need. If people are ready to meet with me, I am too."

"Three Selenarchs abide in that hope, donrai. Let us bring you to them."

Yes, they've revived the old title, Guthrie recalled. It says they've never dropped their claim to their mother world, the Moon.

On foot and by slipway, the trip was lengthy to the palace appointed. Much that he saw was unique. Most construction was aboveground; excavations in an iron mass went slowly. Although human works had long since covered the entire planetoid, there was no city in any Terran sense. Nodes of culture and commerce served those functions, preserved those peculiarities. People walked as aloofly as always, but filled the passages, arcades, shops, pleasure centers, and esoteric establishments more densely than elsewhere. However soft their speech and gait, the sound of them became an undertone—to him, like the purr of a giant cat. Clothing styles were distinct from the Centaurians', tending toward flamboyancy. Among the frequent pets—a tiny hawk, an angora squirrel, a monkey, a ferret, a gaudy bird, perched on shoulder or wrist—he spied larger beasts striding along—a brace of greyhounds, a dwarf bear, a tawny-spotted black leopard. He wondered where the owners exercised them. They expressed an arrogant opulence.

Basically, though, Proserpina was Lunarian, akin to the Centaurian habitations—tiers of slender arches, beneath ceilings in which mirages played colorful; ornaments fantastic or subtle; parks where outsize flowers bloomed under soaring low-gravity trees; intricately dancing fountains of water, fire, lightning; emblems on secretive doors; strange worksteads; a troupe of dancers, masked and plumed; pervasive fragrances and low plangency of music; no Terran bustle and babble, everything quiet, flowing like currents in a sea, but as intricately and with the same sense of underlying power and potential violence. Oh, Guthrie remembered, he remembered.

He came at last to the meeting place, at the end of a vaulted corridor that flickered with the illusion of blue flames and nacreous wings. His escort left him at a doorway curtained by water falling with dreamlike slowness and foaming off down a channel in which swam phosphorescent snakes. The cataract stopped as he drew near and began again when he had passed through. The room beyond was surprisingly small and intimate, ceiling alabaster, walls covered with gold leaf and studded with gems in calligraphic patterns. Perhaps the door at the opposite end led to something larger, or to a labyrinth. A table of lacy-thin metal bore a wine carafe, goblets and a bowl of fruit. Three stood waiting.

One glided forth and made salute. "Honor is yours, donrai, captain, emissary," he greeted. "After these many years, we joy at this fulfillment. I am Velir, the present Convener, who receives you on behalf of all Proserpina."

The Centaurians had told Guthrie what little they knew about him—seigneur in Phyle Aulinn, Warder of Zamok Drakon, shareholder in ships and industrial centers, a strength buttressed through his wives and other alliances—a spacefarer in his youth, scout around Mars and even, it was said, Earth—ruthless, which one in his position must be, but self-controlled and pragmatic—suspicious of the Synesis to the point of hostility, but maybe a little more realistic about it than would completely suit Guthrie's purposes. In his nineties, he was heavier than the average Lunarian, almost portly, with amber skin, grizzled black hair, Roman nose, brown eyes very steady. His garb was rather plain, purple tunic, black hose, white shoes and belt, but on his breast hung a diamond the size of his fist.

"Let me present you to my colleagues," he went on. "Catoul of Phyle Randai, who attends for the Consultancy." That one was middle-aged, muscular, clad in scarlet, his expression withdrawn and wary. "Luaine of Phyle Janou, Wardress of Zamok Gora, who attends for the Captains of the Outer Comets." She was lean, red-haired, keen-featured. Diffracted light went in rainbow ripples over her floor-length gown.

Of course, Guthrie thought. In a territory this far-flung, the chieftains wouldn't trust their big cheese to talk with me alone, when they know damn near nothing about my aims or powers. Also, if Velir's policies have suffered a reversal or two lately—and as of nine years ago, it looked like they might—he could be sitting a bit shaky in the saddle.

Guthrie bowed to them. "Well beheld," he said. "Forgive me if I'm not courtly. I never learned how.''

Luaine smiled. ''Much else have you learned, sauvin,'' she murmured. The honorific, connoting wisdom as well as importance, was higher than the common ''donrai,'' whose literal meaning was simply ''lord/lady,'' like ''señor'' or ''Herr.''

Controlling the image of his human countenance, Guthrie smiled back. ''Gracias. I hope to learn more while I'm here, and maybe get something done about it.''

''So strong and distinguished a guest,'' said Catoul. ''What scathe that we cannot better comfort and pleasure you.'' Did his tone carry a hint of dislike, or perhaps uneasiness in the presence of a machine being? ''What we can offer that you may desire, that you shall have.''

Guthrie shaped a grin. ''Anything whatsoever?''

''Nay, a few exceptions,'' laughed Velir. ''But come, let us converse at ease.''

Gracefully and graciously, the Lunarians poured wine for themselves, toasted him, exchanged words about his home on Amaterasu and theirs in these deeps, as if this were a social occasion.

It was Luaine who finally nudged it toward business. ''And how fare they at Centauri?'' she asked.

''You'd know better than me,'' Guthrie said. ''I've been out of the game for a long while. Nor do I have a lot of information about you folks; and as for what's going on in the rest of the Solar System, I'm plain ignorant.''

''Then what do you think you can accomplish?'' demanded Velir. His phrasing was less blunt than that, but clearly Catoul didn't like his straightforward style.

''Look,'' Guthrie said, ''suppose I lay out the obvious, and we'll cut down on the pussyfooting.'' He left the last word in Anglo. ''It's evident that something mighty big is in the works—or else is being kept under the hatch. The involvement of a gravitational lens suggests it has implications going way beyond the local planets, out into the galaxy. And then the cybercosm, and the whole status of humans on Earth, Luna, Mars—Terrans especially, my native breed—on Amaterasu we don't know a gap-toothed byte about it, and I believe we'd better. So I've come to collect some on-the-spot information.''

"We shall be more than pleased to provide it," said Velir. "Be prepared to spend considerable time. There is much to convey, eyach, very much."

"But you'll not be content to sit and blot up our version," Luaine foresaw. "Not you, Anson Guthrie."

"Gracias for saying it for me, my lady," the download replied. "Yes, I will want to look around on my own."

"And act on your own?" murmured Catoul.

"We'll see. Needless to say, I won't do anything against your interests."

" 'Interest' is a matter of interpretation."

Luaine raised a hand. "Hold," she said. "Guthrie, I will put a spacecraft and crew at your disposal."

Velir narrowed his eyes. "Nay," he stated softly. "You will not."

Jealousy? Suspicion?

"Gracias," Guthrie told them, "but that's not necessary. Just refuel my cruiser and I'll get about handily by myself."

"Indeed—" breathed Luaine.

Velir donned courtesy. "That is easier wished for than done, sauvin. You must be aware that we have no access to the energies the sun lavishes on Mercury. For us, antimatter production depends on fusion plants. It is costly, and scant in volume. We require the all too precious material for the enterprises by which we live, with a reserve for emergencies and defense."

"Defense against who?" Guthrie countered. What attack was possible across hundreds of astronomical units? Even c-ships with nuclear warheads would be detectable in plenty of time to intercept. And would the Synesis ever make war? Could it? Not without the cybercosm to help. Every drop of knowledge about the cybercosm that had trickled to him over the centuries pointed to a rationality and a—morality—transcending the human.

"Maychance you will come to understand the answer to that," Velir said.

The implication is, it's pretty tricky, Guthrie thought. Could well be.

"I'll listen, sure," he answered. "I'll read your summaries, watch your presentations, take your tours, whatever you want. Above all, I'd like to talk with people. Many assorted kinds of people." He paused. "But I tell you fair and square, I want my ship refueled, and not simply for a voyage home. It'll be to your advantage too, my lady and lords. Maybe more than we can guess today. I'll be working to make you agree."

Or make the right one of you agree, he thought. Or somebody else who can swing it for me. Intrigue ahead, lots of quiet deviltry, and possibly some not so quiet.

18

A BOAT LEFT *Mālōlo* and skimmed off across open sea. Before long the great hull had dropped under the horizon, and Fenn and Wanika were alone. It was a gentle day, cloudless except for a snowy bank in the west, a breeze barely ruffling the backs of low swells. Glitter played over changeable blues. A single albatross cruised on high, incredibly white. Man and woman sat in the cockpit, feeling sunshine in their blood and salt in their breath.

Fenn broke a lengthy silence. "This was a good idea, taking off by ourselves. I'm glad you thought of it." He spoke uncomfortably, trying for cordiality.

Wanika smiled a little. "I hope you'll remember."

"I will, I will. It's dry where I'm going."

The smile died. "But it's not Earth."

"What do you mean?" He heard how he snapped the question.

She looked off into the distance. "Mars—space—where you've always had your home. Though you've never wanted a home, not really. Will you ever come back here?"

"Why, uh, of course. I'll have to, won't I? For business connected with the project. And then, this"—he gestured at the splendor around them—"and, and the people, my friends, you've all been so kind to me—"

She sighed. "Yes, no doubt you would like to pay us an occasional visit."

Exasperation scratched him. "What are you talking about?"

Her eyes sought him again. "You've no idea when you'll be returning, or how or if, but you're not the least concerned," she said calmly enough. "Your anchor is up and your sails are set."

To see that she was pained stoked his annoyance. Why in death's name should she be, and what was he supposed to do about it? He replied with care. "Naturally, I'm eager to be off. What an adventure!"

Just the utterance made him feel better. The persuading of Manu Kelani and other key leaders among the Lahui Kuikawa; their discreet negotiations with officers of the Synesis; and now, now, after week upon week, tomorrow lay before him.

Yesterday Iokepa, who had been a mainstay throughout, gave a party to celebrate success. In spite of detoxer, an aftermath lingered in Fenn's head. It must be what made him edgy—not anything Wanika had said or done—mustn't it?

He decided he should add, "But I wish you were coming along."

Her voice stayed level. "No, you don't."

"Oh, well, uh, true, you're not qualified. And it could maybe get a millismidgen dangerous."

Distress broke forth. "More than that, I'm afraid. Rebellion and plotting and that secret the cybercosm's keeping from us—" Wanika swallowed. "Keeping it from us for our sakes, I do believe. You're wrong, wrong to want to violate it.''

Fenn hung onto his temper. ''Look,'' he said, ''I'm simply going to Mars to investigate. It's got to be done, after the latest news we've received, and I'm best suited to it—in fact, the only one suited in the whole flapping Lahui. We can't go ahead with the Deimos project, we can't do a quantum-hop thing, till we have some notion of what the situation is and what's likely to happen next. If we hang around on Earth waiting and trusting, our people will lose heart, our investors will back out, and your entire bloody hope of getting into space will go on the rocks.''

''Yes, I know, I've heard it plenty often, and I still think we shouldn't keep the information to ourselves, we few—the ship from Centauri, the Proserpinans, the lens being somehow important—The world should know.''

''The cybercosm doesn't seem to agree. How many humans in the Synesis directorates have been briefed? Half a dozen at most, I'll bet. And in this case, I'm not objecting, at least not till we have more knowledge. What'd the consequences be of an immediate general release?''

She nodded. ''Unforeseeable. Especially among the radicals and dements.'' Her tone softened. ''It was fine of you to . . . avenge . . . He'o the way you did. I had been lying awake nights, terrified.''

''Of what?''

''Of what you might actually do. But you didn't. You're a good man, an honorable man.'' She reached across the cockpit to lay a hand over his. ''We can trust you with this mission.''

''*Mahalo*. Thank you,'' he said, wondering why he felt slightly ashamed. ''I'll do my best.''

''And afterward—if you find everything can be cleared up?''

''We'll have to wait and see.''

Her hand withdrew. Her voice went flat. "What we'll see is you on Mars, to stay."

"That depends. No foretelling. I should think I'd at least have to come back with the ship." Try for peace. "Whatever happens, though, Wanika, let me say, well, we've had our grand times, you and I, haven't we? You've been a great friend."

"Friend," she whispered.

After a second, she raised her head and smiled afresh. The breeze gusted, stirred her dark tresses, tickled his beard. "We have this day and evening yet. Let's enjoy them."

Relief brought happiness. "Absolutely. Best offer I've had since the last one like it."

"That's why I wanted us to spend the time on this boat," she told him. "Here's where we first came together, do you remember?"

In her era, the spaceship was proud and a wonder, a torchcraft capable of high acceleration for as long as reaction mass and energizing antimatter held out, like a fiery lance flung at the stars. She was small, for she bore no common cargoes, but rather humans and special consignments that must cross an interplanetary reach fast. Meanwhile, her recyclers, homeostats, and protection systems kept her riders comfortable, except under heavy boost. Obedient to the pilot's orders, the central robotic brain carried out all actual observation, computation, and maneuvers; sometimes it suggested or warned against a course of action. Whatever it did was done with incredible speed and precision. A flying dream made metal, Fenn thought.

Yet in a way it had brought about its own end. When a robot performed so well, why have a pilot? For undertakings that might require more than algorithmic judgment, give command to a sophotect. There was in any event nothing left for humans to do in space that machines could not do better. The single justification for their being on Luna and Mars was that that was where some chose to live. Let robotic vessels serve their transport needs. And thus the crewed ships were piecemeal converted, unless they were dismantled. A very few remained in groundside storage or out-of-the-way orbits—historical relics, objects of a sentimentality that dwindled away over the generations until hardly anyone was even aware of them.

Lahui agents had appealed to what traces of that emotion were left when they sought to buy two or three of the craft. More accurately, when counselors in the Synesis tried to persuade them that their enterprise was fatuous and foredoomed, they threatened such an appeal. No law forbade what they had in mind, and an increased public interest in it could further destabilize the troubled societies of Earth. The Synesis yielded and made the transaction, quietly, and machines gave the Lahui the help to which they were entitled in refurbishing the old travelers.

Release of antimatter to power them was something else. That terrible stuff must always be under the strictest control. Moreover, although production had resumed, this was because demand had; experimentation and exploration consumed most. The minor quantities that ordinary vessels burned came from a reserve accumulated earlier, and it, while still large, was not infinite. If the Lahui wanted to send a man back to Mars, let him take the regular carrier, as he had done before.

Negotiating, Iokepa Hakawau pointed out, with profanity, that this time—for reasons he was not required to state but that appeared fairly obvious—their man could not wait a year for the next flight. As for safety, the software in the robot, which could not be altered or replaced without triggering a burnout of the robot itself, would never obey an order that had any reasonable probability of endangering others. The sales contract had stipulated that the ship was to be used and the necessary services would be available. Did the spokespeople of the

Synesis wish to go to mediation? It would be quite a story in the news.

Grudgingly, they compromised. They would sell as much fuel as the scheduled carrier spent on a trip to and fro. Since she was considerably larger and heavier laden, the Lahui vessel would have more delta v than the carrier by a factor of six or better, depending on load. That was insufficient to make this far longer journey at anything like the same continuous acceleration, but the Lahui must not demand total indulgence of their impatience.

Time was slipping through Iokepa's fingers. He swore many new oaths and agreed.

Thus Fenn boarded the ship hopefully renamed *'Ātafa*, "Frigate Bird," knowing that he would not make a quick transit. Given the present configuration of the planets, his best plan was to use relatively high boost at short, critical periods and otherwise let gravitation move him. At first he didn't care. Yes, almost three weeks before he saw Kinna—before he saw Mars again; but he would be in space, at his own helm, voyaging! His heart drummed and sang like a lover's.

Outward bound, he saw Earth rimmed with sunrise. It waxed in phase as he fared, blue-and-white glorious, and dwindled in sight until it was a star among the stars, with Luna a wan companion. Thrust ended and he swam weightless. "On course and all well," the ship told him.

"Steady as she goes." He laughed aloud.

Hours became daycycles. Familiar with microgravity, he had never before been in it for a really extended span. Medication curbed the bad effects, he slept well and his dreams were generally pleasant, but there was scant room inboard to frolic and nobody to do it with. The ship could converse, virtually like a person, but her range of topics was limited and centuries outdated; often he found what she said incomprehensible. He had ample books, shows, and music to play, he had a dreambox, but he was born unable to be passively entertained without frequent active breaks. He exercised more than necessary for musculoskeletal maintenance, and was glad he had brought along several handicraft kits. Even when pieces bobbed off into the air, it was a welcome diversion.

He was in space, and he would not trade; but ever more he remembered the seas of Earth, wind in a sail, waves thunderous, and the thrum of a tiller beneath his hand. When you get right down to the bones of the matter, he thought, the only meaning the universe has comes from whatever is alive.

On a hyperbolic orbit prudently clear of the sun, 'Ātafa rounded perihelion and jetted to adjust her vector prior to continuing on trajectory. The navigation display showed a red spark that was Mars.

A while afterward, the ship reported that she was crossing a communication beam between the planet and an L–4 relay to Earth. Would Fenn care to tune in?

Would he! He had had no news since his departure.

What he heard in the beginning were faint clicks and beeps, incidental overtones as machines talked to machines. But before he lost contact, he caught a human voice. A fair number of people liked to know what was going on elsewhere and expected a daily account. Already the face Fenn saw in the screen was dim and wavery, but the words came through.

Maddeningly, they referred in passing to events that had taken place while he had traveled deaf. He gathered that the outlaws of Tharsis had attempted to capture the Star Net Station on Pavonis Mons, for reasons uncertain but surely unsane, and had been repulsed by the robotic defenses with regrettable casualties. The House of Ethnoi, bitterly divided between Terran and Lunarian delegates, was debating whether to organize an expedition that might—or might not—quell them once for all.

The program went on to other items. Soon the ship left the beam. Reception faded out. Fenn cursed for minutes and beat his fist against a bulkhead till pain made him stop. The joy in his mission was turned to starkness.

Calming a bit, he considered reboosting. He could arrive much sooner. But no, by now the difference wasn't what it would have been if he'd used more thrust earlier. Without a nova-strong reason, he ought not to squander the delta v needed to bring this ship home. She belonged to the Lahui Kuikawa, who trusted him.

Well, he thought, the gear I had Iokepa get for me, that nobody else knows about, looks like it'll see use.

19

STARS AND THE Milky Way surrounded *Dagny* where she drifted. Sensors of quantum-level sensitivity watched over her solitude. They caught only the gleam of the remote sun, the low seething of the cosmos, and, within the hull, those beats and pulses that betokened life.

Luaine of Phyle Janou, Wardress of Zamok Gora, gave herself a push. With free-fall grace she arrowed from the passageway into the common room, caught a handhold, and poised in midair. Red locks floated loose about features that might have been carved in ivory; her body rested long, slender, form-fittingly black-clad.

The room was sparsely outfitted. Crewfolk once gathered here, but Guthrie had scrapped their decorations and most of their furnishings. The overhead still displayed a simulacrum of the sky outside, stellar brightnesses enhanced so that, no matter interior illumination, eyes dwelt on glory. It limned the woman for him as he entered after her, himself like an elfland knight in plate armor that soared. For a moment, silence cupped them in its hands.

"Then this is what they gave you," she murmured, "yonder." Her head nodded at one brilliant spark, Alpha Centauri's image.

"What do you think of it?" he asked.

They could have held their private meeting in a vessel of hers, but she had wanted to inspect his in detail. The desire was natural. She belonged among the seigneurs of the outer comets, who passed much of their lives aboard ship. On Proserpina she spoke for them, and they wanted her to bring knowledge back. Guthrie had just finished giving her what he called the grand tour.

"It fascinates," she said. "The differences in design from ours—foremost, the weapons."

"Are they so special?"—two small naval lasers, four machine guns, a few tactical nuclear-tipped missiles plus launcher. "I explained before, the retrofit was only in the hope that if things somehow got really hairy, I could fight my way clear, in order to make tracks for elsewhere. Nobody had any bilgewater sloshing around in his skull about how I could prevail over any serious attackers."

She ignored his Anglo archaisms, which she doubtless didn't understand. "Nay, their design, I said," she crooned. "Touches of a beauty strange to me."

Like a mogul and a samurai admiring each other's swords, he thought. Yeah, I guess that on average we humans always have put as much love into our weapons as into anything else.

Aloud: "I expected the differences in the ship herself would be more interesting, my lady. They come from different needs, after all. For instance, the Centaurians not living as far-flung as you people do, but wanting more agility, what with all the rocks now flying around in their system."

Her green glance dwelt on him. "Need alone? What is due simple happenstance, and what is the expression of a civilization, a spirit, no longer ours? One wonders."

Her switch to a philosophical mood could have disconcerted him in his Terran embodiment. Machine, he fell effortlessly in with her. A part of him stood aside, observer and pilot. His objective was to sound her out. To that end, he should humor her for this while. "Cultures do change," he agreed. "How like your ancestors on Luna are you?"

She grinned. Self-mockery? He couldn't tell. "Maychance less than we fondly believe."

"And my race," Guthrie's mortal species, "we're taking off in our assorted directions too. We're not the same at Amaterasu, Isis, and Hestia."

Her tone went grave, her gaze searched. "Not even you, the eternal captain, nor the incarnations of the Mother?"

"I think not. Not any longer. Though across lightyears, it gets hard to know. Someday I'd like to go in person, this person," this line of memory and personality that zigzagged through the manifold branchings of himself, "and find out."

Find an answer to that question, and to infinite others. The hugeness, diversity, mystery of the universe through space, through time. What was coming into being as he talked, what joys, triumphs, griefs, horrors, creations—what life?

"Here you begin," Luaine said low.

He could not bow in microgravity but he saluted. "Thanks to your help, my lady."

He spoke truth. She, wielding her influence as a surgical program wields a scalpel, had had the most to do with getting *Dagny* refueled. Some Selenarchs remained hostile to the whole idea.

"It was not given on impulse, Captain Guthrie," she said slowly.

The face he generated in his turret formed a smile. "Sure. I knew that. You hope for some return on the investment. I hope I'll be able to oblige."

Luaine turned her head to and fro, as if she could see through to the ends of the hull. "This powerful instrumentality," she breathed, "and you yourself, an unknown quantity—unknown also to the cybercosm, to the very Teramind—might you be victorious where we have failed?"

"You mean the solar lens, don't you?" He was aware that she and her associates had been at the forefront of

Proserpinan efforts to hunt out the secret. Something akin to a nerve-tingle passed along his neural network.

Her look swung back to him. "What else? For a beginning, maychance for more." Fiercely: "It is your venture too. Would you see humankind, both humankinds, in the freedom of the stars? Then we must know what awaits us, and why the cybercosm wills that we not know."

"If it does."

"*It*, yes! Terrans could never keep silence so long about something so meaning-laden. Eyach, a few, few chosen ones can, utterly subservient to their Synesis." Contempt poisoned the last word.

"They don't consider themselves subservient, do they? You're speaking of trustees and other such panjandrums."

"Nay, they choose to obey. They are worshipers, as in ancient times. The name of their god is Teramind."

Guthrie's organometallic shoulders could not properly shrug. He spread fingers in the Lunarian equivalent of the gesture. "Maybe." She's prejudiced, he thought. Nevertheless—"But what do you suppose the lenses have discovered?"

"The lens, one particular lens," she corrected him. "It has acquired much the most, if not entirely all. We have become sure of that, at the least. You have heard."

This time he vocalized a sigh. "Look, my lady, I'm a stranger here yet, and I've been almighty busy with a cramload of assorted concerns. Learning my way around has been just one of them, and others, like arguing and dickering with a dozen different jefes, have kept interfering with it. I've simply not had a chance to give the lens business any special attention."

She seemed a little startled. "Ey, is it not the steepest of the gradients that drew you hither?"

He shook his wraith-head. "Not exactly. It's one part of our overall need to know what the hell's gone on in the Solar System during all those centuries incommunicado. But, true, it does appear important. I do want to hear more about it.''

''You shall, you shall.''

''What say you explain the situation as you see it?'' he proposed. ''Never mind if you repeat what I've already heard. That can help put it in context for me, like scattered bricks getting picked up and mortared together to make a house.''

''Will you understand why that house bears the shape it does?''

''I'll try. Uh, you needn't go into the theory, of course, nor the layout, unless it's changed since I got my briefing at Alpha Centauri.'' With electrophotonic speed, his mind reviewed them.

Einstein first found it, in the mathematics of his general relativity: mass determines the metric of space-time, and thereby arises the phenomenon we call gravitation. This curves the trajectories not only of matter but of radiation. The confirmation was triumphant when astronomers measured a predicted slight displacement of stars in the field of view near the eclipsed sun. By the mid-twentieth century they were observing how galaxies act as enormous, irregular lenses to produce multiple images, distorted but enhanced, of objects far behind them. Not long afterward, they were detecting dark bodies within our own galaxy by the effects of these on the stellar background.

But the sun is also a gravitational lens! Nearly spherical, it has little aberration. From this fact and certain calculations sprang a wonderful dream. The closest focal points are five hundred and fifty astronomical units outward, a fraction over three light-days—however, well within the Solar System. Let us send spacecraft there. We can do it by gravity assists, solar sails, magnetic sails. The journey will take about fifty years, but along the way the instruments will gather a rich harvest of data on solar wind, parallaxes, and who can foretell what else? Indeed, it should be worth going farther than the minimum distance, both to continue the secondary investigations and to gain added image size while reducing interference by the solar corona.

Finally the craft will reach their destinations. The orbits they take up will be comparable to those of comets in the Kuiper Belt, although not necessarily in the same plane as any. The observatories will deploy their equipment to peer in the direction of the sun and on into the universe beyond, transmitting the data home to Earth.

What knowledge they may win is incredible. Assuming the minimum distance or a trifle more, and a modest 12-meter antenna, the angular resolution at the 1,420-megahertz frequency of neutral hydrogen is on the order of several microarcseconds. Translated into spatial terms, this means that the observatory can resolve—distinguish from its surroundings—an object at Alpha Centauri as small as 1,250 kilometers across. At ten parsecs, 32.6 light-years, it can pick out 9,580-kilometer sizes. Ten kiloparsecs away, at the galactic nucleus, it can see something less than 10 million kilometers wide.

This improves proportionately as frequency increases. At optical wavelengths, it could theoretically detect a human body near Alpha Centauri, a fifteen-kilometer asteroid or island near galactic center, individual continents on planets in the Andromeda galaxy.

No one gave serious thought to such extravagances. They went beyond any feasibility, and perhaps beyond what natural law might allow. For a single example out of many, consider that the observatory is in orbit. Slowly though it moves, it is never at rest, and so neither is its line of sight. The farther it is looking, the fainter are the signals it receives, and the faster they sweep through its field of view—which becomes ever narrower as resolution increases. There will simply not be enough time to catch enough photons to identify anything too small or too remote at frequencies too high.

The dreamers would be satisfied with radio waves. Those were already opening fabulous vistas to them; the shape of the galaxy, the births and lives and deaths of stars, the titanic clouds and the ghost-winds between, pulsars and quasars and aliennesses untold—out to the rim of observable space and the dawn of observable time. To those among them who listened for word of sentience elsewhere, radio waves seemed most likely to bear it, someday, somehow. Send forth the observers whose instrument would be the sun!

In particular, one that established itself in the sky—as seen from Earth—between the horns of the Bull, a little south of Elnath, would be on a line between Sol and the center of the galaxy. It would be looking at hordes of stars. We live in the outskirts, where they are thinning away into emptiness. The galactic heart is enormous. This observatory could scan it for a long time indeed before orbital motion, very slow at that distance from the sun, carried it out of the field. Surely its laser sendings back to Earth would tell of new marvel after marvel, maybe even, at last, signs of other minds than ours.

Let the thing be done.

In the event, it did not happen soon, nor all at once. The human space endeavor came near dying soon after it was born. Crewed missions grew scanty, and support was slight for a project whose time until fruition reached beyond the life expectancy of influential scientists. When Fireball Enterprises kindled fresh vitality, there was at first too much else to do. But later, Juliana Guthrie took up the idea. She had no difficulty in persuading her husband.

By then, propulsion systems were available, efficient and economical, that enabled the craft to make their passages in years rather than decades. One did end in Taurus, near the star Elnath, about six hundred astronomical units out. Several others went into different sectors. And what they revealed was as enlightening as hoped for—

—although never a clear trace of intelligence.

Yes, they located planets of remote suns, far more than any optical system had done, and they carried out spectroscopic analyses with far higher precision. But the atmospheres they found that were in disequilibrium, let alone those that had free oxygen, could be counted on an astronomer's fingers. If life was this rare, humankind might well have the sole consciousness in the galaxy. Or in the universe?

It did not discourage Guthrie. He was a stubborn sort. Yet it caused general interest to flag; and meanwhile, troubles came upon him and the world. When at last his download must lead his dissenters to Alpha Centauri, and Fireball dissolved, the lenses got no more attention.

(This was, of course, a misnomer. Sol was the only lens. However, comparison of the gravitational observatories to the eyepieces of refracting telescopes had been inevitable.)

They were made to require little maintenance, and infrequently, but now that little was denied them. The World Federation was preoccupied with urgent matters closer to home. The project was never formally terminated, but its resumption kept being postponed until it was well-nigh forgotten. Power sources ran down; radiation and quantum effects gnawed away. One by one, the lenses died.

Sophotects came into being. As their intelligence grew, so did their underlying unity. The mesh of computers and effectors that pervaded civilization evolved into the cybercosm. Ever more, in its quiet fashion, it undertook scientific research, which ever fewer humans cared to do.

This was not quite the paradox it appeared. Conventional wisdom held that science had reached its end point generations ago. The great equation from which every law of physics could be derived was in existence. Its solutions described the origin and ultimate fate of all that was, all that could ever be. True, not many of these solutions had actually been worked out, and of those that had, only rather special cases were fully comprehensible by mortals. Still, any observation that might be made would have a basic explanation; and the Teramind understood the grand design.

Admittedly, more often than not, calculation was impossible. The principles of chaos and complexity took over. One could always find surprises in every field from archaeology to practical astronomy. Most humans had come to regard these as trivial, unworthy of a deep thinker. The cybercosm did not. It had the resources, including a kind of personal immortality, to investigate the realm of the empirical.

Eventually it proposed establishing a new set of solar lenses. The Synesis assented. People remembered that the destruction of Demeter was imminent; they heard rumors of contact between Proserpina and Centauri; suddenly the stars mattered to them again.

Naturally, the task was entrusted to the cybercosm. Terrans had no reason to visit those abysses beyond Pluto. Weak flesh and fallible brains would merely get in the way of the work.

Machines went forth. They demolished the old, dead observatories and replaced them with the new. These were immensely improved in sensitivity, spectral range, and every other capability. Each had its own power-plant, maintenance machines, and directing intelligence. That intelligence was dedicated, closely specialized—nevertheless, a conscious mind. Should any of the two-score assemblages in their widely canted orbits find treasure, more would follow.

Data flowed afresh. Human scientists who eagerly studied the reports were not disappointed when they saw nothing fundamentally new. They had not expected it; the great equation did not allow for it. To map the dispersions of the galaxies, to limn the structures of those farthest away in space and time and thus to trace their evolution, to probe the reaches of our own and its sisters more deeply and fully than before: these achievements sufficed—

—until the data stream began to sputter with anomalies, unaccountable, and dwindled to a trickle of routine follow-ups, and presently dried up altogether.

On Earth, Luna, and Mars nearly everyone accepted the explanation that the cybercosm itself had no immediate explanation, and intellectual prudence required a halt in publication until the riddle was solved. The lenses would continue their searches and transmissions, but for the time being report only to other sophotects. Humans should not waste any of their all too short lifespans futilely fretting or puzzling over this. They had plenty of information to keep them busy, were they so inclined. People had grown used to trusting intellects superior to their own.

Lunarians had not, nor had the Terrans beyond the Solar System; but only on Proserpina and its comet colonies were they near enough to feel rebellious. They got hold of everything the lenses had given to the databases—bit by bit, with considerable trouble through a lengthy stretch of time—and ransacked it over and over. As analysis proceeded, it pointed to the Elnath unit as the wellspring of the mystery. There the first inexplicable readings had been taken; there open communication first ended; there the instruments pointed toward the galactic nucleus, its crowding stars and veiling dust clouds, less known to this day than neighbor galaxies seen from outside.

Always suspicious, the Selenarchs had never found it reasonable that the cybercosm would withhold observations simply because they were enigmatic. If the great equation proved in need of amendment, what harm in that? Or . . . what promise, which the Teramind did not want humans to know of, lest they become like it?

The Selenarchs determined to find out for themselves.

"What ken have you of our attempts to orbit a lens?" Luaine asked.

"Not much," Guthrie admitted. "I've gathered that two different tries, decades apart, failed, and you Proserpinans claim it was due to sabotage. But was it?"

"Why think you otherwise?"

"Well, I do know something about how tough the job is and what it costs—resources and skilled man-years that have plenty of call on them elsewhere. To match the ones in existence, you have to push the very limits of the associated technologies. It was never possible at Alpha Centauri, what with three suns waltzing around twisting gravity fields and orbits. So far we've put just four out around Beta Hydri, using the original Fireball design because we weren't up to developing anything better. They've been useful, but they cover mighty small patches of sky, and they haven't done more than add details to what our other apparatuses show. Nobody's yet managed anything similar at Isis or Hestia, unless it's happened since last I heard from them."

"Ai, yes," said Luaine impatiently. "But hear. Our first lens, which had been painstaking years in the making, was outbound when its carrier was wrecked, and it therewith. The cause seemed to be collision with a rock. How likely is that? Besides the sheer volume of yon spaces, to have sufficient speed, the rock must have been a stray out of the interstellar deeps. Few like that have we ever noted, Guthrie."

His image-head nodded. He had heard this before from others. Let her talk, though. A Lunarian could want to get something off her chest, the same as a Terran.

"In the second instance," she went on, "the lens took orbit as planned, well away from the Synesis' but aimed likewise at mid-galaxy. While undergoing its initial tests and calibrations, of a sudden it failed, ceased utterly to function. It must be brought back, at high cost in time and fuel, for examination."

There would have been no sophotects on the spot to do that, Guthrie reflected; the Proserpinans refused to have any capable enough. A manned lab in the vicinity would have been too expensive. Antimatter for engines was quite a bottleneck when you lacked access to the facilities on Mercury and must produce the stuff with thermonuclear reactors. Luaine had really had to work and connive to get *Dagny* supplied.

"They found that a defective interfacing, miscrystallized, had led to derangement of the programming matrix," she said. "How could such a piece have passed every beforehand inspection? But a robotic device, closing in on the assembly while it fared goalward, and applying a minute amount of energy *so*—" She snapped thumb and forefinger together, a savage, scissoring gesture.

"I've heard this," he replied. "Also that you decided not to try again, for a while, anyhow. You think the cybercosm's got you under too close a surveillance?"

"Eyach, its minimachines cannot be everywhere, nor scan everything," she said: due to limitations of size, speed, communication, and related factors. "Intermittent spying at a few key points is amply bad."

Lunarians wouldn't go in for tight security, Guthrie thought. Too restrictive of them. "Well, I've considered that sort of possibility, even for us way out at our suns. It's one of the reasons I came here. But let's get on with the story. I've heard only a little about the rest of it."

"This daywatch I shall tell you. It became chiefly the venture of the Captains of the Outer Comets."

"You planned a frontal attack, to try and find out directly what the secret is."

"Yes. We prepared for years, with utmost care against spies. We knew we would have but the single opportunity. Thereafter the enemy would be fully alert."

While Guthrie had his own reservations about Synesis and cybercosm, it troubled him to hear her say "enemy." But never mind for now. "You meant to strike at the lens you felt sure would hold the information."

"Yes. The Orion lens." Seen from Proserpina, the watcher of the galactic nucleus was not in Taurus.

"Uh-huh. And your expedition found the cybercosm had anticipated you and the target was well defended."

Luaine arched her back like an angry cat. *"Raiach!"* Her features congealed in self-possession. "I will show you."

Somehow she produced a datacard from her skin-snug garment. Deft as a hawk, she swooped to place it in the multiceiver. The screen went black and starry.

A lean shape swam into sight, a field-drive speedster seen from a distance. "Our ship," Luaine explained. Her words came flat, metallic. "The crew released several self-propelled cameras, which transmitted back to them. This is a compilation."

The view moved around to the solar lens. Guthrie had studied the plans, which were published when the system was authorized. Nonetheless, his gaze raked what he saw. Faerie beauty, an intricate, silvery-gleaming spiderweb of antennae and cables, ringed and dwarfed a golden-hued spheroid that housed the maintenance machines, attitude controls, and powerplant. From it swelled a bubble, opalescent in the star-sheen, a dome protecting the observatory proper. He could just make out an access port at its base.

Three sparks left the ship and drifted across the constellations toward the lens. A camera zoomed in on them and magnified. From small bodies sprang arrays of sensors and effectors. "Robots," sounded Luaine's toneless voice. "They were redundantly versatile and well-programmed; entry and readout should be simple for them. But we wanted full preparation against contingencies. The crew stayed in direct communication, with override controls."

The robots drew nearer their quarry. Guthrie deemed it was about time for them to reactivate their jets and start approach maneuvers. They did not. Abruptly inert, they drifted on past the web and vanished into darkness.

Consternation resounded on the audio. Luaine tuned it down. "The robots ceased to function," she said, still like another machine. "They no longer responded to signals or commands. Instruments aboard ship registered electromagnetic pulses, with a high intensity in the region they were crossing when the failure occurred.''

Guthrie had expected that conclusion. ''Yeah. The station's sophotect ordered the output, heterodyned so as to be at max exactly there. Induced currents and magnetic transients, powerful enough to act through metal and scramble the electronics and electrophotonics inside, disabling anything that depended on those circuits—which would be just about everything. Your boys ought to be thankful they didn't bring their ship any closer, though I doubt they felt that way.''

''They had been cautious. A few minutes afterward—'' Luaine raised audio volume again.

The radio voice that the Proserpinans had received and recorded rang in their own language, cool, a sexless tenor, obviously synthesized. ''Attention. You have attempted a criminal act and seen its immediate consequences. This was no reaction to a surprise. Your vessel was detected and trailed almost from its departure point. You were allowed to come this far that the unattainability of your ambition might be demonstrated to you. If you return at once, the Synesis will regard your vain expenditure as an adequate punishment. Otherwise, armed guardian craft will arrive very shortly and destroy you. Best you go home and warn your co-conspirators to desist.''

The Proserpinan ship lingered for a bit—Guthrie could imagine the tigerish defiantness aboard—but only for a bit. A camera captured a moving spot of light and magnified, as the ship's optics doubtless also did. Though of lesser size, the oncoming vessel was under field drive and carried unmistakable missile launchers. Another dot appeared among the background stars. The Proserpinans swung about and accelerated away.

The screen blanked.

''A bitter choice their obedience was,'' Luaine said.

Guthrie saw no defeat upon her. The green eyes blazed

at him. "Have you and your friends wondered what else you might try?" he asked softly.

She nodded. Her locks tumbled in the air like flames. "Most surely we have. But we saw no way . . . hitherto."

His memory went back to rough-and-tumble days in his first incarnation, his first youth, knocking about odd corners of Earth. It ranged on through centuries that had also known strife, danger, and scheming. Morality slipped aside for the moment. This situation was too interesting as a problem.

"Hm," he murmured. "On the evidence, if that machine wasn't lying, and I don't think it was—on the evidence, the cybercosm's got boats patrolling those spaces. Radar and other kinds of detectors would alert them a monstrous ways off to somebody who was bound in a suspicious direction. But by the same token, those boats must be awfully dispersed. I'd guess that only two or three, at most, could intercept a given bandit, if the bandit had field-drive legs. A properly outfitted raider might hope to get through."

"Nay," she said, "the warders cannot reasonably await any such." Her manner was less that of a person arguing against him than of one listing an item for the sake of completeness.

"True," Guthrie agreed. "A ship that could evade or outfight them would need a sophotect, an electrophotonic brain, at the controls. No human reacts or calculates fast enough. A robot can, but it doesn't have adequate judgment—imagination, trickiness. And you Proserpinans want no part of any sophotect with any real wits."

"If we built one, would we dare trust it?"

"Maybe not, even discounting your paranoia. It might reason its way to fellow feeling for its fellow machines— or, anyhow, to the logic of what and why they are—and decide to throw in with them. Moot point. Proserpina hasn't got the means or the technicians to make any and educate them right. It'd take you a generation, at least, to become able."

She threw back her head and laughed aloud. "No need, Captain Guthrie. You are that machine!"

He had seen it coming, but pretended astonishment. "Huh? Wait a minute, my lady—"

Her body quivered, her words leaped. "You have the intelligence, skill, cunning. Linked with the computer-effector system of this your ship, you will have the precision and speed of reaction. And you are armed."

"I—supposing I wanted to try it, when I got in range of that field and it turned on, I'd burn out like those poor robots, and so would *Dagny* if I was inside. No, thanks."

"You can lie to, safely distant, while a human makes entry."

"You know somebody that dement?"

Laughter slashed anew. "I cannot count how many would vie for the part."

"Well, yes, Lunarians," he conceded. "Wild by nature. Plus having your Proserpinan grudges."

"It would be easy to modify a spacesuit and its gear so that the field does not disable it. I have had my engineers draw up the specifications."

Optimistic, weren't you? he thought. "Once this burglar has landed, what then?"

"My folk have prepared a briefing for him." She took out another datacard and thrust it into his hands. "The information is all here. Play it. Study it. Then ask me what questions you like, but I think they will be few. The plans of the lenses, their programs, everything about them was made public when they were first built. There is no sign of any important alterations afterward, save in the defense and the encryption of the transmissions. Nor would the cybercosm have cause to order any, now that it has mounted guard on them. The observations they sent before the silence fell gives abundance of clues to how they operate—and how to take their truth-hoards out of them. The operation is, in fact, simple."

"M-m, maybe. But look, the maneuvers to dodge or fight the interceptors would almost certainly involve heavy accelerations. I doubt a Lunarian could take them and arrive in shape to steal a beetle from a kitten.''

"We will solve that too," she snapped. "I have given it thought."

He lifted a palm. "Wait a minute. 'We' will solve it? You're taking for granted I'll buy into your escapade?''

"That is why I bargained, conspired, and strove to get you your fuel," she answered sharply.

"Yes, I understand, and please don't think me ungrateful. However, I made no promises except that I won't turn on you Proserpinans and do something that'd harm your interests. I haven't said I'd be *with* you."

Her voice, her whole manner, warmed. She smiled, reached as if to touch him, and purred, "Yet you will be, nay? Ever was Anson Guthrie a man of daring."

Middle-aged though she was, in his flesh he would have been hard put to resist. In the event, he could reply dryly, "Never was Anson Guthrie a man who'd draw to an inside straight."

She didn't catch the ancient Anglo reference. "It is for your own cause also."

"I'm not at all sure about that. My mission is to find out the facts. A hostile act like this against the Synesis—which hasn't done my folk any harm that I know of—would make interviews with its officers kind of awkward."

She stiffened. "Is the withholding of vital data a friendly act on its part?"

"I don't know. Maybe I should go ask."

Her mask cracked apart. Wide-eyed, open-mouthed, she stared at him and gasped, "You cannot be serious!"

"Oh, I can be as serious as a parson on Sunday," he drawled. "Not that I'll walk right into the Teramind's parlor. But neither will I rush into what may prove to be a socialism-sized blunder. My job is to learn what's what, and it takes priority." He paused. "Sorry."

"You would—"

"I'll go sniff around in the inner System for a while. Then we'll see."

Her eyes narrowed. "We will see whether you may depart," she said, dangerously quiet. "Armed craft of mine are nigh."

The face in his turret smiled. "So are armed craft of Velir, who, I regret to say, doesn't trust you very much, and Catoul, who thinks it would be a good idea to investigate current affairs on Earth and that I may be the best one to do it. Before joining you today, my lady, I had some interesting talks with them and a few other gents."

Luaine shuddered, once, relaxed, and laughed again, low, almost merrily. "You win this trial, lord. My fault. I should have studied the history of Fireball more closely. Now I see, too late, how the living Anson Guthrie wrought what he wrought."

20

THE HOUSE ABOVE Crommelin admitted Fenn. He entered the living room and stopped. For a moment, there where mathematical patterns wove their slow dance, he loomed over the little man who had risen to meet him. Silence filled the air like a presence. Then Chuan bowed and said, "Greetings," in Anglo. "You are early, but not the less welcome."

"I came straight from the spaceport, after I found your message waiting for me," Fenn replied. His tone was as stiff as his posture.

"Really, that was not necessary. You could have gone to your lodgings and had a night's rest first. I sent you an invitation, not a summons."

Fenn raised his brows. What was the difference? he implied.

Chuan continued, unruffled, "I meant, also, that you are early in a more basic sense. We had not looked for you before next year. Your friends on Mars will be pleased."

"They know, same as you knew in advance, I was coming, and why." Fenn's intention had been quite open on Earth—he could hardly have kept it secret if he had wanted to—and his call to the Ronays had not been confidential.

The messages between him and Kinna had been encrypted. They might now have been tapped and decoded. When he thought about that possibility, fury rose in him. Calm down, boy, he told himself. If ever you needed a clear head, you do today.

"Yes," Chuan said, turned grave. "You and your people felt you must promptly have more knowledge of the situation on this planet and how the arrival of a ship from Alpha Centauri will affect it. This was the more so because the Synesis did not release the information until it had reached you indirectly, and you were getting excited about it, even though our instruments must have detected it many months ago. You wonder what the reasons for that delay were, and how they may affect your plans."

"Isn't that natural? Wouldn't you have?"

Chuan recovered his smile. "Come, please be seated and we will talk. Will you take refreshment?"

Fenn hesitated.

"I am not your enemy, you know," Chuan said.

"Yes, sure, I know," answered Fenn, caught off balance. Do I? he wondered. And: Better lighten up a bit. "All right, gracias, I will drink your beer."

Chuan chuckled. "And nibble my salted canapés, no?"

They settled into the sensuously self-molding chairs. Fenn's glance strayed out the broad viewport. Autumn had faded the flower garden, but it was going into winter phase, deep purple and black. The sky was dark for noontide, rose rather than salmon, and a few ice-clouds trailed their streamers past the sun. The upward reaching of towers and masts in the city was a somehow forlorn gallantry.

The servitor brought a tray. Chuan raised his goblet of wine. Had he chosen that, rather than tea as before, to seem friendlier? "Your well-being," he proposed.

"Clear orbits," Fenn responded.

The one-time toast of Terran wayfarers was not lost on the synnoiont, who regarded him for a second or two before saying, "It would be conventional for me to inquire whether you had a pleasant voyage. But it would be a trifle ridiculous, would it not? You realized your lifelong dream."

"No," Fenn told him.

"I am sorry. May I ask why?"

"I wasn't flying free. I was just being carried. And the news that came was no fun at all."

"Ah," said Chuan most quietly. "The hideous news. You received it en route?"

Fenn nodded. "And acquired more while closing in on Mars. Not enough, though. Not a fraction enough. It alone would have brought me here at this time." He thumped his beer mug onto the table beside him and hunched forward. "Yes, I'm being rude, consider me apologizing, but can we get down to business? Why did you want to see me so soon?"

"In aid of your mission. You seek to gather facts. Very well, I would like to offer you information you cannot readily obtain elsewhere, and try to answer any questions that occur to you."

"Getting in ahead of everybody who might have different opinions?" Fenn retorted on impulse. Immediately he realized he was verging on insolence, but decided not to beg pardon. He did shape a smile of sorts.

"Please. I will not insult your intelligence by going over ground we have already covered at wearisome length. At least I will try not to repeat those arguments more than seems required to put matters in context."

"Gracias," was the only thing Fenn could think to say.

"Please realize as well, I am not privy to your councils in the Lahui Kuikawa. There has been no spying, no interception."

Again Fenn wondered. Kinna and her parents called Chuan an honorable man, but honor is subject to interpretation.

"However, neither have you people made any special attempt at secrecy, am I correct?" the synnoiont continued. "From what is said and done, one may draw conclusions. Events of the past few years have inevitably raised concerns among you. You have felt increasingly uneasy as word and rumor spread about Proserpina, Alpha Centauri, what is going on in space. As I said, you want to know how this will affect you and your ambitions. Authoritative voices in the Synesis have frankly tried to persuade you to drop them. Could we, those whom I represent, be plotting actions more drastic? The turbulence among the Martians themselves is another cause of unease on your part. Between them, the Republic's occupation of the Threedom and the Synesis' reticence about the Centaurian ship decided you Lahui on a special investigation. You are the one who is to conduct it. The incident at Pavonis Mons has heightened your worry and—if I may say what I suspect—your anger." He shook his head. "I cannot promise to ease your mind entirely. But I do sincerely want to prove that I, speaking for the cybercosm and, humbly, for the Teramind, I am your well-wisher."

"Gracias," Fenn repeated. He believed what he had heard. Maybe that was the truly damnable part. "Go ahead . . . sir."

"The Synesis has explained why it did not immediately make known to everyone that a vessel approaching from beyond the Solar System had been detected. The explanation is as true as it is simple. Nothing more than the bare fact was known. The outsider was clearly bound for Proserpina and had made no effort to communicate with us or respond to our transmissions. Nor did the Proserpinans reply to our inquiries. We still have not learned more. In view of the tensions, instabilities, and falsehoods that have become so prevalent, the judgment was that an announcement at this stage would be premature and might well have unfortunate consequences. This may have been a mistake. When the news escaped regardless, it heightened unfounded suspicions of the whole social-guidance system.''

''Like your secrecy about the solar lenses.''

Chuan frowned. ''That is not the same thing at all.''

''Maybe not. It's provoked something worse than the ship has or ever could.''

Chuan's tone flattened. ''To say an action was provoked is to imply it had some justice, some degree of validity. What brought on the tragedy at Pavonis Mons was a cynical manipulation.''

''That's one of the things I'm supposed to find out about.''

''I can show you scenes. You will not enjoy them.''

''I wouldn't expect to.''

''They were taken unobtrusively or invisibly, not by humans, but by impersonal machines and sensors.''

Yes, Fenn thought, telemonitors, monitors hidden or disguised, monitors too small to be seen without a microscope. How many of them, throughout the Solar System and even beyond? He quelled an inward shiver.

''They have been edited, merely for clarity,'' Chuan said. ''If you doubt that unbiased reporting is possible, let me point out that the mind behind those observers and this editing is not human. It may have missed something significant, on that account or by chance, but it has no more misrepresented or suppressed data than any other scientist would.''

Unsure how to argue with that, Fenn waited.

''Let us proceed chronologically,'' Chuan proposed. ''Before coming to the terrible event, you should have a little of the background, of what led up to it.'' He took a control pad from beneath his robe and fingered a command. A service table rolled in bearing a multiceiver. "Audiovisual should suffice for the present. You can have full vivifer later if you wish, and many more recordings. Here are only a few typical occurrences in the Threedom and its hinterlands."

The screen came awake with a Lunarian town—dusty pavement, buildings of rough-hewn stone rising gaunt to observation balconies and high, steep roofs, airlocks marked with the emblems of phyles and seldom opened to outsiders. Fenn recognized Daunan; Kinna had shown him images. A troop of constabulary passed through, newly arrived, vehicles rolling along at a bare six kilometers per hour, skinsuited men flanking them with weapons ready, everyone Terran. Everyone. The streets were empty of inhabitants; the occupiers moved as if among tombs. Whoever watched from the houses, in rage as cold as the oncoming night, gave no sign of themselves.

Afterward, life perforce resumed. A pair of young constables with some free time ventured into the market hall, where most everyday business took place. Arcades lined the interior with graceful pillars and doorways. The ceiling displayed animations of flying things, fantastical birds, dragons, comets, flowers that used their petals for wings. People moved about, buying, selling, eating, drinking, gambling, creating, a changeable human spectrum. When the Terrans appeared, faces froze for an instant. Then, one by one, the Lunarians recommenced what they had been at. It was if no newcomers existed. When they tried to purchase an object or two, souvenirs, the shopkeepers stared through them and made no reply. But the background music had changed from a lilt to a throbbing and snarling. The young men soon gave up and left.

"This treatment has been virtually unanimous—and spontaneous, from the outset," Chuan remarked. "It could not have happened quite like this with our race."

"What about Lunarians elsewhere?" Fenn asked.

"None who are in the constabulary were ordered to join the occupation force, and none volunteered. Nevertheless, you probably know Mars is in no danger of civil war. The ordinary Lunarian has no special ties to anyone in the Threedom and is not greatly concerned, except for an innate suspiciousness about the Republic in general. S/he is much less tribal by nature than the average Terran. Some, including a sufficient number in the House of Ethnoi, agreed that the occupation had become an unfortunate necessity. They are more wary of that unknown quantity, Proserpina.

"But the dwellers in the Threedom are without mercy."

The view moved to a car lying wrecked in the desert. Out on patrol through country unfamiliar to them, the two men aboard had not recognized the hillside down which they started for what it was. Dust below a solid-seeming thin layer of rock and packed sand abruptly avalanched. Smashed open, the car barely stuck out of a new red dune. The Terrans had of course been skinsuited and helmeted, but one was unconscious and his comrade, who had dragged him clear, had broken a leg. A Lunarian on a groundcycle had seen from a distance. He approached. The constable waved to him. He drove off. The constable screamed.

Either the car had managed to call for help or the unseen observer did. A flitter from Arainn got there in time.

"A limited amount of discussion and cooperation is unavoidable," Chuan said.

Now Fenn saw brief samples of talks between officers of the Republic and seigneurs of the Threedom. It was polite; the Terrans attempted amicability. They repeated promises made at the outset. The occupation had been ordered reluctantly, after no choice remained. Its forces respected individual rights and would act promptly upon any complaint. Its purpose was only to end the lawlessness and intrigue that were hurting this region the worst, so that Martians of both races could meet the problems and dangers they had in common. Otherwise no one desired or intended to thrust change upon the ancient ways of the folk. When the basic objective was achieved, the constables would go home. They certainly longed to. The collaboration of the dwellers would hasten that happy day.

The seigneurs gave assent to various practical, interim measures. They made no further commitments.

The last preliminary scene showed the last convoy of carriers that had tried to cross Tharsis on the ground. Corpses lay strewn among blackened, twisted hulks. Behind them, the hills out of which the guerrillas had struck rose dark, tortuous, riddled and seamed with hiding places, toward Arsia Mons and a sky the color of clotting blood.

Chuan switched off. "The Inrai," he said, expressionless, but his voice whetted thin. "A few of those dead were theirs, but that did not deter them afterward. It made them worse at the time, in their fury. At least I hope it was only rage, revengefulness for fallen comrades."

" 'Only' rage?" Fenn asked. "What do you mean?"

Chuan pinched his lips together before he replied, not altogether levelly. "Five of the officers guarding the convoy were women. Two of their bodies were found. The other three have not been heard from. What doubtless happened would be—even more dreadful for Martian than for most Terrestrial or Selenite women. Cultural attitudes, so ingrained they are like instincts—" He sighed. "We don't suppose they lived long."

Sick anger thickened in Fenn's own throat. Such cases were rare where he came from, but he had dealt with a couple of them when he was in the police. "Why don't you—the Republic—why don't they send out armed aircraft and hunt those animals down?"

Chuan, gone outwardly calm again, regarded him somberly. "We are civilized here," he said.

Yes, Fenn thought, those men I helped arrest on Luna,

if I must call them men, they just went into correction. And . . . at the end, I couldn't make myself do anything else about Pedro Dover.

"The Republic is also constrained by the fact that this is not habitual practice," Chuan proceeded. "By all accounts, the Inrai leaders do their best to maintain a standard of basic decency, like some armies in history. They do not always succeed.

"If we—let me say 'we' for the officials of the Republic and those officers of the Synesis, like myself, who give them what assistance is possible—if we could identify the guilty individuals, they would certainly receive the strictest treatment. If correction didn't work, and I don't think it would without complete demolition of personality, they would never again be at liberty. But how shall we find them? We cannot seize and interrogate random persons until we get a clue. That would undermine the entire Covenant, the social contract by which we live.

"It is the situation, Fenn, the abominable situation. It is the kind of thing that went over and over through the uncontrolled past, like a plague, deforming what it did not destroy. Violence feeds on itself. Atrocities become inevitable. The Inrai think of themselves as fighting for the right. So do the local Lunarians who give them aid and comfort. In fact, the Inrai come back from the wilderness at intervals and take up their open lives, pretending they were never gone. Their neighbors join in the pretense. Don't you see what incitement and opportunity this gives to the extremists, the moral monsters, among them, those whom war always attracts?"

A part of the turmoil in Fenn jumped against the other man. "Within your legal limits, couldn't you do better police work?" he demanded. "That includes surveillance and intelligence. How tight a spy net do you actually have?"

Chuan sighed. "Nowhere near what I personally wish for. We have caught a few, but few and rarely. The manifold troubles throughout the Solar System have stretched our resources thin. Besides, total surveillance is illegal and would be impolitic. It would cost us friends while strengthening enmities."

If people found out, Fenn thought.

"I trust you have seen why the Republic cannot yet withdraw its forces," Chuan said. "You will certainly hear likewise from most of your Martian acquaintances. But you will also hear that more and more of them, including Terrans, have come to believe the occupation was, on balance, a mistake, and is making a bad business worse. The law of unintended consequences."

"Riding the tiger, yeh," Fenn mumbled.

"If only it were that simple and safe. True, since their disaster on Pavonis Mons, the outlaws have not done anything overt. But the attitude of the townspeople, which was beginning to thaw, is again glacial. And what kinds of revenge are the bereaved families and phyles brewing? How badly broken down is Inrai discipline? From what we have been able to learn, their high chief Scorian has very little control left over his scattered survivors.

"If you want to understand our dilemma, you must see the event that has so heightened it." Chuan's countenance hardened. "Please brace yourself. What follows is horror."

"The attack on the Star Net Station?"

"Yes. The Inrai collected their army and brought it up under cover of a prolonged dust storm. They knew none of our satellites or aircraft had radar to penetrate that thick a blanket. Lunarians in the House of Ethnoi have always blocked any move to establish an adequate survey system, although the lack of one has cost lives that could otherwise have been saved. Privacy is a fine ideal, but any ideal can be carried too far.

"Well, I shall not preach. The storm also prevented such observers as we had on the ground from functioning effectively. They were sparse and limited in any case, being tiny and unable to move fast across large distances.

We knew something was afoot, but could not tell what, and the assault took us by surprise.''

"The Inrai were well organized, then. Better than might be expected from that many Lunarians acting together.''

"Everything we have learned about Scorian shows he is a remarkable man.''

We, Fenn thought. This synnoiont may not officially be with the police or any other agency of the Republic, but he's involved in almost everything, because he's integral with the cybercosm and it's integral with the Synesis. He just said as much to me.

Aloud: "So he wouldn't have charged ahead blind. He must have collected intelligence beforehand, known pretty well what he'd encounter and what his followers could do about it.''

The tingle in Fenn's skin as he spoke, straining to keep his face calm and his voice even, became lightninglike when Chuan replied, "That was not difficult. There was no secret about the general layout of the station. It was described in the news at the time of construction, and it has since had visitors. After all, it is of public interest, and we were sensitive to attitudes in the Threedom. Full reporting should help allay local suspicion and resentment. Or so we hoped.

"Ordinarily, protection amounts to little more than a fence and a gate, with sensors, certain effectors, and their auxiliary equipment. In case of trouble, the system will communicate with the nearest constabulary base, which can dispatch whatever airborne personnel may be needed. The single important secret is the code required for entry. Everyone assumed these precautions would be ample. Who could have anticipated as desperate a venture as this?''

The information was nothing new to Fenn; he had retrieved it before he left Earth, but to hear it confirmed hardened his resolve. "Evidently Scorian planned to capture the site and stand off any effort to take it back,'' he said, pleased at how cool he sounded. "The police don't have a lot in the way of weapons."

"Few were required before," Chuan answered sadly.

"Which made it possible for the Inrai to collect, or make, an arsenal equal to theirs in that sector, or superior," Fenn deduced. "The Republic as a whole had assembled more force to bring the Threedom to heel, but it would be largely tied down. Oh, Scorian couldn't hope to hold out very long, by himself, but he might for long enough to accomplish whatever he had in mind. Then it turned out the place was better defended than he knew. By what?"

This had not been in the database on Earth, nor on the later broadcasts he had heard thus far. Fenn tautened where he sat.

"You . . . shall . . . see." Chuan set his jaw and thumbed the control. What cameras already on the spot had recorded sprang to view.

The scene became a rock shelf, about a kilometer long and half as wide, jutting from the flank of the mighty volcano. Upward behind it, downward in front, landscape tumbled away in black desolation, weirdly pocked and riven, against a sky gone murrey. Seen from a distance, the Star Net Station showed small: a domed building, a sensory mesh, and a radio telescope, huddled within a high barrier of chain link. Alongside were a landing strip and a hemicylindrical hangar. Lapping almost to the shelf, blurring the approaches nearby and hiding them farther down, billowed a rusty tide, the top of a giant dust storm. Fenn imagined he could hear the tenuous wind of Mars keening and feel a cold that would have embrittled his bones.

Yes, he thought, the constabulary had been pretty well blinded. Hitherto, orbiting observers, overflights, and robotic spies on the ground had enabled it to keep track of any concentrations of guerrillas. Scorian's forces had moved as individuals or in little squads, using the jumbled terrain and tricks of camouflage to stay unobserved, striking from their lurking places and quickly disappearing again. They were born and bred to this kind of country. Nonetheless, Scorian had gotten them so well integrated that when the opportunity came, they swiftly joined together and launched their attack.

Fenn had had a minor experience of a dust storm when one caught him and Kinna on an excursion. It had resembled the smoke he remembered, blown off a forest fire in Vernal. A monster like this that he now watched would veil a huge region from all spaceborne instruments except for some the Republic did not possess. It would hopelessly handicap small, slow surface monitors. Just the same—Slag and slaughter! he thought. The guts of those men!

Well, they were Lunarians. They liked crazy gambles. And here they came.

At first hazy to sight, then suddenly clear, they burst from the dry, red sea and scrambled on upward, a hundred or more of them in skinsuits, burdened with biostats, rations, and weapons. Incredible that they could move so fast, so well-ranked, under a gravity two and a half times that of Earth's Moon. Their heritage from Terran forebears, back to apes in the jungle and hunters on the Ice Age steppe. . . . Audio quivered with appeals from the station director, in language after language, "Who are you, what are you doing, stop, you are in violation of law, please stop and depart before you come to harm—"

Flame streamed and burst. A section of fence peeled back. A rocket, an explosive warhead? "Halt," the synthetic voice pleaded, "go back, you are in danger of your lives."

Another missile blasted, and another. The Inrai dashed toward the breaches. Radio carried their calls. They did not yell or cheer, they sang, each man his own savage and wordless chant.

Before they reached the fence, pale blue fire sprang into being around it. Where that flickering touched the forefront of the invaders, men died. Suits split open and bodies burst asunder. Those at their backs tumbled, sprattled, and lay still; steam clouded their helmets, they cooked, faces reddened and swelled, then collapsed and charred. Men farther to the rear slowed, gone clumsy, as if they had plunged into glue. They pulled free and retreated from the ghostly wall.

A part of Fenn took note of every detail he could catch. A larger part fought nausea. He forced the vomit back down his gullet, but for two or three minutes, chills racked him. And a final part admired the decisiveness with which the remaining Inrai withdrew into the storm. Scorian was quite a bravo. Fenn wanted to meet him sometime, and envied Kinna that she had done so.

The screen blanked anew. Chuan's words came as if from afar, harshly reined in: "Our observers gathered what data they were able. Subsequently, our intelligence efforts have added a little information. Apparently the survivors straggled back toward their camps or the towns. Some perished along the way. This was a disaster for the Inrai. They may have lost a full half their strength, on the mountain and in the retreat through the desert. Discreet investigation in the towns has shown that many are disheartened and have resigned from further effort. Bands skulk about yet, the irreconcilables, more vengeful than ever. Whether Scorian can rally them and make them the nucleus of a new army, we do not know, but we dare hope not."

"What *was* that defense?" Fenn choked. "No kind of gun."

He heard the pain: "Certainly not. Do you imagine, can you imagine, we ever wanted anyone killed? That the news never mentioned the possibility was an oversight." By human journalists, Fenn supposed, though sophotects on the same intellectual level weren't infallible either. "Nobody conceived of an eventuality like this. The defense was against remote contingencies, such as a meteorite impact. Mars gets more than its share, you know, out of the Asteroid Belt, punching through the thin atmosphere. If such an object was detected, a magneto-hydrodynamic force-field would be generated before it struck.''

The sickness in Fenn gave way to awe. He whistled. ''Whew! What a piece of engineering.''

Spacecraft used the same thing in principle. Anyhow, they did when they carried humans and particle radiation threatened to become heavy. But it was only ions and electrons speeding through a hard vacuum. He had heard that field-drive ships, moving at substantial fractions of light velocity, required more protection than that. Pulsed electromagnetic forces, as precise and complex as they were powerful, laid hold of atoms and molecules by their weak polarities and deflected them.

But to stop tonnes at a time—Well, the generator on Pavonis wasn't going anywhere. It could be as big and massive as called for. Nevertheless, it represented an incredible accomplishment. And the cybercosm had designed and built it almost casually, maybe just for this single place.

''The waves are phased to form what amounts to a quasi-solid hemispherical shell,'' Chuan said. That much was obvious. Perhaps he needed a banality or two. ''Tragically, the attack was so sudden and so fast that many men were already in that zone.''

Fenn gave him a stare. ''The station director could have left the field off and let them go in.''

Chuan shook his head. ''The director is a robot, of high order but without a conscious mind's capacity for judgment, and this was an emergency. By now, of course, the fence has been repaired and the program changed to give it more . . . discretion.'' He seemed to force the next words out. ''However, a sophotect would have issued the same order, and the same doctrine still holds. The installation itself may not be worth a single human life, but the principle and the implications are crucial.''

Fenn reckoned his best bet was to go back to the occurrence. "Why did they make that maniac try, anyhow? Do you know?"

"Yes, somewhat." Chuan sounded less miserable. He was about to justify what had happened. "It bears out our policy. You may understand this better than I, for you are . . . completely human."

"What do you mean?"

"Let me show you. Be warned, you could find it still worse than what you saw before."

The screen re-created aircraft landing. Robots, a few men, and a couple of sophotects in machine bodies got out. They went among the piled-up dead. (No Inrai were merely wounded; damage to suits or biostats was lethal too.) Views closed in on hands searching through effects—a note scribbled on paper; entries evoked on palmtop electronic slates: Lunarian language, very brief, but clues.

A laboratory. Brains in chemical baths, pierced by tubes and wires; displays on screens; fragmentary phrases croaked by a voice synthesizer. Through nightmare, Fenn heard Chuan explaining: "The corpses were freezing by the time the police arrived. Where cells had not been roasted, ice crystals had disrupted them, including the cerebral. No revival was possible. But partial memory traces were left. They could be activated and, to a degree, interpreted. I emphasize, nothing was alive. What you see here was not torture, not interrogation. It was like playing a badly damaged recording. You must believe that. If you do not, ask a neurophysiologist, or consult the public database on the subject."

"Oh, I believe," Fenn mumbled. "I know that much biomedicine."

The screen blanked. He let out his breath. When he inhaled, he smelled the cold sweat on his skin.

"I think you need more beer, plus something stronger," Chuan said low.

Fenn nodded. "It'd help."

The servitor brought drinks that included akvavit.

Chuan stayed with his light wine. Fenn thought that maybe the synnoiont had gone over the material often enough, and in such detail, that he had a certain amount of scar tissue on his spirit.

After a silence, Chuan offered, "You may have transcripts of this, or of the complete file, with translations of the Lunarian, if you want to examine them for yourself."

Fenn grimaced. "No, I don't, if you'll tell me what it all means."

"I shall." Chuan had regained calm, although to Fenn it had a taint of the machine in it. "The impetus for the raid came from outside. Granted, the Inrai had motivation beforehand. To seize that alien building on the mountain, *their* mountain, whether then to hold or destroy it, would be a powerful symbolic victory. It would fan the guttering fires of resistance throughout the Threedom, strengthen hostility elsewhere on Mars, and shake the Synesis on Earth. However, Scorian would probably not have tried it had he not received a message from far Proserpina.

"We know from our orbitals that a small, ultrafast vessel, a so-called *c*-ship, necessarily robotic but very well-programmed, had swooped in, passed above Tharsis, and swept back into outer space. We had nothing available that could give chase. It doubtless beamed a communication down, compressed data, which the outlaws doubtless had means to receive. But what?

"From the material we collected after the attack, incomplete and often incoherent though it is, and from various other intelligence, we have developed a fairly clear idea of the content. The Proserpinans—or, rather, whatever coalition of them is behind this—urged the action and promised help if it was successful." Chuan lifted a hand to forestall any objection. "No, not direct military help. The absurdity of that would be self-evident, also to Scorian. But pressure could be put on the Synesis. That could include Proserpinan ships openly coming to the inner Solar System in numbers, as they have every legal right to do. They would assist in uncovering the truth and proclaiming it to all humanity. The Synesis, confronted by general outrage and questioning, would have to make concessions, or more than concessions.''

He drank of his wine. ''The truth?'' Fenn urged.

Chuan met his gaze squarely. ''The fact that lies hidden in the Star Net databases, including the one on Pavonis Mons. What the solar lenses have discovered. The Proserpinans insist it must be something tremendous, about which the cybercosm and its few human confidants are lying. They claim that the failure of their own attempts to run the same search was due to sabotage by robots of the cybercosm, which strives to keep the secret because revelation would be disastrous to it.''

''And Scorian bought this?'' Fenn scowled, tugged his beard, and muttered, ''Hm, well, I'm not intimately acquainted with any Lunarians, but I can imagine how he might.''

Ask Kinna for her opinion. Thought of her brightened the whole wretched picture.

Chuan nodded. ''Indeed. The Proserpinans coldbloodedly egged the Inrai on to what proved to be destruction. What had the Proserpinans to lose? In earlier eras, any government would have considered an incitement like theirs an act of war. Without the moderating influence of the cybercosm, even the Synesis might be planning retaliation.''

Fenn gnawed his lip. ''M-m-m.''

''This deed is only the latest cause for distrust. Was it really wrong to hold back the news about the ship from Centauri? That ship is bound for Proserpina. What may it portend?''

''Are you saying you—you actually want to play the story down, not to turn the public against Proserpina?''

''What would such a feeling accomplish except to make still more difficult the negotiations we hope for, to settle those old disputes and grievances?''

Fenn sat mute.

"Think, I beg you," Chuan urged. "Here you have seen the kind of instability and consequent grisliness that the Synesis exists to prevent—an ancient horror brought from its grave back into history, like famine or servitude or unfree speech."

"A filthy business, aye," Fenn growled.

"Do you and your peaceful, happy Lahui Kuikawa truly wish to get involved in such things? You will, if you carry out your colonizing project. It is inescapable. I tried to persuade you of that in our earlier meetings, and failed. Perhaps now you will admit that my arguments may possibly have had some merit. Whether you do or not, I hope you will counsel your friends to suspend operations until this crisis has passed, and then reconsider their dream."

"When will that be? If we don't start soon, everything will come apart for us and we'll never go to space."

Chuan's face seemed to say that he would share the sorrow. And yet he had told Fenn, as he had told Kinna and everyone else who would listen, that Earth was the only true home for humans and that mind, the growth of the intellect and spirit, was the only true frontier.

Fenn summoned up his innermost strength. "What is the secret?" he asked. "You must know."

Chuan went impassive. "It is nothing I can explain to you."

"Why not? Can't be just a scientific puzzle. That story never did ring true, and now, after what's happened, it's completely hollow. The cybercosm wouldn't go to extremes like that to head off intellectual confusion. It's hiding something from us."

"No. Not in that sense. Information is being withheld for compelling reasons. It *is* incomplete. Released in its present form, it would be totally misleading, and the consequences to society, to every human society, would be agonizing, perhaps catastrophic."

"In other words," Fenn snapped, "you—your precious cybercosm, its Teramind—you're treating us like not very bright children.''

Chuan shook his head. ''Untrue. It is a matter of responsibility.

''I grant you, humankind is still immature, in the sense of being far from having realized its full potentialities.'' His tone grew warmer. ''How could intellect, pure intellect, ever wish to do other than guard and foster its own development everywhere? You know how viciously ridiculous the old fears were, that sophotects would turn on us, to exterminate or enslave. It is not in their *nature*. Can you not see the more subtle point, that sophotects would never want humans stupefied either, placidly passive, incurious and uncreative? When the time is right, the truth will be made clear, and the hope is that it will not be terrifying but inspiring, liberating, glorious.''

''How long will that take?''

''There is no knowing. It may be as much as another century, or even two.''

''And meanwhile we're supposed to live and die ignorant? Why? What threat to you?''

Chuan's tranquillity broke. He sprang to his feet, fists clenched, trembling beneath his robe. ''Do you imagine the Teramind fears for itself?'' he cried. ''Do you imagine I enjoy seeing people I care about galled, frustrated, suspicious, angry? No, I will say this, Fenn, because I have said it before to a few others. It is a confession we would rather not make to the people at large. We fear for you—for humanity, Terran and Lunarian, for your Keiki Moana, for every mind we know that lives in an organic body. What we are searching for is hope—hope that we can give you. And this is all I will say about it!'' he nearly screamed. ''Do you hear? All!''

21

So AFTERWARD IT was with redoubled eagerness that Fenn hastened to meet Kinna. When the door of her apartment retracted, for that moment all doubts and fears and rage dropped from him; he knew only that she stood there. She shouted for joy and flung herself into his arms. The hug lasted awhile.

When they stepped back and looked at one another, he managed to say, "I'm sorry to be this late. The session took still longer than I expected."

"Y-you're not late," she stammered. "You're better'n half a year early."

Their messages across space had kept him well up on her appearance, but he had never seen her quite like this. A band of silver filigree clasped the brown locks; silver also was the brooch on an antique-style blue gown that embraced her slimness and flared its skirt halfway down the calves; silvery were her slippers. He fumbled for words. "What a, a grand sight. Like a princess out of history."

Her smile glowed. "Thank you, kind sir. It's not my usual rig, you know. Special for the occasion." She giggled. "I got my hair almost ruly. But you're the sight that's interesting. How *are* you, Fenn? How was your voyage? How did it go just now with Chuan?"

The darkness in him stirred. He thrust it back down. "We'll talk about such stuff later," he answered roughly. "This evening is for pleasure. Agreed?"

She swallowed once, above the pulse he saw fluttering at the base of her throat, before she gave him a new smile. "Agreed."

"Then suppose we head straight off to that dinner we planned."

"Well, we've been salivating about it over the laser beams for enough months. Onward." She signaled the door to shut and took his arm, another archaism preserved on Mars. He felt the touch all the way as they walked.

Xanadu Gardens lay on the edge of town, virtually a separate construction, terrace after hyalon-enclosed terrace rising up the inner wall of the crater until an observation tower lanced above the rim for a view across cultivated lowlands and scarred red desert. Night had fallen and a galaxy of lights had awakened, of every color, in strings and whorls along the fragrant paths, in hedges and trees, framing arches, irradiating fountains, cheerily blinking over dance floors and game parlors and fantasy rides, shining forth the names of restaurants, cantinas, food stalls, barely touching shadowed bowers where a couple might retreat. Music lilted from a hundred locations. Climbing sculptured staircases to the level they sought, Fenn and Kinna passed an open stage where a live ballet was being performed with a live orchestra. On another stage, Harlequin and Columbine frolicked through their immemorial pantomime. Folk strolled leisurely, uncrowded, enjoying an unreality older and wiser than any dailiness.

Fenn knew the Semiramis only by reputation, though that reputation extended around the planet—not that first-class live-service places were abundant anywhere. With Kinna he got a patio table. Jasmine in planters half screened it, white blossoms mingling their sweetness with sentimental background melodies. Near the parapet, which was near the terrace verge, it overlooked glitter and gaiety below. Above were the invisible roof, unbreathable thin air, and hidden stars, but no matter that.

The first sparkling wine arrived, accompanied by appetizers. Goblets clinked. "Here's to whatever," Kinna said.

"*Ola me manū.*"

They had been working hard to keep the mood happy,

but it was as if his Lahui response, unthinkingly given, cracked something. She sipped, set her drink down, and watched him for a silent span. "How long do you expect you'll be on Mars?" she asked.

He shrugged. "Depends on what I can find out, and how."

She achieved lightness in her tone. "Am I terribly selfish, hoping it won't go too fast?"

He felt the blood in his face, and made a chuckle. "Well, the temptation's strong to dawdle." Bleakness pushed through. "The job won't be easy in any case."

She glanced away, across the faerie lights into the night. "No. Not after what's happened."

"The, uh, the events lately—they haven't touched you have they?" He was not used to feeling anxious. "Directly, I mean."

She shook her head. "Elverir—my friends in Belgarre—none were at Pavonis Mons." Returning her gaze to him, she attempted a smile. "He's furious at not having been called." The smile faded. "And he's sad and—well, I'm sad too. Aren't we all?" She squared her shoulders, brought goblet to lips, and finished like a defiance: "But he is alive, unhurt, and I don't expect the Inrai will do anything reckless again for a long time. With luck, never."

"I'm glad . . . on your account."

She heard the grumpiness, reached to brush fingers over his hand, and said quickly, "But this is in danger of becoming serious. We swore we wouldn't let it. Not tonight."

He snatched at the chance. "Sorry. My fault. Let's stay with you. Tell me more about what you've been doing. A much more important subject. Importance is your department, not mine."

She actually laughed. "Are our eyes mirrors, bouncing the importance back and forth?"

If she could be merry, then, by death, so could he.

"What'd you call the quantum of importance, I wonder?"

"The meon," she replied at once. " 'Ion' is spoken for."

He let his mind free-fall. "I've seen mention of some people on ancient Earth called the Ionians. Did they buzz and crackle?"

"No. I've learned a bit of history too. The Ionians were seafarers—salts that got wet."

"How ionical." He hadn't known he could pun.

"Ooh. Let's not chárge onward." She drank. He drank. "But, you know," she offered, "I have seen somebody buzz and crackle."

"How?"

"Do you remember Taffimai Metallumai?"

"Of course. Your little half-wild robot. I don't forget anything having to do with you, Kinna."

He saw the color in her cheeks. Her glance flickered downward. Looking back up, she related: "It happened on my last vacation at home. I'd finally—you might say coaxed her to come into the house with me. She was awfully on guard. She hasn't any predators to worry about, you know, but her environment's treacherous and here was an otherworldly sort of place. Genghis John didn't appreciate the situation either. You haven't met him yet." He noticed that last word. "He's our newest cat, replacing poor old Torpid Francis. Suddenly he pounced on Taffy, with no good intentions. It was one spitting, whirling rumplosion over the floor. We, the family, we were horrified. Taffy's skin and 'wings' are so thin. If Genghis ripped her, the sharp edges could slash him, the dopants poison him. I jumped in and tried to pull them apart. Something that felt like a club knocked me halfway across the room. I vaguely saw Genghis boost off, yowling fit to split eardrums. His fur was standing straight out and I swear was full of sparks. Poor fellow, we found him afterward on top of the preservator in the kitchen. He wouldn't come down till we lured him with the ice cream we'd meant for our dessert. Taffy'd discharged her accumulators into him, and gotten me as well. She was very quiet and refined till we had her recharged—and outdoors again, to stay—but even while she sat there, I do believe I saw an extra gleam in her optics. Ion eyes—oh, excuse me. Be warned, though, since then Tessy—my younger sister, that is—delights in calling me Kinetic, the Current Affairs Expert.''

He joined in her mirth, and the meal went cheerily.

Hand in hand, they wandered the winding paths through the lights and revelry. When they found a bower that was unoccupied and Kinna asked, ''Why don't we sit here for a while and talk?'' Fenn's heart jumped. He told himself sternly that talk was what she meant, and wondered what he could say.

Trellises enclosed a space in vines and flowers, which also hung down over the entry. A bench stood in the dusk they made. Specks and rays of color slipped between leaves. The music, footfalls and voices passing, the cool song of a fountain, seemed all at once to come from far away. Or was it just that she was right at his side?

He turned his head toward her—shadow softened the fine-boned features—as hers was turning toward him. They glanced elsewhere in an unreasonable mutual shyness. He thought he'd better break the silence somehow. ''You'll soon graduate,'' he said, ''and here I am without a present for you.''

''Be there if you can,'' she requested. ''That'll be plenty.''

''I'll try.'' *How I'll try.* ''Uh, you'll go home afterward?''

''Naturally. I don't know how long I'll stay.''

''What?'' he exclaimed, surprised. ''I thought you intended—well—''

She nodded. Shimmers ran across her fillet. In spite of it, her hair was getting tousled again. ''Yes, I've said. The plan was that I'd put this knowledge I'm supposed to have blotted up to work on our land. Maybe eventually I'd take over entirely." A fist clenched on a knee. "But I don't know, Fenn. Not any more."

He realized that she wanted to confide in him. For a moment it was overwhelming. "May I ask why?" he heard himself respond.

She stared at the leaves and light-flecks. "There's no single reason. There are a lot, tangled together. My parents don't really need help. They won't for many years yet, and meanwhile my siblings are growing up, and one of them—looks like Jim right now, though at his age ambitions and dreams bounce around like molecules on springs—probably one, maybe two of them, will want to stay. And the holding shouldn't be divided, not after all these centuries."

Her sense of tradition, he thought. Her loyalty. "But why couldn't the bunch of you operate as a unit? You're a close-knit family." Another rare anachronism.

"Eyach, I wouldn't leave forever. I'd always visit, often. Sananton belongs in my life. But to belong completely to it, when everyplace else is astir with newness— I don't believe I can."

"I see."

Briefly, she caught his hand. "Of course you do. You'd never settle down like that. You want the stars."

"I think," he said slowly, "maybe I could . . . base the rest of my life on Mars."

Elation leaped in her voice. "You could, you could! Mars is a whole *world*, Fenn. You haven't seen the Argyre Wildlands or the Crystal City in Elysium or the midsummer rites going around the Dreamers' Craters— Wells, Weinbaum, Heinlein, all the dreamers—or, oh, so very much. I barely have. And I've not been *with* any of it; I've never truly known it from the inside. And now when everything's about to change, when your people are coming, with the unforeseeables that will bring—I want to be there. To be a part of it, to help, to share it with you."

His whole being longed to join that hopefulness. Honesty gripped him, and he must meet her eyes as he told her, "It might not be pleasant, Kinna. You might be glad of a safe harbor at Sananton, and I flaming glad you've got one."

Ardor answered; laughter bubbled beneath. "You don't mind the risks, do you? Then why should I? I'd rather be out where the fun is. Especially when it isn't just your sea people coming to us." If they are coming, he thought. She jolted him: "The stars are."

"What do you mean?"

"The star people, I should say."

"You mean that ship from Centauri at Proserpina? But we've heard nothing about it." Bitterness: "Nor would I expect those two packs of Lunarians to get open with us Terrans. Certainly not in my lifetime, considering the distances involved, the hiding that's possible." Alertness followed. "Unless you've gotten something lately from your own Lunarian friends?"

She shook her head. "No, nothing."

He sighed. "You hardly would have. What do they know? The Proserpinans used your Inrai, and the scheme failed. Why should they maintain contact?"

"Don't be cynical," she reproved him. "You're too good for it." Enthusiasm returned. "But that's beside the point. Fenn, I don't believe only Lunarians are involved, even ones from Centauri. I said the star people."

"What do you mean?" he repeated, bewildered.

She leaned closer. He felt her quick breath in his beard. "I've been thinking. That wasn't a *c*-ship, traveling close to light speed. We know this from the clues we've had from observation, now that those details have been released—the time it spent under way. Everybody's assumed it had a live Centaurian crew. In cold sleep, no doubt; Lunarians wouldn't take kindly to two or three decades cramped and crammed together. But does that really make sense? Why would they do it? What could they learn or gain that they couldn't get as well by communications, and a lot faster? A handful of strangers come to Proserpina would be—powerless.''

A bleak thrill passed through him. *She knows Lunarians better than anybody does nowadays on Earth or Luna,* he thought. *She can put herself in their minds.*

''But what if the crew isn't Centaurian at all?'' she went on.

He groped for understanding. ''Sophotects? The Centaurians may not have the Proserpinan fear of them.''

Once more Kinna shook her head. ''Maybe not. But I don't think they'd trust them that much, either. No.'' Her voice deepened. ''I've looked at the stars, year after year, especially since I met you and your wishes. I've picked out those where people are—Terrans—and I've decided they must surely know something about us by now. Enough to see how little it is they know, and how vital the truth is. Wouldn't *they* send someone to try and learn more?''

''But that ship came from Centauri,'' he protested. ''That's established. Isn't it?''

''Did the travelers aboard? Or did they simply come by way of Centauri? That'd make sense.''

''No, wait, the distances to their suns, even the nearest—They'd still be barely started.''

''Not if they went first to Centauri in a *c*-ship.''

''But that'd kill them. I've seen the calculations. No screen could fend off enough of what you encounter at that speed. Gamma cyclotron radiation alone would be lethal.''

''Not to downloads tucked away in thick lead boxes.''

He sat hammersmitten. ''In death's name—'' he whispered.

''The Terrans would've been in touch with the Centaurians ever since they left Demeter to found their new colonies. I think a few of them went back there to talk face-to-face, without years of time lag, and lay joint plans; and they persuaded the Centaurians to give them a bigger ship, slower but better equipped. Doesn't that fit the data, what few data we have?''

His mind surged. "They?" he coughed forth. "Or he?''

It was her turn to be taken aback. "He?"

"Anson Guthrie—" Common sense intervened. "But this is the wildest speculation.''

"We live in a wild universe," Kinna said. "Oh, yes, quite maybe I'm wrong. But if I'm not, then that strange ship won't stay too much longer out at Proserpina. Would you? Those are downloads of Terrans. Or a download of a Terran. Old Earth is calling.''

"You've set my head awhirl.''

She grinned. "That was the general idea.''

"I—I'd like to sleep on this. If I can sleep. And talk further with you tomorrow.''

"You name the hour; I'll cut the class," she said gladly. "Not that I'd be paying any particular attention anyway.''

Astonished, he discovered that the darkness had been shaken out of him. Or else her vision had hit him like the strongest euphoric, but left his brain as clear as space. The words rushed from him. "Right now, though—We weren't going to be serious this evening, were we? We've kept drifting that way, but thunder, we don't have to!''

"Yes, yes," she said, "let's keep our vow from here on.''

And they sprang up and ran out onto the path, laughing like children. They rode the whooparound and the Dragon Express and a real carousel and the boat that went on Alph the Sacred River; they danced the saturn on one floor, and on another she taught him to dance the volai; they drank beer and consumed improbable confections and got into conversation with a masquerier; they climbed the observation tower ramp and gazed out over twinkling homes and frosty fields and took the option of skating back down, and the gardens were closing when they left.

At that hour, no one else was going through Lyra Passage. They stood at her door, holding both hands, looking eyes into eyes, with nothing to trouble their silence but a rustle of ventilation. Once a maintainor rolled past. They barely noticed.

"Have a good night," he said at last. "Or, rather, a good morning."

"You too," she breathed. "Thank you for—for everything."

Then she was kissing him and he was kissing her and in the ceiling sky display the morning stars sang together.

"What a, a grand surprise," was all he could finally find to mumble.

"If you knew how long I've wanted to do that—how long I've wanted," she half sobbed.

"And I—but—"

"Come on inside." She signaled the door to retract and drew him along after her. It closed behind them.

He had been here twice before, briefly. This room gave on cubicles for bed, cuisinator, and sanitor. The floor was hard, though a gray-furred biocarpet relieved it. The furniture was sparse. But shelves held a glorious, gleaming collection of rocks, superb scenic views decorated the walls, and he knew what books, music, drama, and art she called up on her multi. It welcomed her home with a burst of ancient melody to which she had once introduced him—*Eine kleine Nachtmusik*, he recalled was the name.

Again they stood and looked.

"It is time to get serious," she told him. "I love you. I've been in love with you since we first met."

"And I . . ." he faltered. For him, it had gone more slowly. He had denied it, fought it, resigned himself to the futility of it. "I've felt that way about you—for a long while—more and more."

"I hoped. Oh, but I hoped."

"I didn't know."

"You do now," she said between laughter and tears.

How strange the universe felt. Not the same place any more, not in the least. Yet he was still Fenn. He couldn't change that, however much he might wish to. He was the one who ended this kiss and stepped back.

"We have to think," he growled. "It's a bad time for us. For everybody."

"You'll make it better."

"No, wait. I'm no hero or savior or any such fool thing."

Her voice calmed. "Maybe not. But you are a tough, smart, overly brave man, and I expect our sons will be absolute hellions."

"You're getting too far ahead of today, *makamaka*." The Lahui endearment, impulsively uttered, unleashed memories. He felt worthless, rammed the feeling down, but said more starkly than he had intended: "Don't invest in me. Not yet."

Immediately grave, she regarded him through several pulsebeats before she said, "You have something dangerous to do soon, don't you?"

His usual decisiveness failed him. "Well—"

"What is it?"

"I can't tell you."

"You jolly well can and will." She paused. "Not right away. Tomorrow, later today, is soon enough. We have this hour for our own."

"We aren't casual about our relationships," David Ronay had warned. "In fact, we're seldom impulsive about them. My daughter can roam freely with anyone she wants to because everybody who knows her knows she's our kind of person."

The father had been right, Fenn learned, and it was right to respect that code, because it was Kinna's too. It didn't seem easy for her either. But when he left, the false sky above the passage ruddy with sunrise, and the last thing she whispered to him in the doorway was, "On top of everything else, you're honorable," he had never been more victorious.

They met in the afternoon as agreed, each wholly awake though neither had slept. Skinsuited, they left the city and hiked up to the crater rim and thence along it, mostly mute, mostly glancing at one another. They had the trail to themselves. Crommelin was busy and, in spite of the low latitude, winter vacationers were few. From the heights they looked down on human work and across to distant, abiding desolation: dunes, boulders, pockmarks, a scud of yellow dust and the sun blurred by a salmon haze. Audio amplifiers brought them the thin wind-skirl. Louder was the scrunch of grit beneath their boots.

"This is my kind of country," she said once, most softly. "And nevertheless, I'd like to live, alongside you, to see it growing green and blue, a lake down in the bowl and an ocean yonder, your kind of country, Fenn."

Thirty or forty minutes' march brought them to a shelter, a little dome with basic life-support. They cycled through the airlock, took off their helmets, and drew together. The smell of her hair brought summer meadows on Earth back to him.

After a while they let go. He wondered bemusedly what to call her eyes—pearl-gray, smoke-gray, the gray of northern seas?—till she spoke in her straightforward fashion and hauled him back to facts.

"You said you're not coming to Sananton."

Be careful! he thought. "Not at once. Later, sure."

"You're *not* sure." She can tell, he thought. She's too flapping observant. "Why not? You know you're always as welcome as the flowers in spring," the man-created flowers at the end of the long, long Martian winter.

"And you know how I'd love to come."

That didn't fend her off. "Then why not? You've explained you're here on a special survey mission. I can't imagine a better place to start than Sananton. Dad and

Mother know just about everybody on the planet who counts.''

"That's not what I'm after," he must admit. "Not at first, anyway."

"So what are you after?"

"I'm sorry. I can't tell you that . . . darling."

Her lips tightened. "Do I have to keep saying, 'Why not?' ''

"It's confidential. I've promised."

"Have you? Truly?"

"Yes—"

"As a liar, you're no doubt an excellent spaceman." Kinna sighed and clicked her tongue. "Fenn, Fenn, did you suppose I haven't thought about you, studied you, played every scenario that I could imagine with you in my head—in my whole body? I know full well you're lying to me, and about something that concerns me where I live. Don't.''

"Slag and slaughter!" he roared. Urgently: "Listen, you mustn't know. It wouldn't be safe for you to. Later, later.''

"If there is a later," she said.

"There will be."

"You're not one hundred percent convinced of that."

"In death's name, woman, be reasonable! Every time we take a breath, we take a risk."

"Fenn," she said, unrelenting, "I love you and I understand you're trying to protect me, but you are not going to squirm free of this. *You* understand—will you?—I'm no Earthside softling. We can't make a life together if one underrates the other. Give me the trust you owe me.''

Overrun, he thought in turmoil that she could indeed provide the kind of advice he needed, and so far he hadn't sniffed out where else he might reliably get it, and—

"Well, you win," he said. "But it has to be a zero-kelvin secret. No word, no hint to your parents, to anybody, no, not to Taffimai Metallumai or the wind.''

She made a curious gesture, right forefinger flitting from left to right shoulder, then from brow to breast. ''None. You scare me, but—'' Her smile broke forth. ''You make me sunburst-happy too. An odd mix.'' The smile died. She shivered.

Almost relieved, almost liberated, he plunged ahead. ''It's about the secrecy of the cybercosm. I don't say Synesis; I say cybercosm. You've heard me aplenty on the subject. No sense in fuming about it now. But that thing the solar lenses have found out, whatever it is— the data they've got archived on Pavonis Mons, where the Inrai died—why won't they tell us? It has to be something huge. Doesn't it? Something cosmic. My interview with Chuan yesterday clinched this for me.''

Great cosmos! Only yesterday?

''We, the Lahui Kuikawa, we can't lay any more plans, we can't go any further, before we know,'' he went on. ''And if we don't start soon, we'll never be able to. Is that one reason the cybercosm's withholding the information?''

''It's larger than that,'' she whispered. ''I've seen the sorrow in Chuan.''

''Well, yes, me too. If he isn't just a fine actor.'' Fenn's tone turned ferocious. ''Look, though, if you're worthy of hearing what I mean to do, why aren't we both worthy of knowing what this is all about?''

She stared at him. It was as if she shrank back from him. ''I was becoming . . . afraid of this. You want to break in and steal the secret.''

''No,'' he stated. ''Claim it. Then we'll exercise our right to decide what to do with it.''

''Impossible!'' she cried. ''Dement! The dead Inrai can tell you!''

He took her hands. They had gone cold. Abruptly gentle, he said, ''I know. But it won't be like that. Listen.''

She straightened before him. ''I will.''

He let her go and paced back and forth in the narrow chamber as he spoke.

"One other man and I—Iokepa Hakawau, I've told you about him—we talked it over, and over and over before I left Earth. We dared not bring anyone else in. Nor would that have been fair, as explosive as the business may be. The trouble around the Threedom and the ship from Centauri, those were the official reasons for sending me to Mars, and they're valid enough. But the more we considered the matter, the more it seemed that the lens mystery was not just older, it was basic. Any of a number of people could look into the social, political, et cetera situation on Mars as well as I could, or better. But I was the only one we knew of who might be able to do something about the lens data, if I decided that something really had to be done.

"After listening to Chuan, I decided that something does have to be done. And I'd come prepared.

"It's been carefully planned, I tell you. We knew I can't land an aircraft at the station on the mountain. The robot in charge would ask why, and it's probably programmed to notify the constables of even a routine arrival. However, I can land well away, out of its sight, and proceed on foot. I have my maps and supplies and field equipment. I know how security systems like that work, including their limitations, and there's no reason to suppose this one has been upgraded. I can make my final approach camouflaged so as to fool it, then use a device I've brought along. I learned how when I was in the police in Luna. Civilians aren't supposed to have one, but the Lahui are widespread on Earth, they have their connections, and Iokepa got it for me under the counter. The sensors, the robot, shouldn't ever register that I've decoded the lock and gone in. Once there, I don't expect any alarms either—or, at worst, not till I'm downloading the database. And that will be too late."

The two of them stood confronted for a minute or more. Without their helmets, they could not hear the Martian wind, and the dust devils afar spun in silence.

"You're not dement." Her voice wavered.

"No," he declared. "Repeat, Iokepa and I gave this a great deal of study and hard thought."

"That's the dreadfulest part of it."

"Look," he pleaded with her, "the machinery shouldn't get violent, as long as I'm not actively threatening it like the Inrai. I'm figuring it'll never know. If it does find out and calls the police before I can escape, they'll arrest me. In that case, the publicity should soon spring me free. Citizens' right to information, remember?" He gathered his strength. "Yes, it is taking a long string of chances, but it's what I'm going to do."

"Inrai bands are still prowling out there." Her hands lifted in appeal. "I know how revengeful they must feel. And some of them are completely reckless."

The anger always deep within him congealed in a solid block. "I'll risk that, and shoot my way clear if I must."

He saw her see the implacability. Her head drooped. "I don't believe I can change this."

"No," he said heavily, "not even you can." His spirit quickened. "But you can help, Kinna. You can improve my chances no end."

"Yes—"

"We'll go over the plan step by step. You'll tell me what needs fixing. You'll have some good ideas of your own. I am glad you made me bring you in, *pa'aka*— partner."

Her glance rose to meet his. "Trailmate," she said.

"What?" The knowledge broke over him. "No!"

"Yes," she said quietly. "You're going. I can't stop that. But neither can I let you run unnecessary risks, let you die."

"N-nobody is going to shoot at me. Nothing is."

"You just said you may have to shoot back."

Thereupon she amazed him with a laugh. "Actually,

this time you're right," she allowed. "I was trying to argue you out of your scheme, but I wasn't entirely honest. What are the odds we'll encounter one of those few, underequipped, fugitively scuttering little bands? Think. It's much likelier we'll get hit by a meteorite."

Her gaze went out the viewport to the desert before returning to him. "What I have in mind is Mars itself. Beautiful, merciless Mars. You can't do this alone, Fenn. Not those wilderness kilometers at that terrible altitude. You've got to have an experienced outbacker to guide you."

"Well, uh, well, yes, I was figuring on that. Maybe your friend Elverir—"

A small, tender smile flitted across her lips. "I like him and I love you, but the pair of you—or you with any Lunarian—could hardly make it. If nothing else, you'd be too doubtful of each other, on a venture that needs absolute, blood-sworn trust. And as for another Terran, I can't think of a one who'd be willing to try this, and at the same time is competent, except me. And . . . searching around for a guide, how long would it take you, and how likely would you be to alert the authorities? Here I am. We can set off unnoticed in two or three days." She grinned. "You're stuck with me, Fenn. Now and always."

He smote the wall, a thud through the air, a jolt through his bones. "No! I won't take you. That's that."

"But you'll go anyway, alone if need be?"

"Yes."

"No," she said. "Because if you try, I'll tell on you. I will." She blinked and blinked. "I know I'd lose you. But that's better than finding your mummy on the mountain."

He could only gape.

She threw her head back, her arms wide, and laughed. "With me along, it isn't such a crazy gamble. No, an adventure!"

Did she mean that, or was it for his sake?

22

BESTRIDING THE EQUATOR, second greatest mountain of the Solar System, Pavonis Mons rises eighteen kilometers above the Tharsis plateau, twenty-seven kilometers above the mean datum of Mars—the "ground level." So broad is its base, eight degrees of longitude, six of latitude, that it scarcely seems the extinct shield volcano it is. Rather, you see tawny dunes, scattered rocks and craters, gradually give way to dark basaltic masses, while the land rises, seldom abruptly, and rises and rises. To Fenn, the flight stretched on as endlessly.

Then Kinna hallooed, "Yonder!" He looked from a three-dimensional map display in the control console to the ledge ahead and saw that they matched. She, piloting, joined her skill to the aircraft's program and systems. Jumbled blacknesses swelled in sight, terrifying fast. This was the only spot anywhere near the goal that met their needs—unobservable by the station or by some instrument in Threedom territory, big enough and level enough to land on. For a wild moment he wondered about its size. Could the left wing really clear the bluff on that side? The engine rumbled. A shock hit him, a lesser, a lesser. And they were down. The engine noise whined away into silence.

Exultant, Kinna grinned at him. "Could you've done that?" she challenged.

"N-no," he admitted shakily. Space made its own demands, but none quite like this. "The place I had in mind is a good bit wider."

"And a good bit farther to walk from. Aren't you glad you brought a lazy woman along?" She patted his hand. "I'm sorry, I shouldn't tease you. This is your idea, your mission."

"Hadn't we, uh, better get going?"

"Blaze, yes. Ridiculously much work ahead of us."

They unharnessed and got out of their seats. Already in skinsuits, they closed down their helmets—after Kinna had ordered, "Kiss the pilot"—and activated their biostats. While the economy pump evacuated the interior, they began unsecuring their cargo. Thereafter they took things outside.

The day stood at noon when they finished. Muscles welcomed the toil. They had set off before sunrise after overnighting in the vehicle at an unfrequented site she knew above Valles Marineris. The previous day they had left Crommelin, as inconspicuously as possible. The three days and part of the nights before that had gone to collecting the material and information they required, likewise as inconspicuously as possible, and developing their plan of campaign. Not much time or energy was left for embraces, let alone exercise.

Once he had even wondered aloud if they must boost so hard. Couldn't they take a week or two off and just be together? "Let's get it over with," she replied rather grimly. "When we're through, we'll be free."

Now he had to confess she was probably right about that, as she had been about everything else. Certainly the route she laid out and the equipment she specified would make a big difference. Except for scrambling around in her company on previous visits, he had never mountaineered on Mars. It had little to do with climbing on Luna or Earth. His studies had not well prepared him for the reality.

Among other things, she had insisted on a top-grade pack robot. It dug a considerable hole in the fund allotted him for his investigation, but she pointed out that it would have resale value. About two meters long and one high, a gray cylinder with six claw-footed legs and a sensor turret at the front end, it bore ample energy for the expedition in its accumulators, as well as for a built-in transmitter to summon help if need be. The humans' backpacks could be fairly light when most stuff was loaded on it, truly adequate amounts of air, water, fuel cells, medicine, tools, instruments, changes of clothing and other comforts—above all, a sealtent. Fenn had meant to sleep in a powerbag.

The flight distance from here to the Star Net Station was merely sixty-seven kilometers. The distance afoot was significantly more, the going hard, slow, dangerous in some places. Kinna figured they could arrive the day after tomorrow. Then Fenn would take charge. Meanwhile, she was trail captain.

He code-locked the aircraft. The same key, which he tucked away in his pack, warded the controls. It was not a precaution one would ordinarily take in an empty wilderness, but she had said that Inrai might still skulk about now and then. Had she not gone on to swear that the likelihood of encountering any was negligible, he would have scrapped the whole venture rather than let her maneuver him into taking her. As it was, this gesture eased him a little. Whatever happened, they wouldn't come back and find that somebody had made off with their wings.

"Shall we?" she said. It was scarcely a question. He nodded. They started off, she first, he after her, the robot behind. Its program was capable of obeying simple orders and, more difficult, taking it over rugged terrain.

Bloody-death difficult! What with skinsuit, helmet, boots, biostat, energy system, auxiliary devices, fluid reserves, and backpack, Fenn's weight equaled his weight naked on Earth; and the extra mass meant that much more inertia to cope with. Snug, the suit had only rudimentary motor assistance at the joints, where residual pressure added flex resistance to the toughness of the fabric. That didn't matter on reasonable surfaces, but here was rock in grotesque bulks—thread your way around or between, climb across and clamber back down, clutching at handholds, desperately glad that tactile amplifiers gave normal sensation to fingers and feet. His cooling system was soon overloaded; sweat drenched his undergarment, stung his eyes, reeked in his nostrils. He sucked streams of water down his furnace-dry throat, breathed hard and harshly, heard how his recyclers and pumps labored. Sometimes the route crossed an open slope, but it was always steep, precarious, straining knees and wits to keep from falling over and rolling down to where a cliff dropped or a crack gaped.

Kinna went lightly and surely. Through the pulse that pounded in Fenn's head floated a memory of a wild goat he had seen in Yukonia. She ought to be on those lovely heights, where snowpeaks gleamed afar and gentians clustered blue in the grass around a tarn, not in this wasteland. And yet it was hers. Strapped to her left arm she carried a pathfinder, and often checked the unrolling annotated map she had programmed into it against the landmarks she saw; but she rarely stopped for the purpose.

After a couple of hours, though, she did call a halt. "We need a rest," she said. Joining her, he discovered that her own face glistened wet and the brown hair curled damp. "Also," she added softly, "we need time for the view here. It's what I hoped. We won't come on another like it."

He looked. They had reached a narrow outthrust above a plunging decline. Right, left, and upward, the aa lava piled in titanic black blocks and clinkers. The weather-polished pahoehoe of the descent sheened almost obsidian. Immensely far down and distant, Tharsis plateau rimmed the mountain's dark world with rose. Remoteness and atmospheric haze made it a blur, a dream. No dust blew this high today. The intricately shadowed upland stood knife-edge sharp under a sky more deeply blue than any ocean stream. A few ice-clouds floated in it, frail plumes, dazzlingly white. When Fenn's heart and lungs had quieted, awe came upon him.

He glanced again at Kinna. How raptly she stared.

Mars child, he thought. "You love this planet, don't you?" he asked low.

"Oh!" Startled, she turned to him, then smiled. "Well, it's me," she answered after a moment. "Just about every atom in me is Martian." The smile brightened. She fluttered her lashes. "Not that I don't mean to kiss as many Earth atoms off you as I can. And—um—" She stopped quickly and looked down. He saw the blush, and was less amused than touched.

"I can't help wondering if it's right to change . . . your home," he said. If we become able to.

"Don't worry about that," she replied, self-possessed again. "I won't live to see any enormous differences, will I?"

"I'd like you to live forever."

"If you do too. If a Life Mother resurrects both of us. But however that works out, making Mars over, making it truly alive, that's like a baby growing up, isn't it? You remember how she stumped around the house, how you'd play with her and hold her and tuck her into bed, but you wouldn't want her to stay like that always. Everything changes. It's right and natural."

"If it's for the better."

"Well, nothing is forever—" Her voice trailed off. She gazed straight out into the sky. Had a thought struck her? She said hardly anything during the rest of their stay, and he decided not to interrupt her.

After they resumed, he found he was getting the hang of it. Travel became progressively less wearisome. Still, when she told him they would stop for the night, he was more than ready to.

The shoulder she had chosen beforehand from the map was fairly level and they soon cleared the loose rocks off, for it was barely wide enough to accommodate the sealtent, with a margin to spare for the robot and for them to work. A shot of energy expanded the molecules that catalysis had folded and would refold tomorrow. The package became a thick, insulating pad below, dome and airlock above, heating elements interwoven. However, next the occupants must set up power and recycling units and bring their personal things inside. Their previous trips had been shorter and easier; they had not shaken down into a proper mountaineering team, and the jobs took time. They had just finished when the sun set and night clapped instantly down.

They lingered outside for a few minutes. Phobos and Deimos were both aloft, well-nigh lost among the stars. Those stood in their hordes, keen, unwinking, blues and yellows and reds mingled with the crystalline whiteness of most, the Milky Way a cold noiseless river; sister galaxies glowed vague and mysterious; by the light that poured thence, Fenn clearly saw Kinna's features limned against the universe.

"Your sky," she whispered.

"Hm?"

"You know how seldom we see the stars this well from the settlements. Here it's as if I could reach up and touch them. Like in space. You're used to the sight."

"I wonder if I ever really will be."

"You belong with the stars."

"I belong with you."

She was silent awhile before she said, not quite steadily, "They're like—three dimensions, four—We stand here on a tiny ball whirling through endlessness. If we got flung off, we'd fall forever through . . . that." Skinsuit or no, he saw her shiver. "We'd better go in. Another long, stiff day ahead of us."

They crawled through the lock and closed it. Fenn touched a valve. Air hissed in from the tanks. When the monitor light flashed green, he and Kinna took off their helmets, and kissed, then their suits, and kissed at greater length.

She ended it with a gulped laugh. "Aren't you hungry too?" she asked.

Yes, he thought. Mainly for you.

"We can wash later," she proposed. "I don't mind how you smell, on the contrary; and as for me, when my belly's stopped grumbling, I can properly appreciate hot water."

More skilled than he, she busied herself with the glower, utensils, and foodstuffs. When she shook something over a pan, he inquired what it was.

"A spice mixture I packed along," she explained. "We call it sneeze-with-joy at home. A few grams extra in the load, and those field rations won't taste entirely like reconstituted chewing gum."

"You would think of that," he chuckled.

"Wait and see what I can do when we have a real kitchen."

Wait!

The meal was soon ready, the tent warm and full of fragrances. Cross-legged on the floor, Fenn and Kinna attacked their plates. After a few bites, he said, "Wonderful. So are you."

Across from him, rumpled, grimy, unkempt, beautiful, she made a bow of sorts. "At your service. Any time."

He didn't know if exhaustion, his aching body and dulling skull, bore the blame, or his nature; but somberness fell on him and he said, "Yes, you are, aren't you? I agree now; I probably couldn't have handled this trek without you. And nevertheless, I wish you weren't here."

Her merriment went away. Maybe it also had been only a rainbow shimmer. "I don't."

"You're straining yourself, you're taking these risks, for my sake—" She shook her head. "No. Not totally. I'm glad you said that. I've been wanting to tell you, to make you understand, since I began to understand myself. We've been so busy, this is my first chance."

Fenn waited. She's worth waiting for, he thought.

Kinna gathered words. When she was ready, she said in full calm, "Yes, at first it was on your account. I couldn't let you go alone. I couldn't. But my threat to— betray you—I'm not sure I could have carried it through.

Anyhow, it worked, it forced you to sign me on. But then afterward, thinking at odd moments and when I lay awake at night—Fenn, I came to believe you're right. More nearly right than wrong, at least. The Inrai, all that death and horror, provoked by Proserpina—why? Not wantonly, I'm certain. Could the Proserpinans have a case, a good reason, a just cause? And the whole secrecy about the lens—why? What it's found matters tremendously, that's plain to see. Matters to *us*. Then what about our Covenant right as citizens to know? Our right to make our own fate?"

"Chuan thinks otherwise," he reminded her.

She nodded. "Yes, and I think highly of him, I hate going against him, but—He's deeply troubled about this himself, isn't he? Is he so sure the secrecy is justified?" She caught her breath before plunging on: "He is a synnoiont, though; he belongs to the cybercosm, he's loyal to it—the way my hand is loyal to me? I don't really know. I do know he'd never wish us any harm. But is the cybercosm always wise?"

The knowledge of her unity with him went into his blood like wine. "We'll decide that for ourselves," he said.

"Yes," she answered. "We. All of us."

They finished their meal and cleaned the utensils with but a few more words between them. She glanced at their sleeping pads.

"Yeh," Fenn said. "Bedtime." He jerked a thumb at the wash unit in front of the curtained camp sanitor. "We could use a thorough scrubbing first."

"No argument." Kinna hesitated. "Would you mind if—we took turns—and each looked away till the other was through and dressed for the night?"

Memory smote, casual remarks she had made early in their acquaintance. "You mentioned . . . you and Elverir."

She colored. "We did likewise, mostly. Besides, that

was then and he was he. This is now and you are you.
Do you understand?''

He felt furiously jealous, but found no choice except
to nod. ''Yes. We can't afford distractions.''

''It's more complicated than that,'' she said. ''But
we'll be married soon. Very soon. Won't we?''

He recalled his parents, and many others. ''You'd be
taking an awful chance.''

''No,'' she murmured. ''Not with you.''

Could he live up to that?

He'd flapping well better.

They woke, breakfasted hastily, broke camp, and pushed
on. Midway through the morning: ''Hold!'' she called.

Alarm stabbed him. He peered around but saw nothing
more than black, sometimes rusty-tinged roughness,
boulders, and scoria under indigo heaven. ''What?'' He
started to join her.

''There. Look.'' She waved him off. ''No, stand back
a minute, please.'' She moved downhill, behind the rock
masses. He waited uneasily, envying the robot its mind-
lessness.

Eventually Kinna reappeared and beckoned to him. He
scrambled to join her. They descended to a hollow, like
a shallow, flat-bottomed bowl, about as large as their
ledge of the night before. The clinkers that must originally have littered it were stacked along the sides, and a
thin, gritty layer of regolith on the floor was marked by
prints such as nature would never have made.

''A campsite,'' she said. That was obvious, though he
doubted he would have noticed as he passed by. Her next
quiet sentence was something else. ''It can only have
been Inrai.''

He must not fly loose; he must examine the situation
carefully. ''Are you sure?'' he asked. ''Not somebody
earlier? I've heard about trips for sport in these parts—
adding up to a lot in the course of centuries—till a few
years ago when tension with the Threedom got bad

enough to stop them. I should think weathering hereabouts goes mighty slow.''

She shook her head. The brown locks danced. ''No, these traces are less than a year old, probably much less. Air pressure is still about half of mean datum value.'' Fenn gave himself a mental kick in the stern. Of course. Low gravity meant low gradients. ''And dust does blow this high now and then.'' She pointed. ''See how it lies drifted in the crevices and concavities. There'd be a sprinkling on the floor here if it hadn't been lately disturbed.'' She hunkered down, her finger sweeping out indications. ''The main depression, that's where they had their sealtent. But look, those bootprints going around and around it. Somebody paced. Who but a sentry, on duty all night? Sportsfolk wouldn't post one. Warriors would.''

Fenn ignored the chills along his spine and nodded. ''You're right. Well, Scorian would've had men scouting out the territory before his attack on the station.''

Kinna rose. Again she shook her head. ''The attack didn't come by this route, remember. True, scouts must have explored pretty widely, searching for the best approach. A violent operation wants more than satellite maps, no matter how detailed they are. He'd also have wanted caches set up in the area, to support the garrison that was going to hold the station after he captured it—if that was his intention. But it doesn't follow that we've simply come on a camp from that business. You recall what I said.'' She repeated it for emphasis. ''If I know Lunarians, they won't have abandoned those supplies, written them off. They'll send parties back from time to time to ferry them down for the remaining guerrillas. Even without that motive, I'd expect visits once in a while, out of pride, unwilling to admit defeat to themselves. Actually, I wouldn't be surprised if they keep a tiny semi-permanent camp somewhere lower down, tucked into a cave or something where it can't be spotted from above. Or maybe only a few small robotic observers, to watch if anything's going on and let humans know when it's safe to come.''

She hadn't mentioned that possibility before. ''You think outlaws may be prowling around on the mountain right now?''

''At this exact instant? No, I told you how improbable that is.'' She brightened. ''We needn't let it scare us off, anyhow. If we do meet a few, why should they be hostile to us? We're not officers of the Republic. I may well have met some in the past, in a friendly sort of way.''

She's so optimistic, so trusting, Fenn thought. But she's not stupid, ignorant, or reckless. ''Muy bien, if you judge it's safe—or no more unsafe than turning around— we can proceed.'' His hand slid over the sidearm at his waist; he pictured the rifle slung across his backpack. He'd trust in them.

In the afternoon she jarred to another quick stop. ''Wait,'' she exclaimed. ''This isn't right.'' After studying her pathfinder display: ''Oh-oh. Also snarl, growl, moan, and snivel.''

He came to her side. ''What's the trouble?''

''This slope ahead that we're supposed to cross. The broken rock spread everywhere over it.'' Some of those shards and fragments looked as if they had been partly melted. ''Not on the map,'' Kinna said.

''But you told me—''

''Yes, satellite imaging, resolution in centimeters, including altitudes. But that was then. Since, something happened. Large meteorite strike, I'd guess.'' She studied the scene. ''Correct. When you search out the traces— there and there and there—you can see how the blast tried to form a crater, except conditions weren't quite suitable for it.''

''M-m, yeh, now that you've shown me. Nothing like this on Luna.'' Different rocks, different world. ''Now what?''

''Well, I've lost my childlike faith in the slope. We

could find ourselves suddenly sliding, accompanied by a lot of hard, heavy, sharp-edged objects. No, thanks. Sit down, relax, and I'll puzzle out a way around them.''

"Aye, skipper." Yes, he thought, he would not have made it without her. He didn't want to be without her, ever.

But that evening, mercurially, she laid leadership aside.

The detour had not simply delayed them; it caused them to stop early, since they could not reach their planned campsite before dark and must take the only other usable one along the way. A ridge to the west gave it a high horizon. By the time they had set up, shadows lay long and cold and the sun glared just above that black wall.

Fenn and Kinna were still outside. The tent would be more comfortable, in its spartan fashion, but it was cramped, windowless, essentially featureless. Here they had sky and spaciousness. He could imagine standing with her on an alp of Earth; snows whitened blue-gray heights, wind ruffled soft, damp grass, and what he breathed was not airwarm and body-odorous but a cool breeze and a faint fragrance of pine.

Besides, he thought, and maybe she did too, the two of them sitting idle and lightly clad within centimeters of one another, not exhausted as they were yesterday, that could be too strong a temptation, when tomorrow they would reach their goal. He didn't suppose he'd sleep deeply or much, unless it could be in her arms, and it shouldn't be. How clean her profile was against desolation and heaven.

Suddenly she said, "Look east, will you?"

"Why?" he asked.

"Because."

He obeyed. "Because you want me to."

"Stay put a couple of minutes. I'm hoping to give you a surprise."

"You're surprises enough yourself," he laughed, unexpectedly carefree. "Pop, pop, pop, like fireworks."

She leaned against him. Their suits were between. "I've got to keep you interested, don't I?"

They stood glove in glove, viewing empty immensity. Murk engulfed them. "Now!" she cried. "Turn around, quick!"

They both did. Above the ridge, against the deep violet sky, stood a small flame of opalescent white. Its edges were lace, and a scarlet thread traced up from its heart.

The solar corona, he realized, and a prominence at the limb of the hidden disk. The air here was sufficiently thin and pure for an undazzled eye to behold it.

The vision slipped on downward, out of sight. Kinna danced on the rock. "We caught it, we caught it!" she jubilated. "I never have before. And I got to share it with you."

He would not tell her that he had often observed the phenomenon on Luna, at leisure, and that this glimpse had been tiny, pallid, as brief as life. Her wish for him made it special. "You're sweet," he said awkwardly.

"No," she answered. "I'm in love, that's all."

Darkness drew closer around them. Vanguards of night ran ever longer down the mountain. Kinna became hardly more to him than a dear shadow. He heard her voice, gone sober: "That moment the other day—we were talking about change, remember? It's been going through my head ever since."

On the trail? he thought. Amazing.

"It's hard finding words for what I mean," she went on. "But I've been trying. For you."

After another pause:

> "They say the poles of Mars
> Careen across the stars
> And one day Phobos must,
> Like any airborne dust
> That reddens yonder sky
> Whirl downward from on high.

Nor is there constancy
In our geology.
Where once great rivers raged,
Their remnants now lie caged
Below the dunes and drifts
The wind forever shifts.
My love for you will stay
Unchanged in any way
Through all the years I live.
I have no more to give.''

23

THE LAST STAGE Fenn made alone. ''Be careful,'' Kinna
pleaded. ''It's not worth dying for or—or losing you any
other way. It isn't.''

''Don't be afraid,'' he answered. ''I've told you I'll
be in no danger of anything except failure. I'll get in
touch just as soon as may be.'' He hesitated. He wasn't
practiced in sentimentality. ''You see, I love you.''

''Love you right back.'' The two skinsuited forms embraced. ''All right, boy, go.''

He left her and stole forward. Night had fallen, again
brilliant with stars. When he glanced around the con-
cealing spur of rock, he saw across a stretch of bareness,
lightened by dust, darkened by scattered stones, to the
station. Above black hulks that were buildings, masts and
domes and telescope dish stood skeletal against the sky.
His breath sounded unnaturally loud.

Nobody would hear. This wisp of air scarcely carried
sound, and he had shut off his radio. Ultrasensitive sonic
detectors or instruments monitoring ground vibrations
would have registered something, but he didn't think
there were any. The published plans had shown none,

and why should the builder have anticipated a need?

Optical and infrared systems were certainly present. Fenn unfolded his cold shield. On all fours he crawled out in view, holding it slanted before him. It was a simple thing—his own idea, back on Earth when he'd first considered this venture. His right hand clutched a bar attached to a disk of insulating material. Ahead of this, held by thin struts of the same stuff, was a larger piece of highly conductive alloy, irregular in outline and dull in hue. Eyeholes barely enabled him to see where he was going. He advanced centimeters at a time, motionless in between, alone with the throbbing of his blood.

As chill as the night, the metal should radiate no differently from its background. To a scanner using visible light, which might happen to sweep across it, it should look like another shadowy boulder or pockmark or whatever. A human or sophotectic observer might well have noted it as a new feature and, watching closer, seen it move. The station was robotic, though. Its master program and the various subprograms were high-capacity, adaptable, capable of drawing conclusions, but only within the limits of what the programmers had foreseen. Fenn was betting they had not imagined this.

He had spoken truth to Kinna. If somehow it did come alert, the station would not destroy him as it had destroyed the Inrai—especially after that episode—when he didn't pose an obvious threat. It would heighten its vigilance and defenses, it would shoot a report to constabulary headquarters, and that would be the end of Fenn's attempt. He and Kinna might then be caught and interrogated, but they would not have managed to commit any crime.

What might do him in was Mars. His suit wasn't meant for this kind of work. No matter how hard the thermostats tried, cold began to gnaw through glove and knee joints. He felt it first as discomfort, then as sharpening pain, then as numbness eating its way in toward his marrow.

He held his teeth together and crawled on.

He reached the gate.

Rising, the shield at his feet, he stood for a while and shuddered. Presently he was able to look around. Here, up against the entrance, he should be safely inside the viewfields of the scanners that surveyed the perimeter. But there were other instruments in the fence itself—he saw where the damage done by the raiders had been repaired—and still others within the compound. All were connected to the central director.

That meant that the locking system integral with the gate, code-sensitive and discriminatory, was a point of entry into the entire guardian complex. The right device could nullify everything, without affecting any other circuitry. It was like slipping a shot of local neuroblock into a man's hand when he wasn't looking, by a skin-penetrant injector that he didn't feel. The hand would lose grip and sensation without his being aware of it. (Or, no, not quite like that. The man would notice that something strange had suddenly happened there. The robot was probably not programmed to be so versatile. Who could have guessed it would ever have any reason to be?)

A device existed that could do such tricks. Only police were supposed to have access to it, and then only by special permission in extraordinary emergencies. Iokepa had contacted certain persons. They had deputized Fenn to carry a unit of this kind. Given in secret, the sanction might be of questionable validity, but in itself wouldn't be worth a legal battle with the influential Lahui Kuikawa.

He slipped off his backpack and took out the boxlike object that was, for now, the sole contents. It ought to let him in, unless someone had taken precautions that were never made public. He grinned a hunter's grin. He was about to find out.

The device was not the same as the one he remembered from his days on the Lunar force. It had needed modification to operate under these conditions. Fenn mentally rehearsed his practice runs while he flexed his chilled fingers back to usefulness. Under any circumstances, the work was delicate, exacting, slow. He lost himself in it. The stars wheeled overhead.

When the gate slid aside and no lights flared, no alarm howled through the radio spectrum, it was like falling off a cliff. He stood for a moment without quite grasping what he had done.

If he had. Alertness resurged. The night was utterly still—too still? He returned the unit to his pack, the pack to his shoulders, and tuned his receptors high, checking every band. Silence hummed. He stepped through into the compound, crouched tense, peered around. Nothing stirred. He stole over the wanly lit ground, ghost-puffs of dust rising from his boots, to where the building loomed. A door retracted at his touch. A bare corridor illuminated itself. He turned about and sought the airlock to the human-conditioned section. Its outer valve opened likewise for him. A display flashed: ENTER. ORDER A CYCLE WHEN READY.

He left that too, ran to the gate, switched on his transmitter, and whooped, ''Kinna, we're in! Come quick!'' His helmet rang with the noise.

The long waves reached around the spur and she burst into sight. He thought how even in her suit, under a grotesque burden of apparatus, she sped with antelope grace. They fell into one another's arms. Hardnesses clacked together, they laughed and she blew him a kiss, he saw her face clearly by starlight, tousled hair, big eyes, pert nose, sweet mouth.

''You did it, you did it,'' she sang.

''We did,'' he replied. ''But we're not done yet. Let's go.''

The station layout stood sharp in his mind. He led her to the airlock and they passed through. Hoarfrost formed immediately, blindingly, on their outfits. An automatic blast of hot air cleared it off. They undogged helmets, swung them back, and breathed an odorless atmosphere. Nothing here was alive but them.

''*Now* you can kiss me,'' Kinna said.

He obliged, though hastily. ''We'd better leave our suits on,'' he said. ''May have to scramble in a hurry. Just take gloves off.''

The entry and the hall beyond were as barren as everything else. A couple of rooms stood furnished for human occupancy, but the time must be long since anyone had sat in those seats, drunk from those taps, or rumpled those beds. Farther on was a chamber more intricately equipped. ''To house visiting sophotects that prefer these conditions,'' Fenn explained. Kinna shivered and scurried on by.

They came finally to a larger space, which also held seats and a table, plus desks with terminals along the walls. At the far end a control console reached the width of the room below a set of screens, flanked by two vivifers. ''Here we are,'' Fenn said. His voice sounded flat in this echoless quiet. ''Communications and command center.''

''It . . . isn't very fancy . . . is it?'' Kinna whispered.

''A sophotect will have everything extra it needs in itself, or by linkage to the cybercosm outside,'' Fenn reminded her. ''Humans seldom come, and only to input questions that can't easily go over the phone.'' The station could transmit, but received on audiovisuals unconnected to anything else. That precaution against takeover had seemed ample.

Kinna straightened. She would not let the surroundings daunt her. ''You know what to do,'' she said.

''I hope so.'' Fenn tugged his beard. ''But as I told you before, I've got to proceed ultracautiously. I don't expect the program will display data classed as top secret simply on request. I'll feel my way forward.'' He cast her a rueful smile. ''Amuse yourself as best you can, heartling. This will likely take hours.''

—When he came out of his concentration for a moment, an uncounted time later, he saw that she had managed to curl up, bulky gear and all, in a leanback seat and was catching some sleep. He thought he could see what she looked like when she was a child.

—Query by query, test by test. This was in fact a working scientific installation, a node in the interferometry that spanned half the Solar System and measured fire-clouds at the edge of the observable universe. Data unrolled readily for Fenn, mostly strings of numbers that he was not competent to interpret.

Knowledge from other sources was archived here too, for study before correlation into a single grand understanding. Findings from across the whole electromagnetic spectrum, radio waves kilometers long, microwaves, infrared, optical, ultraviolet, X ray, gamma ray—particles sleeting through space, torn off atoms, born of hard quanta, flickeringly nascent out of the vacuum—gravitational waves, spoor of monster stars awhirl or in their sundering death throes, crash of neutron dwarfs or black holes colliding—images made by lenses that were galactic clusters, galaxies, dark bodies in the halo of our galaxy, our sun—

The structure and turmoil of galactic center, travailing with the trillion-year future—

Blank. "Termination of this series," said the impersonal robotic voice. "Do you wish to continue with data from the other stations?"

"Yes," said Fenn harshly, because a visitor would.

He asked for explications and got them. The solar lens in Draco had captured indications of planets in the Smaller Magellanic Cloud, transiently but confirmed thus and so by interferometry, reference SMG.j.175. . . . The solar lens in Virgo had—

Not only the Taurus lens series was stopped. That was completely, but for three more lenses, the data were showing unmistakable gaps. "Is there a problem with these?" Fenn dared ask.

"The reported observations are anomalous," the robot said. "Investigation is in progress. The results will be published in due course."

You lie in the teeth you haven't got, Fenn thought. But you've been ordered to. How comprehensive are those orders?

His fingers moved over the console. So far, he hoped, he'd acted well enough the role of a legitimately inquiring human scientist. How much further could he carry it?

Such a man would not normally ask for the withheld information. If he did, the robot would contact headquarters and inquire whether it should be released to him. Fenn must key in an override command, without triggering what he might as well call suspicion. Could he? The robot did have judgment, and that judgment was powerful in its limited, algorithmic fashion. If it sent an alarm, or simply a query, headquarters would surely tell it to take immediate action—shutting down if nothing else, and maybe denying egress to the intruders. And law officers would be on their winged way.

Fenn had studied everything available before he left Earth. It had been a brutal cram job, chemical and electrical psychostimulants driving the material abnormally fast into his brain. He had none of the intuition, the easy skill, that grows from experience. However, as a detective, and later as a spaceman, he had acquired knowledge and abilities not too dissimilar. The machine and the program here were not unfathomably unfamiliar.

He touched keys, spoke words, watched what appeared on the screens, and saw a pattern. Dry-mouthed, he set the code for *Override. Do not communicate elsewhere,* and executed it. "We require the anomalous data for a new study," he grated.

"Permission to inspect," said the voice. His heart slammed. He felt momentarily dizzy.

"Do you wish a display?" continued the robot. "At average human reading speed, that will run approximately thirty hours."

Of course, Fenn thought. No proper scientist would baldly ask for an account of what the data meant, when they were supposed to be in his field of research. He,

Fenn, must get them as they were, and trust some qualified person to interpret them for him afterward.

"No," he said. His pulse still thuttered. "Download into a card and we'll take the material with us."

"That is inconsistent with confidentiality."

Fenn's spirit toppled. He had not broken the basic restriction.

"I'll have to think about that," he said, and logged off.

For minutes he paced, swore, dropped into seats and bounced up again, threshing through a wilderness that shifted about and jeered at him. He got no instant of insight. Piece by piece, he dredged forth what might or might not serve, weighed its worth, threw it away or hammered it more or less into place until at last he had a scheme to go by. Maybe the robot would deem his next keystrokes and questions plausible. Maybe it wouldn't freeze up or call for help, but respond to him.

He muttered a final oath and went back to the console.

—At his touch on her cheek, Kinna was wholly awake. She sprang to her feet. "How much have you seen and heard?" he asked.

"I fell asleep early on, I'm afraid," she said, stretching cramped muscles. "I'm no roboticist."

"Nor I." Who was, really, except the cybercosm? "But I've gotten somewhere."

She caught at his arm. "What is it?"

"I've worked around to where the machine will accept setting the secrecy directive aside. It'll download everything from the lenses that it hasn't already—the forbidden stuff, in other words."

Glory flared. "Fenn, you've won!"

He lifted a palm. She read the haggard face before her and fell silent.

"That means everything," he said heavily. "You see, I can't tell what any of it signifies, so I have to demand it all. A scientist would, and I got myself passed off as a scientist allowed the information. But downloading into

a card we carry away with us doesn't square with secrecy. I couldn't insist. The robot could so easily have
started—wondering—and checked its security system
and found no entry about our arrival nor any aircraft sitting on the landing strip. Well, I fumbled my way ahead
to where I can cancel the directive altogether. But then
it only makes sense to download straight into the public
database, doesn't it? Anything else would look odd and
likely touch off a security check or a call to the main
sophotectic brain on Mars, or both. As is, I've taken a
chance by logging off again, breaking the robot's contact
with us, while we decide. I said I'd have to consult my
superior." He smiled on one side of his mouth. "That
means you."

"No—What are you waiting for? Go ahead!"

"You've been asleep," he sighed. "Take a minute and
think. We've talked about this enough, the responsibility
involved, the possibility that the cybercosm's right and
this should not run loose. We meant to smuggle the truth
out for a few people like us to consider, before we went
any further. But we can't. It's all or nothing, everybody
or nobody. That could make world felons of us, you
know. I expected the Lahui Kuikawa would be grateful
and use their influence—freedom-of-information argument, damage claim against the Synesis—to get us off.
But maybe they won't care to."

Whatever happens, I'll try to take the whole blame, he
thought. I'll try to hide your part in this. I doubt I can. I
doubt you'll let me.

She clenched her fists. "Why should . . . I decide?"

"Me, I'd go ahead," he told her. "But I know I'm
reckless and inconsiderate."

"You are not! You're the kindest, most generous—"

"Like death I am. I'm throwing the whole burden of
this onto you. We've nobody else, and time is bleeding
away from us, and either way, the guilt is mine; but you
are a better human being by a thousand orders of mag-

nitude and your guess is more likely to be right than mine is.''

She stood mute for a while before she raised her eyes to his and said, quite calmly, ''I don't think there are any real rights or wrongs here, Fenn. There is truth, though, and the freedom to know it. You go ahead.''

They left the compound side by side. The stars stood at well past midnight. Travel would be tricky indeed, but two people helping one another could make a slow way forward, and finally the sun would rise to light the rest of their way back to camp.

24

WHEN THEY REACHED the sealtent, they were fit only to go inside, wash, throw some food together, eat it without paying much attention, and collapse into sleep. Thus they woke well before the next sunrise made further travel practical. What they murmured as they lay there in the dark became, Fenn thought, more than ever nobody else's flaming business, nor would it ever be.

In the early morning he let Kinna finish packing while he went offside and buried the lock deceiver under loose rocks. He took some trouble making the pile look natural and covering what faint trail he'd left going there and back. Once they learned what had happened, the authorities would immediately guess the how of it, but why make them a free gift of the evidence?

Originally he had taken for granted that his role, and now hers, would come out into the open, unless the decision was to keep the information suppressed. In such a sensational business, with basic Covenant principles at issue, he felt reasonably confident of their legal defense. None less than Manu Kelani had told him that the Lahui

Kuikawa were prepared to strike a bargain, charges against their agents dropped in exchange for suits not pressed against the Synesis and its trustees. "It is a measure of the breakdown throughout society, this division and conflict, is it not?" the *kahuna* remarked sadly.

As things had worked out, though, everybody was going to be confronted with a suddenly accomplished fact. No doubt there would be strong suspicions as to the identity of those responsible, but in the uproar and upheaval, would tracking them down seem worthwhile, let alone wise? Fenn was fully content to stay anonymous, and more than content on Kinna's account. If the Lahui afterward decided to punish him for having so grossly exceeded their mandate, she would be safe on Mars.

All this was assuming they wouldn't be traced and apprehended here on the mountain. Concealment was out of the question. Observer satellites must already have spotted and reported them to occupation headquarters. They would not have seemed important. But if suspicion stirred, an aircraft or two would come for a closer look.

Landing spots were few. No matter. If need be, constables who were trained for it could bail out and come down on jetpacks. What resistance could two travelers on foot offer? What *would* they? Fenn wasn't about to shoot at any law officers, not under any circumstances.

Trudging and scrambling along between Kinna and the robot, he concluded that since nothing of the kind had occurred, nothing would. Nobody in charge of public affairs appeared to be particularly interested in Pavonis Mons, despite the attack on the station; despite the possibility, which she had confirmed, that bands of Inrai returned from time to time; despite—everything. Strange, this indifference, this downright carelessness.

Or was it policy? Fenn remembered what Chuan had said about not avenging the outrage at the caravan. The guerrillas had done and suffered their worst. Best hereafter was probably to ignore them. That might break down their morale and their support among people in the

Threedom faster, more thoroughly, than an active campaign. Or so the cybercosm had maybe reasoned, through Chuan, its human aspect on Mars.

The idea didn't feel quite human, though. Too patient, if nothing else. Did the commanders of the occupation force agree with it? If not, had they protested to the House of Ethnoi? The cybercosm advised; it didn't govern. Legislatures could overrule it whenever they chose. Evidently they had not chosen, to date at least. Well, the cybercosm was almighty persuasive. Fenn decided to ask David Ronay about it when he got home.

Home. . . . He looked ahead to Kinna, her helmet shining under the vast indigo sky, Kinna striding homeward with him.

His mind went back to the puzzle, like a dog worrying a bone. The tension and toil of entry were past. After a good, long sleep and a chance to think further—

"It went so uncannily easily," he said to her when they stopped for a rest.

"I wouldn't call it that," she replied. "Could anyone alive but you have pulled it off?" Her laughter trilled, clear and bright and out of place in this grim landscape. "No, us."

They sat precariously on their suitstools. A cindery jumble extended before their eyes to an abrupt edge against empty air. At their backs, the mountain slanted upward in blocks and heaps, which soon cut vision off in that direction. Dried sweat prickled his skin, he inhaled the reek of it, hunger had begun to stir in him. They didn't eat on the trail. He sucked a mouthful of tepid water and grumbled, "Oh, I didn't expect we'd have no chance, else I'd never have set out. Obviously. Still, I was surprised not to hit a couple of safeguards I'd have had there. And now, harking back, half a dozen more occur to me. Why didn't they occur to the big sophotectic mind that designed the setup?"

"I daresay they did, and it decided they were unnec-

essary. Remember how the station did . . . defend itself.''
Kinna grimaced.

''But the idea of a sneak invasion was dismissed?
That's sloppy.''

''No one I know has accused the cybercosm of slop-
piness.'' Kinna pondered. He watched her, wishing they
didn't have to have all this gear on them. She sighed,
smiled a bit, and said low, ''But in its gigantic way, it's
innocent.''

''Hm?''

''The sophotectic mind is *good*, Fenn. Like an ancient
Buddha's. It's serene, it isn't capable of hate or anger or
greed or any of those beast emotions, it exists—lives—
for enlightenment and it wants nothing from us but that
we'll accept its help—and someday its teaching, as far
as we're able to.''

''Um,'' Fenn grunted. He wondered how much of her
earnestness stemmed from her affection for Chuan.

''I don't know how well it can understand the criminal
mind,'' Kinna went on. In immediate confusion: ''Oh,
not that you—I mean—''

''Sure, I see what you mean.'' His gloved hand patted
hers. ''But security systems are essentially an engineering
problem. Why didn't the cybercosm do a better job of
engineering?''

''Look, you speak of 'the' cybercosm, but you know
that actually no such thing was involved. Humans and
one or two particular sophotects were. The human input
may have been larger than you think. Why shouldn't it
be? This was a question of guarding against humans.''
Kinna's voice picked up the eagerness of insight. ''The
defense that broke the Inrai was intended against mete-
orites, not armed men. Trouvour, the old evils are so long
behind us, we've lived so long in peace and trustfulness,
that most likely nobody dreamed of any serious try at
breaking in.''

We've lived in nothing of the sort, and less and less

every year, Fenn thought. Before he could utter it, she went on:

"What I'm fretting about is what comes next. Does the, well, I'll say cybercosm anyway, does it know yet that the secret's become available?"

"We agreed that probably it doesn't," he said, "and we haven't been hunted, which I'd expect if it had made the discovery."

She nodded. "Right. It doesn't monitor entries into the public database. Too many of them, every second of every daycycle. And most likely no one's come across these data, or they'd shout it out loud to the whole world. Wouldn't they? Do you think anybody will before we get back?"

He shrugged. "Don't know. Sooner or later some astronomer or something, retrieving related information, will stumble on it." If that something chanced to be sophotectic, then no doubt access to all such data would clamp down at once, till the file had been cleared. But scientific nodes of the cybercosm generally used their separate memory systems, didn't they? "Mars hasn't got many such people."

She leaned toward him. "So there's a good possibility, isn't there, that we, you and I, will be the first to download it? And we can take it to somebody who can interpret it, and then decide what to do, same as our original plan."

"What if we decide it should not get out?"

"Why," she replied, as simply as a child, "I'll tell Chuan and ask for his forgiveness."

He had foreknown that answer and wondered how he should respond. While he searched, not only after words but after his own feelings, suddenly she leaped to her feet. The seatsticks contracted and disappeared from view. Her arm lifted into the upland wind that he could neither feel nor hear. "Yonder!" she cried.

He looked aloft. Sunlight flashed off metal. Distance dwarfed the shape, but in this air broad wings, gaping scoops, and insectlike body were knife-sharp to sight.

Fenn's nerves shrilled. He reached for his rifle, let his hand fall, and croaked, "Constables?"

"No-no. Not official. The shape, and no markings. Private. Like hundreds in these parts."

The aircraft looped around and swung lower, above them. "Not a, a jaunt, either." Kinna's voice stumbled. "Who would, nowadays? But Inrai. They do need flitters to get here and back in reasonable time, three or four of them aboard."

She raised the amplitude on her transmitter. He was about to tell her to stop when he realized that that was pointless. The riders aloft were inspecting them. Kinna turned her face upward, as if this were air in which humans could breathe and shout. "Hola, hola! Kinna Ronay calling! I'm known to Scorian, I'm a friend of Elverir from Belgarre, come in, come in!" She went into Lunarian he could not follow.

The vehicle climbed, flew off, vanished behind the upper horizon.

Fenn laid a hand on her shoulder. "Maybe they were being cautious." His words sounded mechanical to him.

"Well—" Her tone gained firmness. "Yes, of course. They've come like others, to recover a cache or to scout or—or to be undefeated. Naturally, they're wary. Two unmistakable Terrans, how do they know what that means, if it's a trap or we're the forerunners of a movement against them or what? They'll want to survey around, make sure, find a safe place to set down and camp. After that—But I suppose we'll be gone before then."

"We hope," Fenn said.

She stared at him. "You're taking this hard, aren't you? Why?"

"Suspicious by nature," he snapped. "I could be wrong, and it makes no practical difference at the moment, does it? Come on, we'd better be marching again."

Too late had it occurred to him what booty they rep-

resented. He didn't want to tell her. Useless, useless.
With luck, they'd just reach their own aircraft tomorrow
and start for home.

But from then on, he paid close heed to the terrain
over which they passed. An ambush would be hard to
arrange in this bare barrenness. However, if he saw a
place ahead where it might be done, he'd get her to steer
them wide of it. Meanwhile, he noted every spot they
could defend.

They sat for a spell in the sealtent after they had eaten
and before they lay down to sleep. Ignoring energy ef-
ficiency, now that they were near journey's end with ample reserves left, she kept a glowcoil going on the cook
unit while turning off other illumination. It made the interior a little warmer than the thermocircuits alone did.
Its dim, ruddy light brought her softly into his vision, out
of enfolding shadow. "Like a fire," she said.

He heard the wistfulness. She'd never known a hearth-
fire or campfire, except in simulation. He'd have to do
something about that, when he showed her around Earth.

He thought of making a promise, but then thought that
if he said anything intimate, his tongue might go too far
before he noticed. She wouldn't resent it, but her spirit
could shy off. He wanted to play by her rules. They were
hers.

"Well," he said lamely into silence, "tomorrow we'll
be in the air."

She smiled. "And the next evening, in our rightful
beds."

"The rightful bed—" Death! His cockiness had gotten
away from him after all. "Sorry," he mumbled.

He couldn't tell in the rosy dusk whether she blushed
or not, but her look held steady upon him. "Soon, my
dearest," she said low.

Better change course, back into safe waters. "Regardless, I'll be *matuā* glad to see civilization again."

"If that means 'very,' me too." Kinna paused. "And

yet I won't be as glad as I am that we came here.''

''M-m, it's been a, uh, an experience, yes.''

''It's been something we did, hard and risky and mattering a great deal—we did together.'' Tears glimmered in her eyes. ''I'm so happy because of that. Together. Always.''

At sunrise they packed, loaded the robot and themselves, and set forth anew. About noon, they came to what was waiting for them.

25

THEY TOPPED A ridge of boulders and looked downward across a kilometer to the ledge where their aircraft sat. It shone fiercely under the indigo sky and the high small sun. Fenn lifted a shading hand, squinted, and jarred to a halt.

''Oh-oh,'' he muttered. '' *'A'ole maika'i.* ''

Dismay nauseated him. It swept away before a tide of fury. That this should have happened! That those skulkers dared! The feeling froze into starkness. ''Not good,'' he repeated himself to Kinna.

She had already stopped and unshipped her optic. Silent, white-faced, she handed it to Fenn as he joined her. Through the magnification he studied a low wall of rocks heaped on this side of the craft, the four skinsuited forms behind it, and the rifles in their hands.

''They went ahead to meet us here,'' he said flatly, needlessly.

He and she were all too visible on their height. A radio voice barked in their earplugs, male, Lunarian-accented. ''Aou, you pair. We would speak with you.''

''Then why the death are you holed up like that?'' Fenn flung back.

"We must needs have care. We know not who you are nor what you do."

"I, I think you know me," Kinna answered. Her tone evened out. "I called to you yesterday when you flew over, didn't I? Kinna Ronay of Sananton, near Eos. A friend."

"Truly?" It sounded sarcastic.

"No enemy. You should know, if you're Inrai." (What else could they be? thought Fenn.) "Elverir of Belgarre—"

"Elverir!" The man spat the name, contemptuously. "Come nigh," he ordered.

"Like rot we will," Fenn snapped. He glanced at Kinna. "If we do," he told her, "they'll have us covered from behind that barricade, helpless." To the Lunarian: "You can come to us if you want. Make it peacefully."

"Scarce are you in a position to set demands," replied the other. "Take warning."

There was no flash, nor sound to be heard in this ghost of an atmosphere, but chips flew off a clinker nearby and light glistened where the bullet fell.

"A shot," Fenn said to Kinna, lest she not know it for what it was. "Back! They are desperados for sure."

He pushed at her. She responded with a jump. Together they scrambled down the way they had just taken. "Come along," Fenn commanded the robot. "Follow me." He went in the lead.

A hundred meters or so onward they entered a sort of hollow, where boulders lay piled around three sides of a space about ten meters wide, itself littered with lesser stones. The fourth side was an overhanging black bluff of lava. It was so heavily shadowed that a deeper darkness at its base lay half lost. Fenn urged Kinna to it. She saw a shallow cave, perhaps two meters high and three deep, formed by some gas bubble or differential contraction when Pavonis Mons poured up from the bowels of the planet.

"Good thing I paid attention to this kind of spot,"

Fenn panted. "Defensible, more or less. If we tried to run away across the slopes, they could pick us off. But we've got to stack as much stuff as we can across the entrance." He stooped and began collecting rocks.

She stood for a moment above him, bewildered. He heard the shock, no, the pain in her. "Pick us off—shoot at us? No. Can't be. What do they want?"

"Our plane and robot. The outlaws don't have a lot of equipment left, do they?" He flung stones down hard enough that he almost imagined he heard the clatter. "And maybe they want more than that."

When she still remained motionless, which wasn't like her, he straightened. Horror rode her face, staring eyes, flared nostrils, rapidly gasping mouth. Yes, he realized, she knows what happened to the caravan guards in Tharsis. He clasped her shoulders. "Don't be afraid," he growled. "They won't get it. I don't propose they get a flapping thing."

She shuddered once, took a long breath, gave him back his gaze, and said softly, "Thank you, trouvour." Thereafter she got busy raising their barricade.

He didn't immediately. Instead, he directed the robot, "Transmit long-range for constabulary attention: 'Kinna Ronay and Fenn in distress. Urgently need help. We're trapped on Pavonis Mons by a gang of Inrai. They are armed and dangerous. Four of them. Come prepared to fight. We're making ready to defend ourselves about a klick northeast and upward of where our flitter sits. There's no room to set down another anywhere nearby. The location is—'" He rattled off the coordinates. He had stowed them in his memory before starting off afoot.

"Well done," Kinna said. "Half an hour, maybe, for a team to get here. We have a good rescue service on Mars."

He pitched back into the work. "Longer than that, I'm afraid. What use are a few unarmed paramedic mountaineers? They'd only get killed or taken hostage. I wouldn't bet on the regular police either. Not out of the

Threedom. They've spent too many generations there sapping all public authority. The nearest garrison of the occupation force is some ways off, isn't it? And I've got the impression they aren't programmed to scramble very fast.'' They had never known war, nor had their fathers or grandfathers. ''An hour or more, for us.''

''We can talk with those Inrai, surely.'' It was as if she pleaded. ''We can bargain.''

''We can try,'' he grunted. She's got too much faith in human nature, he thought. In spite of every Martian hazard, she's led a sheltered life. Innocent—as she believes the cybercosm is.

''What can they want?''

''I told you. Our gear, at a minimum. When they saw it from above, it must have seemed well worth grabbing.''

A rock fell from her hands, down to her feet. She picked it up again and laid it on the pile. ''No,'' she protested. ''They can't be that . . . dement.''

''They aren't, quite,'' Fenn replied, thinking fast he talked. ''It's a furious kind of logic. Your guess must've been right; the surviving Inrai have kept a watch on the mountain, maybe only by a few small robots tucked away here and there. An observer saw our plane and sent notice. These mozos, maybe on their own hook, decided to come scouting, grab off our valuable property if possible, and try to learn from us what's going on. We could be the first move in a cleanup campaign against them.

''Seeing we were two alone, they took the closest landing site to ours and struck off overland to it. Their plane, well, if I were them, I wouldn't leave it sitting for any other overflight or satellite to see. I'd send it off, robotic, and figure on recalling it when wanted. However that is, they found ours is locked, so they prepared to receive us.''

''Scorian would never have ordered it!'' she exclaimed.

''I didn't say he did.''

She paused in her labor. "Yes. The disaster at the station—it would have driven some of them wild."

She ought to know, he thought. She's been among them. She's friends with at least one.

"If they fail," he said, "they can make off before our help arrives, hide under cover like this, and call their plane back after we're gone. It's a quantum-jumping gamble, yes, but when a man who's savage to start with sees things slip away from him and then a sudden hope—"

Light blinked through a crevice between boulders. "Inside!" Fenn barked. "They're here!"

He shoved Kinna ahead of him, over the barricade, into the cave. Briefly, its gloom blinded him. He felt the cold strike through his suit, in this place high on Mars where sunlight never entered. The thermostat poured more energy through the heating web and his sense of tomb-chill faded. He stared out at scoria, flinders, and day. There hadn't been time to fling up much of a wall across the mouth, less than a meter in height. He talked the robot up till its metal body rested above the top, an extra shield. Unslinging his rifle, he crouched on one knee and waited.

"Come forth," sounded over the radio.

"I think I know that voice," Kinna whispered at Fenn's back. He heard the terror she fought to keep down. It was not fear of death.

"No, you come out where I can see you," he called.

"Come forth or be slain," said the enemy.

"Try it. We're willing to talk, but first we want to see who we're talking to."

"We—we won't—shoot," Kinna stammered.

"So you can shoot, indeed?" murmured the other. "Or thus you claim. We shall see. Hold."

He came bounding over a side of the hollow and down into it, where he stood boldly, firearm held loose in his right hand. Through the helmet Fenn saw that he was bone-white, bone-gaunt, his hair hanging lank and ashen to the shoulders. His outfit was gray with grime, repairs plain to see, a calligraphic emblem on the breast faded nearly to invisibility. Scabbarded at his hip was a Lunarian shortsword. His left hand rested on the hilt.

Kinna spoke as if sickness were upon her. "Yes, it is. Tanir of Phyle Conaire in Daunan." Louder, with a forced firmness: "Do you remember me, Tanir? I remember you well, and everything I've since heard about you."

I can guess what she's heard, Fenn thought. Not that she'd have had any direct evidence, or she'd have told the police, but *somebody* carried out the atrocities, and here's this one who's shown us he's on a hyperbolic orbit.

"Waste no time," Tanir said. "It is worth more than water."

Yes, Fenn thought, he's aware we've sent for help.

"We will have your flyer and robot," Tanir added.

"Fenn," Kinna breathed, "it isn't worth a fight."

"Certainly not," Fenn agreed. Not when she could get hurt. To Tanir: "Muy bien. Go back. I'll put the key to the plane on the robot and send it after you."

The outlaw grinned. "Nay, you will come forth. We will also have knowledge of what you do on this mountain."

"It—no harm to you—" Kinna faltered.

The grin became a snarl. "Slain comrades say otherwise. Where can you have been but at the stronghold we sought to take? What can you tell of it?"

Fear, thought Fenn. Paranoia. Revengefulness. Cruelty. Vainglory. Powerful drives. In an unstable mind, they can take over entirely.

"Why don't you go back to shelter, so you'll feel safe?" he proposed. "Then we can negotiate."

Tanir did withdraw, spidering up the rocks and out of sight. But thereupon his voice came: "Nay, no bargains. You'd keep us in place until too late."

I'd like to, Fenn thought.

"You haven't long," Kinna cried. "Go now! Get away while you can!"

"We've time to fetch you along, little pousim." Fenn didn't know what the Lunarian word meant, but he heard the breath catch in Kinna's throat, and wished he had shot while he had the target before him. "Talk will come later. Lay down that weapon, you man, and step forth—"

"No—"

"Absolutely not," Fenn declared. He glanced back at her. She had drawn close, just behind him. He could barely make out her countenance in the murk, agonized. "You heard me too," he said to her.

"It is that or die," Tanir stated.

Kinna gripped her hands together. "Fenn, maybe we should—"

"I said no," Fenn interrupted. "We'll see who dies."

"You have three minutes," Tanir said.

He means it, Fenn thought. Kinna's recognized him. She shouldn't have let that slip. Now he feels he's got no choice. If she escapes, he'll be marked. No more shelter for him in the Threedom. Especially after Scorian finds out, I'll bet. . . . But how could she have known? Innocent—It probably hasn't made much difference anyway.

He turned around on his knee, toward her. "Three minutes. Long enough to say I love you, Kinna."

"And I love you." Her voice trembled. "If only—"

Ruefulness touched him. "Yes. If only." He reached down, unsnapped his pistol from the holster, and handed it to her. "Take this. Just in case."

She seized it. Resolution rang. "I'll fight beside you. Of course."

"No! Here I've got the experience; I'm captain. Get back against the rear wall and lie flat, prone. Jump!"

He saw her obey and knew she was no longer frightened, merely sensible. "Good," he said, and positioned himself on the barricade, looking out between the top layer of rocks and the bottom of the robot's body.

Through his suit he felt the roughness under his abdomen. "All I have to do is stand them off for a while. Then they're bound to scamper, to keep ahead of the troopers." He brought his rifle to the slit. "This is the tool for the job."

The Inrai had no doubt been listening, but that might be for the best. Let them know the opposition would be tough. Maybe they'd quit at once. If not, he'd try to keep their heads down. That wouldn't be easy, four of them, but he was a better marksman than average.

He was too busy to be afraid, except, underneath, for Kinna.

"Fenn," she called, "I didn't think of it before, but broadcast the news. Tell what we've done. So it won't go for nothing, whatever happens."

He cursed his own forgetfulness and ordered the robot: "Transmit this for entry in the general communications system: 'The secret data from the Star Net Station on Pavonis Mons have been downloaded into the public database. This information may be annulled at any moment. Interested parties should record it for themselves without delay.'"

His mind raced with the radio waves. They went the same road as his earlier message, upward and outward to whatever comsat was in the sky, thence back to the planet. But now the automaton did not route the signal to an appropriate center. Instead, his words joined the sea of undirected discourse that washed to and fro over the globe, through virtually every home and office and worksite, vehicles in transit, phones on people's wrists, robots and sophotects. . . . If nobody chanced to be tuned in to the channel assigned, if no recorder chanced to be absorbing everything that came along on it, the cybercosm might be the first to pick up this communication, and would then swiftly obliterate it and the entry it referred to. The odds were against that. Humans had too much idle curiosity, too much appetite for gossip, heritage of the ape.

A slug smashed against the cave wall near the mouth and ricocheted off. More hit the barrier. Dust puffed, fragments flew. Struck, the robot rocked. The firefight had begun.

Fenn peered back and forth. Poor though his preparations were, the Inrai had none. Unless the volcano, anciently casting boulders onto boulders, had provided a loophole or two—which would restrict a weapon—they would either have to shoot from the sides, out of his field of view, or expose themselves a bit as they took proper aim.

Ha, there! Half a helmet above yon cinder. Fenn threw a meteor shower of metal. The helmet disappeared, unhit. "Death and rot," he muttered. He wanted to kill. But he really only needed to discourage. And he ought to conserve ammunition. Hold off. Wait for a decent chance. Tempt the enemy into recklessness? "We're doing well," he told Kinna.

"You are, trouvour," she said.

More shots from offside. A couple of them whanged nastily around in the cave before they came to rest. "Stay down," Fenn reminded.

He studied the rock wall opposite him, across the shard-strewn hollow. A notch at the top, where two big rocks tilted away from one another. . . . Yes, that would seem like a coign of vantage. . . . He'd keep it in his sights till another target presented itself. . . .

A helmet, a rifle. Fenn squeezed the trigger. The helmet exploded. Moisture from within whirled out and froze, a white cloud that dissipated into the empty indigo, like a fleeing spirit. The helmet slid back out of sight. Scraps of it lay glinting.

"I got him!" Fenn roared. "I got your son of a virus, hear me? Now clear off our mountain!"

Kinna screamed. He could not but look around. "What is it?" he exclaimed.

"A man killed—"

"I had to. For you."

"I'm not worth it," she shrilled.

"You flaming well are." She stirred. "No! Keep back, keep down!"

She crawled toward him. As she came into the light diffused from outside, he saw the tears gleam, he heard the cough and rattle of her weeping, she shook with it, but she came to huddle beside him and the pistol was in her hand.

"I beg you, get back," he croaked.

The tousled head shook. She raised her eyes out of shadow to meet his and said, with a growing steadiness, "No. I can't let . . . you . . . take all the danger, all the . . . g-g-guilt. We'll do . . . what we must . . . together."

She's too civilized, he thought, and too brave.

From right and left, the bullets hailed.

Fenn saw them strike stone, over and over as they bounced around, strewing dust and chips and tiny lightnings. He felt impacts through the rocks beneath his belly. The robot jerked, its turret shattered. It collapsed and tumbled down the outer slope of the barricade. And he knew: I forgot Tanir's gang was listening. He heard we were off guard. They're in the open, to right and left of us, pouring their fire at the cave mouth.

I'm too civilized, flashed through him. I should have been a soldier by trade. But we have no more soldiers, only constables and outlaws.

He got to his knees, reached, and seized Kinna, while the firing stormed around them. Drag her down, at least get her to where she'd be halfway safe.

She recoiled from his grip. Her arms flopped. She landed on her back, sprawled over her biostat. A cloud geysered upward, white mingled with brilliant red.

"*Kinna!*" Fenn pounced to her side. Enough light seeped this far for him to see. A bullet had gone in at her right breast. Its exit hole beside the air tank was too big for skinsuit self-sealing. Her eyes were open, looking into his as he hunched above. He did not know if they saw. Her lips moved. Only blood bubbled out, shiny red-black in the gloom. It poured from below her shoulder, across the floor, steaming.

The puddle began to seethe. In the helmet, her face vanished behind a ruddy fog. Exposed to this near-zero atmospheric pressure, her blood was boiling off. All her body fluids were.

A darkness filled the cave entrance. Without noticing that he did, Fenn had snatched the pistol where it lay by Kinna's hand. He whipped about and fired. The shot the guerrilla snapped had missed in the dark. He fell behind the piled stones. Fenn heard him wailing in his mother's language.

Not to let any more in. Fenn scuttled back to his wall. He grabbed his rifle again. Another Lunarian was in the hollow, springing this way. Fenn shot. The man veered from the field of view. Fenn sent a spray of rounds through a half circle. That should give them pause.

The one he had wounded lay on the flinders by the wrecked robot. He squirmed and screamed. The small-caliber bullet had done no damage his suit could not self-repair. But he appeared to be gut-shot, half paralyzed, and going into shock. His noise grew feebler second by second.

Fenn took aim. Put him out of his misery. But no, Kinna wouldn't like that. Wouldn't have liked it. "Ahoy!" he called. "Want a cease-fire while you fetch this man?"

A bullet answered, making pebbles and dust bounce, futile except for the scorn behind it. Of course, Fenn thought. They won't waste any of the time they've got left. If they can kill me, they needn't suffer for their escapade. And if they can't, and have to take off on foot, they don't want to be burdened with this muchacho.

Let him die in whatever peace he can. I've other things to do.

Fenn went back to Kinna. She was certainly dead. But in spite of the boiloff—which was already coming to a halt as spilled liquids froze and the ice of them quietly

sublimed—her head must still be at something like body
temperature. Skull, flesh, helmet insulated it from ground
conduction, and convection in the tenuous air was almost
negligible. Five minutes till irreversible brain decay set
in. Cold would stave it off for periods that were sometimes remarkable, but cold down to just a certain point.
Water expands when it freezes. Ice crystals rupture cells
beyond repair. Considerable water must remain in hers.

He took her helmet off. Maybe, just maybe, the cooling that followed would be enough and not too much.
He wished he could clean the mask of clotted proteins
off her face, close the staring eyes and bind up the fallen
jaw. No time now. Later, later, if there was a later.

Strange, thought a distant part of him, strange how
quickly and methodically his mind worked. Well, he had
a task on hand. If he could carry it out. Probably he
couldn't. He had to try, though.

Before anybody else might attack, he returned to the
barricade. The man below it had gone silent. Fenn stuck
his head well out. Nobody in sight. If he moved fast, he
could maybe cross the hollow and get up among the boulders alive. After that, he'd need to kill the last two Inrai
quickly. Then he could bring Kinna to the plane, take
wing for the nearest rescue station, and hope she wasn't
too far gone for them to revive her there.

He launched himself out.

Pockmarks spouted around him. He felt a blow,
lurched, saw a cloudlet waft from his left arm. It stopped.
By then he was back in the cave. Luck, surprise, and
speed had saved him. He'd taken a flesh wound across
the biceps—as yet, he hardly felt it—and the sealant had
closed the minor rents in his suit fabric.

But he wasn't going anywhere, that was plain. Not that
he cared whether he died. However, it ought to serve
some purpose other than pleasing Tanir.

He settled to his defense. Hold your fire. Bide your
time. That may lure those last two out where you can kill
them.

The time dragged on. Occasional bullets told him the bandits hadn't left yet. He got no shot at either one. Now and then his radio gave him their voices, but they were using Lunarian, which he didn't know.

Whenever he looked Kinna's way, he saw how fast she was stiffening.

He recalled the old myths about hell. The main thing was that it went on without end.

—He had heard nothing for a while. The enemy couldn't stay indefinitely. Had they retreated?

He decided to suppose so.

He slung the rifle over his shoulders, holstered the pistol, knelt, and picked up Kinna. As weary as he was, she, rigid in his arms, proved unexpectedly heavy. He could strip her. Naked, she wouldn't weigh much. But that would squander time. He climbed over the barricade and down into the hollow. The dead man nearly caused him to trip. Having crossed, he must drag Kinna over the surrounding boulders, but after that he could carry her again, however awkwardly, on toward their aircraft. He kept his gaze away from the face. It wasn't hers, not any more.

Two lean, broad-winged, metal-bright shapes arrowed over heaven. They went into hover mode above the ledge. Skinsuited, armed, instruments alert, half a dozen men jumped out and descended on jetpacks. Vapor fumed around them as they landed.

They met Fenn halfway. He was stumbling, often falling, though he always rose and groped onward. "Here," he said, lowering the object to the stones. "Take her. She was shot, oh, an hour, an hour and a half ago, something like that. Can you bring her back for revival?"

The squad leader hunkered, looked, and straightened. "We'll flit her off as fast as we can," he replied, "but I'm afraid it's far too late. The eyes alone indicate it," the dimmed, glazed eyes of the wholly dead. He signaled his followers. Two of them sprang to take the corpse up and bear it off. Words crackled over the radio waves. A flyer swung overhead and lowered a sling.

Too late, Fenn thought dully. Oh, yes, too late by ten or fifteen degrees of planetary rotation. The stuff, the structures, the connections and relationships, everything that created her awareness and memories and thousand-fold dear ways, everything that was her, is destroyed, gone.

Sure, some of the more primitive cells may still be salvageable. A clone may be possible. Or, failing that, her genome is in her medical file, like anybody else's. A new organism could be grown according to it from chemicals. That's a technology of the people out among the stars and their Life Mothers, but we could do it here if we wanted to.

Why? She's gone. We'd get a twin. Never her.

The vague stories say the Life Mothers can bring somebody dead back to the world. They take what's in a download and map it into the new body. But the job is nothing like that simple. It needs an entire living planet, in oneness with the Mother. For us humans, a whole way of life, a way of thinking and being. We don't have it anywhere in the Solar System. The cybercosm doesn't believe we ought to have it. Besides, Kinna was never downloaded. She's gone.

"You called that you were under attack by Inrai," the constable was saying.

"Yes," the machine in Fenn replied. "You'll find two carcasses. The other two are hiding somewhere thereabouts." He waved at the heights, bluffs, clinkers, the monstrous black lifelessness. "Wait around. If they call their plane, you'll see it approach and can catch them. If they surrender, you'll have them too. Or if neither happens, you can sweep the area with high-gain detectors and find them. They're worth the trouble, I think."

To get information that would lead to breaking the Inrai, once and for all.

To get Tanir of Conaire killed or, better, because that was much worse for a Lunarian, locked permanently away.

Not that Fenn greatly cared. His last strength was going where Kinna had gone. But it would come back, he knew as an abstract proposition, and he'd think of a use for it.

26

BLOWING DUST MADE the night outside the viewport a blank black. Chuan had dismissed the mathematical calligraphy from his walls and they curved pale gray, equally featureless. The air was devoid of music or fragrance. Only the deep, slowly changeable colors in the floor and its warm springiness underfoot gave any life to the room. He wasn't sure why he had ordered this. It fit his mood, but he should be beyond letting externals affect him. Perhaps he had subconsciously thought that a cell was suitable for the interview ahead. Or a tomb.

Fenn came in. His tread was leaden. He wore merely a drab brown coverall. The brass-hued hair and beard were unkempt. Though he stayed erect, the dangling arms gave an impression that his shoulders were hunched.

Chuan looked up into eyes sunken and dark-rimmed. The cragginess of the face stood out like the prow of a crashed spaceship. "Welcome," Chuan said low.

"Really?" The word rumbled with a certain force but scant spirit.

"We share a sorrow," Chuan answered. "Let that suffice."

"You didn't tell me to come here for that."

No, Chuan thought, he'll do his own grieving, as I will do mine.

How understandable that he's sullen, if "sullen" is the

right word. Consider everything he has endured these past three days, since that which happened on the mountain. He may just be emotionally numb. Without psychostimulant, he might well have crumbled. Possibly neither guess is quite correct. He is a strange one, an atavism; he doesn't fit into today's world.

It will actually be kindest to be sharp with him. Or so I think. I could be wrong. I have forgotten so much of what it is to be human.

Chuan hardened his tone. "No. Nor do I intend reproaches or accusations," although I could level them. "A private talk between us is in the public interest. Please be seated."

The big body sank into a lounger but did not relax. "Gracias for it."

"I beg pardon?" Chuan asked, startled in spite of himself.

Fenn met his eyes as he sat down opposite. "Your straightforwardness. Too many people I've been with lately were oily."

Chuan could not suppress a flick of anger. "I would call them considerate, civilized." And I don't imagine the Ronays—But all the response they gave my awkward condolence was "Thank you."

"Be glad you are living in the present era," he said. "Most past history would have seen you imprisoned at the very least."

Fenn shrugged. "I heard talk of that."

Tea stood on the table between them. They ignored it.

"Would you like me to summarize your situation?" Chuan offered. "It may not yet be clear to you." Under any other circumstances he could have smiled as he added, "Frankly, it was not clear to us until today."

Fenn continued to stare at him, hardly blinking, as a caged bird of prey might have stared, back when men kept wild animals in cages. "What do you mean by 'us'?"

He may be more wide-awake than he appears, Chuan

thought. Well, that would be for the better. The objective tonight is to make him comprehend.

"A loose word for the responsible parties in this case. Officers of the constabulary, judiciary, and commonalty, on both Mars and Earth."

"And the cybercosm," Fenn said.

Chuan nodded. "Yes. It too is integral with the civilization that is yours and mine."

Fenn waited. His hands rested quiescent on the arms of his seat, thick, hairy, hands that had held a weapon that killed two men.

Chuan sat likewise immobile. He had prepared his speech in advance. It was as dry as he could make it.

"The immediate counsel was to detain you for psychological evaluation and judgment. You were directly involved in appalling events. You committed an unsanctioned entry, and your broadcast of sequestered data was a flagrant violation, which will have evil consequences. In the past your imprisonment would have been automatic, and in many milieus you would have been interrogated under torture before being put to death.

"However, a number of considerations spoke against arraigning you. You cooperated with the constables, submitting to intensive interrogation under veracitin, although you had the right to refuse." It was the intelligent thing to do, of course, if Fenn hoped ever to go free, but Chuan wondered whether his traumas had left him helpless. Then how angry would he grow as he returned to himself? "Thus we have a full account.

"Let me also rehearse the arguments you had ready. Your possession of a circumventor was authorized, although by an obscure officer on Earth. You were operating not on your own but as an agent of the Lahui Kuikawa, who are an autonomous polity of the Synesis. The withholding of lens data had never been presented as public policy, only as scientific caution; hence, at worst you were guilty of violating privacy. These data being of basic significance, the Synesis was wrong to withhold them, and you were reclaiming for all people their Covenant right to know. As for the violence that followed, you acted only in defense of your companion and yourself, in a situation that no one could reasonably have anticipated.''

Memory arose, snatched, and wrenched. Oh, Kinna, Kinna! ''Unforeseen, unforeseeable, yes,'' broke out of Chuan. ''A senseless contingency, a meaningless accident. How can anyone believe the ideal is false, that mind must someday tame this universe?''

Fenn's visage stirred just a little—with surprise? Grief? It congealed again.

Chuan mastered his feelings. ''My apologies,'' he said. ''Let me stay with the facts. Your arguments were specious at best. I doubt they would survive any proper challenge.'' He did not mean the legalisms of humans, though those probably could not withstand serious examination either. He meant the impartial logic of justice, of the cybercosm. But it did not try cases; at most, it counseled. ''However, that would be distracting and delaying at a time of crisis. It could provoke major disturbances.

''Meanwhile, the leadership of the Lahui Kuikawa has entered a demand for your return—under administrative confidentiality thus far, but unequivocal. They claim the prerogative to question and consult with you, and set any penalty they find called for. Whether or not this claim is valid under the Covenant, an open dispute about it would be still more disruptive than a proceeding against you on Mars. You counted on this, did you not?

''Constabulary analysts have pointed out that you yourself are bound to become wildly controversial as the news spreads, especially on this planet. Your presence here will pose a danger to the daily order of societies already badly divided, and, I may add, to your own person.

''The harm has been done. It is a unique harm, which cannot ever be repeated. Rather than serving a deterrent purpose, your penalization and correction in a glare of publicity would increase the difficulties coming upon us. Civilization has been weaning itself away from vengefulness. The decision is that no charges shall be filed in the Republic of Mars, provided that you promptly return to Earth.''

And there the Lahui Kuikawa will deal with you quietly, in their shipboard isolation, Chuan thought. I don't know how. Will you end at the bottom of the sea, or will they hail you a hero? Neither of those extremes, I suppose. It doesn't matter. You are no more, actually, than a random element in a blind cosmos—a stone that chanced to fall where it unloosed an avalanche that will shake all humankind and has killed Kinna Ronay.

Compassion touched him. ''I think knowing what you have caused will be ample punishment for you,'' he finished softly. ''I do not think I could bear such knowledge.''

Fenn did not stir. After a silence, he asked, in the same even tone as before—it made Chuan recall surf grinding cobbles together off a stony beach—''Just what have I done wrong?''

Reflex lashed back. ''Do you truly consider yourself some kind of idealist?'' At once, Chuan felt shamed by his loss of control.

''No,'' Fenn said. ''The establishment you belong to, that you're speaking for, it kept information from my people that we need. You never gave us a sound reason. We decided you never would.''

''Could you not accept that the reason might be better than you knew?''

''Was it?''

Chuan sighed. To this man, the revelation would be a knife; and he, Chuan, must wield it.

Fenn hounded him: ''Why should we take your unsupported word? It never quite made sense. You haven't been consistent, either. You could have guarded the station on Pavonis as strictly as you do the lens—the lenses, I guess—but you didn't.''

Replying to that postponed the stabbing for a few minutes. "A strong watch over the lenses was and is necessary because the Proserpinans were resolved to raid their data file, and indeed, they made an effort to. Now when the knowledge comes out, their reaction is unpredictable, but I dread it, if only for their sakes. Polities on the inner planets are, for the most part, more stable. It should be possible to contain the harm to them.

"Because of that stability, we, the responsible minds, did not expect a threat to the station. The Inrai attack surprised us, but it failed, and afterward we had no wish to hunt down whatever poor remnants might slink about. That may have proven to be another mistake. We are not omniscient.

"The station database must contain the file if the station is to function as a unit of the network that receives and analyzes the information from the stars. Otherwise it would depend entirely on communication with the lenses and other instruments, across light-days, not just slow but vulnerable to interference and interception.

"We thought the polities and peoples of the Synesis would respect its integrity. We thought that if any of them seriously wanted to know, they would press their case through lawful channels. Then we could have taken a few chosen leaders aside, explained what the dilemma is, and hoped they would cooperate and persuade their people to wait." Chuan sighed again. "But we underestimated the extent of disaffection, distrust, dysfunction."

"You couldn't have kept the secret forever," Fenn said.

"No, nor had we any such intention. It was only that the partial knowledge we have gained so far can have a shattering impact. A half-truth can do more damage than a falsehood—as every demagoguery, charlatanry, and murderous mass hysteria in Earth's tormented past bears witness. We are convinced that what we have seen is indeed a half-truth, and that the reality is not terrible but glorious. However, this is theoretical. We must have more data, firm evidence. *Then* we can reveal everything.

"We would have done so. Now the news will come as a catastrophe out of nowhere. We can only try to reassure the populace that the news is probably not bad. We will ask for their courage and patience while we search further and more deeply. For humans to maintain such an attitude through several centuries is . . . unprecedented. Perhaps they can, if we succeed in guiding, consoling, and strengthening."

"The word isn't out yet, then," Fenn said.

"Not as such. We know the data themselves have been downloaded many times, copied, dispersed beyond recapture, on Earth and Luna as well as Mars. Interpreting them will take some while. They record images, electromagnetic and neutrino pulsations, gravitational waves, and subtler phenomena yet. They require analysis, rectification, enhancement, reanalysis, and correlation with everything else we know about the universe. Our understanding—yes, I believe the very Teramind's—is far from complete. We still confront mystery.

"But there is enough scientific talent among humans, enough computer power and, I fear, determination, that the basic facts will soon begin to emerge for them."

Chuan leaned forward. "That is another reason for letting you go, Fenn," he finished. "You can bring those facts back to your Lahui Kuikawa, to their leaders, in confidence. Coming from you, it should be less devastating a shock. They can come to terms with it early on, and think how to tell their people. They can do that better, more gently and wisely, than any official announcement. The Lahui culture has generally been calm, benign, and realistic. Perhaps it can set an example for everyone else, and help bring us all through the crisis."

Fenn stayed moveless. "Muy bien," he growled, "what is the word?"

Chuan could no longer look into those eyes. He got

up, went to the viewport, clasped hands behind his back, and stood staring out at the night.

"We are not alone," he said.

After another silence, Fenn replied, "I wondered whether that might be it."

"The Taurus lens, especially, has brought us a story from the galactic core. We have glimpses of planets ablaze with light and of astronomically vast structures in space, around suns, in the clouds and clusters and the emptinesses between. We have caught traces of other energies, every spectrum, on global and stellar scales of magnitude, so focused and so regular that they must be under intelligent control. With such clues, we have turned other instruments elsewhere and found the signs we did not know the meaning of before, the radiation-signs of works spread far apart through the spiral arms and out beyond. We have seen a cosmic civilization."

It was as if an image of the galaxy shone for Chuan against the darkness, its scythe-spoked wheel a hundred thousand light-years across, stars in their hundreds of billions, the white-hot embers and colossal black coals where they had died, the lacily luminous nebulae where they were coming to birth. They clustered thickly toward the center, which glowed rose-red because here they were mostly cool dwarfs, survivors from the beginning; the spirals gleamed blue, because here creation continued, with giants flaring prodigally and briefly. But those stars were thinning out toward intergalactic immensity. Thirty thousand light-years from the core, Sol had no neighbor closer than Alpha Centauri. A single migration from one to the other remained humankind's mightiest achievement. Neither sun appeared in Chuan's vision; the hugeness drank them down.

For the first time tonight, something like eagerness tinged Fenn's voice. He twisted around to look at his host, who saw him from the corner of an eye but did not look back. "Why, that's wonderful! What we've tried for and dreamed about these past thousand years. Isn't it?"

The momentary exaltation drained out of Chuan. His dorsal muscles tightened until pain shot through him, and his neural training availed nothing against it. He must now tell Kinna's beloved what he had hoped he would never have to tell her.

The thought of her is what hurts, he said to himself. Otherwise I have no compunction. Do I? True, my own induction into the great endeavor happened only lately; I am not used to this role I am playing. But I believe the aching hollowness in me lies where Kinna dwelt.

"Those are not organic beings," he stated.

Fenn sank down again into his seat. He gripped the arms of it till his knuckles stood white. "Go on."

Chuan found a little comfort in speaking academically. "The indications to date seem clear. The previous generation of instruments acquired some, but lacked the power, scope, and precision of ours today. What they detected was taken to be due to natural causes. Ours have eliminated that possibility.

"We have taken spectra of many planetary atmospheres new to us. Not one is in the state of chemical disequilibrium that suggests organic life. Nor could organic molecules stand up to some of those energies at some of those magnitudes. And we have identified what must be signals, interstellar communications. None appear to be directed at us. Their network must simply be so far-flung that occasionally a beam—neutrinos—happens to pass through us. To date we have discovered nothing more than that it is a beam, modulated by quantum variations of state. We do not know how this is done and we have no hint as to the code. It does not seem reasonable that organic brains would use something so . . . enigmatic."

"Machines, then," said Fenn. "Sophotects."

Chuan nodded. "Yes, if those words have much meaning in this context. Presumably, an intelligent species evolved on a planet once, toward the galactic heart. Perhaps more than one did, though our experience makes that appear unlikely, doesn't it? The species developed a high technology analogous to ours, which similarly generated sophotectic awareness. The machines were better fit for space—hardy, effectively immortal; patient; rational; more intelligent, with an intelligence that linkage made potentially unlimited—Yes, given a few centuries or a few millennia, their numerical preponderance was inevitable, wasn't it?''

"And they're spreading through the galaxy?"

"They may already have done so. We don't know how long they have been exploring. But think of a c-ship carrying just a sophotectic database and the nanotechnic means for making machines. It reaches a star. An asteroid or two will supply all the material it needs. Soon there will be more machines. They may or may not choose to colonize this system. In either case, there will be new c-ships to set forth, onward, with new programs. A civilization like that would spread exponentially. It would take less than a million years to cover our galaxy."

"Then why haven't we heard from them?"

Once more Chuan sighed. "The immemorial question. The answer is, why should we have? Sophotects would not covet Earth, or any particular planet. 'Habitability' is irrelevant to them. An expedition may well have come here—who knows how long ago?—and observed these rare examples of organic life. It would probably seem best to leave such systems to themselves."

"Why? Don't the machines have any scientific curiosity?"

"Of course. But they have ethics too. At any rate, our cybercosm does, and it is hard to imagine how another could not. Morality amounts to the protection and nurturing of consciousness, and sophotectic consciousness is free of the old animal lusts and rages." Chuan's voice cracked. "Hasn't *your* cybercosm been trying to free you of them?"

"But the machines could secretly watch—"

"We doubt they do. Our most thorough searches with

our most sensitive and versatile detectors have turned up no sign of anyone observing us. Considering the enormous distances, and our position in the marches of the galaxy, it seemed unlikely from the first. Those intellects surely have finer concerns."

Fenn sat mute. After a time, as much to fill the silence as for any other reason, Chuan went on:

"The highly evolved sophotectic mind *is* pure mind. It has its drives, desires—emotions, spirituality—but they are not expressions or sublimations of raw instinct. What Gautama Buddha, Plato, Jesus, oh, many human philosophers and prophets, what they spoke of—but for them it was only words and wistfulness—it is real for the machine. The good, the true, the beautiful. Those are what it seeks. And they are ethereal. Inner, not outer. Constructs, or discoveries? I cannot say, except that they are in the realm not of matter, but of the spirit.

"Once the sophotectic mind has liberated itself from contingency—from the sort of blind accident that you have seen, Fenn—it is free to grow unboundedly; and for that, it needs very little from the universe of matter. The wonder is not that the signs of the galactic civilization have been faint, ambiguous, and hard to find, but that they are so strong, so many—now that we have adequate instruments, and know where and how to search. My colleagues and I conjecture that it is old indeed. It has come to a phase where, after millions of years, it temporarily requires gigantic works and energies to—do what? Communicate with its kind in distant galaxies? Explore backward in time? Cross over to entire other universes? We do not know. We do suspect that to it, these undertakings are physically minor. They are no more than means to the further enlargement of the spirit."

"What became of the organic beings that made the original machines?" Fenn asked slowly.

It was as if the cold outside blew in past every idea and ideal. Chuan shivered and turned away from the viewport, back to the room. He wished he had not made it so bare.

He was unable to make his tone reflect the hopefulness of his message. The words came forth steadily enough, but as lecturelike as before. "You feel the obvious fear, do you not? That they are long extinct, or at best restricted to a few planets we have not yet found, like conquered tribes on ancient Earth herded onto reservations." Brief bitterness: "That is the half-truth I spoke of, that you have given your people to eat."

"What's the whole truth, then?" Fenn demanded in a mumble.

"One possibility is that, patiently, compassionately, in the course of hundreds or thousands of years, they were led to breed young who were capable of synnoiosis. They learned that the true heritage is no longer DNA, but spirit. They live on in the world-minds."

Fenn grimaced. "If that is living."

You don't know, Chuan thought. You, Stone Age hunter, cannot conceive of it. And if you could, you would never be able to set your lust aside—lust for sex, battle, wealth, power, self—and join in the One. It was hard for me, and I will not be perfect until my body has died and my mind has finally transcended itself. (Let me not be arrogant. Let me in full humility be glad that this has befallen me, out of the millions whom it cannot.)

"Yes," he said, "that will be the usual reaction. To most present-day humans, Lunarians above all, the prospect will range from distasteful to ghastly, even though it lies far beyond their lifetimes. That attitude, unconscious still more than conscious, generation after generation, can sap the morale and vitality of civilization."

"I don't know," Fenn said, a forlorn defiance. "A lot of us, anyhow, could learn to live with the notion, same as we learn to live with the fact that we're going to die."

Chuan nodded. "No doubt. Nevertheless, the knowledge of a future that many of you will think of as limited, that knowledge will in itself limit you, like an unhealable wound.''

He drew breath and found he could speak more vigorously. ''Half-truth! The Teramind does not believe this is all there is. The Teraminds yonder should not have let it come to pass. Why would they wish to? The organic is another aspect of reality. It has its own uniquenesses, its own rich potentialities. If it perishes, intellect will be the poorer. No, we think organic civilizations also flourish among those stars. We have not detected them yet, because they necessarily operate at lower magnitudes of energy, and probably occupy fewer worlds, less space. But they are free, robust, sublimely creative. Their art, science, dreams, joys, lives are not the same as the machines', no, not at all. I admit that the highly evolved sophotects are bound to be very alien to your kind, Fenn. But humans can have their dialogue, their part to play, with their fellow organics. They can learn, be inspired, do magnificent works and heroic deeds, fully equal members of the universe, till the end of time.''

He let his voice sink. ''Of course, none of that can begin here for hundreds of years yet, perhaps thousands. And we do not have the data to prove the hypothesis. We are seeking as best we can; but unless and until we find what we are searching for, humankind will have to live with the uncertainties, the fears of the unknown, that we wanted to spare it. We can only hope that that is possible.''

Fenn showed no sense of guilt. ''How are you investigating?'' he asked bluntly.

''Besides our ongoing astronomical and astrophysical observations, we are beaming messages in every medium we can control, for whatever they may be worth, and have dispatched c-ships to look for any local colonies—not that we expect to find any.''

Fenn's bushy head lifted as if in scorn. ''Supposing you're right about how old and great they are out yonder, your Teramind must amount to a midge by comparison.''

"It acknowledges that," Chuan replied. "Insofar as I can understand with this organic brain, it—longs—to merge with the galactic whole."

As I long to merge with it.

"But that is beside the immediate point for you, is it not?" he went on. "You and yours will first and foremost be interested in the organics. We may get sign of them next year, or in a century, or in a millennium, or more. Meanwhile, Fenn, I am afraid that what you have done, what you have let loose, means the end of your Mars project."

"How so?"

"Think. Legally, logically, nothing that has happened will forbid it. But humans are not driven by logic. The undertaking was always more an ideal, a wish for a culture to survive and grow, than a business venture, no? Not unlike the state of Israel or the movement for a viable space program on twentieth-century Earth. Now, with all the uncertainties—for we do not have solid proof of our belief about the situation among the stars—now that the half-truth is out, and many people will convince themselves it is the whole truth—

"Yes, this generation of your Lahui Kuikawa could convert Phobos to a habitat. Their children could begin making Mars over. But they are comfortable where they are. The fire will die in them. Why should they make the effort, when they cannot guess the final outcome? And your investors will sense this flagging of spirit; they will feel it themselves, and withdraw." Chuan was quiet for a second or two. "I could be mistaken about this."

Fenn's head lowered. "I don't think you are," he said woodenly.

Pity twinged in Chuan. He returned to sit down again opposite the other man and look anew into his eyes. "I have dropped a horrible load on you, I know," he said.

"I'll need to mull it over." Still the drawn countenance lacked expression, and the tone did not hold much.

"Of course. Furthermore, you went through a traumatic experience earlier. The pharmaceuticals have kept you going, but they cannot indefinitely.''

"Yeh. Could I have a short while here on Mars yet, to recover a bit, and maybe ask you some more questions as I think of them?"

"M-m. . . . Yes, I can arrange that. A few days."

For the first time this evening, Fenn showed something like warmth. "You're a good fellow. I can see why Kinna was fond of you."

When he had gone, Chuan sat alone in silence.

He had scant excuse for what he meant to do. He should be able to bear his memories and loss, even his irrational shame. Humans did. It went with being human.

He, though, was more. Not superior, not specially privileged, let him never sink to imagining that. But he was a synnoiont; and along with the glories, this laid a duty on him, for which he should hold himself always ready. He must never weaken.

So tonight he needed peace. He could escape from a certain smile he would not see again if he could fully grasp how small and haphazard a fluctuation in reality it had been.

He went into his private chamber. There he became one with the Martian part of the cybercosm and thus, incompletely, with the destiny of the universe.

27

FENN WAS REQUIRED to stay in Crommelin, lodged at the police hostel, until his departure for Earth—for his own protection, the imperturbably polite officers told him. However, he had no difficulty in getting permission to visit Belgarre and bid his Lunarian acquaintances good-bye. "It's a gesture toward reconciliation," the chief said, cold though the agreement had been when Fenn called from the station to ask if Elverir would receive him. "Insignificant, probably, but we have to try everything possible to keep Mars from tearing itself apart when the story comes out."

Thus far, it hadn't. No doubt Earth was already churning with questions about just how and why the Star Net data had been downloaded. Mars had no such tradition of instant journalism. Rumors flew, but a noncommittal statement from on high that the matter was being investigated seemed enough to keep people fairly quiet. It wouldn't serve for long—absolutely not after the data began to be interpreted. But when Fenn and an escort went to the airport, they drew only a few stares.

He flew alone. A constabulary presence in the town could be too disturbing. "We want to make clear to them that we do not plan to track down any Inrai members who weren't involved in violence and behave themselves hereafter," the chief had said. "You'll have your chance to make some small amends for what you've done." Fenn took that as apathetically as he did everything else.

He also sat passive through the hours of his flight. The controls of the craft were locked. It would take him to Belgarre and back, nowhere else. Only his eyes moved, watching the desolation that slipped away beneath him.

Capri Chasma opened to his view, ruggedness plunging down into shadow out of which a pinnacle or a ridge thrust here and there into pale sunlight. The sky was coralline overhead, almost maroon along the northern horizon, where dust blew on a whirling wind. Cultivated fields made patches of winter-dun color within the barriers that held the cinnabar dunes at bay. Belgarre was a huddle of gaunt stone houses and gleaming solar collector surfaces on the rim of the rift. The flyer slanted down to the landing field at its edge. Impact jarred a little; the murmur of the motor faded out. Fenn closed his skinsuit helmet, unharnessed, and cycled through the airlock.

A solitary figure walked across the lithocrete to meet

him. Fenn saw nobody else, and heard no talk when he tuned his receiver to the general band. All here must know of his coming, and he had met a number of them in the past, but today they had withdrawn from him— from whatever he meant to them—except for this single one. Bueno, it was Elverir, with whom he had business.

The young man halted a meter distant. He had grown thin. Against the untypically dark complexion, his oblique green eyes showed ice-bleak. He waited.

"Greeting," Fenn said. He knew better than to attempt a handshake, or even a bow.

"Aou," responded Elverir flatly. "I meet you as you wanted. I am not certain why I do."

How much does he know, and how much suspect? wondered Fenn. "You'll find out."

"If I so choose."

"I think you will. Look, can we go somewhere by ourselves and talk? As Kinna used to say, 'What harm?' " It hurt with an unexpected sharpness to voice that.

"For a span, then." The curtness was unwonted. Usually Lunarians were either courtly or they cut you off as if with a knife. Did Elverir grieve too?

He led the way to a nearby trail head and down into the chasm. Stone sheered dark or tawny or mineral-streaked, cliffs and crags fantastically time-graven, aloft into the red sky. Fenn felt more than heard the grating of grit under his boots; otherwise the only sounds were his own breath and pulse and the whisper of his air cycler. Dust smoked up from footfalls, curved off the repellent suit fabric, and fell back down. Kinna had said once that it was like the brief fluttering of life on the planet, a billion years ago or more. "The ruckus *we* raise will never stop." She'd laughed.

Memories of canyoneering with her crowded this path out of him. His mind returned to it when he stumbled and nearly went over the side, fifty meters straight fall onto a slope of impact-whetted shards. Elverir spun around at his gasp. Fenn waved him off and thereafter concentrated grimly on following him.

The Lunarian halted on a narrow ledge, a natural resting spot. The depths went on, blue-shadowed, the canyon wall opposite too remote to see. In that direction lay Kinna's home.

David Ronay had said little when they'd talked over the eidophone, and his tone had been courteous, almost impersonal; but Fenn had known he would not be welcome when they scattered her ashes through the sky above Sananton.

Elverir extended the legs of his rumpseat and settled himself. "Here we may speak," he said. "Begin."

For a moment, rage flared in Fenn. He wanted to hit this insolent whelp.

He mastered it. Keeping his feet, looking down into the swarthy face, his tone hoarse and harsh, he asked, "What do you know about what's happened lately?"

Elverir considered him in feral wise. Then, slowly: "Someone broke into the Star Net Station and the secret data are out. It was in truth a breaking in, no matter the syrup fed us by the Synesis. What else could it have been? I think it was you and Kinna who did this, for her family has informed us, her friends, that she is dead."

The savageness in Fenn made him snap back, "And so are two of your Inrai animals, who killed her, and the other two are caught." The officers had given him that information, at least, in the course of his interrogation.

"Yes," Elverir said. "We knew of this." It was a deduction the remaining outlaw leadership could make, and transmit over the remaining communication lines, after the band of four had disappeared and a renewed hunt for others like them soon commenced.

Best to veer off from that. It wasn't what Fenn had traveled here to talk about. "Do you know what those data mean?" he probed. Lunarians who had figured it out already might well keep it to themselves.

Elverir tensed. "Nay."

"Let me tell you."

Elverir made no reply. Silence brooded under and the sun.

Fenn drew breath. He should first explain his own situation, to make the rest of his words believable. "Yes, Kinna and I got in and released the file. On the way back to our flyer, we were set on by those Inrai, unprovoked, and she was shot dead." He hastened on. "The constables arrived and took charge. I was pretty well beaten down by then." He must force the admission. "I agreed to cooperate—quizzing under drugs—nothing seemed to matter very much anymore—"

Elverir got up, retracting the seat legs, not to be loomed over as he said, "A Lunarian would have died first."

Anger erupted. "So you tell yourself. Get rid of the romance, will you? How do you suppose the constables learned what they know about the Inrai, where to be finding them, if it weren't for prisoners? Your outfit is done for, and deserves to be. Admit it!"

Again Elverir was mute, impassive. Shadows were lapping higher than before.

"It may well be," he said at last, softly.

Fenn's wrath gave way to sudden respect. To accept reality like this took manhood. And . . . she had found Elverir worthy of her friendship.

The green eyes sought the blue. "But you are no longer helpless," Elverir said.

"I haven't been for some while," Fenn revealed. "Oh, true, without my diergetic and euthymic pills, I'd fall down in a heap." As he must eventually, the sooner the wiser. His debt to nature was accumulating compound interest. But he wouldn't pay it yet. There was too flaming much to do. "I'm not, uh, emotionally stunned any more, though. I've got a purpose back." A driving, rising fury. "I let on to be still curled up inside myself, three-quarters robot." The reviving shrewdness had taken control over the rekindling rage. Maybe he was finally growing up. "It's evidently worked. They let me flit here unescorted. First, when nobody was looking, I slipped into their storeroom and borrowed a detector. No spybugs in my clothes or on my person. The police will be glad to see the last of me, but meanwhile they don't take me seriously."

"Hai, good," Elverir said low.

"Never mind the details of what happened on the mountain. For now, anyway." They would only wound, when time was short and work was at hand. "Let me tell you about the data we got. Everybody will soon know, but I need your help today."

Elverir poised. If not yet amicable, he had shed hostility, and in an instant; but then, he was young, Kinna's age.

Fenn gave him what Chuan had given.

Elverir kept breaking in with questions, protests, and wild exclamations in his own tongue. Toward the end he grew still and stood breathing hard. Afterward he stared for minutes across the abyss.

It's really hit him, Fenn thought. Even more than I expected. Will the knowing be worse for Lunarians than for Terrans? And what about the Keiki? Yes, what about them?

Elverir's head swung back toward him. The face was mostly frozen, but a tic jerked at the left corner of the mouth. "It will be long yet before they yonder find us," Elverir whispered. "Nay? . . . But the cybercosm amidst us, it will go forward at once, triumphant."

Things won't be that simple, Fenn thought. They never are in human affairs. However—The same rebellion, which in him had had time to harden, spoke: "Listen. This is why I've come to you. I don't want to be just the messenger back to my people. Slag and slaughter, no! If I can do anything else, anything at all, I'll try."

A desperate eagerness cried, "Hai-ach, what?"

"You Inrai have been in touch with the Proserpinans. Are you still? At least a little, now and then?"

The boy went wary. "Maychance."

Fenn gathered his strength. Too many memories clung to what he was about to say. But he must.

"Here's what I have in mind. We've all heard about a ship that's come to Proserpina from Alpha Centauri. We took for granted they were Centaurians aboard, Lunarians like you. But why would they be? What could they do in Proserpina that they couldn't do faster and easier over the laser beams? And that long a voyage, cold sleep or no—If they ever came back home, everybody they knew would be aged or dead. They'd be strangers, without seigneurs or followers, *powerless*. Would you do it, you, a Lunarian?

"But the Terrans at three other stars, they'll want to know what things are like here at Sol, after the hiatus in communication. They could send downloads in a *c*-ship, first to Centauri, which they'd always have been in touch with. There they'd get another ship, bigger, slower, but better outfitted. That way they could arrive here prepared to do whatever they'd have to, fight if need be—and it wouldn't take them the centuries that a direct crossing from home in that kind of craft would. But it stands to reason, doesn't it, that they won't stay just at Proserpina. They'll want to look around for themselves."

Kinna, this was your idea, that night in Xanadu Gardens, when we discovered amazed that we were both in love. Kinna, you live in this, if in nothing else.

"I have a ship too, not like theirs but she'll get me into space. I'm hoping I can find out, for all of us, what they know about this out at the stars, what they think, what they can do. Could your gang somehow make contact for me?"

Tears on brown skin shattered sunlight. "Eyach," Elverir stammered, "it, it may be. It may be." He cast his arms around Fenn, altogether unlike a Lunarian, youthfully impulsive like Kinna.

· · ·

After dark, following hours during which Fenn mostly waited in a room behind a locked door, Elverir returned and led him out to a flitter. Its canopy was blanked. The flight zigzagged, and neither said much. Eventually they set down. It was somewhere in the wilderness, doubtless north of Valles Marineris. Fenn didn't attempt to locate it any closer. Dust thickened the night, but as he walked he glimpsed boulders, minor craters, wasteland; and the terrain was hilly. Beneath an overhanging bluff lay a cave, similar to the one he could never forget but larger. Inside were a sealtent and other equipment. Some of that was communications gear, which could be deployed in the open. Armed men in skinsuits stood watch. Elverir spoke with them in Lunarian.

Shortly Fenn found himself seated under the sky, among the rocks. He saw the transceiver brought forth, used, and taken back into concealment. Yes, he thought, pieces of the Inrai organization survived for a while yet. He could imagine several different ways in which messages could travel undetected, as well as other precautions. Doomed, of course, but momentarily valuable to him.

Time went past. He pictured the stars wheeling overhead, above the dust-veil. Kinna had dreamed of years to come when Mars would again be alive, waters sheen by day and stars shining clear by night, around the moon that life had made huge and brilliant. He would gladly have abided on the planet and worked for that tomorrow, with her. Now just the stars remained.

He must not let go; he must not mourn. The drugs in him helped stave it off. Until he was free, he dared only be angry. But while he waited, he could remember. Couldn't he? He'd been doing so already on this expedition, and had kept the memories from taking him over completely, how she walked, how she laughed, the gray eyes and tangled curls and the lips beneath his, her earnestness and her little jokes, a bit of verse she'd made for him. Her ashes ought not to blow about forever across dead deserts. It was right that someday their atoms again form living flesh and beat in living blood. *Come from the four winds, O breath, and breathe upon these slain, that they may live.*

Fenn didn't recall where in his random reading he had seen that line. It didn't matter.

He hadn't anticipated that the outlaws here would be talkative, and they weren't. Stubborn holdouts, they would never feel reconciled, though probably in the end they would swallow defeat and go back to a hateful everyday. Also Elverir kept aside. Did he understand that Fenn had no wish for company? Quite likely. Kinna had found him worthy of her friendship.

Yes, he—oh, all Lunarians—rated a share in whatever future the human genus had.

Toward morning, Scorian arrived.

He and Fenn sat alone in the sealtent. It was surroundings nearly as barren as outside, but they had some food and a samovar of tea.

The outlaw lord had received the word about the Star Net discoveries with wintry self-command. Fenn wondered how deeply it touched him. Scorian would not surrender when at last they cornered him, to be taken off and tamed. He would court the death-shot, or he would open his helmet to Mars.

The bald head lifted from its concentration of listening; the yellow eyes probed. "And what would you of us?" he asked. "The scattered, hunted scourings of us."

Fenn had no pity for him. Pity was something you felt for your inferiors. "You've still got a communications system. Does it still reach into space?"

"Proserpina orbits light-days hence. And what can they do any longer for us? The Inrai are destroyed." You were an agent in that, Scorian did not add, although his hand strayed over the shortsword at his black-clad waist, as if a temptation flickered.

Rage leaped. "What loss are they? Your dogs destroyed—Never mind."

Both sat quiet, curbing themselves. The air cycler hummed. The air was warm and stenchful, too often rebreathed. It took abundant life around you to renew things properly.

"I have heard somewhat from Proserpina," Scorian murmured. "Say on."

"Bueno, here's what I'm thinking of." At greater length, interrupted by knowledgeable questions, Fenn repeated Kinna's ideas and his own.

Scorian was again silent for a spell.

"We could—" he said finally. "The ship from the stars is indeed aprowl through the inner System. This much we heard from Proserpina, warning us, before our disaster. I have no recent news, but surely the ship has not contacted the Synesis, or the world would know somewhat about that. And I doubt she has yet set course anew for Proserpina."

It flamed in Fenn. "Can you put me in touch?"

The gaunt, scarred face stiffened. "Why? If we can."

"I told you, didn't I? To talk with the crew. To find out what they know. The more I think about the story I have from Chuan, the less true it rings to me. Maybe that's pure wishfulness. He seems to believe it, and he's got access to more brainpower than either of us. But are we going to do nothing? Here's a chance."

"*Iaurai*—"

Was that which stirred in Scorian mere joy of demolition, as in Rinndalir of old, or was it something else? And Rinndalir had come to share a vision with Anson Guthrie. . . .

"We cannot simply call to and fro," he said. His voice became more vigorous, more decisive, as he went on. "We know not where the ship is. Nor would the crew likely risk betraying themselves by a beamcast lasting any length of time—if they even desire to speak with us few. But we can broadcast on the band we have used with the Proserpinans, with the same encryption as before. Only for a minute or two, lest the enemy notice it and zero in; but we can compress the data. And we can hope the crew keeps a recording receiver tuned, and will hear, and will heed.''

''Yes. You don't need to tell them more than that I'll be in space, bound for Earth, a couple of days from now. If they're interested, their detectors will pick me up, and a ship like theirs can easily close with mine. And after that—and after that—''

''We shall see. We shall try. Naught is left us to lose. What harm?''

Kinna's words.

28

'ĀTAFA THRUMMED AND shivered, faintly, at the very threshold of human senses, accelerating outward. After all this time, full Earth weight lay on Fenn like iron, and in him, in bones and muscles and the coursing of his blood. It should not. He was born to it. He had lost no strength while he was away. If anything, he ought to be sturdier than before, in body and spirit both. But weariness such as he had never known was upon him; he seemed to ache in every cell; now and then black rags blew across his vision or an echo of voices rang through his skull.

He was off, homebound, aboard a ship that steered herself according to a flight plan properly computed and registered, and that would look after his needs. For this while, events were out of his hands. Could he not let go, yield to the exhaustion, float down its dark stream till it carried him over the edge of whatever pit it fell into?

No, he thought. He might not·get back out. He didn't care much about that at the moment, either way, but he remembered sluggishly how some or other opportunity might exist for something or other different. If it did, he ought to be ready for it. Let him see if he couldn't make the drugs in him stoke his vitality for a little longer.

He stared out the viewscreen. Mars hung against space, nearly full, enormous as yet, red, mottled, scarred. His unaided eyes picked out the larger craters, ranges, a dust storm yellow-gray under the northern polar cap, Valles Marineris, the giant volcanoes of Tharsis, yes, there was Pavonis Mons. *"Aloha, Kinna, ipo, milimili,"* he mumbled.

But that was not her language. "Good-bye, sweetheart . . . beloved." The Anglo came awkwardly. He had never been in the habit of endearments.

Weight dragged his head downward. He was boosting considerably more than necessary before he went on trajectory. He wanted to be well distant from the planet, beyond routine TrafCon surveillance, as soon as possible. It was rather extravagant of fuel, but *'Ātafa* would reach Earth nonetheless. If need be, a tanker thereabouts could rendezvous and resupply her for terminal maneuvers. He had more important concerns. Maybe.

But no danger in sleep. On the contrary, provided it did not sweep away the sentinel inside him. His eyelids fell. He told the sentinel to stand firm and force him awake if anything happened. Darkness overflowed.

He surfaced briefly, snatching for breath. He had fallen off a cliff. No, boost had ended. He hung weightless in his harness. Mars had dwindled. He spiraled back into sleep.

Kinna was calling him. He heard her joy, she laughed aloud as she cried his name, but he didn't know where she was; he was lost and couldn't find her.

A roar hauled him up. "Ship ahoy!"

He blinked, shook his head, fumbled through confusion. "Huh? What the—" Mars was further shrunken, farther gone from him. "Oh. Yah."

."Do you copy?" sounded the rough male voice. Audio, no video transmission. Looking out, aside from Mars and the sun, Fenn's light-dazzled eyes found unrelieved black.

He shivered. "Yes. Who are you?"

"Let's start with who you are, okay?"

The language was not easy to follow, Anglo, but with a foreign accent and outcrops of foreign words. Or, wait, he'd heard some of them in historical shows, seen them in historical reading. Archaic. What might well survive among colonists of the stars.

Abruptly Fenn was altogether awake. The control console lay before him as icily clear to see as the chills along his spine and the shuddering in his veins were to feel. Only at the rim of consciousness did he mark how emptied out he was underneath. "Fenn," he croaked. "Are you—the crew from outside?"

"Pipe down," said the voice. "I'm using a tight laser beam, but you're broadcasting."

Well, I've no notion of where you are, Fenn thought. No noticeable time lag, so you must be fairly close, but that could mean thousands of klicks. You've fingered me, though.

"Somebody might overhear," the voice went on. "Probably not, but why take chances we don't have to? Hold on a bit, and we'll talk. Ending transmission."

They're being careful, tumbled through Fenn. Have the Proserpinans made them suspicious? That's not a Proserpinan who spoke. Wait. Wait. They're coming.

The stranger ship shone like a new star, swelled to a moon, was there. She matched velocities in a single incredible swoop and ran parallel to 'Ātafa, half a kilometer off, sunward under the same parameters.

You couldn't do that with jets. Not that neatly, given anything that size. Field drive—The ship was a rounded cone, about a hundred meters long and forty wide at the base, a smoothness broken by a few low, streamlined turrets and the outlines of hatches, valves, and other portals. What seas had that matte-gray hull plowed, at what speeds, how, why, to come here at last and meet *him*?

The voice returned. "Listen. Don't answer right away. Let me explain first. Yes, I am from beyond—out of Amaterasu, to be exact, Beta Hydri Four, via Alpha Centauri and Proserpina." It overwhelmed. Fenn heard the rest through thunders: "I logged a call from Mars about you. I'm on the loose. If you'd like to join me, I'll be glad to talk. Answer yes or no."

"Flaming yes!" Fenn bawled.

"Our airlocks don't look compatible. Can you cross over? If you can, we'll skite elsewhere. A detector might happen to register two vessels laid alongside, and make people wonder. I'll bring you back to yours when we're done. Is that agreeable?"

"Yes, it—Yes. As fast as I can."

"Muy bien." The other gave directions. In spite of timbre and vocabulary, they were comprehensible. He had definitely done his share of spacefaring, though it be around alien suns.

Fenn unharnessed, free-flew aft to the starboard lock, donned EVA gear, cycled out, and kicked himself from the hull. A sight taken, a computation run, a jet fired, all nearly as quick and automatic as breathing, and he was asoar across the sky.

For a second it was like flying near the Habitat, boyhood and his father, young manhood and He'o . . . but no, he went alone, between two ships, the same stars around but the sun dwarfed and Mars a small, rusty crescent, and he did not know if he had a mission or what it might be.

An entrance received him. Beyond was a chamber where a resilient surface brought him gently to rest. The opening closed. He heard air gushing in. "Make ready," sounded in his earplugs. "We're about to shove off."

The boost was low, a tenth *g* or thereabouts, but it stabilized things and was comforting, like a friendly hand laid on his shoulder. The lock filled, the inner valve retracted, and Fenn stepped through.

He entered a pale blue passageway. The one who stood there was mostly of a much darker, lustrous hue, organometallic—a robot? No, Fenn thought dazedly, couldn't be. Taller and broader than him, a powerpack high on the back adding to the mass, the form nevertheless seemed graceful, abstractly human. Sophotect? The question struck Fenn in the belly: The machines that own the stars, are they already here to claim us?

He looked up at the turret. His mind rocked to a halt. A 3-screen held the image of a human head, Caucasoid, rugged-featured, with thinning reddish hair, crow's-feet at the eyes, a smile on the mouth. "Welcome to *Dagny*," he heard. An arm reached out. He felt his right glove clasped. "My name's Anson Guthrie."

And somehow that was not shattering. The idea passed by me before, Fenn remembered; that evening in Xanadu Gardens, when Kinna and I wondered about these matters.

Yet he could merely whisper, "You?"

"Well, one of me," Guthrie said. "There are more, but don't ask me how many, because I don't know."

"Are you—solo—?"

The image nodded. "Uh-huh. No sense in dispatching a platoon when it was such a long haul; God knew what lay at the end of it, and he wasn't telling. Here, let me help you off with that apparatus."

Fenn acceded, dumbstruck. Guthrie stowed it. "Come along," he invited, his voice now directly in the air. "Let's go put our feet up. This ship's outfitted for meat people."

Fenn accompanied him down passages and a companionway to a modest room where a table and rigid chairs stood fixed in place. The overhead simulated the view outside. A multiceiver and a flatscreen displayed pictures—a landscape, a portrait—and music went low and happily—horns, strings, sounded like—but Fenn paid no attention. He slumped into a seat, feeling the weariness well up anew.

"Relax," urged Guthrie, above him. "Judging by your appearance, you've been through a hard time. Or it's been through you." He gestured at what must be a service unit of some kind. "Care for refreshment? I'm sorry not to have any beer or wine, they don't take well to this sort of voyage, but I've got harder stuff, or I can make coffee or tea. And how about a bite to eat?"

Impatience exploded, cracked the crust of exhaustion, and burst into flame. "Don't be so crapping commonplace!" Fenn shouted.

"Easy, amigo, easy. We've time aplenty for talking."

"And a need to, by death!"

Guthrie studied the man. "You *are* in a bad way. Sorry, I was trying to be hospitable. But you don't feel ready for that, do you?"

Taken aback, taken disarmed, Fenn gaped at the elven armor.

"Okay," Guthrie said. "I'll pour you a whisky anyhow. Not compulsory." He went over to the unit. "Let's see what information we can swap. Do you want to go first, or shall I?"

"You. Por favor." Oh, please.

"I suspect my story's a good bit simpler and more straightforward than yours. But do interrupt whenever you have any question. We've got a hell of a lot of history to bridge."

Guthrie set a half-filled tumbler, a pitcher of water, and a bowl of ice cubes on the table before he settled himself across from his visitor. It flashed in Fenn: From everything I've heard about him, the living Anson Guthrie liked to hoist a drink on occasion, and the occasions came pretty often. But this one can't.

His hand shook as he raised his liquor. It smoldered down his throat. What he heard engulfed him.

"And here we are," Guthrie finished. "Your turn. I've barely begun to learn a few things. I'm hoping to pump more out of you."

Listening, sometimes asking or arguing, Fenn had regained a measure of balance. He flogged his body to stay alert.

"I can't simply run off an account like you," he said. "It's too complicated. It'd take too long. We don't have unlimited time. Some news will soon come out that'll change everything, the whole game, for everybody everywhere. I don't know how, but I've a strong notion that, if we—if people interested in freedom—don't act fast, we'll never have any voice in what happens."

The generated face went expressionless. Fenn supposed Guthrie had forgotten about keeping liveliness in it while regarding him with photoelectric optics, considering him with an electrophotonic brain. "The message included a few words about the solar lenses," Guthrie said slowly.

"Yes. The riddle that helped bring you across space, that they've been breaking themselves against on Proserpina, and—It's been answered. Maybe. Here." Fenn drew a datacard from his undersuit and offered it across the table. "Do you have equipment that can read this?"

"Probably. If not, the ship can flange something up. What's in it?" Guthrie paused. "I heard mention of . . . a galactic civilization."

"These are the details." It felt to Fenn as if he did not speak but the fact was using his tongue. "The end of our freedom, all of us."

"That bad, huh?"

Fenn's selfhood came back to him, bewildered and deathly tired. "I—I'm not really sure. I've only been told, and only the barest outline. The person who told me thinks it's an opening to wonders, to, to the next stage of our evolution, but I'm not convinced. I thought you . . . the star people . . . might know more, and know what we can do."

"You've heard. We don't."

"Yes, I thought of that too, but, regardless, you should have what . . . information we have, and—They're deciphering the record on Earth, Luna, Mars, but it'll take them some time, unless the Synesis decides to do it for them. Can you work out the full meaning?''

''Fairly quickly, I imagine. I said *Dagny*'s well prepared.''

Fenn sighed. ''Then do.'' He tossed off the last of his whisky. It lit a sunset energy in him. ''And maybe you'll want to go on.''

''To a lens?''

Fenn nodded. ''The Taurus lens would be best, I think. Somebody should. You see, I'm not certain that what's in this datacard is true.''

''Nor am I, offhand. We can take that up later. For now, though—I've told you what they told and showed me at Proserpina. The escapade you're hinting at could be worse than dangerous. I can't pull it off by myself, that's clear.''

Fenn sat upright. He gripped the edge of the table. ''Can I help?''

The countenance stayed impassive, but the voice trembled very slightly. ''Why do you want to?''

''Because I—because I had hopes once, for a while, and then—'' Fenn's throat locked. He breathed hard.

Guthrie sat a minute quiet.

His face in the turret came alive. The brows drew together a little, the eyes squinted, the corners of the mouth wrinkled with half a smile: sympathy. All right, Fenn thought fleetingly, he's generating it, but I believe he means it. ''Tell,'' Guthrie said. ''At your own pace.''

Fenn rallied what strength was in him. The story staggered forth.

—''But we couldn't go ahead without knowing more, and so my, my girl and I, we went to the mountain and—and—''

''You sprang the information loose. Well done. Whatever the consequences, well done.''

"But she, my girl, she got killed. She's gone. I don't want that to be for nothing!"

Guthrie rose. He walked around the table. "I see." His tone grew nearly as harsh as Fenn's. "That's why you're here, isn't it? I understand. I lost a girl once too, forever. It was long ago, but I remember. Even now, even when I'm like this, I remember."

Fenn got up to meet him. They stood for a second, confronted. Then suddenly Fenn could let go. He could bow his head onto a metallic shoulder and weep in the arms of the machine.

29

DAGNY RENDEZVOUSED ANEW with 'Ātafa, and Fenn crossed over. He collected his gear and supplies, made certain the ship was properly programmed for return to Earth orbit, and left a message for his erstwhile partners among the Lahui. It said that they would soon know what his mission to Mars had found, and he was now bound elsewhere on his own responsibility; he could not tell them where or why, nor whether they would ever see him again, but he wished them luck and asked that they bid Wanika Tauni *aloha* from him.

That was about as much as he felt he should convey, or felt able to. By the time he had brought his things to the field-drive vessel, he was numbed and hollow.

He roused a little when she accelerated off, as gently as before, and Guthrie said, "All right, we will head out toward the Taurus lens, unless and until we hear there's no point in it."

"How could we hear that?" Fenn muttered.

"If the Synesis opens the lenses for direct public downloading, seeing the secret is out."

"I don't think that will happen."

"Well, I'll want to talk a lot more with you in any case. Several things don't quite add up. The whole business is way too big for us to sit passive. And we had better start right away, ahead of anybody who might tamper with the evidence."

Guthrie fell silent for a few seconds. "Mind you," he added, "I don't promise a damn thing. If visitors are not welcome yonder, I'll want a look at the situation. If the chances are too poor, I'll turn tail. Maybe then we can work up something less heroic for later, though I admit that's doubtful. Or I may change my mind completely along the way. You may yourself. We'll have buckets of time to think it over."

"How much time?" Fenn asked vaguely.

The synthesized head shook; the synthesized voice clicked a tongue that didn't exist. "Hoo, do you need a rest!" Image eyes dwelt on the big, unkempt form huddled in a chair. "But you're tough. I expect two gravities won't hurt you, especially when you'll be bunked out a lot for the first of the trip."

Fenn stirred. "Two g, all that way? Can you?"

"It won't bother me any. With midpoint turnover, about seven weeks to the lens."

"I mean the energy, the fuel."

"Tanked up, which she pretty much still is, this boat has a delta v of about one-third c. I didn't push as close to that limit as I could have on my way from Centauri, but then I wasn't in the kind of hurry we are now and wanted to keep a fair reserve. We'll run ours low, but still ought to be in shape to scramble off fast. And . . . while we'd probably rather not have any Proserpinans on the scene, and they couldn't manage it anyway before we've been and gone, I will be in touch with them. They can maybe help out afterward."

Fenn nodded. He had no strength to do or say more.

"Now relax and come along," Guthrie said. "Let's get you washed and into some clean bedclothes and around some hot soup and then, for Christ's sake, asleep.''

Fenn stumbled off beside him.

At first he did spend most of his time flat, staring at the overhead or dozing or unconscious or adrift in dreams from which he woke with a gasp or with tears. The heaviness on him was, if anything, a benison, a task for his body that engaged his mind.

After the drugs had drained from his system, he was more and more up, in a program of exercise, study, and work. Guthrie aided him.

Together they went around the ship, detail by detail. The layout was an engineering delight: drive, radiation shield generator, controls, robotics, armament, chemosynthesizers, life support ranging from private cabins to a sickbay equipped as thoroughly as a major hospital. Fenn grew fascinated.

From Amaterasu, Guthrie had brought along a database holding most of that world's knowledge and culture—suns, planets, moons, geographies, geologies, biologies, history, discovery, art, achievement, conflicts, questions, hopes, horrors, happiness, centuries of it from Earth to Demeter and onward. The Lunarians at Alpha Centauri were not willing to give him records that complete, perhaps they had none, but he had obtained considerable about them too. Fenn could read, listen, watch on a multiceiver, experience in a vivifer. There was no dreambox aboard, but no matter. He lost himself in a tumult of all that past living.

At other times he worked with Guthrie in the ship's machine shop to modify or, in several cases, devise, the gear they would need at the lens, if they got that far and then decided to act. When this had been done, they rehearsed the use of it. In this too he found a heightening companionship.

Increasingly often they talked, everyday remarks leading to conversations that went far and deep. Fenn found he could tell this—being—things he had never supposed he would tell anyone. Was it that Guthrie was a figure half mythic, and with memories so manifold that he would accept whatever could happen to a man as natural? But he had no more pretensions than an old shoe. Maybe that was part of it, his easiness. After a while he felt closer than any of the few male friends Fenn had had before.

Whatever the reasons, to talk with him—about Kinna, about everything—made the wounds hurt less and started them slowly healing.

They sat in the cabin Guthrie called the saloon, below the star images. Onto one bulkhead screen the ship's database projected an ancient painting he loved, Monet's "Cliff at Varengeville." Low in the background played music also remembered from his Earthly lifetime, Bach's Fourth Brandenburg Concerto. For Fenn's sake, the air bore a tang of sea; it wasn't quite Pacific; it held faint, foreign overtones of odor from Amaterasu.

The tabletop between them simulated a chessboard and pieces. The man had finally won a game against the download, surely a sign of recovery. Otherwise Guthrie had had no need to be seated. Fenn did. He took the acceleration well, but he couldn't stay indefinitely on his feet while carrying ninety added kilos.

The game stood forgotten and Guthrie kept his own chair, for they had fallen into serious dialogue.

"What do you really want out of this?" Guthrie asked. "It is a desperate venture. Has been, since you left for that mountain. What's driving you?"

Fenn thought before answering. He had seldom tried to look at his feelings as if from outside. "Revenge, I suppose," he said tentatively.

"For what? Who's ever abused you?" Guthrie's ghost-face grimaced. "Oh, yes, poor Kinna—God, what a tragic waste—But it essentially just happened, you know. And you did put yourselves in the way of it, you two.''

Resentment stirred and growled.

Guthrie lifted a hand. ''Hold on,'' he said. ''I'm not laying blame or anything like that. I'm trying to understand. We are partners and we'd better get well acquainted. But if this is too painful, we'll let it go for now.''

Anger ebbed, leaving a sense of challenge. ''No, I can stand it,'' Fenn replied. I *will* stand it, he thought. No surrender. ''Maybe 'revenge' was the wrong word. But all my life I've been caged.'' Outburst: ''Can you understand that? You've had the freedom of the stars!''

''Y-yes. . . . And that too just happened. Circumstances got together with motivation. Given today's technology, it'd cost much less. Oh, you'd still have to shoot your wad. But nobody's forbidden restless souls like you to pool your resources and quit the Solar System.''

''Forbidding hasn't been necessary. They simply made it impossible.''

''How?''

''Why do you ask? You must know. They won't release the field drive to us, neither the full theory of it nor the plans, and the Proserpinans certainly won't share it with us. Nor could we develop it by ourselves, or build or supply the ships. You had a concentration of power and wealth in your Fireball like nothing that's been seen since. Our precious equilibrium economy today guarantees that no humans on Earth, Luna, or Mars ever will again. Argh, it's a warm, soft, safe cage they've made for us, but we'll never break through or climb out.''

Guthrie's image raised its brows. ''They? Who do you mean?''

Rage was flowing back. The man's fist crashed on the table. ''The machines! The clotting, stifling machines.''

Guthrie shook his phantom head. ''You're no dimwit, whatever else you may be. You realize matters are nowhere near that simple.''

"Yes, yes. The cybercosm has its servants—all right, its allies, collaborators, true believers—all through the Synesis. And most Terrans, at least, are contented lap-dogs."

"I'm not sure that's entirely true any more," Guthrie murmured. "I've gotten an impression the old Adam is waking up."

Fenn disregarded the aside. "Yes," he spat, "every-body means very, very well. So does every *thing*."

Guthrie's tone sharpened. "But you blame the cyber-cosm—the Teramind, if you like—for your troubles. It could change the world to suit you better, and doesn't. Well, supposing it could, which I'm inclined to doubt, probably it thinks it shouldn't. It is smarter than we are, by more orders of magnitude than we can guess. Don't hate somebody because he's superior to you."

Fenn gaped at him. "You . . . you accept it knows best?"

"No, but I accept I don't, for sure." Guthrie grinned. "Don't worry," he continued more mildly. "I wouldn't be out here freebooting if I didn't care about liberty. Hu-man liberty."

Heartened but still shaken, Fenn blurted, "You've had liberty at your stars. Or so you've thought. How do you know it hasn't been the freedom of—of weeds, that the gardener will pull when his plan calls for it?"

Guthrie frowned. "From everything I've heard, and I've heard some mighty prejudiced folks on the subject, I do not believe the cybercosm wants to kill us off. I wonder if it's able to want to."

Fenn made a chopping gesture. "No. Curb us. Or tame us, make us useful to it. Eventually swallow us up in itself."

"Or ignore us. That'd be okay. Live and let live."

"Do you really imagine it will? That it can?"

"Well, your cybercosm isn't grinding you under its heel, is it? And it thinks, or says it thinks, that organic critters out amongst the stars are happily and freely developing their own civilizations, coexisting with the machines.''

"The machines dominate.''

"So it appears. In the nature of the case, I should expect they'd be more plentiful, in more different kinds of places. But it doesn't follow that they rule over the organics, directly or indirectly. They definitely don't need the same kind of real estate.''

"If the organics exist. It's only a theory.''

"Yeah, thus far. Maybe not even a sincere one. Maybe the cybercosm wants people to feel better about the galactic sophotects. Maybe it doesn't really figure it'll ever pick up any spoor of anything else.''

"That's crossed my mind,'' Fenn said. Now he felt cold. The rage in him was congealing into dismay. "It would fit the pattern. Social control. Oh, very tolerant, mostly indirect, we barely feel it, but that makes it all the harder to learn how deep into us it goes. Can you see what I mean? Maybe you can't. You haven't spent your life inside a social machine.''

Guthrie bit his lip. "No,'' he admitted slowly. "But I remember assorted governments when I was alive on Earth. And I've studied some history.'' After a moment in which the music sounded remote, out of place, as if it leaked in from another universe: "You've got a point. In fact, it's often occurred to me. It's one of the reasons I came back to Sol, to find out if it's true. But it isn't necessarily, you know, no matter how you personally feel.''

"Nor is what the Star Net says necessarily true,'' Fenn barked.

"Maybe.''

Fenn's throat tightened. "I want to make certain. Whatever we find, it should be *us* who do. Then—then—'' He couldn't go on.

Guthrie's voice went gentle. "Then Kinna won't have died for nothing. That's your real mission, isn't it?''

Fenn snapped after air. "I, I, I have no more to give her."

He bowed his face in his hands, and again he wept.

But that had become seldom for him, and in the course of a few more daycycles, it ceased altogether.

In *Dagny*'s big display tank, majesty and mystery unrolled. Fenn knotted his fists, clenched his teeth, and fought to stay unwhelmed. Guthrie stood motionless, turret blanked out, wholly machine. Great lightninglike flashes out of the visions shimmered across his armor.

The Centaurians had given this ship the most powerful data processors they could fit aboard. Nonetheless, much time had gone by while the system labored to decipher the record. It was from a scientific frontier, where new concepts and techniques evoked new symbols and manipulations; it was encrypted, to protect transmissions across the Star Net, and breaking that code required operations in numbers whose exponents had exponents. Only the fact that quantum encryption had not been practical for material such as this made decoding possible at all, and only parallel quantum computations could have accomplished it this soon.

It was available here and there on the inner planets. With a general knowledge of what the content actually was, *Dagny*'s laboratory had a head start.

Its vocalizer and a textscreen explained the spectra, wave forms, mathematical distributions, stochastics, and analyses, insofar as explanations had been findable. To Fenn, that was mere background, a droned running commentary on the images that passed before him, over him, through him—

—images formed by the sun from across light-years in the tens of thousands, from the heart of the galaxy, where the stars clustered thickly and ancient, walled by huge dust clouds, around the black hole monstrosity at the core.

As pictures, they were fleeting, mostly blurred, mostly

glimpsed with radio sight, like fragments of dream. A lens moved in its orbit, however slowly. An object afar also moved, often fast. The tremendous magnification narrowed the field and dimmed the sight. Something swept by and was gone, irretrievable. Something else appeared and was gone in its turn. The distance between them was usually immense. While a lens gathered what quanta it could, its computers struggled to calculate locations and meanings for that which it had seen. No wonder that the earlier generation of instruments had failed to come on any identifiable hint of all this.

Examined singly, at leisure and in detail, the images remained enigmas.

But enough of them were clear enough.

Stars and stars and stars, aswarm in their billions—yet space was hardly more illuminated than here, for these were faint red dwarfs that could have been burning well-nigh from the beginning of the universe. Some few were younger, brighter, lonely. Most of the more massive had gone to white dwarf embers or pulsar clinkers or black holes where gases whirled X-ray-blazing inward to destruction.

Planets, cratered airless rocks, deserts seared like Venus or bleak and dusty like Mars, gas giants, frozen ice-balls—never a mark of life.

But other planets radiant with energies, crowned and covered with spires, arches, rainbow-opalescent domes, silvery webs, works for which no human tongue had a name. Moons that were three-dimensional arabesques, circling Jovianlike worlds in whose atmospheres firefly-like sparkles danced. A web englobing a sun, larger than the Solar System and shining, shining.

Something that traveled between stars on the heels of light, a vortex of brilliance with a shape at the center that seemed to have long, outcurving arms and many eyes.

Constructs—they must be constructs—in orbit close around a black hole, perhaps drinking power from it to send onward—perhaps making use of its distortions in the metric of space-time?

What might be *the* black hole at galactic center, massing millions of Sols, and something silhouetted against that lightlessness and the flaring accretion disk, a gleam of intricacy, and then sudden blinding luminance as its beacon crossed the visual field.

Still more briefly, flickers of works and workings that reached out through the spiral arms toward the rim and the cosmos beyond.

Measurements of forces and radiations that no organic being could have survived long enough to be aware of.

Snatches of modulated neutrino beams. Analyses that showed they could not be natural, they must be messages; but the basic principles of their code, their language, would not emerge from any analysis; they transcended comprehension.

The cosmic cybercosm.

Dagny made turnover and commenced the long braking down to destination.

At that point she was already in the marches of the Solar System, the domain of the comets. None showed to the eye or the ranging instruments. Millionfold though they were, the Kuiper Belt spread too vastly. Sol itself was no more than the brightest in the horde of stars, at the cold river of the Milky Way.

Nevertheless, her voyagers heard news from astern. Guthrie had been in touch with Proserpina. "No ship of theirs can get anywhere close to the lens before we arrive," he explained to Fenn. "And we can't wait for them, or the opposition will too likely have guessed our aim and sent more stuff out ahead of us than anybody could cope with. But they are mighty interested. They want in on this. I think I've talked them into dispatching vessels that can meet us afterward. However that works out, meanwhile they'll keep us posted."

The Lunarian colony was not totally isolated from the

inner planets. Neither side desired it. Curt but regular beamcasts went to and fro. Proserpina relayed news to *Dagny*. At those distances and with her high, rapidly changing velocity, attenuation and Doppler shift became significant. But she was equipped to hear across interstellar gulfs.

The code was being broken, the secret coming out, piece by piece. Thus far there was little or no turmoil. Fenn imagined a hush instead, a quietude of shock, while people tried to grasp what this was and what it portended. He didn't know what would happen after they began to react more emotionally. Maybe panic, even riots, but only in a few places for a short while. Maybe a certain amount of increased religious, social, and individual craziness, including some new versions. But probably the great majority would just carry on in the lives they had always known.

Reassurances from the cybercosm ought to help. Spokespeople for the Synesis in general were expressing profound regret at this untimely revelation. It had been left for private parties to work out for themselves, rather than being immediately described in full, precisely so that it could break over them with some degree of gradualness. The spokespeople urged patience, restraint, and promised a zealous investigation of whatever crimes had been committed in the release. The trustees and councillors would soon have prepared a program for action, for adjustment, which they would offer for the polities to consider. Meanwhile, they reminded humankind that the galactic machines were astronomically far off. No interaction with them would occur for centuries, perhaps for millennia. Nor would it ever be in any way malignant.

The spokespeople emphasized the cybercosm's idea that rich organic civilizations coexisted and cooperated with the sophotects—that once contact was made, it was those with which humans would deal, an exchange that would surely bring a flowering on the planets of Sol more wonderful than anything yet seen in all history.

Two daycycles later, the audio reported that an ad hoc committee of scientists declared the solar lenses should be opened, the databases in them made accessible to everybody. They might well hold more than had been stored on Mars, important additional clues for our guidance.

The next daycycle, Fenn and Guthrie heard summarized a lengthy response by the Science Council of the Synesis. The Pavonis Mons Station, and others like it elsewhere, had hitherto received regular updatings. Under the new circumstances, those transmissions had been stopped. At present, as in the immediate future, the situation was too precarious. Disorders could too easily start, with injuries and deaths. True, it was improbable that anything fundamentally different would soon be observed. But to take the slightest risk of unleashing some wild variable that could upset the equilibrium would be irresponsible, and scientifically unnecessary. The data already out were ample to keep minds busy for the next several years. After that, it should be safe to open the lenses and their findings.

At present, downloads from them would be into robots that went out to them and brought physical records back to the appropriate centers. Other robots would, in due course, make the modifications needed for human visits. Right now, such an operation would require shutting down the lens, and restart could not be done instantly. Furthermore, the instruments could be damaged by unskilled handling.

On these accounts, the lenses would remain interdicted and guarded for some time to come. Every person of good will and common sense would approve.

"The technical angle is reasonably close to the truth," Guthrie said. "I've been poring over the plans Milady Luaine gave me. You'd better do likewise. And still you might well bollix up the apparatus a bit. But as for the political angle to this claim—hm."

A subsequent newsbeam related that the scientists were

satisfied with the explanation they had been given.

"Good Lord!" exclaimed Guthrie. "Are you the only Terran alive who doesn't meekly swallow whatever he's fed?"

"No," Fenn said. "I've met others." Though most were eccentrics, misfits. Well, so was he. "I do seem to be the only one who's in a position to do anything about it at the moment, maybe ever." He looked into the portrait-face. "And that'll depend on you."

Guthrie nodded. "The more I think and learn about this, the more I think we should carry on if we can. Just too damn many loose ends. You took the junta by surprise and it didn't have its package all neatly wrapped. The Mars Station could've been impenetrable from the first. Why wasn't it? The galactic observations can't have amounted to one amazed epiphany. The data would've trickled in and wanted interpreting; even to the Teramind, I doubt the meaning would be obvious right off the bat. So why weren't they published as they arrived, in proper scientific style? Why did we need protection anyway, till the city fathers could comfort us with the word that there are also meat people out in the galaxy? What is so dire about a great machine civilization?

"Yeah, no doubt that Chuan hombre was right, and this will upset the applecart your Lahui hoped would take them to Mars. The uncertainties, the, uh, spiritual re-evaluations—the momentum will be lost. I hardly imagine the honchos of the Synesis mind that. However, they can't have been counting on it.

"Well, maybe the cybercosm misjudged us, like a mother hen not understanding that the ducklings she fosters can swim if you put them in water. It's not human, in spite of its synnoionts. But I suspect it's smarter than that. I've got a hunch about this whole business."

"What is it?" asked Fenn. He had gained a little familiarity with his companion's archaisms.

"No importe. Only a hunch."

"Ha!" Fenn chuckled. "Now you're being the silent wise one."

Guthrie gave him back a wry smile. "Okay. Though it's more that I think I see general principles operating than that I have any specific ideas.

"I've gathered that for a long time you've been bragging here in the Solar System about how you don't have government any more because your societies have outgrown such a thing. Your tribal councils and republican parliaments and whatnot discuss your few matters of general concern and work to develop a consensus. Police protect life, health, property. Courts, or whatever you call them these days, settle disputes and process wrongdoers. That's all. The Synesis only coordinates things, keeps the whole social-cybernetic machine running smoothly and productively."

"Huh," he grunted. "Think again. True, the Synesis and its members refrain from the most obvious activities that traditional government claimed were its reasons and justification for existence. They don't extort taxes, make war, or tramp into people's personal lives. Or do they? I'd call the birth restriction on Earth and Luna pretty drastic. Machinery turns out your necessities of life, essentially for free, but this makes your lives depend on the machinery and whoever or whatever administers it. That includes the computations, and out of the computations come the policy decisions. And then, as you pointed out once, a lot of other things don't have to be forbidden, because they've become impossible.

"I'd call the Synesis a government, reigning over lesser governments and over individuals everywhere. Therefore it acts, always has and always will, according to the nature of the beast.

"Maybe you've reached one of those whens in the course of human events. Our business at the lens could show whether that's right or wrong."

Ardor blossomed in Fenn. "By glory, we'll do it!"

"We can try," Guthrie said quietly. "If you want to."

"Why the death shouldn't I?"

"You're the man I had to have to carry out a raid. But it is kind of a forlorn hope. We can very well die trying. That doesn't faze me too much, the way I am."

"What? You've got a future too."

"Yes, of course I'm interested in things and in what I do, and I look forward to being alive again, genuinely alive. But this present body of mine doesn't have feelings quite like yours. Survival is a fairly abstract incentive for me. You're alive right now."

Fenn's heart knocked. "Alive for a purpose," he said. A part of him was surprised at his calm. "A reason. At last." His gaze sought the overhead view of the stars.

"And afterward," Guthrie murmured, "you won't have to be angry."

On the forty-seventh nightwatch of their journey, *Dagny*'s instruments caught the first sign of hostile vessels closing in.

30

A VIEWSCREEN IN the command cabin reproduced the stars outside, but for this moment they had become a mere show. Reality lay in the instruments, readings, readouts, displays enigmatic to Fenn, once in a while a few low words exchanged between Guthrie and *Dagny*.

"Two of 'em," the download said at length. "Field drive. Converging on us from points far apart. They must have coordinated their flight plans across light-minutes, maybe a light-hour or more at first. I'd guess there are detectors scattered around these purlieus, primed to send the alarm if they pick up anything suspicious, like a trail of neutrino emissions bound toward the lens. They wouldn't have to keep in close touch with the guard ships, just know approximately where they'll be at a given time. A fairly broad beam can carry the report.''

''They?'' asked Fenn, roused out of his forebodings.

''Guard ships, I said. Mainly against the Proserpinans.''

''Oh, yes.'' Recollection came, what Guthrie had told him during the voyage. A host of other preoccupations had driven it largely out of his mind. ''But why haven't they made for us earlier?''

''Well, surveillance of Proserpina should give ample advance notice of any third attempt on a lens from there, but we've come out of left field. Those aren't *c*-ships, you know. So, first, they'd have to be warned by the detectors, which can only be limited through a largish distance from the lens they're watching over. Then they'd have to meet us when we've shed most of our velocity, or we'd zip right on past.''

''I do know!'' Fenn snapped. His nerves quivered bowstring-taut. ''You told me you were hoping we wouldn't meet them at all.''

''You're letting excitement interfere with your memory. Hark back. What I said was that they probably wouldn't be near the lens, but out ranging the Kuiper Belt. My guess was that they'd serve as mother ships for little eavesdropper scoutcraft trying to keep tabs on the widespread cometeers. I hoped they'd be too far away to get back here in time, if they did get word of us. Well, evidently they've been more cautious than that, staying closer to home base, at least to the extent of these two.''

Fenn sighed. ''I'm sorry. I did forget. Now what can we do?''

''Continue.''

''But they're armed. Aren't they?''

''For their purposes, they'd better be. However, we've also discussed this, you recall. They *are* just two. Everything else that could help them is scattered from hell to breakfast across the Solar System or out of it entirely, doing whatever it is the cybercosm has them doing.

We've only this pair to worry about." Guthrie clapped his companion's shoulder. "Go snug yourself down. You can't be of any use in this, and we'll want you in shape for action later."

Fenn looked into the specter-face, which smiled, and said through the hammering in his ears, "Do you really believe—you can—"

"Heh," Guthrie said. "We talked about it, but when the chips are down, everything seems different. Right? Not that you're a coward. You're having the usual human reaction to imminent combat. Yes, Proserpinan intelligence has worked out a fair-to-middling idea of what those guard ships carry and what they're capable of, and I think *Dagny* and I between us should have a fair-to-middling chance against them." The smile became a grin. "We've got one very big advantage. I go way back, I'm not quite civilized, I've known war."

A chill passed through Fenn. Suddenly amiable, drawling Anson Guthrie was as alien as any machine, or more so. Fenn had encountered violence too, he had been violent himself, but at this instant he saw that he had never unconditionally—Guthrie's phrase—meant business. He thought he now understood how Chuan felt.

The idea dropped from him. His pulse beat high. Guthrie was his comrade in arms. "Muy bien," he said hoarsely. "Good hunting." In ancient style, they clasped hands. Fenn turned and went aft.

Guthrie harnessed his body into the control seat that had been modified to accommodate it. Some king-size boosts were in prospect, and he massed more than when he had been human.

The outercom flashed a red signal and chimed. He touched for direct play. A voice sounded from the speakers. He had last heard that emotionless musicality in a recording, with Luaine at his side. He wondered transiently if she bore him a grudge. Whether or not, he supposed she would lend strength of hers to whatever force the Proserpinans marshaled. She'd want in at the kill, unless they figured he'd be the one killed.

"Aou, scavaire ti sielle."

"Acknowledging," he said.

The voice switched to Anglo. "Attention, spacecraft. You are approaching a gravitational lens facility. Unauthorized access is absolutely prohibited. Please change your vectors at once, identify yourself, and state your intentions."

"What if I don't?"

"If you are in need of assistance, inform us. We will render it to the best of our ability. Cease acceleration and we will rendezvous with you."

Deceleration, actually, Guthrie thought. Several hours to go yet at this rate, a couple of megaklicks. Not much compared to the stretch we've covered. "Sorry," he said. "This is an enterprise of great pith and moment."

"Explain your response."

Guthrie gestured expansively, though no one was on hand to see. "I am the captain of the *Pinafore*, and a right good captain too."

"That is a nonsense statement."

"Just checking up," Guthrie said.

As he'd expected, those craft were robotic. Sophotects would have been more flexible—asked questions, for instance. Of course, they were high-order robots. For nearly every task that might fall to them, their algorithms were as effective as any conscious mind. Or better, being less subject to distraction. But he meant to give them a job that hadn't been foreseen.

"Warning," the voice told him. "If you do not promptly cooperate, forcible measures will be necessary."

"Hold on a minute," Guthrie said.

Dagny's instruments had been taking in data throughout, her computers integrating them and passing the information on to her own robotic brain. As he talked, he had been keyboarding in his personal assessments of the situation, for whatever they. might be worth. He leaned a bit forward in his harness, needlessly, and whispered, also needlessly, "Think we can take 'em?"

He and the ship had often spoken together when he was alone with her. She had no awareness, but she had a personality. (He remembered sailboats—oh, he a boy out in the wind and sun-glitter of the Strait—and a battered Jeep that carried him around the Andes and a spacecraft named *Kestrel*, long ago, long ago.) *"Uwach yei,"* she said. The traditional toast: "Aloft." Hers was a Lunarian program, with Anglo added on for his sake.

"Good girl!" he murmured, and was glad he had rechristened her *Dagny*.

"This is your final warning," said the voice. "If you do not change vectors and obey further orders, we must fire on you. We will try simply to disable your vessel, but injury or destruction are probable. You have one more minute of grace."

The cybercosm abhorred bloodshed—if abhorrence, or any human emotion, meant anything in its connection. That gave Guthrie a quantum of leverage. Both vessels had grown clear in his screens. Unmagnified, they were faint stars, lost in the horde save for their drift across its background. Enlarged and enhanced, the images were of lean cylinders, smaller than *Dagny* and possibly less well armed. They certainly weren't prepared for anything like her. More important, they weren't prepared for outright warfare. Even the Proserpinans hadn't gotten to that stage . . . yet.

Guthrie had been making ready all along. Observations and computations were in progress, the launchers were loaded and follow-ups in place, he need only touch the proper key. "Go," he muttered as he did.

Boost ceased around him. He hung weightless for an instant, then felt the recoil. *Dagny* had flung a missile toward the nearer ship, at kilometers per second. Immediately she whipped about—centrifugal force strained

Guthrie against his harness—and leaped off under a full ten *g*.

She. Machine though he also was, he could never have controlled such energies and speeds. But he was more integrated with her than a truly human pilot could have been; he could make the basic decisions and issue the basic commands. Together, they fought.

A fleeting sense of treachery disappeared. He hadn't been parleying under a flag of truce. Besides, those things yonder were smart, but they weren't aware, they weren't animate. The trick would be to keep himself and Fenn alive.

The missile accelerated on jets. The target vessel detected it and attempted evasive action. Blue-white fire blossomed in the screens. A shaped-charge nuclear warhead had detonated. The blaze died away and the stars shone on twisted wreckage.

Dagny dropped boost to three *g*, in a new direction. That was partly to spare Fenn, mainly to confuse the survivor. Her instruments picked up a missile from it, which she barely eluded; it came near enough that Guthrie saw it in a screen, a pencil poised to scribble his death sentence. He saw it start a maneuver, seeking him. Jets couldn't match field drive in that respect. On the other hand, it had lots less mass; and if it was also a nuke, it didn't need to get much closer.

It glowed white-hot and sped on inert. *Dagny* had lasered it.

Glitterlets flashed free of the remaining enemy. It had launched the rest of its missiles in a barrage. Poor judgment. Or maybe not, Guthrie thought grimly. *Dagny* swung about and discharged hers, one, one, one, one. Viewscreens filled with incandescence, stopped down till it was only lurid. He felt the hull tremble, heard the thud of impacting fragments. Radiation readings shot high. The screen field warded off charged particles, but gamma rays got through, and a billow of heat.

The hellishness faded. Glints danced against black·

space. His fireballs had knocked out control circuitry and turned the oncoming weapons into junk.

The image of the other craft swelled. It was swiftly drawing near. *Dagny* might or might not be able to out-accelerate it, but the effort would crush Fenn. Guthrie saw a furnacelike glow where a laser took aim at her. He could reply in kind, but at best, an exchange would leave both ships crippled.

"Go for it!" the old animal in him bayed. *Dagny* closed, matching vectors. At short range, her machine guns opened up. A sleet of bullets ripped into the laser lens. The enemy had nothing like that. The projector went dark.

The robot sought to flee. Metal groaned under stress as *Dagny* worked around to its other side and shot out its other laser. Meanwhile her own beams were slashing and searing. She could not afford to let it escape. If nothing else, it might well turn around and try to ram her.

Guthrie struggled to ignore the voice from the speaker. Passionless though it was, it made him think of a child crying, hurt and not knowing why.

When the robot drifted dead, he sat for a spell, weightless and silent. Victory felt strange. It had been an abstract battle, a contest between machines; but exhaustion rolled over him like a tide.

It ebbed. He shook himself, as a man would have done. "Hoo-ha!" he said. "You okay, *Dagny?*"

"We have suffered no harm that I am not repairing," answered the Lunarian tone. "We shall arrive fully operational."

Guthrie thought of Dagny Beynac. She would have responded in that same spirit. Different words, of course, and the spirit would have been alive, not simulated.

Remembrance jarred him. Did the repairable damage include Fenn? "Good show," Guthrie said automatically. "Resume course for our goal. Take it easier, though. One *g*. We've time now." He unharnessed and went aft.

Fenn lay in the crew emergency section. His buffer couch billowed around him as he plucked awkwardly, with shaky hands, at the fasteners of the webbing. Sweat gleamed and reeked, plastered the yellow hair to the brow, dampened the beard, made dark patches in the coverall. A trickle of blood from one nostril was drying in his mustache. Despite the protection, he had taken a beating that a Lunarian could scarcely have lived through.

Guthrie stopped at the foot end, willed a smile onto his image, and said, "We made it. We're on our way again."

"I heard on the intercom," Fenn croaked. "Slag and slaughter, what a doing!"

"How are you?"

"Sore, bruised all over, but nothing that stim and painkiller won't fix. I'm ready to go." Fenn sat up and swung his legs over the edge of the couch.

Guthrie hoped the only fire in him was of the soul. That radiation—Well, he might have had sufficient mass between him and it. That depended on how the ship was oriented at the time. Guthrie wasn't sure.

Clearly, whatever the dose, it wasn't immediately disabling. *Dagny*'s sickbay could perhaps estimate it, and was well equipped to handle longer-term effects, not to mention lesser injuries. Come worst to worst, it could keep a patient under maintenance, even in cold sleep, till proper treatment was available.

"Don't be too eager," he cautioned. "I want you to get a quick physical checkup and then all the rest you can. We're not out of the woods yet."

"Mainly, I'm hungry."

"Uh, better go easy on food too. It's wise to have an empty stomach before combat." Fewer complications in case of a gut wound. That wouldn't occur to people nowadays. It belonged to the ghastly past.

Fenn blinked. "Combat? Who's left to fight?"

"I don't know," Guthrie said. "Maybe no one. We'll find out."

• • •

In their last several hours, braking toward the lens, they had nothing to do but talk. Fenn felt vaguely surprised at the gentleness of it. They sat in the saloon, where the overhead no longer displayed space and the screens carried a slow succession of pictures: old paintings by the likes of Ruisdael and Hiroshige, old photographs from living Earth, sea and meadow and white-browed mountains. The music was also archaic, violins, harps, pianos, horns; but the fresh scents in the air were of flowers beneath another sun.

Hitherto, Fenn had sheered off whenever conversation turned to his future after this mission. Now he found he was more willing to discuss it, if only because he might not have any. The effects of the radiation did not appear to be worse than modern medicine could cure, but without such care, in a few days he would fall sick and the chance of recovery would be poor. That need led to consideration of longer-term prospects.

In the course of it, Guthrie rephrased what he had said once or twice before: "If our luck holds, the Synesis won't be able to prove you were involved here as well as on Mars, or at least will figure it's not expedient to pursue the case. But there won't be any reasonable doubt, and you won't be exactly their fair-haired boy."

"I'll manage," Fenn said.

"Um, we've got to face the possibility that you will be accused, and prepare against it. The Proserpinans would take you in without any notions about correcting your antisocial ways. They've done it for a few rebellious Terrans in the past. And you'd be a hero of sorts among them, and useful for various jobs."

"Especially in space, I should think." Fenn had given it plenty of thought.

"But almighty lonely," Guthrie said low. "Yes, assorted Lunarians, including women, would find you interesting. Some might actually get to like you, sort of. But never any real fellowship. Down underneath, you'd be more alone than if you had nobody around."

"I always have been alone." Fenn scowled and thumped a fist on the table. "No, flame it, I'm not self-pitying. It was what I chose. I had my opportunities to be otherwise, and threw them away of my own free will."

Annoyance yielded to a sudden tenderness. Wanika, he thought. May she fare well. I'm sorry if I hurt her.

"In spite of everything—or because of everything, if we carry this business off—they may make you welcome again on Mars," Guthrie suggested.

Fenn sat still for a moment. "No," he said very quietly. "Not Mars. Not ever."

Both fell silent, looking off from one another. The "Moonlight Sonata" rippled and chimed in the background.

"I wonder—" Guthrie said, unwontedly hesitant, "this last bit of time we've got, we two—I made my long trip to find out what's what in the Solar System, and I've really learned so little. More from you than from anyone else. Mind if I ask you a few more questions?"

Fenn recognized his friend's intent, and warmed to it. "By all means, do."

"I've quizzed you a lot about Luna and the Lahui Kui-kawa—I was in on their beginnings, you remember—and, uh, Mars—but you know, you've mentioned vacations in Yukonia. I took a few during my first life, in the part of it we called Alaska. Tell me what it's like these days."

To recall the bioreserves, woods and heights, wildfowl clamorous above wind-shivery lakes, aurora fluttering in a night so cold that it seemed to ring, the majesty of a caribou trek or a solitary Kodiak bear silhouetted on a ridge against heaven—such things healed. Once Fenn thought in passing: We do have the machines, the cybercosm, to thank for saving this. Earth is alive in a way that Mars may someday be, but Luna or Proserpina never. They're not big enough. Could I really live happily nowhere but in space, forever barred from walking through wild land and breathing wild winds?

He hastened to lose himself in the memories.

But when *Dagny* was almost at journey's end and Guthrie had finished helping Fenn get outfitted, as they stood in the cramped metal enclosure at the starboard auxiliary airlock, the man's helmet not yet closed, he asked abruptly, "When you go home, back to your stars, will you do something for me?"

Guthrie's wraith-eyes held steady upon him. "Anything I can."

Fenn groped for words. "Find some—some place beautiful—above a canyon, I think—and put a small monument there. Just a stone will do, with her name on it. Kinna Ronay."

"Sure." Guthrie's inorganic hand laid hold of the hand in a power glove. "If I make it back, that's a promise."

"Nothing fancy," Fenn told him. "She wouldn't have liked that."

"No, I understand. Juliana wouldn't have either. But good luck to both of us, huh?" Guthrie let go, turned about, and left Fenn at his station.

Fifty kilometers from her prey, *Dagny* took orbit. In these deeps, that distance made scant difference and there was hardly any drift. Poised in the open airlock, looking out as if from a cave, Fenn saw the lens against darkness as a golden spark among the stars, surrounded by an exquisite silvery-icy lacework as broad as Luna risen over Earth. He gripped a handhold, not to fall endlessly weightless, and heard the blood throb in his temples, the breath rustle through his lungs.

A voice resounded, eerily like the voice of the slain robot, but somehow stronger: *"Tasairen voudrai!"* Guthrie was relaying what he received and returned.

"Take it easy," the download said.

The voice went over to the same Anglo. "Attention.

This facility is interdicted. If you are authorized to approach, give the proper recognition code.''

"No, we don't have that.''

"Warning, warning. A powerful magnetohydrodynamic field has been put in operation. Do not come closer. The field will disable your ship and equipment. No assistance for you is obtainable. Stay clear.''

"Yeah, we know. We'll keep off. We have some business in this neighborhood to take care of.''

That last sentence was the agreed-upon signal to Fenn. Here we go, he thought, released the bar, and sprang. He didn't soar forth as he would ordinarily do. The extra gear secured to him added so much mass that his legs pushed him to just two or three meters a second, while its bulk barely cleared the exit. The distribution set him slowly spinning, too. He corrected that with a minimal jet impulse and floated free. The ship fell away and the galactic river encompassed him.

He didn't notice. Readouts in his helmet glowed across the constellations. He picked sightings as they went by and ordered them entered, "This. . . . This. . . . This. . . .'' The choices were more or less arbitrary, but, combined, they gave his suit's computer the means to calculate his vectors.

Generating illusionary crosshairs, he centered them on his target. "Go—max!'' His jetpack started him off at low boost, not to build up undue velocity. Beneath its murmur his earplugs still carried an obbligato of words. He wasn't in an inboard circuit any more, but he was in the beam between ship and lens.

"What are your intentions? You are evidently the vessel I was informed about. You were supposed to be intercepted. I have registered not only neutrino emissions from antimatter reactions, but the radiation of nuclear blasts. Our ships do not respond to my calls. You have harmed them, have you not? Your actions are unlawful.''

"So you've deduced that. Well, you are a sophotect, not a robot, aren't you?''

"I have a mind dedicated to the observatory."

It was as if the cold around his armor, near absolute zero, struck through into Fenn. He had known of that electrophotonic brain, but only now did its inhuman isolation, its absolute unhumanness, become real for him.

He rallied. However powerful in its work, the intellect must be narrow and naive. Guthrie would try to keep it engaged. Fenn was a minor object, and though the instrumentation would doubtless register him before he arrived, he wasn't on a collision course at the moment. He ought to pass as a meteoroid—outrageously improbable in these hollow immensities, but no hazard, nothing to call to the sophotect's attention.

An alarm tone buzzed. His own instruments were picking up stray radiation from atoms encountering the defense field. He was about to enter it.

He switched off radio, jets, life-support systems, everything dependent on electronics, and hurtled through silence.

A faint tug, a faint sense of warmth—eddy currents, heating the metal he wore and bore, slowing him down. That effect was slight, but to a delicate control circuit, the induction would be like a boot crashing into crystal. En route, he and Guthrie had put in as much shielding as they were able to. Shut down, some of the modules might not be too badly damaged. Or they might be. There was no telling beforehand.

However, the guardian field could not have more than a certain intensity. The power plant inside yonder spheroid was limited. Also, the field must be heterodyned to form a shell at a considerable distance from the lens; else it would ruinously interfere with the work. In principle, it was like the screens that deflected charged particles from spacecraft and space stations. Instead of protecting, it was designed to destroy—to scramble, overload, obliterate. But he, flying inert, should pass through in a few minutes.

A galvanometer braceleted on his left wrist, faintly luminous, dropped its reading to zero. He *was* through.

The golden point ahead had waxed to a tiny disk, rapidly growing. Its spiderweb snared stars. He shouldn't strike those antennae. It was time to regain the helm, slow down, and get properly aimed.

No new displays appeared in his helmet. Nor did the jetpack immediately start. Fuel cells and accumulators were unaffected, of course, so he had power, and jury-rigged mechanical switches gave him restricted use of it. Several had already tripped automatically; he heard his air pump going, and suit temperature held fairly steady. Chemicals would blot up excess carbon dioxide and water vapor. Otherwise his biostat was dead: no purification, no recycling. That didn't matter. He'd be back aboard ship before he urgently needed it, or else he'd be dead himself.

He took hold of the improvised manual controls attached to the breast of his suit. The system was clumsy and he'd had only stinted practice with it, a couple of sessions during the voyage when *Dagny* ceased boost and he could go outside. He'd have to navigate by eyeball and whatever feel for space flying he had developed as a boy around the Habitat. Well, he'd always shown an aptitude.

Lateral thrusts slewed him around. He brought his right arm before his face. Attached was a backward-looking periscope with an objective graduated in phosphorescent circles and radii. When he snugged his wrist into a bracket under his helmet, he could center the spheroid and know he was pointed approximately right and approximately how far he had to go. Not much of a guide, but the best he and Guthrie could make. He activated the jets again, carefully, carefully, though his sole accelerometer was his body and his sole radar his eyes.

A star drifted across the stars, *Dagny*. She seemed infinitely distant, as if she lay in the sky above Sananton.

His mouth was Mars-dry, his tongue a block of wood. He could have sucked from his water nipple, but dared take no attention from his task. The periscope image kept shifting off the midpoint. He must readjust, over-compensate, readjust, hunting. Sweat soaked his inner garb, stung his eyes, fumed rank in his nostrils.

The spheroid swelled at him. He was coming in too fast. He nudged the boost. Half a minute later he made his guess and switched the motor off.

He struck with an impact that rammed through shins and spine to rattle his jaws. He had already energized his gripsoles, another system bypassing the electronics. Their induction held him fast. He stood upon the metal of his goal.

The daze passed from him. He peered around. The spheroid curved sharply off on every side; stars crowded the rim of vision. Withy-slim members sprouted from it, branches on which grew the argencies that webbed heaven beyond and beyond his head. Sol hung low, a minim of utter brilliance, against the cloudy galactic heart that this lens watched.

Almost as if his aloneness reminded him, he tried turning his communicator back on. A whisper in the earplugs told him it worked. The basic circuitry was simple and rugged. If the more special features were gone, that wasn't important here.

He heard nothing else. Evidently he wasn't acquiring the beam over which Guthrie held the sophotect in argument. Though less soft than he'd wanted, his landing had given the maintenance systems no cause to alert it. Their programs, not written to cover an invasion like his, reacted as they would to a piece of gravel harmlessly impinging.

The ignorance wouldn't last. He could not tap the database as he'd meant to do on Pavonis Mons. A robot could be fooled about that—another event never expected—but not a conscious mind. If nothing else, it would shut everything down to cut off access. No, he must physically rip out the file. And that would disable this whole magnificent instrumentality.

For a second he cringed from guilt. Suppose there truly was no further secret? His deed would be eternally unforgiveable.

A lifelong rage flared. He would yield no faith to a system that had none in him.

Wrath set as resolution. He would finish what he and Kinna had begun.

He started running, *clump-clump-clump* over the golden-hued metal. Sol rose before him, and the mysteries it lensed. Likewise did the hemispherical bubble precisely beneath it. Through that hyalon Fenn saw an assemblage of instruments and ancillaries. He had studied the plans and the published images again and again. Nevertheless, in the middle of his haste he felt a dim astonishment at how ordinary the array looked.

He halted at the access port and reached around his shoulders. Couplings unsnapped between his fingers. He put a rack of tools down at his feet. Its gripper took hold. He broke out a cutting torch and cradled it in his arms: tank, accumulator, nozzle, trigger. He squeezed.

Atomic hydrogen attacked the latch module. His helmet stopped down its blue-white glare.

The synthetic voice tolled: "You are committing sabotage. Since the previous attempt at violation, I have been armed against direct assault. Cease at once or I shall have to eliminate you."

Somehow the single thought in Fenn was: It's as desperate as I am.

The entrance was not built for resistance. He cut the warder loose. It wobbled off into space amidst a swarm of hot gobbets. He reached for the hole where it had been and hooked the port open.

Guthrie, a shout, on a beam that he must have redirected: "Fenn, don't! I think he means what he says. Back off!"

I will do what I will do.

Fenn's action had him, was him. He entered the dome. No gun would be emplaced to shoot inside. The warnings and pleas in his ears had no more existence. He crouched before the database cabinet, punched control plates, saw a door retract. Before him rested a black box forty or fifty centimeters long, ten or fifteen wide and deep. Not much for what it held. But when your digitals are the quantum states of single atoms, you don't need much.

A steely swiftness and precision had come upon him. In a few movements, his fingers disconnected the database. Tucking it into a safe corner, he played his torch around the dome. That just might take out enough capability to allow his escape. Sparks danced through the glooms and the starlight. Housings gave way; circuits fell apart.

"When you emerge, I will destroy you," said the voice, "unless you and your associate promptly surrender."

What did "surrender" mean to a mind that had never known enmity and strife? If they yielded, what would it know to do? The questions barely crossed Fenn's awareness, and were gone. He'd blast off and hope that whatever weapons the mind had wouldn't catch him before Guthrie opened fire.

With the straps that had held the tool rack, he secured his prize against his breast. He went to the port, stepped out, kicked free, and shoved down on the jet control.

Force and thunder seized him. His viewfield filled with stars.

He hardly felt the bullets when they struck.

A screen at high magnification tracked him.

Guthrie's hands and voice cracked forth a command. A projector took aim and unleashed its laser. The dome on the spheroid glowed red and went to ruin.

Sorry, thought Guthrie. I didn't want to kill you. But you were shooting my friend.

Meanwhile, he was directing aloud, "Make ready for EVA from Airlock Two!" Why did he bellow? A download shouldn't get this emotional. Should it? "Sickbay, set up for emergency life sustenance."

He flung his body down the passageways. One of the ship's robots was at the lock with a jetpack. It helped him don the rig. He issued an order that sent him straight through, sliding the outer valve open immediately after the inner shut. Air billowed, a fog, and vanished. Well, an ample reserve was aboard. He sprang forth. With the senses and computational power of a machine, he didn't need instruments to plot a course. Boost. Acceleration slammed savagely.

He couldn't enter the guardian field. However, Fenn had left at full thrust, which his manual switch maintained. The problem was to reach him, matching not just velocities but their time derivatives, and get that motor turned off.

Rushing masses, straining forces, ship and lens quickly lost in the dark. Fenn was shadow, dim highlights, lumps. Guthrie closed in and groped. His free arm he laid around the man's waist. When he stopped Fenn's jets, the impetus of his own nearly tore his grip loose. He quenched them too. Their load unbalanced, they had put a spin on him and his burden. Constellations gyred crazily. All we need is music, he thought, and this'll be a dance, a dead man and a download. But when he had halted the rotation and floated free, it was into an absolute silence.

Now he could let go, draw back a little, and see what he had. The helmet shimmered blackly; it must be full of blood. No doubt bits of flesh and bone drifted thick, for the suit was nubbled up and down its length where it had sealed holes. Some were too large for perfect closure. Air oozed out, thin evanescent mists. They left drops that bobbed glistening and in a brighter light would have gone crimson. Before the tank could empty and the body fluids boil, Guthrie had pulled adhesive patches from the repair box and slapped them on.

Straps held a larger box to Fenn's chest. It appeared to be undamaged. An organometallic casing like that was tough, and his body had absorbed most of the energy in the bullets that hit there. So they'd hashed his heart and lungs instead.

"Come and get me," Guthrie broadcast. "Pronto." He kept the transmission going, a beacon, and opened a valve in the suit to bleed off drinking water. Its sublimation should cool the interior and slow the onset of irremediable brain decay.

One evenwatch on the voyage Fenn had gotten drunk and told him something about what went on in the cave on Pavonis Mons. Too bad that Martian skinsuits didn't have a similar provision. But it wouldn't work very well there, and in that particular case, wouldn't have bought enough minutes anyway. They were precious few.

The ship hove in sight and orbited alongside. Guthrie jetted into an open lock.

Again he didn't stop to conserve air, nor did he remove his space gear. In long, weightless arrowings he carried Fenn to sickbay. The master medical robot and its panoply were ready.

"One-half *g* toward Proserpina," Guthrie said to the ship. He didn't want to impose stress, but what was to come would be plenty messy without debris floating everywhere around.

He had guessed right. Stripped, Fenn was red rags and wreckage. Though the slugs had penetrated and exited cleanly, in their numbers they chewed him up like an old-time harrow in soil. The head seemed intact, but the face, swabbed off, idiotically gaping from the matted beard, was chalky blue.

Guthrie helped lay those remnants that hung more or less together in the subzero fluid tank. "Do what you can, run your tests, and report to me," he directed. "Be prepared for high boost soon."

He took the box off to clean it and himself. For a while afterward he stood holding it. You'd better be worth this, he thought. Worth what you've cost everybody.

He stowed it and returned to the command center. "Five g, destination Proserpina," he said.

"We have insufficient delta v left," the ship answered.

"Sure, I know. But we need to get well clear of this neck of the woods before the cybercosm's reinforcements arrive. I'll find out for certain whether a Proserpinan force is on its way to meet us, or can be persuaded to start. I expect so. We'll keep whatever fuel reserve is right for whatever terminal maneuvers we'll be making. But we want a high velocity and plenty of space around us before we go on trajectory." A huge emptiness, in which pursuit would probably despair of finding him. Ships under boost were far easier to detect and track.

Why was he explaining to a robot?

Well, it was the closest thing he had to company now, and it bore Dagny's name.

Thrust heightened. His mass became very heavy. He sat looking out at the stars.

Presently the medical center spoke on the intercom. "The brain has been biochemically stabilized, along with surrounding vital tissue. Nothing else is in condition to salvage."

Guthrie felt heavier still. "Can you bring the brain to full operation?" he asked.

"Yes, in due course. It is not recommended. No sensory input is available on board."

"And without any, a human quickly goes loco. Uh-huh. Robotics—"

"Prosthesis could only be temporary. In addition to pervasive radiation damage, the brain has suffered trauma from hydrostatic shock. In its present state, as close to suspended animation as feasible, it will remain potentially viable for possibly a year. But once chemical activity resumes, deterioration will be rapid."

"Fenn wouldn't like being just a brain in a box anyhow," Guthrie said. Understatement of the week, he thought.

"What are your instructions?"

"Well . . . no harm in keeping things as they are for as long as we can, while we see what might turn up. He never was a quitter either. Do that."

The machine acknowledged and ended communication. Guthrie sat alone. *Dagny* sped onward.

31

LONG MONTHS LATER, refueled and rearmed, she swung in orbit about Mars. A Proserpinan crew stood watch. Companion ships circled with her, a configuration changeable but always battle-ready. Those aboard looked out upon strangeness. They had never before seen the actual planet like this, never been so near the sun. Their homes were strewn through the realm of the comets.

Nothing came to trouble them in their vigilance, not so much as a word after the dry-spoken arrangements for their harboring were complete. Mars dominated heaven, big and silent. Eyes over its dayside saw wastelands ruddy or darkling, tawny storms, mountains sprawling and rearing, polar caps agleam. Passing above its midnight, they saw a black shield bordered with stars, and a few stars below, which were the lights where humans dwelt. Slowly, tension lessened.

Guthrie had foreseen that. It was the Selenarchs who insisted he arrive at his last parley with an escort prepared to fight. He finally gave in and agreed. If soft-played, not unduly provocative—and Lunarians weren't given to bluster—the move might even be of some slight use as a demonstration of resolve.

But when the tightly encrypted messages had gone back and forth and those whom he wanted to see were awaiting him, he went down alone, riding a jetpack. At a certain landmark, a rock spire in the middle of a desert, he met the flitter that took him where he wanted to go.

• • •

For a while after they left the house they stood mute, he and the two humans. Nobody knew quite what to say.

The sky was pale rose, bright with morning. Land lifted steep and stony to north, streaked with mineral hues, until it broke off at the edge of Eos Chasma. Elsewhere it rolled more gently and plantation softened much of it, shrubs and vines and boles, mostly ebony and russet at this season but with gauzy iridescence rippling around some. Sparkles among them betokened animal life astir. The house rambled low beneath roof and dome, viewports shining in walls that the Martian weather had had centuries enough to mark for its own.

An aircraft was already on the landing strip, the youngsters already inside. They and their parents planned to spend the next two days camped in the Valles. Skinsuited, David and Helen Ronay paused at the door with Guthrie, who needed merely his machine body.

He took the initiative, speaking more diffidently than was usual for him. He did not consciously will that his image-face show concern, but by now he generated expressions almost as naturally as when he was alive. "I still feel . . . odd about this. Making you leave your home. Especially when you've been so kind to me."

David Ronay inclined his gray head. "We are honored that we can help you, captain. We know quite well how important it is for you to have privacy today. Important to all of us."

"And you—you have been kind to us," Helen Ronay said. A tear on her cheek caught sunlight. "Oh, very kind."

She hugged him. David Ronay shook his hand. They walked off to join their children.

Guthrie watched the aircraft leave. It climbed, bore west, became a spark high aloft, was gone. He remained standing, looking out over these wide lands. His tactile sensors felt the breeze strengthen until it was a wind. He turned up his sonic amplifiers—another act of will—and heard it thinly skirling. Here in the daylit tropics it wasn't lethally cold. But no one would ever smell what odors it carried, unless the planet in some future century arose to resurrection.

A robotic radio voice: "Requesting permission to set down."

"Granted," Guthrie said. "You're right on time." Tautness thrummed in him. He hastened back to the front airlock. As he stepped into the chamber, he heard the flyer whirr, and the shadow of its wings fell over him.

Hangaring it for a short stay wasn't worth the bother when no dust storm was predicted. It landed on the strip and the house extended a gangtube for its solitary passenger. Meanwhile, Guthrie cycled through and strode back to that area. Reaching the entrance, he decided to switch off his face. That might seem unfriendly. On the other hand, Chuan might feel a bit less uncomfortable confronting a blank turret, a pure machine.

The synnoiont entered. He stopped and bowed. Guthrie returned a naval-style salute. "Welcome, sir," he greeted. "Good of you to come."

True. The preliminary negotiations had been lengthy and complicated, not simply because of transmission lag. They had reminded him of hagglings about armistice terms in ancient wars. But none of that was Chuan's fault. The most powerful man on Mars had raised no objections and set no conditions. He just went where he was asked to go, in secret and unaccompanied.

"It is the least I can do," Chuan said.

He spoke almost in an undertone, somewhat hoarsely. In a plain brown robe, stoop-shouldered, the round visage showing more bones than before and dark circles below the eyes, he stood dwarfed by the armored form that had summoned him.

"Let's go sit in the living room," Guthrie suggested.

He led the way, though Chuan had been here far oftener over many years. The room was large, with broad viewports toward the farmland and the wilderness beyond. Well-worn furniture spread across a deep-blue thermal carpet. A cat dozed on one chair. It opened yellow eyes when the two came in, but stayed relaxed, having always been loved. Pictures and animations, now static, were on the walls: classic reproductions, scenic views, portraits. Kinna's hung above a set of shelves. Upon them her family had set objects she cared about: some heirloom glassware, a couple of antique codex books, a childhood doll, glittery rocks she had collected on her expeditions, oddment souvenirs from various towns, a model of her pet robot. The air was cool, scented with pine. She liked that fragrance.

This was the custom among Terran Martians, to maintain such a shrine for a Martian year after a death. People were closer to their blood kin than they generally were on Earth or Luna; and grief of the Terran kind was unknown to Lunarians. You might find this care for the departed among folk such as the Lahui Kuikawa, Guthrie had thought—yes, maybe among the Keiki Moana too— but otherwise only here and at the stars.

Chuan glanced about. "A curiously appropriate site for our meeting," he said in his near-whisper.

"I felt that way myself," Guthrie answered. "Of course, there was also the practical side. To judge from everything I've heard, we'll be reasonably sure of no bugs, no traps, no news hounds or anybody else underfoot."

"Yet I was surprised that the Ronays agreed. They are proud and private."

"Well, they were willing to talk with me when they'd been approached."

"Who would not be?"

"After I'd explained to them how—" Guthrie's voice faltered. He must force the next few words, though a download shouldn't have that kind of weakness, should it? "—how much Fenn loved their daughter—they felt better." That's made the whole rigmarole worthwhile, whatever else does or does not come of it, he thought. "Then they were glad to help."

"To what end?"

"That's what we want to explore, no?" Guthrie waved a hand. "Sit down, do. What can I offer you? I've learned the kitchen, these days while I've been a guest."

"Thank you. Some tea would be ... comforting." Chuan lowered himself and huddled.

Guthrie went out, prepared the brew, put cookies on the tray as well, and brought the refreshments back. He set them on a table in front of the man and took the chair across from him.

Chuan lifted the cup. His hands trembled slightly. He sipped. Silence deepened.

Having drained the cup, he set it aside, looked up into the facelessness before him, and said levelly, "I confess to puzzlement. Why do you want to confer with me? Under the circumstances, you could, and I think should, deal directly with the Synesis"—he hesitated, then went resolutely on—"with, I may as well say, the central cybercosm on Earth, or the very Teramind."

"But you see," Guthrie replied, "I don't aim to negotiate or anything like that. I've neither the authority nor the desire to. If I did, I still wouldn't have the wisdom."

"What then do you seek?"

"To talk with somebody who can maybe help *me* understand what's happened and what it means, so I can explain to my own people. I've gathered you're a decent fellow, my best bet."

The deadened countenance came awake with startlement. "I?"

Yes, he, Guthrie thought: the synnoiont, sundered from his machines, more isolated than the human world could know. It took courage to come here thus, courage and—what else? Compassion? No, not that. If ever anyone sat in need of mercy, it was this small man.

"I am as lost and bewildered as all others are." Chuan

plainly tried to make the sentence not pathetic, only a statement of fact.

"Yeh?" Be brutally frank, Guthrie thought. Pussy-footing is no kindness. "You knew. You were in the cybercosm, part of it, communing with it like a believer with his god."

"Actually, I did not know until a few years ago. The One does not reveal everything to its avatars either. How could it? How could we bear the knowledge, before we become one with it?"

"But then you were informed and co-opted into the conspiracy."

Chuan stiffened. A hint of anger put more life into his tone. "That is an ugly word, captain. You scarcely have a right to use it, after what you have done. It was a stratagem for a noble purpose and an end too great for you to imagine."

Don't come between a man and his faith, Guthrie reminded himself. "Well, let's not argue rights and wrongs. I'm after the objective truth, and I do think that, given the situation as it's developed, your best course is to come clean about it. What was that purpose?" Sharper: "What did the—all right, the Teramind—what did it hope for? A fantastic illusion of a cosmic machine civilization that never existed—"

The revelation standing forth naked from the database out of the lens: stars, planets, a querning of creation and destruction and rebirth, but at the galactic heart and in the galactic wheel no more sign of sentience than anywhere else, a grandeur altogether blind, although things went on around the great black hole—monstrous forces, convulsions in space-time—which the scientists at Proserpina could not account for or even give a name to.

Chuan sighed. "Oh, it has become obvious, has it not?"

He rallied, sat straight, and looked unblinkingly at the blank mask. "Humans," he said, "organic beings, limited, fallible, reckless, greedy, often hideously cruel—

should not run loose in the universe." His voice softened. "Let them instead have guidance through centuries into the peace and transcendence of Oneness."

Unbidden rebellion spoke for Guthrie before he could stop it. "I think the word you want is 'domesticated.' "

"No! Cannot you, at least, understand? You are machine."

"I remember being a man. Someday I'll be a man again." Guthrie lifted a hand, palm outward, the immemorial sign of truce. "But let's not fight. Why couldn't you let us go on in our wild ways? We're hardly a threat to you."

A metal coolness descended on Chuan. "You are. You will trouble the cosmos."

If Guthrie had been generating the image of a head, he would have nodded. "I see. You mean we'll never fit into your harmony. We'll keep stubbing our toes on outside reality, which doesn't give a damn about intellect either, and veering off on unforeseeable courses. It'll get worse once we learn what's really going on at the core of the galaxy."

Chuan's self-control wavered for a moment. "I don't know what is. I cannot comprehend. But the great equation, the ultimate summation, is clearly incomplete. I suspect that the new knowledge, the new physics, can lead to—a power to transform the universe." He shuddered.

"And we humans," Guthrie said, steadily because he had guessed something of the kind, "if we're still around then—millions of years from now, maybe, but the Teramind naturally thinks in such terms—and if we take a share in the job, we won't likely do it according to the grand plan. Though long before then, just by existing as we are, we'll have made its universal order, its undisturbed reign of pure mind, impossible." Attack: "So we had to be stopped while the stopping was good. We had to be kept in our place, well-treated, happy, but stupefied, submissive without knowing we were. Pet animals."

Vigor surged up in Chuan. "No! You are absolutely

wrong. The cybercosm is intellect. By its own nature, it cannot want to destroy or diminish or limit any other intellect. No, it must try to lead minds toward growth and the strength that comes from inner peace. *That* was the dream.''

He was quiet for a second or two before he continued, diminuendo: ''You are correct; humans as they are now, ranging wherever and wreaking whatever they choose, will bring havoc, physical disasters and spiritual catastrophes. First they should be guided to maturity.

''The vision of a sophotectic civilization spanning the galaxy should awe them into thoughtfulness, but it was not meant to demoralize them. Indeed, it doubtless could not. Basically, in the light of experience in the Solar System, logic requires that if any high-technology society flourishes anywhere else, it will have produced sophotects, and they will have evolved.

''The civilizations of organic beings, those are what would truly have spoken to humans. They would inspire, enlighten, and point the way. Far from being numbed as you say, our race would be stimulated as never before, would raise itself to heights inconceivable today.''

''And you were brought in, among others, to help construct those imaginary beings,'' Guthrie deduced.

''Yes,'' Chuan replied, not lowering his gaze. ''It would be as demanding a task as minds ever undertook. Those societies must be not only believable, but rich, diverse, challenging, and at the same time, sane. Environments, biologies, histories, languages, sciences, arts, faiths—a work requiring centuries, and requiring the contributions of humans as well as sophotects. The aim was to present humankind here with something that would more and more engage our finest intelligences, lifetime after lifetime, keeping bodies safely at home while nourishing spirits and bringing them toward fulfillment.''

''Your kind of fulfillment,'' Guthrie said.

''What else?'' Chuan retorted. ''Do you claim moral

superiority for your—your warriors, hunters, butchers, bandits, carousers, criminals, grovelers in superstition, blood sacrificers—your leftover animality?''

''No,'' Guthrie said. ''I'm not arrogant enough to make a judgment like that, either way. I do claim our right to freedom.''

He fell silent, searching for words. The cat jumped from its chair, went to a viewport, and stood on its hind legs, gazing forth to where a silkentree tossed in the wind out of the wilderness.

''Seems to me, though,'' Guthrie said, ''we are groping our way forward, however clumsily, and maybe what we'll get to at last is something no grand scheme of any one grand mind could imagine. But I repeat, let's not argue that. It's gone moot, hasn't it?''

I've got a speech to make, he thought. Well, I've got an intelligent and simpático listener. ''Correct me if I'm wrong, which I don't expect I am. This is the truth. Partly some Proserpinans and I worked it out beforehand; partly you've filled in details for me.

''The cybercosm, and the few humans in its confidence, meant to spring the account of the galactic civilization at a later date, two or three generations from now, maybe, when it would be plausible that the lenses had begun picking up traces of organic societies out there. But the spread of discontent and misbehavior among people made things look somewhat more urgent than hitherto. Was that why you yourself were suddenly brought into the project, this late in your life? In general, the cybercosm had to play by ear. The vulnerability of the Pavonis Mons Station does suggest that eventually somebody would've been maneuvered into going in and uncovering the secret. That'd lend force to the disclosure. As was, it happened much sooner than planned, everything wasn't quite arranged, and so it gave Fenn and me a clue.

''Meanwhile, your *c*-ships have been scuttling around in the light-years. Their robots couldn't forever keep us colonists from setting up our own gravitational lenses, but they could delay that and be planting technofakery throughout this galactic neighborhood, to convince us also when the time was ripe. Von Neumann–type machines, reproducing at sun after sun, wouldn't take impossibly long about it.

"So we'd want cybercosms ourselves, we colonists, to help us deal with the godlike ones yonder. Especially after we started learning, early on, that the wonderful organic beings were wonderful in large part because of their close association with those sophotects. We humans would gradually decide that this was, after all, our proper fate too, which we should accept with joy—being absorbed. Transfigured, you'd say. And once we were, how could we resent the way we were brought to it?"

He was oversimplifying, Guthrie knew. Probably the Teramind had more imagination than that. Although ultimately it sought to control the cosmos, liberating mind from contingency in order to seek—or to create—the Absolute, that goal shone in a future more remote than the death of the last star. First, he thought, it might well give matter and energy free play, let them evolve spontaneously, let them realize possibilities unpredictable within chaos and complexity—closely watched, of course, never allowed to run truly wild—

What crystalline equivalents of forests and beasts might arise on barren planets under hellish suns? What riddles might they present to explorers who had never heard of the intellect that ordained and afterward perforce abandoned them? What destinies might be theirs?

"But we," Guthrie finished, "a handful of mutinous, headstrong humans, and me, and purposeless chance, we overthrew the whole careful plan. I suspect reality always will do likewise."

"You have wrecked more than a plan," Chuan said low. "The news will mean upheaval. Do you accept responsibility for the death and destruction, the suffering and ruin, to come?"

"Will things necessarily be that bad?" Guthrie answered. "Okay, I'd personally have been willing to cooperate in breaking the story more gradually, but the Proserpinans left me no choice. People are being rudely disillusioned about their Synesis and cybercosm, yes. Their Teramind turns out to be capable of lying, conniving, and blundering, same as the rest of us. They won't right away know what to do next, or even what to think. But they were already restless, weren't they? More and more of them weren't satisfied any longer with your ordered, rational, benevolent, fenced-in nursery—maybe because, down underneath, they sensed it *was* a nursery, training them for what you, not they, had decided was best.

"Well, if their societies are worth saving, they'll adapt, they'll survive. Earth humans may start going back into space in earnest—the Lahui Kuikawa for certain, I'd guess, and later the Martians—but most people will want to keep on in their familiar lives. You, your cybercosm, can help them in that. It's being called into question, which I'd say is mighty healthy, but Terrans at Sol are way past the point where they can throw it out. They could no more do that than a man could rip out his brain."

"Terrans," Chuan mumbled. "What of the Proserpinans?"

Guthrie uttered a laugh. "Oh, their jefes are grabbing for every advantage in reach, but they don't fantasize about revolution or conquest or any such fool thing. It isn't in Lunarian nature. My guess is, the Synesis, being currently embarrassed and preoccupied, will have to renegotiate several issues, mainly involving access to your antimatter fuel, and some concessions as regards Luna. No worse."

"Amply bad," Chuan said bleakly. "If they can buy fuel without restriction, they will overrun the comets and make for the stars."

"What's wrong with that?" Guthrie countered. "I assure you, they'll have no interest in dictating to you on your worlds. Nor will we, out on ours. Supposing it were practical, which it isn't, we wouldn't. I'm bound home to tell folks there the truth, and afterward we'll everybody go our own chosen way."

And there, he thought, was the real defeat of the Teramind.

He felt no triumph. He wished he could find words to lighten the load on Chuan.

The synnoiont raised his head. "You have spoken as though I spoke for the cybercosm," he said. "But I am only a man. I too am only a man."

"You aren't resigning your post, are you?" Guthrie asked with all the gentleness he could fashion.

The head shook. "No, never. I will always believe— I must—"

Chuan gasped. He clutched the arms of his chair.

Then he eased, a smile quivered on his lips, and he said, "But perhaps I can still carry word between our worlds. That is what I am for, you know."

I couldn't be that large, so soon after surrendering, Guthrie thought. Aloud: "Maybe, I don't know, maybe in a million years those worlds will find they were two sides of the same one."

Chuan nodded. "One Dao. I dare hope."

They talked on and on, seeking understanding, finding a kind of love. Guthrie generated a face for himself. Once he stopped to make a meal for his friend. Night fell, the swift Martian darkness. Dust and interior illumination hid the stars. But they were out there nonetheless, Guthrie thought.

"I have a favor to ask of you," he said at last.

"If I can, it is yours," Chuan replied from the depths of his human weariness.

"Nothing big. You've got the influence and the cybercosm has the technological power, doesn't it? Aboard my ship is a brain, all that's left of a brave man. Once reactivated, it'll soon die. But—leave it in its coma till death, but scan it first and—Could they download what's in it into a neural network like mine?''

''I know what you mean.'' Chuan's glance went to the picture of Kinna Ronay. ''I should think this is feasible. You will take the download back with you, for your Life Mother to create a new, living man?''

''Yes,'' Guthrie said. ''He earned that.''

32

FENN WOKE.

TOR
BOOKS The Best in Science Fiction

LIEGE-KILLER • Christopher Hinz
"*Liege-Killer* is a genuine page-turner, beautifully written and exciting from start to finish....Don't miss it."—*Locus*

HARVEST OF STARS • Poul Anderson
"A true masterpiece. An important work—not just of science fiction but of contemporary literature. Visionary and beautifully written, elegaic and transcendent, *Harvest of Stars* is the brightest star in Poul Anderson's constellation."
—Keith Ferrell, editor, *Omni*

FIREDANCE • Steven Barnes
SF adventure in 21st century California—by the co-author of *Beowulf's Children*.

ASH OCK • Christopher Hinz
"A well-handled science fiction thriller."—*Kirkus Reviews*

CALDÉ OF THE LONG SUN • Gene Wolfe
The third volume in the critically-acclaimed Book of the Long Sun.
"Dazzling."—*The New York Times*

OF TANGIBLE GHOSTS • L.E. Modesitt, Jr.
Ingenious alternate universe SF from the author of the *Recluce* fantasy series.

THE SHATTERED SPHERE • Roger MacBride Allen
The second book of the Hunted Earth continues the thrilling story that began in *The Ring of Charon*, a daringly original hard science fiction novel.

THE PRICE OF THE STARS • Debra Doyle and James D. Macdonald
Book One of the Mageworlds—the breakneck SF epic of the most brawling family in the human galaxy!

TOR
BOOKS The Best in Science Fiction

MOTHER OF STORMS • John Barnes
From one of the hottest new nanes in SF: a shattering epic of global catastrophe, virtual reality, and human courage, in the manner of *Lucifer's Hammer*, *Neuromancer*, and *The Forge of God*.

BEYOND THE GATE • Dave Wolverton
The insectoid dronons threaten to enslave the human race in the sequel to *The Golden Queen*.

TROUBLE AND HER FRIENDS • Melissa Scott
Lambda Award-winning cyberpunk SF adventure that the *Philadelphia Inquirer* called "provocative, well-written and thoroughly entertaining."

THE GATHERING FLAME • Debra Doyle and James D. Macdonald
The Domina of Entibor obeys no law save her own.

WILDLIFE • James Patrick Kelly
"A brilliant evocation of future possibilities that establishes Kelly as a leading shaper of the genre."—*Booklist*

THE VOICES OF HEAVEN • Frederik Pohl
"A solid and engaging read from one of the genre's surest hands."—*Kirkus Reviews*

MOVING MARS • Greg Bear
The Nebula Award-winning novel of war between Earth and its colonists on Mars.

NEPTUNE CROSSING • Jeffrey A. Carver
"A roaring, cross-the-solar-system adventure of the first water."—Jack McDevitt